John Payne Collier

An old man's diary

Forty years ago

John Payne Collier

An old man's diary
Forty years ago

ISBN/EAN: 9783337118860

Printed in Europe, USA, Canada, Australia, Japan

Cover: Foto ©Andreas Hilbeck / pixelio.de

More available books at **www.hansebooks.com**

AN OLD MAN'S DIARY,

FORTY YEARS AGO;

FOR THE FIRST SIX MONTHS OF

1832.

Omne meum : nihil meum.

LONDON :
PRINTED BY THOMAS RICHARDS.
1871.

PREFACE.

Nothing but the fact that the circulation of this
fmall work is limited to the number of my private
friends, could warrant fuch a piece of apparent
egotifm : even fince it has been in type, I have
almoft repented that I entrufted it to my excellent printer. Thofe who receive it muft therefore
be fo good as to confider it *ftrictly in the light of
a manufcript communication.*

No part of it is of a later date than about
forty years ago, and I am not aware that more
than two individuals mentioned in it are now alive.
This confideration ought to make me, and has
made me, more careful as to all perfonal references
and obfervations ; and I have been moft anxious
to exclude whatever could be objectionable to fur-
viving relatives.

For nearly thirty years I received moft bountiful
and generous encouragement (not to call it patron-
age—a word he never tolerated) from a nobleman

of the higheft rank, whofe title often prefents itfelf
in the courfe of the enfuing pages : the facts
there ftated fpeak for themfelves, and I can find no
words that will half exprefs my gratitude to him : I
may perhaps be allowed to add that his noble fucceffor, almoft without perfonal acquaintance, and
entirely without folicitation, has liberally continued
to me the fubftantial means of purfuing thofe avocations, which, for many years, have never had in
view the acquifition of the ordinary rewards of
literary exertion.

As to the particular contents of the tract in the
hands of the reader, it may be fit to fay that at
various periods I have been in the habit of keeping
memoranda relating to perfons, incidents and papers;
frequently tranfcribing the laft (even when they were
my own property) for the fake of better prefervation,
or more immediate reference. Many of them will
be found here inferted, including unprinted productions by fome of our moft diftinguifhed poets, and
unknown letters by men whofe great names need
not be repeated. For the trifles I have added
of my own, I have only to folicit the indulgence
ufually accorded to young authors (I am now pretty
far advanced in my fifth fcore), recollecting alfo
that they contain nothing that can give offence
(excepting, perhaps, to good tafte) and that I was

unwilling to exclude what I did not myfelf diflike, and what formed a portion of my original record.

It is to be obferved that the day of the month preceding the various entries is not always to be implicitly trufted, and chiefly for this reafon : I was fo much engaged upon matters entirely difcordant, that I was fometimes obliged to make up arrears by inferting notices belonging to different dates at the fame date : this courfe I generally took once in feven days, and in a comparatively few inftances memoranda belonging to the middle of the week may have been inferted on the firft day of it.

There are, of courfe, many omiffions in my Diary, fome intentional and others accidental : one of the latter, which now turns out to be curious, I may here fupply. In the winter of 1813-14 I was in Holland, where I purchafed feveral books : one of them was an imperfeét copy of Tyndale's *Gofpel of St. Matthew*, to which the date of 1526 has been affigned, and which feems to be the very earlieft tranflation into Englifh of any portion of the New Teftament. Many years afterwards, I think in the fpring of 1832, I happened to fhew it to Rodd, the learned bookfeller. I was at that time ignorant upon the fubjeét, and Rodd offered me books to the value of two or three pounds for it. I gladly accepted them ; and on farther inquiry Rodd became confirmed in his opinion, that my fragment of a volume was of the greateſt hiſtorical and bibliographical importance—ſo much ſo, that it has juſt been reproduced in fac-ſimile by Mr. Arber. Rodd, finding what a treaſure he had procured, ſold it to Mr. T. Grenville, as I heard, for £50. In Holland it had only coſt me a florin; but I no more blamed Rodd for benefiting by his ſuperior knowledge, than I blamed myſelf for giving ſo little for it to the Rotterdam bookſeller. I ſometimes entered the purchaſe of books in my Diary, but in this inſtance it was only an exchange. It carries the hiſtory of Tyndale's tranſlation one ſtep farther back, and proves how, and when, it reached this country.

J. P. C.

Maidenhead, 1st May, 1871.

Per tutta volta un tal desio mi mena,
Ch' io credo, forse andando, poter corre
Qualche arbuscel di che la piaggia è piena.
Macchiavelli, Cap. della Ingratitudine.

OLD MAN'S DIARY,

FORTY YEARS AGO.

1832.

January 1.—I have feveral times refolved to keep, and have kept, a journal or diary. I began one before I was 18, and perfevered for feveral years, recording in it fome of my boyifh effufions : one of them I remember to this hour, and, if I miftake not, it has merit in its way. It is in the old ftyle, which even then I affected.

THE REMONSTRANCE.

WHY so scornful, lady fair ?
    Can thy servant never please thee,
Bending humbly whensoe'er
    Walking forth, perchance, he sees thee ?

Doth he not at distance stand,
    Ever ready still to aid thee,
Waiting only thy command,
    His sovereign lady having made thee ?

Doth he not his duty fill,
    As a foot-page to obey thee,
Asking only for thy will,
    Never daring to gainsay thee ?

B

Doth he ever near advance
  Till he sees some sign of favour ;
Anxious watching for the glance,
  Makes him blest—aye, blest for ever ?

Doth he not forego his books,
  Other friends alike forsaken,
Reading only on thy looks,
  Whence are all his lessons taken ?

Grant him, then, at length some boon
  For his love, vow'd in this ditty,
Lest, he dying over-soon,
  Thou be known to have no pity.

What became of my early diary I know not, nor do I recollect to what date it was brought down. I neglected it long
before I married (not the lady above addressed, who was
the sister of a friend in the Foreign Office) in 1816, and I
kept no record until several years after that event, which
made me the father of six children, all born before the date
at the head of this page. I was too busy with newspaper-
work, with my *Poetical Decameron*, published in 1820, and
with my *History of English Dramatic Poetry*, which came
out about a year ago, dedicated to the Duke of Devonshire,
who was kind and generous enough to present me with a
cheque for £100 for it. I never dreamed of any such
bounty, concluding that the date of giving money for dedi-
cations had long expired.

Some months subsequently I sent the Duke a copy of
my *Poet's Pilgrimage*, and on the fly-leaf opposite the
title-page I ventured to place the following Sonnet.

TO THE DUKE OF DEVONSHIRE.

Accept, my Lord, the tribute I now send,
  Nor deem that " poem " (such in early days
  I dared to call it) far beneath thy gaze,

Which I with toil, tho' not ungrateful, penn'd :
Accept it, too, because I not intend
  With your just praises, even, to smooth my lays,
  As if my panegyric could be praise,
And a new lustre to your dukedom lend.
  You need it not; for rank and wealth can gain
Tedious applause, since flattery is cheap.
  I know that you would scorn a servile strain ;
Or did you not, I then would silence keep :
  Low as I am, I would not so descend,
  High as you are, you still are lowness' friend."

The Duke told me that he had a poetical relative, William Spenfer, and he gave me a MS. copy (made for him, I think, by Lady Blanch Cavendish) of the pretty poem beginning,

  Too late I stay'd : forgive the crime ;
  Too swiftly flew the hours :
How noiseless falls the foot of Time,
  That only treads on flowers.

The Duke defired me, in the moſt friendly manner, to call upon him again in a few days.

We had a large merry party to inaugurate the new year, all near relations.

Jan 2.—I read in George Dyer's Poems, 1802, ii, 233:

  " Oh Law ! tho' sages are so fond to prove
That thou in nature's bosom hast thy seat,
  And that thy voice, inspiring awe and love,
Preserves the world in harmony complete ;
  That heaven and earth to thee their homage pay,
That great and small alike thy care employ,
  That every being gladly owns thy sway,
And hails thee mother of their peace and joy."

What is this but a verſification of that noble profe passage at the cloſe of Book I of Hooker's *Eccleſiaſtical Polity* :—

"Of Lawe there can be no leffe acknowledged, then that her feate is the bofome of God, her voyce the harmony of the world : all things in heaven and earth do her homage, the very leaft as feeling her care, and the greateft as not exempted from her power : both angels and men, and creatures of what condition foever, though each in a different manner, yet all with uniforme confent, admiring her as the mother of their peace and joy." (Edit. 1594.)

Surely Dyer ought here, as he does in fome places, to have made a foot-note acknowledgement of his obligation. Yet Dyer was in general the most confcientious of men. I saw him not unfrequently before his fecond marriage, when his wife took the management of a queer-looking abfent little man, and kept him in better order. C. Lamb used to tell moft wonderful ftories of Dyer's ftray-faculties, efpecially how one night he took away Basil Montague's footman's laced hat inftead of his own, and did not fcruple next day to carry it home on his head. He was the moft kindly, fimple-hearted, and truthful of men. He wanted originality, but his verfe is generally harmonious : I have two volumes of it, dated 1802, but he had begun authorfhip ten years earlier, when he was a liberty-boy.

Jan. 5.—I bought yefterday fome very old and curious theatrical documents, commencing even as early as the reign of Henry VII—the precife year is not given. I wifh they had come into my hands before I publifhed my *Hiftory of English Dramatic Poetry and the Stage.* The names of the king's actors are only four, hardly fufficient for the performance of the comic interludes of that day ; but no doubt they were affifted by others, whom they employed,

if they did not pay them. The men who were then rewarded quarterly were

John Englifſh,
Edward Maye,
Richard Gibſon,
John Hammond.

They are called, curiouſly enough, "*Luſores Regis, alias
in linguâ Anglicorum,* Pleyers of the Kinges Enterludes."
The document is only ſigned by two of them, Maye and
Inglifh, who received the money, 10s. 4d., for themſelves
and their fellows: this is the earlieſt player-autograph that
I remember to have ſeen ; but Richard III had players in
his pay ſome years before.

The next document is alſo without date, but of the
reign of Henry VIII; and the name of Cardinal Wolſey is
at the head of it, as one of the perſons entitled to " lodging
in the King's Houſe": here no players are mentioned, but
their place ſeems to have been ſupplied by a company
called "The yong Mynſtrells". After the name of Wolſey
come thoſe of the Duke of Norfolk and "his wife", and of
the Duke of Suffolk and "his wife", for the ladies have
there no higher titles.

Of the year 1550, there is a very intereſting paper preſented to the king, and containing a proteſt againſt many
enumerated abuſes in Church and State: among them
are the two following articles.

" The players playe abrode in everye place everye lewde, ſediciouse
fellowse devise, to the daunger of the kynge and his cownsaylle.

" The prynters do printe abrode whatsoever any fond man deviseth,
be yt never so folishe, so ſediciouse, or dangerouse for the people to
knowe."

A third paper relates to the paffing of Anne Bullen through London, and prays that the Lord Mayor may have the fervices of "the Kynges Mynftrelles for the furnyfhing of the Pagents and the Barges."

The next document does not relate directly either to players or theatres, but to the vicinity of thofe places of entertainment, which, about the middle of the reign of Elizabeth, were built in Southwark, on the weft fide of London Bridge. It is the copy of a leafe for ninety-nine years of a piece of ground, "abutting on Maiden Lane", upon which the Globe Theatre was actually built in or about the year 1594 : the leafe is dated twelve years anterior to that event; but, befides "the Stews", the known refidence of proftitutes, it mentions five or fix public-houfes near adjoining, and among them the " Rofe", from which one of the play-houfes occupied by Philip Henflowe (juft previous to Shakefpeare's era) was named.

Jan. 8.—Thomas Munden, the fon of the famous comedian lately dead, gave me three original letters by Addifon, in his large and moft diftinct handwriting. I did not keep copies of them; and I am forry for it, becaufe I lent them to a perfon (well introduced to me), who profeffed to be abdut to write a new life of Addifon, and I never could recover them after the fomewhat fudden death of the borrower. I have not heard of them fince ; and the lofs makes me now more particular as to lending anything, whether in print or in manufcript.

I cannot rejoice too much that I did not lend him on the fame occafion, what he very much preffed, an original letter from Dean Swift to Ambrofe Phillips, which, in the opening paragraph, speaks highly of Addifon: it bears date, " London, Sept. 14, 1708", and runs as follows :—

> "Nothing is a greater argument that I look on myself as one whose acquaintance is perfectly useless, than that I am not so constant or exact in writing to you as I should otherwise be ; and I am glad at heart to see Mr. Addison, who may live to be serviceable to you, so mindfull in your absence. He has reproached me more than once for not frequently sending him a letter to conveigh to you. That man has worth enough to give reputation to an age ; and all the merit I can hope for with regard to you will be my advice to cultivate his friendship to the utmost, and my assistance to do you all the good offices towards it in my power."

The letter enters into many other particulars, relating to war, peace, and love ; and, as " Namby-pamby" was then in Yorkfhire, it exprelfes a hope that he would marry fome lady of that county with £10,000.

Jan. 11.—My birthday, kept by me and all my family with due cheerfulness and hilarity.

I mentioned on a former page my "poem", *The Poet's Pilgrimage.* I originally had it printed anonymoufly (to ferve a ftruggling typographer) ten years ago, and fent copies to a few of my friends who knew it was mine. C. Lamb wrote me word that, while reading it, "he almost forgot he was not reading Spenser"! Wordsworth highly praifed the two firft cantos, which he had finished just before writing to me ; and H. C. Robinfon was "fure it muft raife me in the opinion of all my relations and acquaintances." Thus encouraged I "took heart of grace", and in 1825 had the title-page reprinted, with my name upon it, and a few alterations made in the preliminary matter. I was afterwards foolhardy enough to carry it myfelf to a literary bookfeller,

and read to him the firſt canto. He aſſured me that it
would not ſell as verſe, but added that, as it was all very
good ſenſe, I might put it into proſe, and then he would
conſider of it again. I was diſappointed, took up my hat,
and called in the fifty copies of which I think the whole
impreſſion conſiſted, and have kept them by me, excepting
a few given away as preſents, until this day. Let me add
that the four cantos (and more that I afterwards deſtroyed)
were written between the ages of eighteen and twenty-four,
after I had juſt read Spenſer. Therefore, if there be (as I
dare to hope there is) ſome ſmall likeneſs to the "Faery
Queen" in the verſification, it was owing to the echo of thoſe
3600 delightful ſtanzas in my heart and ears; for I read
aloud to myſelf every line of them, swinging and swaying
in my chair to the time and meaſure.

Jan. 16.—I am delighted with a volume juſt preſented
to me from Paris (one out of a hundred copies) with the
general title of *Poéſies des XV et XVI Siècles, publiées
d'après des Editions Gothiques et des Manuſcrits*, brought
out by Silveſtre, in the beſt ſtyle, and with the beſt ſkill. It
begins with a French Art of Rhetoric, *pour faire Rimes et
Ballades;* after which we have *Le Caſteau d'Amours*, by
Gringoire, and about a dozen other pieces, dramatic and
undramatic, the moſt curious and intereſting to me being
an old morality, entitled *La farce du Munyer de qui le
Diable emporte l'ame en Enffer.* The original is a unique
manuſcript, occupying thirty-ſeven pages in the printed
copy. Another drama, called in the title "Moralité", is of
L'Aveugle et du Boiteux, illuſtrated by a moſt capital and
characteriſtic wood-cut; and a third production of the ſame

clafs, called *La Farce de la Pipée.* By whom it has been fent to me I know not; but it feems one of the moft fingular and amufing books of the kind ever iffued by the French prefs : it is, befides, in fo handfome and permanent a form. I heartily thank the donor.

Jan. 20.—I was in luck yefterday morning. Paffing along Holywell Street, I caft my eyes over fome books expofed on a ftall for fale : the firft I took up was a very nice clean copy of Hughes' "Calypfo and Telemachus", 8vo, 1712, for which I paid 2s. 6d., and walked away with it in my pocket. I did not reach home, or look at it again, for fome hours. I faw then that there were two fly-leaves, fomewhat fhorter than the pages of the book, and, examining them, I found that they were covered with writing, in a hand that I recognifed in an inftant. It was Pope's! and it was headed by him,

" To Mr. Hughes,
on His Opera";

it confifted of thirty-eight couplets. This is the fecond piece of original compofition by Pope *in his own autograph* that has devolved into my hands quite accidentally, and I am duly grateful. I tranfcribe the whole of it here, exactly as it ftands in the original, left by any chance that original fhould be loft. To whom the book had belonged firft I know not : probably to Hughes himfelf, who pafted in the fly-leaves, but the name of a former owner, whoever he was, has been cut away : poffibly it was Pope's own book, and he may have depofited in it his tribute to Hughes. It has no great originality, and one of the rhymes, "fons" and "mourns", is unlike Pope in his

later day. In 1712, when "Calypſo and Telemachus" was
acted and publiſhed, he was in his twenty-fourth year.

" *To Mr. Hughes, on his Opera.*

"When, dearest Hughes, you strike the tunefull strings,
 And, taught by you, our British Opera sings,
Th' Italian Muse is forc'd to quit the stage,
 Whilst charms superior captivate the age :
Music and Verse no longer disagree,
 Nor 's Sense thought useless now to Harmony.
In your Telemachus both parts unite,
 And charming sounds are joyn'd with solid wit.
These Nature studied, and those powerfull arts
 Which strike the secret springs that guide our hearts.
Sooth'd with your verse fierce factions peace proclaim,
 Rough Whiggs grow mild, and hottest Torys tame :
At your command their conquer'd passions move,
 With you they rage, they pity, hate, and love.
Then such instructions flow from Mentor's tongue,
 Minerva only could inspire the song ;
Whilst each description shines so clear and bright,
 We fancy every thing before our sight.
How gayly drest the first bright scene appears,
 What wanton beautys all the island wears !
Methinks I hear the murmuring waters flow,
 And echoing rocks repeat Calypso's woe.
Now the fond goddess lost Ulysses mourns,
 But quickly for the younger hero burns:
What art doth she not try ? what charms put on ?
 To make the beauteous haughty youth her own.
Then, what fierce furys in her bosom rise,
 To find the prince her profferd love despise.
See in Telemachus the best of sons,
 With what true filial piety he mourns ;
Whence Eucharis coquet, gay, young and-fair,
 Finds means to trap him in th' enchanted snare :

With greedy looks he draws his ruin on,
Sucks in the charm, and hasts to be undone.
　Here Mentor for a while withdraws his face,
And lets him feel the dangers of the place ;
But, as he seems just sinking in the waves,
Exerts the goddess, and the hero saves."

Jan. 25.—I twice faw the famous Mrs. Abington at parties given by Serjeant Rough, in Bedford Row. She was fhrunk by age into a fmall woman, but was very fprightly, and, in fpite of her wrinkles, attractive to all the company. She had quitted the ftage in 1798, having played *Scrub* for her benefit two years earlier : her moft celebrated characters were *Eftifania* and *Beatrice*, and fhe was fond of referring to her theatrical triumphs. She died early in 1815.

I have alfo feen Mrs. Garrick, but only when I was quite a boy, helped into her carriage on the Adelphi Terrace.

The Duke of Devonfhire, to whom I mentioned the fact, gave me a theatrical curiofity—viz., a handfome oval ticket, furrounded by a well-engraved border of fhell-work, for the benefit of Mrs. Garrick, about a year and a half before fhe was married : it is fubfcribed " Violette", and runs merely thus :

" For the benefit of Mademoifelle Violette, at the Theatre Royal in Drury Lane. Wednesday, February the 11th.

　　　　　　　　　　　　　" VIOLETTE. (L.S.)"

By reference to the bills of the day, I fee that the performances on the 11th February, 1747, were " The Carelefs Husband" and " Dancing by La Violette". She had come out on the 3rd December, 1746 ; and Horace Walpole, in a letter, dated June 5th in that year, fays :

" The fame of the Violetta increases daily : the sister Countesses of Burlington and Talbot exert all their stores of sullen partiality in competition for her : the former visits her, and is having her picture, and carries her to Chiswick, and sups at Lady Carlisle's."

La Violette was married to Garrick in 1749; and I have feen the original fettlement, dated June 20th in that year, where he is fpoken of as David Garrick, Efq., and his wife is called Eva Maria Violette : it is figned by them, and by Dorothy (Countefs of) Burlington, who agrees to give Garrick £5000 as the marriage portion.

As I have room on this page, I will copy here the following letter from Garrick to Clutterbuck, on the fale of his half of the patent early in 1776 : Garrick died as nearly as poffible three years afterwards.

"Adelphi, Jan. 18th, 1776.

"My dear Clut,—You shall be the first person to whom I shall make known that I have at last slipt my theatrical shell, and shall be as fine and free a gentlemen as you would wish to see upon the South or North Parade of Bath. I have sold my moiety of patent, etc., etc., for £35,000, to Messrs. Dr. Ford, Ewart, Sheridan, and Linley. We have signed to forfeit 10,000 pounds if the conditions of our present articles are not fulfilled the 24th of June next—in short, I grow somewhat older, though I never played better in all my life, and am resolved not to remain upon the stage to be pitied instead of applauded. The deed is done ; and the bell is ringing, so I can say no more, but that I hope I shall receive a letter of felicitation from you. Love to your better half, and to the Thorpes and all friends.

" Ever most affectionately yours,

" D. GARRICK."

The original has been lent to me by J. Hamilton Reynolds, author of " The Mermaid".

Jan. 29.—Where is Creffida fpoken of as a widow ? I find two or three paffages in Chaucer's firft book of *Troylus* that feem more than to intimate it, and even that fhe may have had children. Thus :

> " And as a widowe was she, and al alone,
>   And nyst to whom she might make her mone."

This may mean only that fhe was lonely as a widow : then, two ftanzas farther we are told that fhe wore black :

> " In wydowes habite large, of samyte brown ;"

i. e., bruno, meaning black ; but three ftanzas onward we find what looks very queftionable :

> " She kept her estate, and of yong and olde
>   Ful wel beloved, and wel men of her tolde ;
>   But whether that she children had or none
>   I rede not; therfore I let it gone."

Six ftanzas farther on we read :

> " Among these other folke was Creseyda,
>   In wydowes habite blacke."

And in the next ftanza :

> " As was Creseyde they sayden everychone
>   That her behelde in her blacke wede."

I muft look to *Filoftrato* and the old romance. Shakefpeare does not reprefent her as a widow.

Is not the following the original of Goldfmith's " Clown's Reply", or is it ftill older ?

" A noble lord asked a clergyman at the bottom of the table, why the goose, if there was one, was always set next the parson. ' Really,' said he, ' I can give no reason for it ; but your question is so odd, that I shall never see a goose for the future without thinking of your lordship.' (*Polly Peachum's Jests.* 8vo. 1728.)

A few of the jokes in this fmall volume are very grey and venerable.

Feb. 1.—My friend Amyot introduced me formerly to Mr. Allen, the Mafter of Dulwich College, and I have fince confulted the books and manufcripts frequently.

The original of the following tranſlation is preſerved there: it is in the beautifully clear handwriting of Ben Jonſon, and as it is ſhort I copy it.

"MARTIAL.

"The things that make the happie life are these,
Most pleasant Martial : Substance got with ease,
Not labour'd for, but left thee by thy sire ;
A soil not barren ; a continuall fire ;
Never at law; seldome in office gownd :
A quiet mind, free powers, and body sound ;
A wise simplicity ; friends alike stated ;
A table without art, and easy rated ;
Thy night not dronken, but from cares layd wast ;
No soure or sullen bed-mate, yet a chaste ;
Sleepe that will make the darkest howres swift-pac't ;
Will to be what thou art, and nothing more,
Nor feare thy latest day, nor wish therefore."

I have not found that the lines have been anywhere printed, though I have looked for them in every likely place, and in ſome unlikely places.

Feb. 2.—A friend of mine has juſt purchaſed a beautiful French engraving of Raphael's admirable picture, "The Marriage of St. Catherine", and underneath are the following lines. My Italian muſt be pardoned, and I only quote from memory.

"Se di tai fregi adorno
Fu Sanzio imberbe encora,
Non mai precorse il giorno
Tal luminosa Aurora."

Which I thus Engliſh :

"If beardless Raphael could display
Such powers his youth adorning,
We ne'er again shall see a day,
With such a glorious morning."

Raphael, as he proceeded with this divine painting, muſt have woiſhipped, as it were, every touch of his own miraculous pencil.

I always quote Italian with fear and trembling, never having gone through the drudgery of the "grammar rules", but relying upon my knowledge of Latin and French. At one time, and for two whole years, I never read anything but Italian, whether in verſe or proſe, and thus I got through Arioſto, Taſſo, Doni, and various other romanciſts; beſides many noveliſts, in hopes of finding the original ſtory of Shakeſpeare's *Tempeſt*. I need ſcarcely add that I did not find it.

Raphael worked himſelf to death at the age of only 37, and it is the more wonderful to think of the aſtoniſhing number of the pictures—to ſay nothing of their finiſh and excellence—that he left behind him. How many men of genius, too, in nearly all departments, have finiſhed their career about as early. It would be eaſy to add others ; but at once I can name Purcell, Mozart, and Orlando Gibbons, as muſicians, and Burns and Byron as poets, to ſay nothing of painters, becauſe theirs is an unhealthy ſedentary employment.

Feb. 5.—The following ironical ballad may be worth preſerving, and that is all I will ſay of it.

ON A WELL-KNOWN AND WELL-TRIED PROVERB.

I'm rich, hale, and jolly, no starveling like you,
   With straight back to great people above you;
For this proverb I ever held prudent as true,
   Take care of yourſelf—friends will love you.

Number One is, of course, the first number with me;
　　Aside do not let people shove you:
When you can, take advantage of every degree;
　　Take care of yourself—friends will love you.

Push on in the world; push up, never down;
　　Well settled let nobody move you,
Unless to a place you prefer to your own:
　　Take care of yourself—friends will love you.

When at school, if you know you've committed a crime,
　　Lay it on to some boy that's above you;
Get him punish'd, and you'll be rewarded in time:
　　Take care of yourself—friends will love you.

If at College, look after the greenhorns who dash;
　　The result, you will find much improve you,
And fill both your pockets with other folk's cash:
　　Take care of yourself—friends will love you.

When out in the world you may cheat, rob, and lie;
　　Seem simple as any young dove, you,
And not care a rush who may live, or who die:
　　Take care of yourself—friends will love you.

If you wish to be lov'd, therefore, love Number One,
　　And ne'er let that point be above you;
Let others' misfortunes but add to your fun;
　　Take care of yourself—friends will love you.

Thus to love and be lov'd is the blessing of life,
　　And all ranks will soon hand and glove you;
And 'tis sometimes convenient to have a fair wife:
　　Take care of yourself—friends will love you.

The following, which I copy from the original signed by the peer, ferves to show how poor the Lord Treafurer of England was in the ninth of Henry VII, 1493: he was obliged to borrow ten marks.

"Be it underftanden and knowen that I John Lord Dynham, Tresorer of Englande, have borrowed of Thomas Stokes ten marc sterling, to be payd unto the saide Thomas, or unto his assignes, at Whitsuntide next commyng ; to the whiche payment wel and trewly to be made, I bynde me, myne heires and executors, by this my writing, sealed and subscribed with my owne hande this xxvjᵗⁱ day of Februarie, in the xiᵗʰ yere of the reigne of our sovereign lord King Herry the vijᵗʰ.

" DYNHAM." (L. S.)

Feb. 8.—John Hemming, the old actor, and the joint-editor with Condell of the folio of Shakefpeare's Works in 1623, had a fon named William Hemming; and his father obtained riches enough at the Globe to fend him to Oxford, where he took his degree in 1628. William Hemming became a dramatift, and produced three plays, one of which, printed in 1662, he called "The Jew's Tragedy", taking the facts of the deftruction of Jerufalem from Jofephus, but interlarding monftrous abfurdities of his own, intended, by their grofs comic character, to relieve the blood and flaughter of the tragic fcenes : he alfo introduced a mafque and fongs ; and, perhaps, in the whole hiftory of our early ftage, there is no parallel to the extraordinary mingle-mangle he compounded. It muft have been reprefented juft before the Reftoration, though printed two years after it ; and no production can fhow more clearly the abfurdities exhibited at our public theatres after the plays of Shakefpeare had been forgotten. I fay forgotten, becaufe young Hemming takes the greateft liberties with his predeceffor: thus in act ii, fcene 2 (it is moft irregularly divided) he has this fort of parody upon Hamlet's foliloquy,

" To be or not to be ; aye, there's the doubt," etc.

debating, not indeed the queftion of felf-flaughter, but the

advantages or difadvantages of fovereignty. Further on
he has an imitation of the quarrel fcene in "Julius Cæfar",
ufing the very words of Shakefpeare, but put into the mouths
of his own characters:

> "*Eleazer.* Muft I endure all this?
> "*Jehochanan.* All this and more". Etc.

In feveral places, Hemming introduces a Dogberry of
his own; but his moft impudent attempt is a burlefque of
Falftaff's famous fpeech on honour, which is affigned to
the loweft of low comedians:

> "Call you this honour? A pox of honour", etc.

Numerous fcraps of ballads are inferted, fometimes in
the fpeeches of ferious perfonages, and the following is intended as a parody on that in "Hamlet" (act iii, fcene 2):

> "Why, let the mongrel curs go play,
>   And lordly lions fight;
> The braver beaft shall win the day,
>   And so, my lord, good night."

We have alfo "a rat behind the hangings", followed
by fome ridiculous rubbifh from a fong of the day. All
this proves to what a pitiable condition our ftage was reduced prior to 1660, tending to reconcile audiences, juft
afterwards, to the reprefentation of anglicifed continental
commodities.

Feb. 10.—Lord Glengall, author of "The Follies of
Fafhion", a comedy brought out with fuccefs a feafon or
two ago (Nov. 30th, 1829), having another dramatic piece
in profpect and progrefs, very courtier-like fent to inquire after my health, and afked me, if I were at leifure,
to call upon him in Upper Brook Street. I, therefore,

went there yefterday morning, or rather afternoon, about three o'clock. I was ufhered, in fome ftate, into a back-drawing-room, and prefently his lordfhip joined me. He is what ladies call a very pretty man, with regular fea-tures (not without clevernefs of expreffion) and a cheerful complexion. He was evidently in an undrefs-drefs—*i. e.*, in a green filk robe, lined with pink, and faftened round the waift with a cord and taffels. He was very friendly, and even familiar, in his manner, and it was fome time before he let me know that he had written a confiderable portion of a new comedy : he read a fcene or two and one or two fketches of characters to me, but unfinifhed, though lively and pleafant. Then he wifhed to know whether I thought it would fucceed on the ftage, and I anfwered at once in the affirmative, if the reft fhould be as good, and well compacted into a comedy. This opinion feemed to give him pleafure ; and he told me that James Wallack, who had acted the hero of " The Follies of Fafhion", was alfo well fatisfied with the new part he was to take. There was in the projected piece the character of a miferly money-lender, and I told Lord Glengall that I thought it a little too much like *Sir Francis Gripe*, in "The Bufybody", in which character I faw Suett in the year 1805, and Munden in 1808, juft before Lewis played *Mar-plot* for the laft time. Lord G. fmiled at my early ac-quaintance with the ftage ; but I added that I could go back even to 1797, and in the year 1803, I well remembered J. P. Kemble as *Rolla* and Mrs. Siddons as *Elvira*. My inter-view ended by Lord G. afking me to dine with him on a future day—an invitation which I intended to receive, but not to accept. He did not tell me what name he meant to give to his new comedy, and I thought it premature to make the inquiry. He knew very well that I had written a criticifm on his "Follies of Fafhion", and that I might have to perform the fame duty for his projected comedy.

Feb. 12.—The Duke of Devonfhire called at my houfe yefterday, and left his card, ftating that he wifhed to fee me.

I went to Devonfhire houfe, and was received, as always, cordially. The Duke faid that he wanted to put the whole of his English Dramatic library, ancient and modern, under my care, and he fhowed me John Philip Kemble's Catalogue, which had been fent to him with the Plays, and which I faw at a glance was the *Biographia Dramatica,* by Stephen Jones, 8vo, 1812, with manufcript notes. As J. P. Kemble obtained the Plays there enumerated, he had put a cross againft each in the margin of the book, and marked under the particular edition included in his collection. This book the Duke wifhed to be my guide in procuring plays to fill up vacancies, for he faid he had made up his mind to buy every play of every age in our language, not caring much what price he gave for the rarer ones anterior to the Reftoration. I faid that I would moft gladly undertake the duty, but added that I could not know what Plays were, or were not, already in the bookcafes, unless I had the ufe of J. P. Kemble's Catalogue. The Duke told me to take my own interleaved copy of Jones's *Biogr. Dram.,* and to tranfcribe into it all J. P. Kemble's MS. marks and memoranda, fo that my Catalogue fhould be an exact counterpart. I undertook to do fo, but obferved that the procefs required time. The Duke added that, to fhorten the labour, he would himfelf write into my copy of vol. i all J. P. Kemble's MS. notes, while I might take home with me vol. ii for the fame purpofe.

I was then afked in how many days I could finifh with vol. ii (the thickeft of the two), and I anfwered "in a week", the marks and notes being numerous. " Well," faid the Duke, " you take home vol. ii, and come to me again this day week, and I will have vol. i ready for you." Thus this matter was arranged much to my fatisfaction.

In the courfe of converfation the Duke told me how he had originally obtained J. P. Kemble's Collection of Plays. Before the great actor went to Switzerland, where he died, he offered them to the Duke for £2000, and the Duke agreed to buy them ; but gave J. P. K. his choice whether to have the fum down, or an annuity calculated upon his life. J. P. K. preferred the laft, and inftead of the £2000 he received till his death, I think, £400 a year : as J. P. K. died earlier than was expected, the Duke faved money by the annuity. This he cared little about.

Feb. 16.—The Duke fent me a note afking me to call upon him, "if I happened to be paffing," as he wanted to fhow me a volume of old plays which he had purchafed on his own refponfibility. I went, of courfe, directly, and found that the volume was one of which I had already heard as in the market, but which I had never feen. He had had it rebound, and, in confiftency with all the rest of his Kemble plays, had had all the old leaves inlaid, a courfe that, to the Duke's furprife, I regretted.

I think that there were five dramas in the volume, two of them of the highest value and curiofity ; viz., the firft edition of " Hamlet", 1603, wanting only the laft leaf, containing but twelve lines ; the firft edition of " The Merry Wives of Windfor", 1602. Thefe are confidered *unique,* and the " Hamlet", 1603, until recently has never been

heard of. The third play was Robert Greene's "Alphonfus",
1599, the only edition and a moſt ſcarce play, while the
two others were of later dates, and of much ſmaller value
—the titles I do not recollect.

I congratulated the Duke on his purchaſe, for which he
told me he had given only a hundred guineas ; and I left
him continuing his labours on vol. i of the "Kemble Catalogue." I aſked him if he wanted any more time than the
week to complete it, and he anſwered me in the negative,
ſaying he liked the job, that he was at it early and late,
and ſhould complete it before my vol. ii was ready.

The popularity of Shakeſpeare's "Venus and Adonis" and
"Lucrece" (its counterpart) muſt have been great in the
reign of Queen Anne ; and there is an edition of them in
1707 of which no notice has been taken, perhaps becauſe
it appeared in ſuch unlikely company ; viz., in *Poems
on Affairs of State*, vol. iv, p. 143, where "The Rape of
Lucrece" is made to follow a long piece headed "The
Miſeries of England from the growing Power of her Do-
meſtic Enemies", while "Venus and Adonis" preceded
"The firſt Anniverſary of the Government under his High-
neſs the Lord Protector".

This reprint of 1707, in faɛt, was the earlieſt appearance
of theſe two poems after what may be conſidered the old
impreſſions. About 1709, Lintot printed, without date and
ſeparately, two little volumes in 12mo, under the title of
A Collection of Poems, containing "Venus. and Adonis",
"The Rape of Lucrece" (it had begun to be ſo called as
early as 1616), "The Paſſionate Pilgrim", "The Sonnets",
and "A Lover's Complaint". Rowe's edition of the Plays
was followed by the Poems in 1709, and again in 1714 ;

but in the interval—viz., in 1710—Curll publiſhed his edition of the Poems from the copy of 1640.

Feb. 17.—I quote the following from the original manuſcript: it is by Charles Lamb, engraved upon the tomb of
his firſt love—perhaps his laſt. She died at the age of 19,
Lamb being a trifle younger. The lines deſerve preſerva-
tion, if only for the ſake of the gentle, ſuffering author.

"Epitaph for Mary Druitt.

" *Buried at Wimborne, Dorſet*, aged 19.

> " Under this cold marble stone
>   Sleep the sad remains of one,
>   Who, when alive, by few or none
>
> "Was loved, as she might have been
>   By lovers many, rich I ween,
>   If she prosperous days had seen.
>
> " Only this funereal stone
>   Tells the simple grief of one
>   That loved her, and her alone."

I am not aware that the above has been printed, certainly not in the edition of Lamb's Works in 1818 ; nor do
I find that the name of the young lady has been elſewhere
recorded. I have heard from my mother that Mary Druitt
died of the ſmall-pox, and ſhe muſt have had the ſtatement from Mary Lamb. Originally, the epitaph contained
another triplet, but Lamb eraſed it, as leſſening the ſim-
plicity of the tribute :

> " Death will prey on flesh and bone,
>   Hateful to be look'd upon ;
>   And where then her beauty ?—Gone."

To have added the preceding would alfo have made one part of the epitaph inconfiftent with the other, by introducing the image of death in its deformity.

The fame manufcript contains Lamb's fweet Sonnet to his Sifter, which Coleridge, for no very good reafon, objected to infert in his *Anthology :* neverthelefs, I have feen it in print.

Feb. 18.—The Duke, by appointment, took me with him to fee Mathews's collection of theatrical pictures and portraits at the actor's cottage, Highgate, and we found them in nearly all the rooms. Some of the pieces, fuch as thofe really by Zophany and Gainsborough, are good, but moft of them are only tolerable, as the reprefentations of perfons who had been popular performers, male and female: two or three are by Hogarth, and highly characteriftic, fuch, for inftance, as Peg Woffington and Quin: a few feem to have been chriftened by Mathews, both as to perfon and painter, fuch as the Nell Gwynne imputed to Sir P. Lely, etc. The fcene from Macbeth, with portraits of Garrick and Mrs. Pritchard, I did not believe to be by Zophany; but the Duke was too polite to exprefs an opinion, and took the fhewman's word. Mathews and his wife (who only appeared once for a few minutes) were quite upon their hind legs. Winfton, the Secretary of the Garrick Club, of which the Duke is Prefident, happened to come in: his father had been an actor, but of fmall repute, and he was well verfed in all the tranfactions of the ftage during the laft thirty or forty years. It was mentioned by Mathews that he had been recommended to make a public exhibition of his acquifitions, and for this purpofe that a catalogue had been fome time in preparation. The picture that on the whole gave me the greatest pleafure was the portrait of Woodward as *Petruchio*, by Vandergucht.

Feb. 21.—This was the day week, and when I called at Devonfhire houfe the Duke, with an air of triumph, produced his annotated vol. i, and I fhewed him my annotated vol. ii : he obferved that I wrote the beft, and he the neateft hand. He told me again that he fhould put the whole of his Dramatic Library under my care ; adding that he had bought with the plays a good many volumes of modern play-bills, which he wifhed to have indexed, and that if it were not inconfiftent with my other engagements, he would pay me £100 a year for the trouble he gave me at leifure times : he added, that he now and then wanted a little literary advice, and that in that way alfo he might avail himfelf of my fervices.

Of courfe I expreffed myfelf very much flattered and bound to his Grace for his liberality, reminding him that he had already prefented me with a large fum for the dedication of my "Hiftory of English Dramatic Poetry and the Stage." He would not hear of it, told me to call upon him, when convenient, at any time between 11 and 1 : if he had nothing elfe for me to do, I could procced with the indexing of his play-bills.

I tranfcribe the following from the original in the handwriting of John Day, the old Dramatift and contemporary with Shakefpeare : it is in the hands of a friend, and it is efpecially curious becaufe it mentions a work by Day of which no bibliographer has given any account.

SIR,—It hath become an antient custome in this great Ile of Man, the World, for men in any fashion acquainted, at the birthe of the new

E

yeare to new date the band of theire loves, and by some present, or gifte new seale, and more strongly condition them : which custome to contynew, and to pay some part of the duty in which I stand obliged to your worshipp, I am bold to present you with this small Poeme contayning *The Myracles of our Blest Saviour.* And hoping you will receyve it as gratefully as I tender it willinglie, I cease your trouble.

Desirous to be all youre
JOHN DAY.

The "fmall poem" here mentioned may or may not have been a manufcript, but it feems not now known: the address at the back of the note has been torn away, only leaving the words "very good" and "Efquire". I add here, from my own collection, an acroftic, alfo in Day's handwriting, to Thomas Dowton, a well known actor in many of the dramas produced at Henflowe's theatres; which fhows alfo how very ancient the name of a great comic performer, of our own time, is in connexion with the ftage.

ACROSTIC VERSES UPON THE NAME OF HIS
WORTHIE FREINDE, MAISTER
THOMAS DOWTON.

T he wealthie treasure of America,
H idd in the vaines and artiers of the earthe
O r the ritche pearle, begotten by the sea,
M ade round and orient in its naturall birthe,
A re not all valewde in the eye of arte
S oe much, by much, as a compassionate harte.

D etermine, then, to keepe that wealthie mine,
O f all Exchequers in the worlde the beste ;
W isdomes the quoine, the stamp upon 't devine :
T he man that owes it beares this motto—*bleste.*
O f all my freindes ('t weare shame to wrong desarte)
N ot one of all beares a more passionate harte.

JOHN DAYE.

Day feems to have been poor all his life, but efpecially near the clofe of it.

Feb. 24.—Even I, in a fmall way, have been of affiftance to eminent literary men in my time. Not long ago Douglas Jerrold called upon me and afked me to give him an introduction to the *Morning Herald*, as he fadly wanted employment. I did fo at once, telling him however that perfonally I knew nothing of the editor, though I was well acquainted with the gentleman whom I believed the proprietor much confulted on fuch occafions. Jerrold afterwards faw me again and thanked me, as his application had been fuccefsful, and he had engaged to write theatrical criticifms for the paper.

Something of the fame kind happened with Thackeray, at a time when he was chiefly known as the writer of the " Yellowplufh Papers " in *Frazer's Magazine.* He wifhed me to introduce him to the *Morning Chronicle*, but I do not think that his application there was fuccefsful: I, however, one day met him near Somerfet Houfe, walking along at a prodigious pace, when he ftopped me and faid, "Collier, I know that you will be very glad to hear that I have this moment come from concluding an engagement with a publifher, who will give me £200 " (I am not fure that it was not £300) "a year, if I will fill only eight pages of his monthly publication." I, of courfe, congratulated him, for I knew that it was juft then of great importance to him, as he lived in rather an expenfive houfe in Coram Street and kept a man fervant. I dined with him there, in company with John Mitchell Kemble and his firft wife, the daughter of a German profeffor ; but who had the dirtieft nails I ever faw any body fit down to table with. There were three or four other diners, but it was one of the dulleft parties of the fort I ever remember.

I fubfequently afked Thackeray how, confidering his circumftances, he could afford to keep a livery-fervant (who by the way wore very old-fafhioned cut clothes, with broad worfted lace down the fronts and round the pockets), and he told me that the old man (at leaft fixty) had been a fort of heir-loom from his father; and that, rather than not ferve the fon, he was content with his keep, and almoft no wages. Thackeray fupported him while the old fellow lived.

Feb. 28.—The following is worth copying : it is from the original now before me, in the handwriting of King Charles I, and it is dated :

> " Holdenby, Feb. the 17, 1646.

" Since I have not diffembled nor hid my confcience, and that I am not yett fatisfied with thefe alterations in religion to which you defire my confent, I will not loofe time in giving reafons (which are obvious to every body) why it is fitt for me to be attended by fome of my chaplains; whofe opinions as clergymen I efteeme and reverence, not only for the exercife of my confcience, but alfo for clearing my judgement concerning the prefent differences in religion. And I have at full declared to Mr. Marfhall and his fellow minifter, having fhewed them that this is the beft and likelyeft meanes of giving me fatisfa'ction (which without it I canot have) in thefe things whereby the diftractions of this Church may be fettled. Wherefore, that in all haft two of thefe reverend divines, whofe names I have here fett downe, may have liberty to wayte upon me, for the difcharging of their duty to me according to their functions.

> " Bishop of London.
> " Bishop of Salisbury.
> " Bishop of Peterborough.
> " Doctor Selden, clerke of my closett.

" Doctor March, Deane of Yorke.
" Doctor Sanders.
" Doctor Bayly.
" Doctor Heywood.
" Doctor Seale.
" Doctor Hammon.
" Doctor Taylor."

The above is upon half a ſheet of foolscap, but the back of it is blank without any addreſs.

Mar. 1.—There has been lately a conſiderable ſtruggle on the part of the Major Theatres to put an end to the performances at the Minor Theatres, and the Duke of Devonſhire, as Lord Chamberlain, has had ſome trouble with both. On the 23rd of laſt month was held a meeting of the proprietors, actors, etc., of the minors, to`petition Parliament for the repeal of the exiſting law againſt them. The Duke aſked me what I thought upon the queſtion, and I ſubſequently put into his hand the following

MOCK PETITION FROM THE MINOR TO THE MAJOR
THEATRES.

Theatric Giants —mighty Majors,
   Look with pity from your height
On some pigmy struggling stagers,
   Now, alas ! in woeful plight.
Let us still sometimes be diners,
Do not starve the humble Minors.

True, we yet have little merit,
   But our wish to please is known ;
Yours you certainly inherit ;
   And you need it—where's your own ?
With your full cramm'd bags of shiners,
Don't extinguish the poor Minors.

You support the nation's drama,
 Alias call'd "legitimate":
We've but *fames*, you have *fama*,
 And in every sense are great.
Be not, therefore, mean repiners,
And extinguish the poor Minors.

We'll not touch your noblest features,
 Lions, elephants, and stuff :
Let us act with human creatures,
 And we shall do well enough.
Ye dramatic law definers,
Don't extinguish the poor Minors.

We have hopes from the Committee,
 Since to them the point 's referr'd.
Why are authors to be witty
 Only where they can't be heard ?
Why are gaudy scene-designers
To extinguish the poor Minors ?

Why is 't fit that naughty people
 Have good lessons but from two ?
Sure, the props of church and steeple
 Should prop us as well as you.
With them be not you combiners,
Don't extinguish the poor Minors.

We'll submit to Mr. Colman,
 Would but that the mischief cure :
He *was,* and *is* a devilish droll man,
 Once so wicked, *now so pure.*
Oh ! most whining of the whiners,
Don't extinguish the poor Minors.

Sure we are his Grace of Devon
 In his heart must wish us well :
We won't use " angel"; no, nor " Heaven";
 Too polite to mention " Hell".
These are for profane designers,
Not for us, poor moral Minors.

We can have few private boxes,
  So, few friends 'mong the polite,
Who must take their titled d——
  Where they may be out of sight.
These morality refiners
Would extinguish the poor Minors.

If the public don't approve us,
  Sans your help we fall with ease :
If they do, you can't remove us,
  Prelates, peers, or patentees.
Still we pray—petition-signers—
Don't extinguish the poor Minors.

The committee alluded to above has juſt been appointed by the Houſe of Commons to inquire into and report upon the ſubjeƈt, and Sir Edward Lytton Bulwer is the chairman, and the Honble. George Lamb one of the members. The Duke took my paper into his own ſtudy, and after he had read it, he came laughing into the long library where I was ſitting—praiſed the verſification and humour of the ſuppoſed petition, but expreſſed no opinion. I, however, well knew what were his wiſhes, as Lord Chamberlain, upon the ſubjeƈt. He will of courſe wait until the report of the committee has been preſented to the Houſe of Commons. In reference to the ſtanza where the *modern purity* of "George Colman, Junior" is laughed at, it may be allowable to mention that he is at this very time living with Mrs. Gibbs, the actreſs, in Brompton Square.

  Words and actions don't agree,
  But what is that to you or me?

March 2.—William Hazlitt called upon me; and, as I had not been able to procure one, I aſked him for a copy of his *Liber Amoris*, publiſhed ſeveral years ago ; he ſaid

he had not one, and feemed fhy of talking about it, as he
probably knew that I was acquainted with the object of his
romantic attachment.   In fact, fhe was the daughter of a
tailor, at whofe houfe he had lodged, near Clement's Inn,
whom my father had employed when the girl was quite a
child : I had the ftatement from him.   She grew up to be
pretty, with a nice oval face and a good complexion, but the
portrait oppofite the title-page of *Liber Amoris* was fancy
more than reality.   Hazlitt practifed as a painter of portraits, but without much fuccefs. I have feen his head of C.
Lamb in his Blue-coat School drefs, and though a likenefs,
it is too manly and mafculine ; he alfo painted portraits of
H. C. Robinfon and his brother, but they were confidered
failures. He vifits and criticifes galleries and collections of
pictures for the newfpapers, and has an admirable eye for
art.   His brother John was a miniature painter in Great
Ruffell Street, Bloomsbury.   William Hazlitt was a warm
admirer of three pictures in my father's drawing-room :
one was a Vandyke-drawing of Belifarius, another a land-
fcape by Pohlemberg, and the third an Italian portrait of
a lady, which he faid *might be* by Leonardo da Vinci. I
never have feen any other fpecimen of Hazlitt's poetry,
but, like Lamb, he was very partial to my mother, and one
day, when parting, put into her hands the following lines :

"ON AN ITALIAN PICTURE.

" This picture, by Da Vinci painted,
Shews a woman almost sainted :
Half a saint and half a woman,
Having virtues both in common.
Note her air divine ; while Nature
Strives, as 'twere, in every feature

To display a double power,
Earthly, yet no earthly flower !
Mark her forehead, heavenly, noble,
Yet touch'd as with some mortal trouble :
See her eyes cast down, not weeping
O'er the treasure in her keeping ;
And her hands and taper fingers,
Where angelic softness lingers :
Then her grand and wide-spread shoulders,
Her bosom heaving to beholders.
Surely, nothing can be finer,
More of mortal, or diviner ;
And no genius can be vaster
Than two-fold shown by this great master.

W. H."

This picture and feveral others had belonged to my grandfather, and had been left to him by Mr. Way, formerly a Mafter in Chancery, living clofe to Lord Erfkine in Lincoln's Inn Fields.

Bayle's article upon Pietro Aretine is a capital one. I tranflated the two following from the notes : it is the fuppofed epitaph upon Aretine, in the church of St. Luc at Venice.

Hic jacet Aretine, whose keen abuse
  Nothing escap'd, in many a Tuscan poem,
Excepting God ; and this was his excuse.—
  " I can't abuse Him, since I do not know Him."

Or, better,

Here lies Aretine, men call'd the divine,
  Who on everything living pass'd sentence,
Excepting his God, and 'tis not very odd ;
  With Him he disclaim'd all acquaintance.

There is a good ftory in Alexander Barclay's *Eclogues* (the tranflator of Seb-Brandt's *Ship of Fools*) which would

tell well in the manner of Prior. While Adam was out at
work, and Eve at home combing their many children, fhe
faw the Deity approaching their dwelling. She was afhamed
of appearing to have fo large a family, and put fome of
them among the hay, others under tubs, and kept only two
or three of the beft looking about her. God congratulated
her on her nice family, and patting one on the head faid
that he fhould be an emperor, another a king, a third a
great warrior. Eve, hoping that the fame good fortune
would be conferred on the reft, made them come out of their
hiding-places, all dirty, uncombed, and in other ways offenfive to fight. The Creator was difgufted at their appearance,
and decreed that thefe fhould be the hewers of wood and
drawers of water of the world, the hedgers, ditchers,
and ploughmen : hence, according to Barclay (who does
not quote his authority) the different and difproportionate
degrees in fociety were eftablifhed.

The *Ship of Fools* appears to have been tranflated by
Alexander Barclay, prieft, in 1508 ; but the edition I ufed
(with the *Eclogues* at the end) was printed by Cawood,
1570.

March 5.—Coleridge recently recited to me the following, not very good, epigram by him on his godmother's
beard ; the confequence of which was that fhe ftruck him
him out of her will.

> " So great the charms of Mrs. Munday,
>   That men grew rude a kiss to gain :
> This so provok'd the dame, that one day,
>   To Wisdom's power she did complain.

> " Nor vainly she address'd her prayer,
>   Nor vainly to that power applied :

The goddess bade a length of hair,
In deep recess her muzzle hide.

" Still persevere—to love be callous,
· For I have your petition heard ;
To snatch a kiss were vain (cried Pallas),
Unless you first should shave your beard."

The following was written by him on the late Earl of Lonfdale. I had it alfo from his own lips :

A very old proverb commands that we should
Relate of the dead only that which is good ;
But of the great Lord that lies here in lead,
All the good we can say is, that he is dead.

I was at the Britifh Mufeum to-day, and fending for Coles's Diary, Add. MSS. 5487 (quite for another purpose), I met with the following amufing notice of Horace Walpole and Kitty Clive : fhe had quitted the ftage as nearly as may be ten years before. She was a clofe neighbour of Walpole's, and fhe was often at Strawberry Hill, and " turned a card" with its owner. The Rev. Mr. Cole, a great goffip, under date of 29 Oct., 1779, thus writes :

Mrs. Clive, the celebrated actress and comedian, has a little box contiguous to Mr. Walpole's garden and close almost to the chapel : here she lives retired, and her brother, Mr. Raftor, with her. He called at Mr. Walpole's while I was with him, with a message from his sister to spend the evening with her, but he was not disposed to stir out. * * * * While I was at Strawberry Hill, I saw on the table a scrap of paper, with the following verses on Mrs. Clive, which I took a copy of, though I had no leave from Mr. Walpole for so doing ; yet as they lay publicly for any one to see them, I thought it no breach of honour to copy them. They seemed to me, from the blotting and alterations of the writing, to have been lately composed, probably the evening before, while Mrs. Clive was present, and meant as a sportive and innocent amusement to divert the time. They were written by way of epitaph, and on a supposition that Mrs. Clive was dead. They are as follow:

EPITAPH ON THE DEATH OF MRS. CLIVE.

Ye smiles and jests, still hover round,
This is Mirth's consecrated ground.
Here lived the laughter-loving dame,
A matchless actress, Clive by name.
The comic Muse with her retir'd,
The tragic wept when she expir'd.

Walpole, as he fays in his *Short Notes*, had written the Addrefs for Mrs. Clive on quitting the ftage.

March 6.—When I am working at Devonfhire Houfe, I fit in the large library, and the Duke in the outer room. He asked me to take luncheon daily, but I replied that a glafs of fherry and a cruft of bread was even more than I required. He takes me, therefore, at my word, and every morning, when his own luncheon is brought up, inftead of fending the fervant to me, he himfelf brings me a large glafs of wine and a crust of bread on a plate. I told the Duke once that it pained me to be fo waited upon, and that it better became me to wait upon him. He fmiled, and afked, "Why fo? You are much more worth waiting upon than I am: and, excepting on the fcore of money, more fit to· be a duke than I am. Every day when you are here, I fhall bring you bread and wine." I ufe his very words; and he always does his utmoft to leffen the diftance between us, and to put me at my eafe, on a level with himfelf. I do not call it condefcenfion (he will not permit the word), but kindnefs, and I should be moft ungrateful not to make all the return in my power. Yet, if he thinks any persons prefuming, and difpofed to make too free, his noble noftrils dilate like thofe of a finely-bred racer, and he at once looks the fools down to their level. People in general, even fome near friends, do not know him—I flatter myfelf I do—and he is really open-hearted.

To-day he came into the large library where I was at work (bringing, as ufual, my luncheon of a glafs of fherry and a bifcuit in his hand), when he said : "I have juft finished your poem, and although I do not like allegory in general, you have done much to reconcile me to it. I am efpecially pleafed with the opening, where the flowers, growing on the bank of the stream, are reprefented as saluting their fhadows in the dancing waters :

> —— " The flowers made haste to kiss
> The leaping waves, and many kisses took, `
> As if they lov'd upon themselves to look,
>   And own their shadows in the waters fair :
> Then, having kiss'd, tears from their bright eyes shook,
> To see the stream away their beauty bear;
>   Then kiss'd, and kiss'd again, to see it still was there."

This he repeated by heart ; and while thanking him for his criticifm, I inquired if he did not think the paffage would ftand better as I had originally written it ?—

> " As if they lov'd upon themselves to look,
>   And own their shadows in the running glass :
>   Then, having.kiss'd, tears from their bright eyes shook,
>   To see their beauty with the waters pass ;
>   Then kiss'd, and kiss'd again, to see still there it was."

He liked the firft beft, and urged that the laft line, with "was" as the rhime to "pafs," was quaint and objeﬆionable on all accounts. I obferved that the whole feven lines were but a prettinefs—not in the higheft ftyle of poetry—adding, that of the firſt canto, and perhaps of all the four cantos, I liked beſt the imaginative ſtanza, where the Pilgrim himſelf was ſo moved by the hero's apoſtrophe in praiſe of poetry, that for a moment he ſeemed to forget his diſguiſe, which, fading from him, almoſt betrayed the preſent Muſe :

> " While thus I spoke this wild apostrophy,
>   With earnest tone and gesture void of art,
> And warmth so truly token'd by my eye,
>   The hoary Pilgrim seem'd to feel a part
>   Ev'n of the burning love that from my heart
> Flow'd in a torrent ; for I could behold
>   A light celestial o'er his visage dart,
> That made him look no longer grey and old,
> But features of fresh youth and beauty's beam unfold."

For this ſtanza my memory was put to the teſt, and the Duke did not ſcruple to expreſs his opinion warmly. He added that the uſe of the word "ſeem'd", in the fourth line, reminded him of a line in the laſt canto, where, as it appeared to him, it was injudiciouſly employed. He fetched the book from his table in the next room, and pointed out a line at the end of canto iv, st. 32, where "ſeem'd" ſounded to his ear very tamely and poorly :—

> " And the bright waves seem'd proud of every gilded prow."

The two lines introducing the above made him think that *ſwell'd* was preferable, as it marked the triumph of the waters in the bright burdens they ſuſtained :—

> " Banners and silken sails and pennants shake
>   In the delighted airs that freshly blow,
>   And the bright waves *swell'd* proud of every gilded prow."

I at once admitted the great improvement, and ſaid that I would gladly alter my own copy the moment I reached home: "feem'd", I admitted, was very inexpreffive, while *fwell'd* converted to the purpofe of poetry the natural heaving of the waves. Thus, I faw that the Duke had not only read my poem, but liked it; and had the good tafte to fuggeft an admirable emendation. I cannot refrain from recording this incident, and I do not know why I fhould not. I am, perhaps, too fond of my poem, which is unknown, like the ring in the fifh's head of the Arabian tale. It may yet be difcovered, as that was: if not, I am content to know that I wrote it.

To-day I was elected a member of the Garrick Club, my fponfors being the Duke of Devonfhire and the Earl of Mulgrave. This is entering grandly.

March 7.—I have juft bought a manufcript of the time of Elizabeth and James I, containing a great many valuable and curious poems, fome known and many unknown, fome with the names of the authors appended, and fome without: a few are not quotable, and others fupply important deficiencies in productions hitherto fuppofed to be complete. I will give one fpecimen from a fhort piece, imputed, in *England's Helicon* and in Ellis's *Specimens* (ii, 221, edit. 1811), to Sir Walter Raleigh: as it there ftands the meaning is equivocal, but in my MS. there are ten additional ftanzas, moft of which alfo have a double application, but the following may be extracted.

> " Now, what is Love, I pray thee note?
> Tis lyning for a petticoate;
> Tis armour but for pistoll shott,
> It is a semy quaver note,
> It is both falsèd and by rote,
> And this is love wheron men dote."

The whole is in fifteen ftanzas, and the laft runs thus :

" Yet, to conclude, say what Love is ?
A thing of woe, a thing of blisse,
A thing won and lost with kisse ;
A fiery wavering thing it is,
A thing that burnes and nere cryes hisse,
And this is love, or else I misse."

I was at a theatrical dinner of twenty ladies and gentlemen, two of them being the treafurer of Drury Lane and his wife ; the latter fo ignorant that, when Otway's "Venice Preferved" was mentioned, fhe occafioned a ftop and a ftare by simply obferving, "That is one of Shake-fpeare's tragedies, is it not?" Nobody anfwered the queftion. Several good fongs were fung, one by Mathews, who told, in a very amufing way, the manner in which he contrived that his *Monopolylogues* fhould not be anticipated by being fent in to the Licenfer acting under the Lord Chamberlain, and thus publifhed. Mathews only forwarded for approval the mereft fketch of the performance, without one of the fongs. This was in the time of the Duke of Montrofe, who, on inquiry, was aftonifhed to find that, when he fent to Colman for the copy of the forthcoming performance, he got nothing but the bareft outline. Mathews declared to-day that all that related to the old Scotchwoman had never yet been in black and white, and that he trufted entirely to his memory and to the promptings of the moment. His fon Charles, according to his father, has a surprifing talent at compofing fongs, almoft *ex tempore*, keeping them in his head as he invents them, and repeating them afterwards entire. Of this faculty he gave us a particular inftance in one of the moft popular productions of the kind : he fang it, and this he afferted was made by Charles as they were on their way to Edinburgh in a postchaife. The father merely gave the fubject, and the fon had the fong, cut and dried, by the time it was wanted.

Mathews faid that he ferioufly projected the writing of his own reminifcences, but added that he had not yet put pen to paper with them.

Lord Glengall tells me that he has fufpended the finifhing of the new comedy on which he was engaged in consequence of the fad condition of the theatre.

I may add here that I was prefent when a boy at the first appearance of both Mathews and Lifton in London—Mathews as *Jabel* in "The Jew," in 1803, at the Haymarket; and Lifton in 1805, as *Sheepface* in "The Village Lawyer," alfo at the Haymarket. They both came from what was then called "the York Circuit," and there my father and mother had feen them play.

March 8.—At the Garrick Club for the firft time, where I saw Sir George Warrender, C. Kemble, James Smith, Poole, Barham, and others, play-patrons, actors, authors, and amateurs. It promifes to be fociable and agreeable. C. Kemble told me that his daughter Fanny (whofe play of "Francis the Firft" comes out very foon) has alfo completed a tragedy, which is better conftructed, with a very ftrong leading intereft, as well as a ftriking cata-ftrophe. The fault of "Francis the First" certainly is that it has neither beginning, middle, nor end: there is no entire-nefs or coherence in the ftory, and the intereft, fuch as it is, is double: for the firft half of the piece it belongs to one fet of characters, and for the other half to another. De Bourbon is the hero of the firſt half, and Francis the Firſt of the laſt. It has been in type many months.

C. Kemble alſo told me that the leaſt ſum the two theatres of Covent Garden and Drury Lane are likely to loſe this ſeaſon is £10,000 each—that is ſuppoſing there be no material improvement in the audiences. He imputes the laxneſs of the public in coming to the great theatres to the low prices at number of the ſmaller ones; and he ſaid that if he had his way he would to-morrow reduce the admiſſion of the boxes at Covent Garden to five ſhillings, of the pit to two-and-sixpence, and of the gallery to one ſhilling; but then he would take off about the firſt half-dozen rows of the pit to be let out in ſtalls, as at the King's Theatre.

He is miſtaken—all this would not do : he muſt reduce the ſize of the theatre, not the price of admiſſion. Sheridan's "School for Scandal" was brought out in a houſe holding at the utmoſt £350 : Covent Garden eaſily contains £700. Since the firſt enlargement of the two houſes to this extent, they have been nearly every ſeaſon loſing concerns.

C. Kemble, who knew that I was for free trade, and no monopoly, or duopoly, talked of himſelf as a ruined man.

March 9.—Pleaſures-of-Hope Campbell told me that he was ſeriously ſetting about a Life of Mrs. Siddons, which he had *to her* undertaken to write, and for which ſhe furniſhed him with ſome papers. I promiſed to give him anything I could find among the Larpent Plays to contribute to his purpoſe; but I do not believe that he has induſtry to get through it. He has, however, been two or three times at the Britiſh Muſeum collecting materials. He ſays that Mrs. Siddons' letters are good for little, and that thoſe

of her correfpondents are not much better ; and he complained generally of the want of character and variety of
incident in the life of his heroine.

Does the following refer to an anceftor of the Kemble
family ? I copy it from *Domeftic Intelligence, or News
both from the City and Country*, of 26 Aug., 1679.

" By letters from Hereford, we have advice that upon Tuesday the
22 inst., one John Kemble, a Popish Priest, condemned the last
assizes, was hanged, and afterwards beheaded there."

What follows is in the handwriting of the famous Henry
Lawes, compofer of "Comus," and fubfcribed with his initials.
There is no mufic appended : the words are doubtlefs thofe
of an anthem he had composed.   Is it now known ?

" PARTE OF THE 27 PSALME.

" *Vers for a Man.*	Harken, O harken unto my voice, O Lord, when I crye unto thee have mercy uppon me and heare me. O hyde not thou thy face from me, nor cast thy servant a waye, nor cast thy servant a way in displeasure.
" *Chor.*	O hyde not thou, etc.
" *Vers for a treble.*	Teach me thy waye, O Lord, and leade me in a plaine path, because of myne enemyes.
" *A base and a treble.*	Deliver me not over into the will of myne adversaries, for there are false witnesses risen up against me ; for there, etc.
" *A meane.*	I had fainted, unles I had beleevde to se the godnes of the Lord in the land of the livinge.
" *A base and countertenor.*	I had fainted, unles I had beleev'd, etc.
" *Chor.*	I had fainted, etc."

I have, however, a piece of Henry Lawes' compofition in
the tune to a political fong of great popularity, at the time,

the words of the first verfe being thefe, as he writes them under his original score :

•
> " Farewell to the parlyament, with a hey;
> Farewell to the parliament, with a hoe.
> Your dear delight the cittye,
> Whose wants have made us witty,
> And a figg for the close committee.
> With a hey tronny nony noe."

On another fheet H. Lawes fupplies the whole of the words, confifting of no fewer than twenty-one ftanzas. They may be feen printed, with many variations, among the *State Poems* : it has no date either in the MS. or in the book. If Henry Lawes had not been the author of the fong, as well as of the mufic, it feems ftrange that he fhould have taken fo much pains in writing out the whole of the words: it feems, too, a strange condefcenfion on his part. He was born in 1600, and died not long after the Reftoration.

March 10.—There was, as I learn at the Garrick, a curious *rencontre* between Poole (author of " Paul Pry", etc.) and Lifton, the actor, this morning at the Olympic Theatre, while they were rehearfing a new piece by the former. They did not come to blows. but words ran high. Lifton complained that Poole had faid of him in fome " respectable fhop" that he (Lifton) was entirely indebted to him (Poole) and Kenney (the author of " Love, Law, and Physic," " Sweethearts* and Wives," etc.) for his reputation as an actor—that Poole had called him " a vagabond", and thirdly, that he had faid that John Reeve was a better actor. As to the fecond and third charges, Poole met them by the lie direct, and defired Lifton fo to tell his informant : as to the firft, he maintained that it was true to a certain extent, fince both he and Kenney had written the pieces entirely for Lifton. The fact is that the obligation is pretty mutual, only authors cannot fee it on one fide, nor actors on the other. But for Lifton neither Poole nor Kenney would have been half fo popular. Poole's piece called " Young Hopeful" was afterwards brought out and acted three nights : it was then withdrawn, and Poole wrote a letter to the *Morning Chronicle*, afferting that the want of fuccefs was owing to Lifton's intoxication, if not to his wifh to damn the piece.

What follows is a theatrical curiofity—an autograph letter from Barton Booth, the great performer of *Cato* for twenty fucceffive nights—to Lord Lansdowne, reprefenting the hardfhip of his cafe, as excluded from the patent granted to Wilks, Dogget, and Cibber. The immediate refult was the iffue of a new patent to the four actors, with equal advantages to each. The point is an interefting one in theatrical hiftory.

"Tuesday, Dec. 16th, 1712.

"MY LORD,

"I cannot forbear returning you my most humble thanks for your kind promise of assisting me, tho' at the same time I cannot but be concerned at the trouble I give you.

" Let me humbly beg leave to give your lordship some further light into this affair : a short history of my misfortunes, since I first undertook this unhappy business I am now engaged in, may prevail on your Lordship's good nature and generosity to redress the oppression I now labour under, with more dispatch than perhaps might seem necessary to you, if you were unacquainted with my present condition.

"After having been six years at Westminster school, instead of going to either University to pursue my studies, my folly led me to the profession I now must stick to while I live. As the world goes, actors are very rarely preferred to any other employment. I blush to own my indiscretion : I was very young, but since I have brought myself to a bad market, I must make the best of it.

" I have been thirteen years an actor : five years in Lincoln's Inn Fields, under Mr. Betterton ; and during that time I did not receive, *communibus annis*, thirty pounds by my salary : from thence I removed, under Mr. Vanburgh and Mr. Congreve, to the playhouse in the Haymarket for four years. I fared not much better than before : these misfortunes threw me materially behind-hand in the world, and had I not married a gentlewoman of some fortune, I must have perished : for the four remaining years I received my full pay, which amounted to one hundred and ten pounds per annum, or thereabout. I have had success in my benefit plays for the four years past, but never yet was able to retrieve the losses I sustained. Before I was always cheerful in my misfortunes, and endeavoured, by much industry and application in my business, to render myself acceptable to the town, still flattering myself with hopes that one time or other actors would be encouraged, as they were at the restoration and for many years afterwards. *Volvendos dies en attulit !* But Mr. Wilks, Mr. Doggett and Mr. Cibber only enjoy the benefit of this alteration in our theatrical government : those gentleman have been and are in possession of what has already made them happy in their circumstances, while I must act and labour to divert the town for a bare subsistence only : this, my Lord, is hard upon me ; yet I have something to urge further, to satisfy your Lordship that my case is still worse : my present livelihood depends upon my health, and even at this time I lie too much at the mercy of my creditors.

" Thus, my Lord, if I am not redressed, I must be a sacrifice to my equals ; Mr. Wilkes, Mr. Cibber, and Mr. Dogget, must raise fortunes to themselves and families while I starve.

" I know the worth and honour of the Vice Chamberlain, but not being so well-known to him as your Lordship, I have humbly begged of you to be my patron, and advocate to him ; and I am well assured he has ever had a just and true regard for your Lordship.

" I must beg leave to tell your lordship, that you are an honour and an ornament to Dramatic Poetry in particular : the knowledge of that

naturally inclined me to believe your Lordship would readily endeavour to help an oppressed actor, who has had the good fortune to
please the town, and sometimes your Lordship, whose judgement I
would willingly stand or fall by.

"I never could hope to be forgiven the freedom I have taken were
not your Lordship one of the best tempered noblemen living.

"I humbly beg that my necessity and the justice of my cause may
prevail upon your Lordship to pardon my presumption of writing to
you.

"I am, my Lord,
    "Your Lordship's most obedient and most humble servant,
                                    "B. BOOTH.
"To the Right Honourable the Lord Lansdowne."

March 11.—The Duke of Devonſhire took me with him,
when he went to viſit the ſtudios of ſeveral great painters
and ſculptors, Landſeer, Calcot, Bailey, and Chantrey, to-
day : he gave ſome commiſſions and ſome works in progreſs,
but he did not remain anywhere long enough to pleaſe me.

No man living can have enjoyed a finer opportunity, than
I have had, to worſhip the nobleſt ſpecimens of ſculpture and
painting ; becauſe I ſaw, under every advantage, the whole
contents of the Louvre before they were again diſperſed
over Europe. I arrived in Paris in 1814-15, juſt as the
exhibitions were cloſed—the very day when they were ſhut.
I was bitterly diſappointed (for I then wanted to ſee nothing
elſe), and reſolved to put a bold face on the buſineſs, and
to wait upon the Baron Denon, the official keeper of the
treaſures, to ſtate my caſe and to aſk his aſſiſtance. He
received me moſt politely ; but when I diſcloſed my object
in troubling him, he at firſt very gravely ſhook his head.
However, I urged my appeal as an Engliſhman who might
never have another opportunity, and in the end he gave

me a card, which he faid would admit me on any day between twelve and four for three whole weeks. I remained
in Paris for the three weeks, and no day paffed that I did
not avail myfelf of the kind Baron's card.

There were not twenty ftrangers in the Louvre on any
day, fo that I had the advantage of feeing everything at my
leifure, and without the inconvenience of the flighteft
crowd. The Baron had alfo given me a catalogue; and
thus I faw, not copies, but *the renowned originals*, among
fculptures, the Apollo, the Venus, the Torfo, the Diana,
etc., and, among pictures, "The Transfiguration", "The St.
Peter Martyr", "The Defcent from the Crofs", "The
Stoning of St. Stephen", and hundreds of others. I look
back upon this expedition to Paris as one of the luckieft
events of my life ; and on queftions of art in fculpture and
painting, I plume myfelf no little upon my tafte and judgment, thus improved. I did not fail to make the Duke
aware of the advantage I had enjoyed fo many years
before I was introduced to him. I never can be fufficiently
thankful for the wonderful opportunity : it will be a fource
of happinefs to me as long as I live.

I had the fatisfaction of being introduced to Talma, not
on this vifit to Paris, but fome years before his death, which
happened in or about 1827. His figure was not good, too
fhort and ftout, while his face was by no means handfome,
and could never have been fo, but expreffive. I only faw
him act two parts, in "Athalie" and "Les Horaces", and I
did not thoroughly relifh either ; but I muft own to a pre-
judice againft the ferious productions of the French ftage.

I have had an offer for a new edition of Shakefpeare. My anfwer was, that I am not yet prepared

to undertake fuch a great work, and I added that the pro-
pofer might come to me again in two years. In the meantime, I will read through and collate every play in the
oldeft impreffions, all, or nearly all, of which are now
within my reach at Devonfhire Houfe.

My friend Amyot and I, between us, have bought all
Larpent's Dramatic Manufcripts, he having filled the office
of Licenfer under various Lords Chamberlain for many
years, fo as to carry us back quite to the time of Thomfon
and Goldfmith. We have found among them fome curious
pieces, efpecially in the fhape of prologues and epilogues ;
but the collection is fadly deficient in fterling old comedies:
thus, we can difcover no production by Goldfmith, neither
"She Stoops to Conquer" nor "The Good-natured Man".
The fame of Sheridan's "School for Scandal" and "Rivals";
but there is a copy of "The Critic", with fome of the author's dafhes, and a direction at the end refpecting the ex-
plofion. Of modern farces and melodramas, there are a
fuperabundance ; but, on the whole, they are hardly worth
the money we have given for them (£400). There are two
or three copies of "Lethe", in various fhapes, and fome of
them in Garrick's handwriting. There are many prologues
and epilogues that were fpoken, but not printed ; and two
by Sheridan (not in his handwriting) to feparate plays,
where the paffage,

> "While his left heel, insidiously aside,
> Provokes the caper it affects to chide,"

is repeated ; the fact, apparently, being, that, as the comedy
for which it was firft written was damned, the author
thought he might fairly ufe the fame fimile for another

II

production, which might have better fuccefs. The Larpent Manufcripts fill fix or eight immenfe bundles, and I hardly know how to find them houfe-room, particularly as Amyot leaves his fhare to my keeping. Sheridan became a patentee after Garrick retired in 1776.

I have a very diftinct recollection of Sheridan as a Parliamentary orator ; but the laft time I heard him fpeak was after the burning of Drury Lane Theatre in the fpring of 1809. This was Holland's Theatre, which I well remember, with its lofty arches above "the flips" on each fide of the houfe, giving it an appearance of great lightnefs. I was prefent at the fire, to which I ran from my father's houfe in Hatton Garden.

Mar. 10.—Fanny Kemble, who made her firft and moft fuccefsful appearance on the ftage as Juliet, two years ago, and who has been continuing her career in many of the principal parts of tragedy and comedy, is about to teft her talents as a dramatift, and has written a tragedy which fhe calls "Francis the Firft". It has been put into type, firft as fhe originally wrote it, and afterwards as it is to be acted : as fhe wrote it, it is only in proof, and fhe has given me a copy, in order that I may compare it with the other and more complete impreffion, which is to be reprefented in a day or two. What has been done to make the piece more *actable* does not in fact make it more readable ; and if I am rightly informed, Sheridan Knowles has lent the authorefs a helping hand in a new fifth act, which is very buftling, and confifts mainly of four fcenes relating to the battle of Pavia, and the capture of Francis I. Act v is merely meant for the ftage.

I am told, and believe, that the whole was written before

the authore∫s was eighteen; and it is a mo∫t clever performance, if we cannot quite ∫et it down as a work of genius.
F. K. is a charming woman, with a face better than hand-
∫ome, but her complexion a little ∫warthy : ∫he talks well
and confidently, and is of cour∫e an obje&ct of attra&ction now
in all companies.

I have ∫ome mi∫givings as to the continued ∫ucce∫s of
" Francis the Fir∫t" as an a&cting play, but it de∫erves great
encouragement.

March 13.—I heard from Abbott (who when fir∫t he
came to London was called the "Bath Ro∫cius") the following anecdotes of Sheridan Knowles, author of "Virginius,"
" William Tell," " Alfred," etc.

Knowles was for ∫ome time on various country ∫tages,
and played ∫ubordinate chara&cters to Kean. On one occa∫ion
he was de∫irous of making his inferior part more prominent,
and accordingly in∫erted, in every place where he could
make room, ∫oliloquies of his own author∫hip, which he delivered much to the ∫urpri∫e and di∫∫atisfaction of Kean and
the other performers, and ∫ometimes of the audience.

He was playing *Macbeth* at Bath (Abbott was the *Mac-
duff)* the la∫t night of a not very pro∫perous engagement,
and after the fall of the curtain he addre∫∫ed him∫elf to
Abbott and ∫aid, " I'm off to-morrow, my dear boy: can I
take any letters for you ?"—" I thank you" (∫aid Abbott)
" but where are you going?" " Why to be ∫ure now—
upon my ∫oul, I don't know exa&ctly," was the reply.

Knowles has dined with me ∫everal times to meet people
who wi∫hed to ∫ee him, and he always did his be∫t to
make him∫elf agreeable : he generally ∫ucceeded ; indeed,

he was rather fond of fhowing off, and mimicking fome of the leaders of the profeffion : his Irifh imitations of John Philip Kemble were really ludicrous,˙ and he was apparently not at all aware of the brogue he introduced into the foliloquy in "Hamlet." He infifted that John Philip Kemble had a Welfh brogue. Somebody played off a harmlefs joke upon him by quoting the following couplet from Chaucer :

> " It is great harme, and eke great pytè,
> To set an *Irous* man in hye degree."

The joker said it was a very unfair exclufion of Knowles's countrymen from high office ; and Knowles entirely agreed with him, fancying that "irous" meant *Irifh*, and not paf-fionate.

March 15.—Fanny Kemble's play did not fucceed as well as her friends expected. I thought, indeed, that the houfe would have fhown more *toosy-moosy*, as Braham calls (or ufed to call) "enthufiafm." Much of the poetry (and there was a good deal of it) was loft in the huge area of the houfe. They fay that Covent Garden muft be fhut up in a few days, unlefs " Francis the Firft" fhould draw extraordinarily. Drury Lane is nearly in the fame condition, only the leffee there has capital, upon which he can, and does, draw, if the performances do not.

March 16.—The following is founded upon a paffage in Burton's *Anatomy of Melancholy* (part i, feét. 2).

THE CREATION OF MAN.

> Before the creation of man ('tis a fable
>   Not founded on Scripture, as what fables are ?)
> A circumftance happen'd, for which I'm unable
>   To mention my author, whoever he were.

Dame Care took a walk by the side of a river,
  Till weary she sat herself down for a time ;
And then for her pleasure (we ne'er should forgive her)
  She moulded a form from the clay and the slime.

Two arms and two legs she affix'd to the figure,
  But wherefore I do not pretend to explain ;
Some five feet in height, or, they say, rather bigger,
  A head on its shoulders—without any brain.

The tide would have soon wash'd away the frail image,
  But Jove, coming by, gave it motion and life ;
And by all the traditions brought down from that dim age,
  Betwixt Jove and Care there arose a warm strife.

'Twas merely on this—having made such a creature
  Between them, they could not agree on its name ;
And Care, who was rather perverse by her nature,
  Refus'd ev'n to Jove to relinquish her claim.

At length Jove propos'd to refer it to Saturn :
  Dame Care with reluctance came into the plan;
And Saturn decreed that all after this pattern,
  Should be call'd ('twas a monstrous absurdity) MAN.

The ownership next was as stiffly disputed :
  Dame Care wished for ever to make him her drudge ;
But her scheme with the notions of Jove little suited,
  So Saturn again was call'd in as the judge.

This course, too, appeared far the best to the others,
  For Terra stepp'd in and demanded her share :
The stuff Man was made of she swore was his mother's,
  Nor would she resign it to Jove or to Care.

" Man's but Man (said the Father of Gods), not immortal,
  And Care's shall he be from the day of his birth ;
But his soul shall be Jove's when it enters heav'n's portal,
  While the body returns to its mother, the earth.

To this sentence the parties disputing consented.
Poor Man for himself had a few words to say ;
But Jove would not hear him, and Care soon prevented
His murmurs by stopping his mouth up with clay.

See alfo, for the profe verfion, the Epiftle to the Reader, before the *General Hiftory of Women*, by Tim Touchit : 8vo. London, 1742. This book is ftolen chiefly from Thomas Heywood's Γυναικειον. 1624. Folio.

C. Kemble fhewed me a note from his admirable fifter —the laft fhe wrote. I once or twice faw her at private parties ; but fhe was nothing in fociety, or rather fomething too much of the tragedy queen. Latterly fhe became haggard, and I am told did not bear the vifitations of age at all patiently ; she could not (as fhe wished) carry her ftage deportment as Queen Catherine into private life, and fancied that fhe was ill-ufed by infirmity. She preferved her fine voice nearly to the laft. My earlieft recollection of her was as *Elvira* in " Pizarro" at Covent Garden in 1803-4, but she and her brother John had previoufly produced the play at Drury Lane in 1799. Among Larpent's MSS., I found Sheridan's copy of " Pizarro", with a few corrections hit off in the moft flashing way and dashing hand. Mrs. Hatton (Anne of Swanfea), with whom I formerly correfponded, ufed to tell aftounding and incredible ftories of her fifter, Mrs. Siddons : fo did Winfton, Secretary of the Garrick Club, neither credible nor creditable, and I disbelieve them all.

March 18.—I went again, as my cuftom of a morning now is, to Devonshire Houfe to continue my work on the plays and play-bills—the laft becomes rather tedious.

The Duke is never weary of making me feel at home in his houfe, always treats me with kind, yet refpectful familiarity, and if he have any friends with him, introducing me to them. This he did with Lady Blanch Cavendish, afterwards married to the Duke's coufin, heir prefumptive to the title. He alfo introduced me to Lord Mulgrave, who had feconded me, at the Duke's inftance, for election to the Garrick Club. The Duke feldom had a ftranger with him that he did not make me acquainted with : fuch was the cafe with Lord Clare and Lord Milton.

Charles Lamb and his fifter were with us this evening, but I do not ufually mention fuch incidents unlefs, as in this inftance, they lead to fomething elfe : they are vifitors we are always rejoiced to fee. I told C. L. that I had very recently had an offer from a publifher to edit Shakefpeare, and I told him alfo my reafon for declining it, which he applauded ; adding that eight or ten years hence would be time enough, and I fhall take his advice.

This led him to afk me, whether I remembered two or three paffages in his book of books, Burton's *Anatomy of Melancholy*, illuftrating Shakefpeare's notions regarding Witches and Fairies. I replied that if I had feen them, I did not then recollect them. I took down the book, the contents of which he knew fo well that he opened upon the place almoft immediately : the firft paffage was this, refpecting Macbeth and Banquo and their meeting with the three Witches : "And Hector Boethius [relates] of Macbeth and Banco, two Scottifh Lords, that, as they were wandering in woods, had their fortunes told them by three ftrange women." I faid that I remembered to have feen that paffage quoted, or referred to by more than one editor

of Shakefpeare. "Have you feen this quoted," he enquired,
"which relates to fairies ? 'Some put our fairies into this
rank, which have been in former times adored with much
fuperftition, with fweeping their houfes and fetting of a pail
of clean water, good victuals and the like ; and then they
fhould not be pinched, but find money in their fhoes and
be fortunate in their enterprifes * * * and, Olaus Magnus
adds, leave that green circle which we commonly find in
plain fields.' Farther on Burton gives them the very
name affigned to one of them by Shakefpeare, for he adds,
'Thefe have feveral names in feveral places : we commonly
call them *Pucks*' (part i, fect. 2), which Ben Jonfon degrades
to *Pug*." I told Lamb that this quotation was fo applicable to fome parts of "A Midfummer Night's Dream",
that I could not but think it muft have been extracted in
the notes upon that play.

I affured Lamb that, if I ever plucked up courage enough
to edit Shakefpeare, my firft principle would be to reprint
as nearly as poffible the ancient text; and that now I had
in my power ample means for doing fo, becaufe the D. of
D. had placed all his original editions, 4to and folio, at my
difpofal. Lamb did not profefs to be well read in the notes
of any impreffion, but he faid, with unaffected modefty, that
both he and his fifter were pretty well acquainted with the
text. The fact is that a new and illuftrated edition of their
charming *Tales from Shakefpeare* has juft been brought
out, but Lamb obferved that it had been of little or no
pecuniary advantage to them.

There is a clafs of admirers of poetry, as they call themfelves, who perhaps poffefs fufficient tafte and knowledge,
but are afraid of giving an opinion until they have had an

opportunity of feeing in print, or hearing in converfation, the judgment pronounced by others. I have known hundreds of fuch people, and I could name fome of them among my particular friends. The Rev. John Mitford is not one of thefe: he is a fcholar and himfelf a verfifier, and he has liftened with apparent pleafure when I fometimes have read to him pieces of my own compofition, and efpecially ftanzas in praife of poetry in my early allegorical poem. I do not believe that there is a particle of envy in the compofition of his mind. I cannot fay the fame of another friend of mine, who is prone to "damn with faint praife", and to hint faults rather than to point out excellences. Both were with me to day, and to both, and at their requeft, I read my defcription of the Stream of Popularity in my *Poet's Pilgrimage*. I gave Mitford a printed copy of it, and Dyce, who joined in while we were talking of it, afked me to perform the promife I had once made to him, to let him have the original manufcript. I prefented it to him, and he carried it away.

Dyce owns to having himfelf been "guilty of the weaknefs of verfe"; but I never could prevail upon him to fhow me a line of his own; excepting once, when he put into my hand fome annual, where he pointed out about twenty couplets figned with his name. I remember that they defcribed a ftorm at fea, and there was a pretty fimile in them, where he likened the froth of the waves, whipped into the air by a guft of wind, to the fudden flight of a flock of white fea-fowl.

He gave my wife fome time ago a copy of his *Specimens of Englifh Poeteffes*, but at the fame time profeffed himfelf by no means proud of it.

I add here an imitative paftoral dialogue which Mitford pronounced fuccefsful, after he had read it over twice. Dyce was reading fomething elfe, viz., a very diminutive copy of George Peele's *Tale of Troy*, 1604 (only an inch and a half high, by an inch and a quarter broad), which I had borrowed for his ufe, and of which he afterwards made a collation, prefenting a copy of it to me: it was the fmalleft book he had ever feen, and he grieved fadly that he had not known of its exiftence before he printed his fecond edition of *Peele's Works* in 1829.

A Pastoral Dialogue.

Damon.   Ah! fairest Chloris, if I die,
      To thee my death I owe,
  Though thou canst look with tearless eye
      On me, and on my woe.

Chloris.   Young Damon, prithee do not fear ;
      For this full well I know,
  Thy death, fond youth, is not so near,
      Though thou persuad'st me so.

Damon.   Look on this pale and hollow cheek,
      Look on this sunken eye ;
  Look on these limbs so wan and weak :
      Do they not say I die ?

Chloris.   And if thy cheek be sad and pale,
      Should that compassion move ?
  Unto thyself thou ow'st thy bale,
      And to thyself thy love.

Damon.   In words, I own, thou did'st not teach,
      Still, thy command I took ;
  For feeble words can never reach
      The language of thy look.

Chloris.   If words could tell thee what I mean,
        Then short had been thy pain ;
    And in my look was nothing seen
        But anger and disdain.

Damon.   Farewell, farewell, proud shepherdess;
        My woes will soon be o'er :
    I would to heaven I lov'd thee less,
        Or thou did'st love me more.

Chloris.   Nor more nor less can I thee love,
        That love thee not at all.
    Though tears, and prayers, and looks you prove,
        Thy profit will be small.

Damon.   Then, let me die : my suit forgive ;
        In death I still am blest :
    Though by all others I might live,
        To die by thee is best.

    And though no love nor pity flow
        In life to thy poor swain,
    Still, some compassion thou shalt show
        In ending thus my pain.
             Sic moritur Damon.

March 19.—Bronzino, the author of the following stanzas, died in 1621 : they are addreffed to the Grand Duke of Florence, who had promifed to give him a horfe, and had forgotten to keep his word. Nobody could be offended at a hint thus conveyed, and the conclufion is capital.

ON A HORSE PROMISED, BUT NOT GIVEN.

    A new way has been found out by your Highness
        Of giving to your faithful servants horses :
    No money's wanted ('tis your Grace's slyness
        To keep their little cash within their purses)

For saddle, spur or bridle : but some shyness
  Is needed still in asking, which of course is.
We've only to accept—with faith to boot—
And for the rest we still may walk on foot.

Blessed, thrice blessed, be this rare invention
  Of giving horses with such generous ease !
It must have been discover'd with intention
  To mount as many horsemen as you please.
Sans saddle, rein, whatever one can mention,
  We may not only ride o'er land, but seas :
Mountains can never stop us, and we gallop
O'er ocean safer than in ship or shalop.

I know it well, for I have often tried it,
  Since me my Lord ten times a day dispatches :
I go and I return—so fast I ride it,
  The very wind my wondrous horse ne'er catches.
The Emperor's self might glory to bestride it ;
  In all his stud he has not one that matches :
It leaps and gallops with me—oft hath done it;
And yet, 'tis strange, I never was upon it.

Perhaps you thought that for this noble creature
  I must buy hay and corn, and could not do it,
And, therefore, to maintain it, it might eat your
  Forage—'tis worse than deadly poison to it.
What above all must seem quite out of nature,
  It never eats—at least I never knew it ;
And yet it grows no leaner, which is stranger :
It costs me nought for either rack or manger.

This is, perhaps, because it has resorted
  To courts, where little can be had to eat ;
And where by drink folks chiefly are supported,
  Because it costs a great deal less than meat.
Oft has it made confusion when it snorted
  (And but for this defect it is complete)
And started from its shadow in the water :
Water it hates, when found in any quarter.

But while I praise my steed, with joy elated,
 I fear I may do harm by what I spoke,
Making it seem as I no truth related,
 And so my praises only end in smoke.
I fear lest when this topic is debated,
 It may be thought I only meant a joke :
On this account I'll drop the subject, slily
To get a horse I can't praise quite so highly.

The ironical flattery of this epiftle can hardly be too much admired. Bronzino was one of the many painter-poets of Italy : his pictures are rare.

March 20, 1832.—I copy the following epitaph, or elegy, or what you will, "Upon Sir James Mackintofh," from the original in Coleridge's handwriting, lent to me by H. C. Robinfon. I do not profefs to be able to underftand who was brother-bard, but Coleridge could not endure Dr. Parr's "turncoat"; poffibly becaufe he himfelf had turned.

" The Devil believes that the Lord will come
 Stealing a march, without beat of drum,
 About the same hour that he came last,
 On an Old Christmas Day, in a snowy blast :
'Till the trump then shall sound no body nor soul stirs,
For the dead men's heads have slipped under the bolsters.

" Brother bard, brother bard ! in our churchyard
 Both beds and bolsters are soft and green,
 Save one alone, and that's of stone,
 And under it lies a Counsellor keen.
'Twould be a square grave, if it were not too long,
And 'tis fenc'd round with iron, tall, spear-like, and strong.

" This fellow from Aberdeen hither did skip,
 With a waxy face and a blubber lip,

And a black tooth in front, to show in part
What was the colour of his whole heart.
This Counsellor sweet, this Scotchman complete—
The Devil *scotch* him for a snake !
I hope he lies in his grave awake.

" On the 7th of January,
   When all is white, both high and low,
As a Cheshire yeoman's dairy—
   Brother bard, ho ! ho ! believe it or no,
   On that tall tomb to you I'll show
   Two round spaces void of snow.
I swear by our knight and his forefathers' souls,
That in shape and size they are just like the holes
   In the house of privity
   Of that ancient family.

" On those two spaces, void of snow,
   There have sat in the night for an hour or so,
Before sunrise and after cock-crow,
   The Devil and his grannam,
   With a snow-blast to fan 'em,
Expecting and wishing the trumpet would blow,
For they are cock-sure of the fellow below."

Coleridge had an intolerable and inexplicable averfion to anything Scottifh ; and I have heard him fay more than once, " When I fpeak of a Scotch rafcal, I always lay the emphafis on Scotch." He had a notion that Mackintofh had done him fome injury, but I never could learn any particulars. He abufed Dyce only for being a Scotchman, the grandfon of an Aberdeen linendraper.

March 29.—W. Dunn, treafurer of Drury Lane (where, by the way, they might as well be without a treafurer, the theatre being kept open nightly at a great lofs), told the

following ſtory of the late John Philip Kemble, of which he
was an eye and ear-witneſs—Dunn was then a young man,
ſpending a family evening at old Richard Peake's. About
half-paſt nine, after not only the wine but the tea was done,
in came J. P. Kemble half-cocked. " My dear Dick" (ſaid
he) "don't diſturb yourſelf. Mrs. Peake, pray go on with
your cards; but I have an appointment here with Sheridan,
and I ſhould be ſorry if he came and found me abſent. He
may not come, but I am reſolved, at all events, not to
neglect my duty. You know, my dear Dick, that we have
a great deal at ſtake juſt now." Peake ſaid that he was
very glad to ſee him, and apologiſed for having done tea,
offering at the ſame time to have ſome made for Kemble.
"Oh, no, my dear Dick" (replied Kemble), "I don't much
care for tea." "Then will you take a glaſs of wine?" inquired Dick. "You are very good, my dear Dick" (returned the other) : " the fact is, that I have not had time to
take my uſual quantity to-day, ſo I do not care if I do."
The bottles and glaſſes were produced, and Mrs. Peake,
&c., retired, well knowing what was likely to happen.
Kemble talked long and vehemently about himſelf and his
talents as an actor ; and at this moment, being peculiarly
angry with Pope for ſome ſucceſs in "Othello", he threatened
to cruſh him, and to show the town what he (Kemble) could
do, which they had never ſeen yet. Bottle after bottle diſ-
appeared, and finally Kemble, Peake, and Dunn got "mortal
drunk", and all three fell faſt aſleep. Kemble, who had
occupied the floor for ſome hours, was the firſt to wake, and
opening the shutters, he obſerved that it was broad daylight. He rouſed his companions, and on looking at their
watches (when they had wound them up does not appear),

they found that it was eight o'clock. "Well" (faid Kemble
gravely), "this is really very provoking; but Sheridan is
always too late for his appointments, I do not think it
likely that he will come now; but if he should, my dear
Dick, tell him how long I waited in expectation of feeing
him." And fo, flopping his hat on his head, and hardly
knowing whether it was the wrong or the right fide before,
he marched off. Dunn was a good *ftory*-teller.

April 3.—I own that I grow a little weary of my barren
duty of indexing modern play-bills; and the Duke of
Devonshire, who is a very keen obferver (partly, no doubt,
occafioned by his deafnefs, which makes him sharper with
his eyes) feems aware of it, and told me to-day (when he
brought in my sherry and cruft of bread) that he did not
like to fee me always fo drudgingly employed.

The Duke hears on fome days better than on others, but
he tells me that he can always hear me, becaufe I pronounce
my words diftinctly, forming each fyllable, not elaborately,
but completely; and this is the fecret of making deaf people
hear what otherwife would efcape them. This is the fecret,
too, of being well heard in large affemblies.

To-day I for the firft time faw on the library fhelves feveral
thin folio volumes, in parchment, of a diary kept by the famous Lord Halifax; and the earlieft entry I noted ftated that
the Earl had gone to the theatre and feen one of Dryden's
plays. I mentioned that diary to the Duke, and he obferved that it was known to be in poffeffion of the Caven-
difhes. I fpeak of the matter, becaufe it went out of my
mind for fome time, and when next I looked for the books
they were not in their place.

The Duke told me that he had juſt received from Leigh Hunt one of the pleaſanteſt letters he had ever read: he ſhewed it me, and it certainly was very playfully humorous. I aſked him how and when he had become acquainted with the author of *The Story of Rimini?* He did not make me any anſwer, and I fancied that I had been wrong in aſking: he ſaw what was paſſing in my mind, and relieved me inſtantly by adding, that he had once lent Leigh Hunt £200. He went on to tell me that, without any perſonal introduction, the author of *Rimini* had written to him ſome years ago, ſaying that he was in a pecuniary ſtrait, and that nothing would get him out of his difficulty but a loan of £200. The Duke was charmed with the ſtyle and frankneſs of the letter, and wrote to L. H. to call upon him: he did ſo next day, and explaining the matter to the Duke, the latter conſented to advance the ſum required; but aſked when it could be repaid? Leigh Hunt replied that he had a drama nearly finiſhed which had been accepted, but that in his preſent circumſtances he could not promiſe to return the £200 in leſs than two years. "Take three," ſaid the Duke, "and let me hope to ſee you here again on this day three years." That day three years arrived, and L. H. came, money in hand; and "ever ſince," added the Duke, "he has been a delightful correſpondent of mine."

I had heard ſomething of the tranſaction before; and Leigh Hunt had himſelf told me, what the Duke did not tell me, that when L. H., at three years end, carried the money back to Devonſhire Houſe, *the Duke would not receive one penny of it!* I was therefore ſomewhat prepared to hear from the Duke of a loan; but Leigh Hunt never informed me what a large ſum he had borrowed. I knew

K

too, from other fources, that this was not the only time when L. H. had been indebted to the confiderate generofity of the Duke of Devonfhire. In fact, the letter, which had fo much pleafed the Duke this day by its happy expreffions, was an indiftinct requeft for a comparatively fmall fum, with which I know the Duke intended to comply, though he did not tell me fo.

To us, who generally have no more money than we know what to do with, the Duke's generofity to poor applicants feems extraordinary. I have feen him give away £10, £20, or even £30 of a morning to people, as I thought, not always very deferving. Howard Payne was at one time a conftant recipient, and on one occafion told the Duke that he had come from America with dramatic pieces worth, according to his eftimate, £500, but which had only realifed £75. Poor foreigners were efpecial objects of the Duke's bounty:. he never could refufe anybody ; and now and then he afked me to fee people he did not know, and to give them what became his rank and their claims. He required no account of what I had expended, and I am fure I faved him a confiderable fum.

April 5.—H. C. Robinfon called to tell me of the death of his old friend Goethe; and it is fomewhat of a coincidence that at that very moment I was finifhing a tranflation of one of the youthful fongs of the noble German poet. It is that which H. C. R. often mentioned to me, and particularly the happy figure of the mill-ftream at the end. I read my verfion over to him, and he liked it; and as I do fo too, I copy it here, obferving only that it is fuppofed to have been fung at a jovial meeting of young poets, to which Goethe had travelled from a diftance. The meafure of the original is peculiar, and as it demands four double rhymes in each ſtanza, it was not very eaſy to put it into Engliſh.

DRINKING SONG.

A heavenly rapture fires my brain,
  Your inspiration merely ;
It lifts me to the winking stars,
  I seem to touch them nearly :
Yet would I rather stay below
  With you, I vow sincerely,
My song to sing, my glass to ring
  With those I love so dearly.

Then, wonder not to see me here
  To aid a cause so rightful :
Of all lov'd things on this lov'd earth
  To me 'tis most delightful.
I vow'd I would among ye be,
  In scorn of fortune spiteful ;
So here I came, and here I am
  To make the table quite full.

When thus we should together meet,
  Not quickly to be sunder'd,
I hoped at other poets' songs
  My joy, too, should be thunder'd ;
For friends like us would never grudge
  To travel miles a hundred,
So eager some this day to come ;
  Nor is to be wonder'd.

Long life to him who guards our lives !
  My doctrine's not learnt newly ;
We'll first do honour to our king,
  And drink to him most duly.
May he his foes without o'ercome,
  Within quell all unruly !
And grant support to every sort,
  As they shall serve him truly.

Thee next I give, thou only one,
   Who all thy sex defeatest !
Each lover thinks right gallantly
   His mistress the completest :
I also drink to her I love,
   Thou, who some other greetest,
Ne'er drink alone; still deem thine own,
   As I do mine, the sweetest.

The third glass to our friends is due,
   Who aid us when we need it.
How quickly flew each merry day,
   When such were by to speed it !
When fortune's gathering storm was dark,
   We had less cause to heed it :
Then fill the glass, the bottle pass,
   A bumper !—and I'll lead it.

Since broader, fuller swells the tide
   Of friends as life advances,
We'll drink to every lesser stream
   The greater that enhances.
With strength united thus we'll meet
   And brave the worst mischances ;
For oft the tide must darkly glide,
   That 'neath the sunshine dances.

Since all are met together here,
   And all as one united,
We trust that other's toils, like ours,
   With joy may be requited :
Upon one stream, from source to sea,
   Full many a mill is sited :
May we the weal of all men feel,
   And with it be delighted.

April 7.—Sheridan Knowles's play of "The Hunchback"
(brought out at Covent Garden on the 5th inft.) was in an

unfinifhed ftate even a month ago, as he had not concluded
the fifth act. He began it nearly two years ago, and about
a year fince he read the firft part of it to C. Kemble ; who
liked it very well, but not well enough to advance Knowles
(as he wifhed) £50 upon it. Knowles then took his play
away rather in a huff, and having rewritten the four acts he
fent them to Drury Lane. There they remained (Dunn
the treafurer *tefte*) for four or five months on the table un-
looked at : at length Dunn fent the four acts to Capt. Pol-
hill, who placed them in the hands of Bunn, his man of
bufinefs. Knowles afterwards called to know whether his
play would be acted at Drury Lane, and he was told that
the chance of fuccefs was little, if it were brought out, and
that it must at all events ftand over until the run of " Der
Alchymift" (which, by the way, lafted only three nights)
was concluded. Knowles was again in a huff—took " The
Hunchback" away from Drury Lane, and one day in his
Irifh energetic manner entered C. Kemble's room at the theatre and faid without preface, " By God, they want to infult
me at Drury Lane ; they have had my ' Hunchback' for
months, and now they refufe to bring it out. Will you play
it ?" C. Kemble faid that he could not give him an anfwer
without feeing the piece again, and Knowles put the four
acts into his hands. C. Kemble read and liked them,
but even then (about the end of February) Knowles had
not written the fifth act. Kemble again refufed to advance
money upon them, and Knowles was again ftarting away,
having fnatched up his MS., when C. Kemble faid fomething to foothe him, and in the end it was agreed that
Knowles fhould complete the play, and that then an offer
fhould be made to him. In about a week afterwards

Knowles again fuddenly burft into Kemble's room with "The Hunchback" finifhed (the fifth act is unqueftionably the worft, and was clearly money-hurried), and with an offer, quite unexpected by anybody, to perform in it himfelf. "By God," (faid he) "I am fure it will be a hit : I know I fhall create a fenfation, and I'll play in it myfelf." C. Kemble was ftartled, but the propofal was too promifing to be rejected, and fo Knowles's play was brought out, he being paid nightly fo much for his authorfhip, and fo much more for his actorfhip.

April 14.—Kenney the dramatift, as he informs me, was originally a banker's clerk, and his duties were fo active and laborious that he could have no time to himfelf in the courfe of the day. He therefore ufed to coax the porter in winter (as K. lived in the houfe) to let him have a fire in his bed-room, and then he ufed to fit up reading and writing. He was induced to quit this clerkfhip, partly by its irkfomenefs and partly by the perfuafions of Tweddell, brother of ("Remains Tweddell"), who was an attorney at Durham, and Kenney was to go into partnerfhip with him. Tweddell, however, made a more profitable arrangement, and left Kenney to fhift as he could. About this time he had written "Raifing the Wind," and it was, as Kenney fays, the origin of all his misfortunes ; for it prevented his obtaining feveral fituations, as it was thought that the author of fuch a piece muft be unfit for fteady bufinefs. Warner Phipps, actuary of fome infurance office, endeavoured to get him a place ; but did not fucceed, and plainly told him that another perfon had been preferred by the Directors, merely becaufe Kenney was the author of "Raifing the Wind".

Thus he was driven to dramatic writing in felf-defence; and Kenney defcribed very feelingly, when he found himfelf thus circumftanced, the fears he entertained left he never fhould be able to do anything as good as what he had already produced.

I may add here a lively fong, written lately at the requeft of a dramatic compofer, who wifhed for fomething that might be introduced into any fuccefsful mufical piece. Whether he did not like it, or whether he could not adapt it to any air of his own invention, I do not know, but I never heard of the fong again. Perhaps it was too old-fafhioned.

Cupid's Darts.

When beauty enters but the eye,
Cupid leaden darts lets fly :
Well he knows a shaft of lead
Sharp enough for such a head.
Love like this we know remaineth
But till fading beauty waneth.

When within the heart of heart,
Man's and woman's noblest part,
Cupid means a shaft to plant,
He wounds with point of adamant :
Love like this for ever stayeth,
Till adamant itself decayeth.

April 30.—I have juft quitted old Colman (*i. c.*, George Colman *Junior*, as he was called in the lifetime of his father, the author of "The Jealous Wife") and Mrs. Gibbs in Brompton Square. My bufinefs was peculiar : it was, if I could, to get him to refign the office of Licenfer of Plays, which the Duke of Devonfhire intimated he would give me

if I fucceeded. I did not fucceed, although, at the inftance
of the Duke, I offered Colman every farthing of the income
the place produced, while he lived. The Duke told me that
he wifhed me all fuccefs, but felt pretty fure of failure, if
only becaufe Colman was fuch a ftaunch old Tory, that he
would grant nothing to a Whig Lord Chamberlain : at the
fame time, as he wanted me back foon, he fent me from
Piccadilly to Brompton in his own brougham. The moment I broached the matter to Colman (Mrs. Gibbs did
not come into the room until he fent for her), he put a
negative upon it : he heard my propofal without interrup-
tion, and then faid, "Mr. Collier, I will not do it : I give
you no reafon, and I am not bound to give you one, but
I can not do it." I obferved that, under the circumftances,
I was not furprifed, and I hoped that he would not take
my propofal amifs, as I was not unauthorifed to make it. He
added, "No, no; you are quite right in afking, and I think
I am quite right in refufing. The Duke of Devonfhire is
a very kind man, as you know, but in this inftance I cannot
oblige him, nor you."

I was taking up my hat, when he faid (hobbling to the
bell, for he was very gouty, and then clearly fuffering),
"Wait a minute : I want fomebody elfe to know that I have
refufed." When the maid-fervant anfwered the bell, he faid,
"Tell your miftrefs I want to fpeak to her"; and in came
Mrs. Gibbs as if fhe had been waiting outfide. Colman juft
introduced me by name, but did not utter that of Mrs.
Gibbs, yet every body knew that fhe lived with him : fhe
was ftill good looking, but fat, and not well dreffed. "I have
juft had an offer" (faid Colman) "to give up my place, on
condition that I fhould ftill receive all the emoluments, and

I have refufed the offer: am I right?" "Certainly," faid
the lady. "I fee no reafon why you fhould relinquifh a
pofition fo appropriate to a man of your character, reputation, and connexions." Of courfe there was no more to
be faid: I took up my hat, fhook Colman by the hand, who
politely hoped I would do him the favour to call again
when I happened to be in Brompton, and quitted the houfe
with a bow. He fubfequently wrote me a civil note.

When I faw the Duke, he repeated that he had felt pretty
certain how the propofal would be met, but he wifhed me
to make it, as it was poffible that Colman, at his age and
with his infirmities, might like to avoid the trouble and
refponfibility of his office.

The Rev. R. Barham, for fome time, but under the rofe,
has written dramatic criticifms for the *Globe* when they
are wanted; but in general that evening journal takes them
from a morning paper. If Barham wifhes to do a good turn
for any actor or dramatift, he has thus the power without
refponfibility: his payment is only the ufe of the "bone",
or free admiffion, given to every newspaper. His company
is much liked, and he much likes company—efpecially theatrical, and he is often at the Garrick Club. He is a rather
fhort thick man of between forty and fifty, with a very droll
expreffion of face, to which a drop in one of his eyelids gives
additional effect. He is fond of a humorous ftory, and tells
it well: he is befides a genealogift, and when I lately
bought Ford's poem on the Earl of Devonfhire, publifhed
in 1603 *(Fame's Memorial)*, and wanted aid as to the hiftory
of the Blunt family, Barham drew up for me a ftatement
regarding it, with a regular pedigree. He feems a thoroughly
good-natured man, and rejoices to do a fervice to anybody:

L

he is an efpecial encourager of younkers; and I never knew him detract from other people's merits, or make a really ill-natured fpeech of anyone, who did not more than thoroughly deferve it. His verfes are very droll.

May 4.—I was invited to meet a large party and James Sheridan Knowles, whofe play, "The Hunchback" has juft been fo fuccefsful. He told me that he was born at Cork—that he was educated very much in England, where he fpent eighteen early years—that he was at one time in the militia—then in the Tower Hamlets—that he fubfe-quently left the "featherbed forces", and was made a Doctor of Medicine, with an Aberdeen diploma, in order to qualify him for fome fituation, I forget what, which he did not get. He informed me alfo, that his firft play was "Caius Gracchus", which was performed at Belfaft fome years be-fore it was brought out in London. His ufual habit was to write in bed, or walking, and he compofed the greater part of his "Hunchback" on the fands off Newhaven. He was delighted with Fanny Kemble, and never expected that fhe could have done as well in *Julia* as Mifs Phillips of Drury Lane. Knowles has a wife and eight living children (having buried three) and his eldeft fon of one and twenty is affiftant furgeon to a fhip of war now in the Eaft Indies. He dotes upon his fecond boy, and pronounces him a moft remark-able youth. Knowles was in capital fpirits all the evening, and while he admits that his acting is not the beft, he fays that he has greatly improved fince the firft night: according to his account, it is twenty years fince he trod any ftage until he came out at Covent Garden; but in the interval he has delivered many dramatic lectures, and accompanied them by recitations. He fang feveral fongs with a pleafing and not unpowerful voice—one of them his own words, intended to ridicule difputes about creeds, and with a chorus combining the rofe, fhamrock, thiftle and leek. He has already laid the firft ftone of another drama, but as he will be acting in the country all the fummer in "The Hunchback", he will perhaps not have time to complete it. He is engaged to go to Ireland and Scotland, as well as to many parts of England, and he fays that he means to play *Virginius* as well as *Mafter Walter.* He muft not rely upon his attraction as an actor only; and fo I told him. He gave me a copy of his "Hunchback," and promifed to fend me "Caius Gracchus," "William Tell," "Virginius," etc. "The Hunchback" is publifhed partly on his own account.

Knowles jokingly complained that the friend to whom he had entrufted the correction of the press, etc., of the "Hunchback" had cut out of the preface two good fimiles, one of them about a fhip after a ftorm reaching port, etc. At all events, that was not very new.

I may add, on the author's authority, that when the *Hunchback* was originally written, and as it was firft prefented to Drury Lane, the under-plot was entirely different, refembling in fome degree, and therefore too much, the fcenes in *Much Ado about Nothing* between Benedick and Beatrice. Thefe Knowles was advifed to alter, and he did fo, re-writing the whole under-plot in a fortnight.

I faw in the State-paper Office a letter from Sir Dudley Carlton, then at Oxford, dated 8 Nov. 1596, which mentions a particular collection of Sonnets that had been fent to him and that he liked. The notice is curious, becaufe private letters of that period fo feldom contain anything like literary criticifm or information. It is poffible that he refers to Henry Lok's " Christian Paffions," which bear the date of 1597, but had undoubtedly been printed earlier. Carlton's words are :

"I thank you for having me in so good remembrance as to send those Sonnetts, which I did much desire. . . The verses please me the more in that they treat of unaccustomed matter, and doe make that the subject of Poetrie, to which loosenes, which doth accompany the best writer, cannot learne to frame ytselfe. For, in this much writing age, that Poett is in great straites who tieth himself to such a matter, that he cannot use the libertie of old-fashioned poetrie as to speake of Goddes, Goddesses, Muses and Cupids, and is therefore the more to be liked by how much the more he is debarred of common helpes."

It is pretty clear, therefore, that the "sonnets" were, if not Lok's, like Lok's, of a facred character.

May 5.—Winfton, Secretary of the Garrick Club, shewed me a curiofity connected with our more modern ftage, viz., Garrick's Account-book for the feason 1772-3: by which it appeared that he and his partner that year divided £5000 odd hundreds between them, befides paying £1000 out of the profits to Clutterbuck. The largest receipt of the feafon was towards the clofe, when Garrick played *Richard III* for the Theatrical Fund, and when £313 were taken. The ufual receipts were from £250 to £280 when Garrick performed, and at other times from £170 to £240. This was the firft feason of the *Grecian Daughter*, and it never drew lefs than £230, while Murphy netted, every time it was acted for him, not far short of £200. It is to be obferved that on the author's nights £73 10s. were charged for the expenfes of the Houfe : on benefit nights, to the actors the charge was only £63 10s. The Houfe could contain from £300 to £320.

May 10.—I wrote an anonymous rhyming epiftle to the Earl of Mulgrave, perfuading him not to accept the go- vernorfhip of Jamaica which had been offered to him: he fhewed it to the Duke of Devonfhire, who knew the hand- writing, and betrayed the authorfhip. It was not good, and I tore it up, and burned the only copy I had kept of it. Lord M. did not go, but I do not fuppofe that my epiftle had anything to do with detaining him in England: I cannot recollect a fingle couplet of it. I hope it is gone the way of all flefh (of all wicked flefh)—to the fire. The following, in a very different ftyle, is, I think, worth copying.

THE LOVER'S DREAM.

It was the Spring, and birds did sing
　　On every tree and thorn,
When forth I stray, ah, well-a-day !
　　In love,—and all forlorn.

The Lark on high was in the sky,
　　Singing with cheerful glee ;
Unseen his song, the clouds among,
　　Seem'd heaven's minstrelsy.

As if each cloud, in rosy shroud,
　　Did utter forth a sound,
And with a smile did greet the while
　　The music of the ground :

For there the Thrush his notes did flush,
　　And strained his speckled throat,
The while his mate did burden take,
　　And answer'd with her note.

The Black-bird, too, his bride did woo,
  And fill'd the air above ;
Alas! and why, then, may not I
  Thus win my own sweet love ?

Ah! why should I but weep and sigh,
  When all is full of glee ?
Why doth the Spring them gladness bring,
  And bring no joy to me ?

This woful thought sleep to me brought,
  Sleep ever friend of woe :
A tuft of grass my pillow was,
  And tears all ceas'd to flow.

Then in a dream my love did seem,
  Like Goddess of the Spring,
On me to shower each scented flower
  She in her lap did bring.

" This rose," said she, " I give to thee
  Emblem of love and youth,
The lily white, the maids' delight,
  And pansy for my truth.

" Now end thy woes ; for like this rose
  The constant love I bear:
Though leaves decay, nor colours stay,
  The perfume still is there.

" This love of ours is like the flowers
  We know that wise men say.
Do flowers grow for only show ?
  Now take them while you may."

But when I strove to kiss my love,
  Since she so kind did seem,
I did awake to my mistake :
  Such love must be a dream.

Oh! could but I in slumber lie
  For aye such dreams to view,
And never rise, till arms and eyes
  Could prove the vision true !

May 15.—At Rev. W. Harnefs's, at dinner, I met Mary Ruffell Mitford, Fanny Kemble, Col. Harnefs, S. Rogers, Kenyon, C. Kemble, the Rev. Mr. Sandby, defcended from Paul Sandby, and two or three others. The only perfon I had not met before was Mifs Mitford, a moft agreeable and unpretending woman, though the authorefs of *Our Village*, of various novels, and of two or three tragedies, including "The Fofcari" and "Rienzi", played with confiderable fuccefs. I was charmed with her natural manners, and ladylike (not fine-ladylike) fimplicity. She did not talk much nor loud: her father is wholly dependent upon her, having run through feveral fortunes, and loft various good chances. Col. Harnefs, the brother of our hoft, is a very fcientific foldier. Harnefs himfelf was one of the chief talkers, and Kenyon is always full of anecdote : he is an habitual diner-out, and knows everybody. I had met him feveral times before, once at H. C. Robinfon's. In the evening, the Lambs joined the party, and Charles was joked about the charming young quakerefs who had lived in the fame ftreet in Pentonville where Lamb had lodged : fhe generally wore white, and fomebody prefent called her "a white witch". "No" (faid Lamb) "if a witch at all, as fhe lives at *the laft houfe* in our ftreet, fhe muft be the Witch of *End-door*."

The pun occafioned much laughter, but Lamb feemed almoft afhamed of it : it brought to my mind another joke of his, of a fimilar kind, of which I had been the occafion a great many years before. My father, mother, Robinfon, and the Lambs, were juft ftarting to fee Holcroft's "Vindictive Man" on its firft night : I was then a boy of about fixteen, and a queftion arofe whether I fhould not go alfo? it was decided againft me, and when Lamb was quitting the houfe he called out to me, " There; go along, you are a French Proteſtant". I did not take the joke until it was afterwards explained to me, that a French Proteſtant was a Hugonot (*You go not*). Lamb turned on his heel, and ran away, as it were, from his own joke.

While upon joking, the ſubſequent clever trifle, alluded to by Rogers at the above dinner at Harneſs's, may be worth quoting: it is tranſlated from the *Facetie del Barlacchia*, which has gone through hundreds of editions in Italy.

> Barlacchia was so very ill,
>   'Twas said that he had died one day,
> And had not left behind a will,
>   Not having aught to will away.
>
> But getting well, he came to court,
>   And when the Duke saw him arrive,
> He star'd, and cried, as if in sport,
>   " Barlacchia ! are you still alive ?"
>
> " No," said the Jester—" 'tis my ghost,
>   And not my mortal frame of sin.
> I've been to heaven, and came back post :
>   St. Peter would not let me in."
>
> " Why, how is that ?" inquir'd the Duke :
>   Barlacchia answer'd : " When I knock'd,
> He ask'd, in voice of stern rebuke,
>   Who 'twas would have the gate unlock'd ?
>
> " I said ' Barlacchia.' His reply
>   Was how I'd acted down below ?
> And how I'd left my family,
>   Whether provided for or no ?
>
> " I said I was a servant poor
>   To a great Duke of liberal mind,
> But that I'd nothing to secure
>   To wife or child I left behind.

" ' How can that be ?' St. Peter cried :
  ' You served a duke, almost a king.'
' I ask'd for nothing,' I replied,
  ' Or he 'd given me anything.'

" ' Go—get away ! be off down stairs !
   Heaven has no joys for such in store !'
St. Peter bawl'd ; and unawares
   I found myself at court once more.

" Therefore, great Duke, without delay
   Make me some gift from your estate :
My soul to heaven will then away,
   And be admitted at the gate."

May 21.—I had a good deal of converfation with the Duke on the fubject of major and minor theatres, and "free trade" in wholefome dramatic amufements. It arofe out of the opening of a new fmall play-houfe in York Street, Weftminfter, by a perfon of the name of Davenport. The Duke, for the firft time, expreffed himfelf decidedly in favour of not compelling the minors to clofe, becaufe he wifhed that people might be able to buy innocent pleafure at as cheap a rate as any other commodity ; only he faid that good-nature had led the king to take part with the patent theatres, under the belief that they were ruined : people ought to hear, as well as fee plays.

I fuggefted a doubt as to the exiftence of any patent, and referred to a document Winfton fhewed me, in which, in 1713 (I think), the patentees, who derived their rights from Davenant and Killigrew, furrendered their patents to Queen Anne, agreeing in future to hold under the ordinary licenfe. I alfo urged that, if the major theatres were ruined by the minors, it was in a great degree their own fault, inafmuch as the law gave them a remedy in £50

M

penalties againſt all performers upon unlicenſed boards; which law they had themſelves neglected to enforce, while they called upon the Lord Chamberlain to take upon him-ſelf the odium of cloſing profitable minor theatres by his own authority.

The Duke ſaid that he was placed in a difficult ſituation, owing to the wiſhes of the king and the urgency of the patentees; and aſked whether I thought he ought, or ought not, to proceed againſt the new Weſtminſter Theatre, as he was proceeding, by the ſlow proceſs of law, againſt the Strand Theatre? The opinion I gave him was, that he ought to wait the iſſue of the pending ſuit in the Common Pleas againſt the Strand Theatre, the objeƈt of which was to eſtablish the Lord Chamberlain's powers: if in the mean-time it were required of him to proceed alſo againſt the Weſtminſter Theatre, he might have a two-fold anſwer—firſt, that he delayed until the pending ſuit was decided; and, ſecondly, if this proceſs ſeemed to the Winter Theatres too dilatory, that they had the remedy in their own hands, by ordering actions for penalties to be commenced againſt the performers.

May 28.—I bought a copy of Petrarch's Will, which is quoted by De Sade in his life of that poet. It is entitled *Teſtamentum illuſtris. Poetæ Franciſci Petrarchæ, ab eo ipſo multo ante, quam e vitâ decederit, conſcriptum. In ejuſdem monumento, quod Arquadæ viſitur, ita inſcriptum eſt.*

> *Frigida Francisci lapis hic tegit ossa Petrarcæ.*
> *Suscipe Virgo Parens animam. Sate Virgine parce*
> *Fessaque jam terris, cœli requiescat in arce.*
> *Men. Aug. An.*
> M.D.XXXi.

It confifts of only 8 pages 8vo, and at the end is "*Cum Privilegio in Quinquennium.*" I have a notion that it is a curiofity : whether, and how often, it was printed before I have not yet afcertained.

I have tranflated in my time a good deal from Petrarch; but I do not think any of it fatisfactory : you may render the fenfe, but not the grace of the original. I have elfewhere mentioned that for two whole years I devoted my reading exclufively to Italian, profe and verfe; and I may fay that I found no author so eafily rendered into our language as Ariofto, nor any fo difficult as Petrarch, Dante not excepted. In tranflating Ariofto into the Englifh octave ftanza I obtained fo much facility, that it became quite a pleafure to me : not fo with Taffo, but I hardly know why. Of Ariofto I kept by me for fome years my translations, but I finally burned them, because, even if good, they were not wanted. Sir John Harington, who firft printed his verfion in 1591, is wonderfully clever in parts, efpecially the comic ; but people in general are not aware of the number of original ftanzas he thruft in, as if they were to be found in Ariofto. Taffo I never liked as well. I even read down to the time of Marino and his *Adone*, which ran very well into Englifh. I tried to imitate the eafe and fpirit of Cafti, but not with much fuccefs ; and I alfo went over all the novels of Boccaccio, Sachetti, Cinthio, and many more, putting not a few of their tales into Englifh : when I fhewed them to H. C. R., he advifed me not to print them, becaufe they were of a kind and character ill fuited to the fobriety, not to call it feverity, of our age. Thofe, however, I could not bring myfelf to deftroy. Stewart Rofe has done well in this department, and there is no need for more of his clafs.

I confider the following one of the beft of my tranflations from the Sonnets of Ariofto : Op. fo. ii, 336.

> Oh gladsome prison where entranc'd I lie !
>   Nor fate nor foeman's rage have here confin'd me,
>   But love, compassion, beauty, only bind me,
> A captive to my sweetest enemy.
> In other prisons the sad inmates sigh
>   To hear the rusty key : I have resign'd me
>   To life and joy, leaving all grief behind me.
> I wait no judge severe with steady eye,
>   But my lov'd mistress' greetings and caresses,
> And converse free from all restraint of crimes,
>   Smiles, blandishments, delights that sense encumber ;
> Sweet kisses, which most sweetly she impresses
>   A thousand thousand, and ten thousand times :
>   They would be few, if I could count the number.

May 30.—I forgot to mention, under its proper date, that the Duke was kind enough to carry me with him to the *Converfazione* of the Duke of Suffex at Kenfington Palace. H.R.H. was very courteous, and received all his vifitors in an ante-room near the head of the ftairs : he wore as ufual his velvet cap, his blue ribbon and his garter. I had an invitation fent to me through my friend Amyot and Mr. C. Greville. The company was very numerous, and of all ranks and degrees in politics, literature, fcience and art. I was introduced particularly to Sir Robert Peel, to whom I had fent a copy of my *Hift. Engl. Dram. Poetry and the Stage,* who thanked me perfonally (he does every thing of the fort very coolly, not to fay coldly) and faid that " he had been greatly interefted by it", though I may doubt whether he really had read one word of it : my anfwer was, that I had met with few people who could fay as much of it. There were a good many foreigners of diftinction in various departments, and H. C. Robinfon introduced me to Schlegel, the brother of the author of the lectures on dramatic poetry: he rather oftentatioufly wore all his decorations—his Englifh, French, and German orders. There, too, was Ramohun Roy, in his Hindoo coftume; but the perfon who moft attracted my notice was Prince Talleyrand, in his diplomatic habit, and very large neckcloth to fupport his double chin. All went away at about eleven o'clock.

June 1.—I had the opportunity to-day of reading a letter from the Rev. George Crabbe, the poet, who began writing verfe and publifhing it as early as 1775. The letter was merely dated 1781, without month or day, and was addreffed to Edmund Burke: it befought him to aid the writer, then in great pecuniary diftrefs, but it was written in an admirable ftyle of manly grief for the wants of himfelf and his family. He faid that he had come to London in April of that year, and that his father had defigned him for the medical profession, but had not been able to afford to allow him to complete his ftudies. At the time Crabbe wrote he had been earneftly feeking for literary employment in London, having brought with him fome new poems, which he had been advifed to publifh by fubfcription: he complained that a printer had deceived him, and that he had imprudently given a bill for £7 to a perfon to whom he owed £14, which bill was on the point of coming due. He apologifed to Burke for entering into thefe painful details, adding that the compulfion of mentioning them was, perhaps, fufficient punifhment.

He acknowledged that he knew nothing of the perſon he was addreſſing beyond his public character; but ſtated that he was induced to apply to him in his extremity, becauſe he believed him to be a good as well as a great man. There was nothing at all fulſome in this part of the letter, but the requeſt was very humble and earneſt in its tone. Crabbe went on to ſay, that a peer to whom he had applied, and of whom he knew ſomething through his lordſhip's brother, had left his appeal altogether unanſwered. He ſubjoined that, if Burke conſented to advance him the money to take up the bill (and he propoſed to call in a day or two to aſcertain the reſult of his application), he promiſed to repay it out of the firſt receipts from the ſubſcribers to his poems. The character of the whole letter was moſt deſponding, for he declared life a burden ; obſerving, in concluſion, that it was uſeleſs to reſort to his relations, ſince they were as poor as himſelf.

The whole ſtatement occupied two ſides and a half of foolscap ; and the perſon who ſhowed it me ſaid that Crabbe told him that, before he wrote it, he had walked for two hours upon London Bridge, unable to bring his mind to ſufficient reſolution to throw himſelf headlong into the river. What had been the reſult as to Burke the owner of the letter did not know : we will ſuppoſe that it was favourable to the entreaties of the excellent poet ; and Crabbe's " Library" was firſt publiſhed in the year of the date of this letter to Burke.

June 4.—The Duke gave ſeveral very large muſical parties during the ſpring, to ſome of which he perſonally invited my wife and myſelf : we borrowed the carriage of a friend and went. The attention the Duke paid to fuch "no-bodies" as we were was remarkable, and he introduced us to the circle round the fingers (Grifi, Tamburini, La-blache, etc.), where the Duchefs of Kent, the Princefs Victoria, and the Princefs Mary, formed the centre. On another occafion, when my wife was not there with me, the Duke fpied me out, ftanding at the door with old Sam. Rogers, and purpofely came from a throng of vifitors to bring us into the room. I afked him afterwards in what way he paid the performers? and he anfwered that it was not ufually in hard money, but in jewels, which were often more coftly; and he fhewed me the bracelet he was about to prefent to Grifi for finging three fongs: the chief ftone in it was a fapphire, and the value of it exceeded £50.

The Duke was even more kind to my wife and me on a Court-day, when he was in office as Lord Chamberlain. He fent his carriage for us, which took us to St. James's Palace, and there he received us at the top of the great ftaircafe, led us into an anteroom through which the nobility, minifters, and ambaffadors, muft pafs; and not only fo, but when not officially engaged, he placed himfelf befide us, and told us the names and ranks of the courtiers, efpecially foreigners, as they paffed into the prefence-chamber. On another oc-cafion, he met us at Windfor Caftle, and took us into all the moft private apartments: in one of them the King's fhirt was actually hanging before the fire.

He fhowed us over the fireproof room at Devonfhire Houfe, filled with piles of gold difhes, plates, etc., into which, he informed us, his father, I think, had converted the boxes containing the freedom of the corporations in Ire-land, prefented to him when he was Lord·Lieutenant. On the fame day he placed before us the original *Liber Veri-tatis* of Claude, and we were at leaft a couple of hours engaged in looking over the works in biftre of that great mafter. In the meantime, the Duke had gone out to fee Mrs. Coutts (as fhe was then called, and had become), who was his next door neighbour.

June 7.—Spent the evening at Robinfon's, in company with Wordfworth, the Lambs, Moxon, Burney, and fome others, and proved myfelf a good liftener : Lamb and his sister faid little or nothing, being engaged at cards. Words-worth was very talkative and agreeable, fpeaking much less of himfelf and of his own works than ufual : he made only one quotation of his own, from the introduction to his "Peter Bell", then in MS. He has much aged within the laft four or five years, and his nofe, always large, bears now a greater difproportion to his face, which has fallen away in the cheeks : his eyes are better, but ftill weak and red.

He told us, among other things, that, on the mother's side, he was defcended from the old Cumberland family of the Crackenthorpes. De Quincy, the opium-eater, has taken fhelter within the precincts of Holyrood Houfe, in confequence of debt, where his mother allows him £200 a-year. He was resident in Wordfworth's houfe when he wrote the greater part of his book; and the poet feemed to make it a complaint againft De Quincy that, in thofe articles out of which his book was manufactured, he had gone into painful circumftances of a domeftic nature, par-ticularly with reference to the death of Wordfworth's daugh-ter. Confequently, Wordfworth faid, that after he had once read the book, he put it away. De Quincy's father had been a manufacturer in the north.

Wordfworth fpoke much of Hartley Coleridge, the poet's fon, and faid that he was a man of high genius, and a fellow of Oriel, till he was obliged to relinquifh it in confequence of his peculiarities, or irregularities. It feemed that the fellows of Oriel were very ariftocratical, and objected to H. C., among other things, becaufe he had bought apples at a ftall, and had eaten them as he walked along the High Street. However, he gave moft offence by the unreftrained freedom of his fpeech, and by threats to introduce all forts of changes into the College.

Wordfworth took an opportunity to fpeak of my *Poet's Pilgrimage*, and efpecially praifed the conclufion of canto iv, where the hero firft difcovered that he had been led by the Mufe. Almoft the only word Lamb uttered in the midft of his beloved game of whift, was to fay that the whole was Spenferian.

Wordsworth paid a tribute to Sir Egerton Brydges, and applauded the eloquence of fome of his profe writings; but was aftonifhed when I told him that in one of his late letters (which I have feen) he afferts that he had written above two thoufand fonnets. This letter, dated from Geneva, contained fix or eight fpecimens.

Speaking of ftories he had read in early life, Wordfworth faid that no tale had ever affected him more than that of *Patty and Peggy*, two fifters, who were induced to vifit London and became proftitutes. He told us that it was "full of vulgar forrow", and that he had in vain tried to get through it fince his youth : neverthelefs, when he was young, "he had literally wafhed away the book with tears."

N

I mentioned having heard Coleridge very happy in cenfuring the tautology of Johnfon's couplet—

> " Let observation with extensive view
> Survey mankind from China to Peru ;"

and Wordfworth claimed to have been the firft to make the
criticifm in Coleridge's company, urging that the lines in
faƈt only faid, " Let obfervation with extenfive obfervation
furvey mankind extenfively." On the other hand, Dryden's
commencement of the fame fatire was admirable :

> " Look round the habitable world, how few
> Know their own good, or knowing it, pursue."

Wordfworth repeated by heart feveral of the couplets that
follow thefe lines. He admired Dryden more as a writer
of paraphrafes than as a tranflator : he read the paffage he
wifhed to render, until he took in the full and entire meaning
of the author, then threw afide the original, and expreffed
the thought in his own happy and truly Englifh phrafeology.

Wordfworth is a good talker and is fond of talking, but
he is not fo gently overbearing as Coleridge, and allowed
me now and then to interpofe a remark: fo did fome others,
and all were well fatisfied.

June 8.—I have feen to-day in private hands an interefting
document in reference to the biography of R. B. Sheridan,
viz., an unexecuted agreement between him and Grant
Raymond, by which it appears that in 1809 Sheridan was
anxious to publifh an edition of his own works. Raymond
was to undertake the management of the whole affair, and
to give Sheridan (whofe objeƈt of courfe was to raife money)
certain fums as the bufinefs proceeded. Two hundred
pounds were to be paid to him at the commencement, to

enable him to furnifh the prefatory matter, amounting to
at leaft one fheet 8vo.: then, he was to have only another
£100 when the printing of the work was completed ; but
£250 as foon as 2500 copies had been fold, and £250 more
when 5000 copies had been difpofed of. In furtherance of
this bargain Raymond was to be furnifhed with a correÊted
copy of " The School for Scandal"; and Sheridan alfo undertook to provide correÊted copies of "The Rivals", "The
Critic", etc., as they fhould be needed by the printer.

If this document have been mentioned in any of the
memoirs of Sheridan, it has efcaped my obfervation.

Winfton has among his theatrical relics two fongs,
said to be the authorfhip of Mrs. Siddons when very
young. He obtained them from an old aÊtor of the name
of Jones, who, in the commencement of his career, belonged
to Roger Kemble's company, and was afterwards employed
at Drury Lane for many years. He had all his life kept
a journal, and had carefully inferted thefe fongs, which
Winfton copied : fuch is the authority for attributing them
to Mrs. Siddons, who at that date was courted by Siddons,
and by a young farmer in the neighbourhood of Hereford.
She gave the preference to Siddons. There is no merit in
either fong, but the beft runs in thefe lines. •

> " Say not, Strephon, I 'm untrue,
>   When I only think of you :
>   If you do but think of me
>   As I of you, then shall you be
>   Without a rival in my heart,
>   Which ne'er can play a tyrant's part.
>
> " Trust me, Strephon, with thy love,
>   I swear by Cupid's bow above,
>   Nought shall make me e'er betray

1 hy passion till my dying day :
If I live, or if I die,
Upon my constancy rely."

Winſton ſays that he has given a copy of it to Campbell for his life of Mrs. Siddons. I doubt if C. will think it worth a place there. Jones stated that Mrs. Siddons wrote it before ſhe made her firſt appearance in London in 1776, which ſeems likely, becauſe ſhe was, I think, at that date married to her Strephon.

June 10.—I was under examination, by the committee of the Houſe of Commons on major and minor theatres, on two ſeparate days for ſeveral hours. I mention it as a proof of my good memory, that though I had to ſpeak of many particulars and dates regarding our early ſtage, I was able to do ſo without referring to a ſingle book or memorandum. I took none with me. My recollection has always been good, and it began early, for I bear in mind with perfect clearneſs incidents and places ſome months before I was three years old. Then it was that I had my hand ſtung by a bee, and that my father ſhewed me a dead bird, the firſt dead thing I had ever ſeen. I was born in the year when the Baſtille was burned, and I never ſhall forget an engraving of the execution of Louis XVI, with all its blood and horror ; but then I was four years old, and rather more, and was living at Thames Ditton.

I thought at one time of making, and printing, a ſeries of tranſlations from Italian poets anterior to Dante, and I bought a collection of books for the purpoſe. I carried out my plan, to a certain length, ten or a dozen years ago, and then I abandoned it in consequence of difficulties in the old language, and some other discouragement.

To day I came acrofs a few of my old fcribblings, and after the lapfe of time, I am fo pleafed with the following fonnet by Guido Guinizelli that I copy it here.

SONNET TO HIS LADY.

Fain would I late my lovely lady praife,
 Comparing her to lily and to rose :
As Dian far exceeds a dim star's rays,
 So she I love is fairer far than those.
Whether I liken her to earth or air,
 When all the sky in purple glory shines,
Or brightest jewels,—she is still more fair:
 Ev'n love itself she betters and refines.
Where'er she moves with such a gentle grace,
 Pride pays its homage and submissive sues,
 While firmest faith in her could none refuse.
None can approach her, none however base,
 But her sweet presence with new worth endues,
And none can think of ill that sees her face.

One more, not quite fo good, from Guido Cavalcanti.

CUPID'S COURT.

My silly eyes, which on that day abus'd me
 When first I saw thy form complete in beauty,
In Cupid's Court of pallid looks accus'd me,
 Where all his loyal subjects pay their duty.
They instantly made it appear before him,
 I was your loving servant ; and in fitness,
Showing my heart 'mong those who there adore him,
 They call'd against me my sad sighs to witness.
They would hear no defence ; and I was taken
 Where many more, in dismal place and shady,
Complain'd of Love, in company or lonely ;
 But when they saw me, pity gan awaken,
And all exclaim'd : " If thou dost serve that lady,
 Death is thy hope and refuge—and death only."

June 17.—The Duke of Devonſhire having invited me to ſpend a week with him at Chatſworth, I went down to Bakewell and from thence to the inn at Barlow, within a mile of the mansion : thither a carriage was sent for me, and I arrived at the end of my journey about half-paſt ſeven: the Duke, ready dreſſed for dinner at eight, welcomed me at the top of the great staircase. He told me, however, that I had no time to loſe, and that the groom of the chambers would ſhow me my room, and appoint a ſervant to wait upon me conſtantly. I was only dreſſed juſt in time for grace, and I was making my way quietly to the bottom of the long table (there were about thirty gueſts), when the Duke ſignalled me to take a chair which had been left vacant next to Lady Carliſle. I had no formal introduction, but Lady Carliſle ſeemed to know who I was, and was very talkative and agreeable. There was a ſervant, either of the Duke's or of ſome of the viſitors, behind each chair, and at my back was the man who had been appointed·to attend to my wants, whether at dinner or at any other time.

After the ladies (ſome twelve or fourteen) had retired, we did not ſit long, but adjourned to the muſic-room, where the Duke's private band was performing. Lady Carliſle did her beſt to make me feel eaſy and at home; which I own I did not feel, in ſpite of her endeavours. Some of the ladies and gentlemen went away early, as they had diſtances to go, but the whole party broke up before eleven, and I was ſhewn to my bedroom.

Next day was Sunday, and all the ladies and one or two of the older gentlemen went to Church at Edensor (where the Chaplain preached) in the Duke's curtained omnibus drawn by four greys: the Duke walked with me and feveral others. After luncheon everybody betook themfelves to what they liked best, reading, walking, or lounging; and the Duke afked me to accompany him to a cottage, about two miles diftant over the fields, where he had a litter of favourite puppies at nurfe. On the way the Duke faid, "We fhall be quieter to-morrow."

So we were; but ftill there were fixteen at dinner, and one of the guefts was Prince Bonaparte, who fat nearly oppofite me, but confined his converfation entirely to the gentleman who fat next to him, and who, I think, came with him. In the morning the Duke had taken me over to the intended fite of his great Confervatory, and introduced me to Paxton, his head gardener, who had entered the Duke's fervice a fhort time before at the wages of only twenty-four fhillings a week: he had married the houfekeeper's daughter, and was now eftablifhed in his place.

Next day we had little or no company, and in the morning the Duke fhowed me all over the flower gardens, and the fountains were fet playing: the "Emperor," as it is called, threw the water far above the loftieft lime trees. Lady Carlifle had gone away; but a family had arrived of the name of Beaumont, defcended, as the Duke informed me, from the Judge, the father of the two poets, Sir John and Francis. Perhaps, however, I miftook.

On Thurfday we had company again, confifting of about fix or eight ladies and gentlemen of the county, who were very cheerful, efpecially during the mufic in the evening. I took a candle, unperceived by any body but the Duke, and went into the room devoted to the books' which had belonged to Bifhop Dampier. In the morning the Duke had walked with me to the very ancient oak woods behind Chatsworth, where he shewed me trees which he said were four, five, or even six hundred years old; and I dare say some of the youngest had seen Mary Queen of Scots when she was residing, under *surveillance*, at Chatsworth. Here the Duke pointed out to me a huge flat slab of rock, which was called Robin's, or Robin Hood's Stone, on the opposite side of a wide chasm. Out of the legend which the Duke narrated to me, connected with it, I wrote the following imitative ballad, which I gave to him after we returned to London.

ROBIN HOOD'S LEAP.

Now, listen ye of gentle blood,
　And I a tale will tell,
Of Robin Hood in Chatsworth Wood,
　And what him there befell.

From Nottingham, a score and ten
　Long miles, he journey'd o'er,
To 'scape as then from the Sheriff's men,
　And came to Edenshore.

Sweet Edenshore, by Derwent's side,
　Brings joy to every heart;
For all around each foot of ground
　Seems of old Eden part.

Here Robin came, known well to fame,
　Full weary and way-sore,
And sat him down on a mossy stone,
　In the vale of Edenshore.

His hand he rested on his bow,
　Upon his arm his head,
And he thought again of his merry men
　In Sherwood how they sped.

While thus he sat, a pit-a-pat
  He heard on the stony way :
'Twas the dainty feet of the blithe and sweet,
  The winsome Kitty Ray.

From out his stound he woke at the sound ;
  No armed foe he saw,
But the prettiest face in that lovely place,
  And it cheer'd the sad outlaw.

" Good morrow to thee, fair maid," said he,
  " And a thousand on thee light,
For thou hast the bonniest face to see
  I have met by day or night."

His feet were cover'd thick with dust,
  And dusty was his brow.
" Thou hast journey'd far," quoth she; " I trust
  That thou may'st rest thee now.

" My father dwelleth here hard by,
  And my mother can brew and bake;
Then with me haste our ale to taste,
  And eat of our oaten cake."

" Bethink thee, maid, whom thou wouldst aid,"
  Returned the archer good :
" An outlaw I am doom'd to die ;
  Men call me Robin Hood."

Sweet Kate grew pale to hear his tale,
  But soon her fears gave place ;
She felt deep ruth for his trust and truth,
  And honour'd his manly grace.

" Hie hence (cried she); this place forsake,
  And wend to my home with me :
My heart would break should they thee take ;
  Lie there from danger free."

Bold Robin thank'd the maiden kind,
    Who never thought of ill :
Her hand he took with a cheerful look,
    And went with right good will.

He soon forgot his lawless lot,
    And oft-times blest the day,
When, tir'd and hot, he reach'd the spot
    Where he met with Kitty Ray.

And Kitty, too, so frank and true,
    Her love did soon avow.
Her maiden heart of Robin seem'd part ;
    She never had lov'd till now.

Three weeks at last were gone and past,
    How wondrous quick they flew !
When Robin had ken of the Sheriff's men,
    Who him did still pursue.

He saw them hurrying down the hill,
    He saw them on the lea,
He saw them hasting toward the house,
    And his heart was woe to see.

" One kiss, one kiss, my Kate ! and this
    Is all I have time to take :
Yet could I stay and perish to-day,
    And freely, for thy sake.

" Behold you yonder men ?—I ween,
    My life that they pursue ;
But reach me down my arrows keen,
    And eke my bow of yew.

" Remember, Kate, if their hands I 'scape,
    As I am Robin Hood,
My horn so clear thou at night shalt hear :
    I'll sound it in Chatsworth Wood."

His arrows long, and his yew-bow strong,
  She brought with trembling knee :
He swam the tide to the other side,
  And soon was far and free.

His foes too late arrived ; and Kate
  At her spinning sate apart :
'Twas well they marked not her tangled yarn,
  And heard not, as she did, her heart.

She listen'd long after even-song
  To hear a bugle wound ;
And blam'd each leaf, in fear and grief,
  That rustling made a sound.

At length she heard it, shrill and clear,
  Resound from the echoing wood,
And at break of day she took her way
  To meet with Robin Hood.

She cross'd the Derwent at the ford,
  Her kirtle above her knee,
And ne'er stood still till she climb'd the hill,
  Where Robin she hoped to see.

The rugged rocks on rocks were piled,
  With giant oaks between ;
A scene so noble and so wild
  May scarce elsewhere be seen.

Her Robin true she quickly knew,
  Like an eagle perch'd on high :
On a table of stone he stood alone,
  When her he did espy.

He leap'd at once into her arms,
  O'er a chasm wide and deep ;
And to this day the old folks say
  That this was the Outlaw's leap.

> Seven yards I ween, as may be seen,
>   It is from side to side :
> His joy so great to meet his Kate,
>   He heeded not how wide.
>
> For two months' space, in this wild place,
>   Conceal'd good Robin lay,
> And those in chase could find no trace
>   Of him and of Kitty Ray.
>
> Each following morn she brought him food,
>   His green retreat unknown.
> That this tale is true that I tell to you,
>   You may see by Robin Hood's Stone.

Let me acknowledge here, that for unqueſtionably the
prettieſt ſtanza in the ballad I was mainly indebted to the
Duke: originally it was without the lines—

> "His foes too late arrived ; and Kate
>   At her spinning sate apart :
> 'Twas well they marked not her tangled yarn,
>   And heard not, as she did, her heart."

The Duke remarked that Kate ſhould be employed
about ſome houſehold duty, ſuch as knitting, on the arrival
of the Sheriff's men ; and that ſhe ought to be ſo nervous
on the occaſion as to keep dropping her needles, and thus
run the riſk of diſcovery. I at once took the hint, but
thought that ſpinning would be more picturefque, as well as
appropriate, and hence the ſtanza. The whole was poor
payment for all the Duke's kindness, eſpecially during this
viſit; but *quanto io poſſo dar tutto vi dono.*

On our return from Chatſworth to London we ſtarted
on Friday morning, and we slept on the road. The Duke
would ſet me down at my own door; the firſt time, as I

imagine, that a travelling carriage and four fine horfes had ever stopped there. He infifted on coming in and fhaking hands with my wife, and thus ended a moft pleafant expedition. I never attempted to thank the Duke, and could have found no adequate terms.

June 25.—During my abfence I found that I had been fent for to one of the government departments; but as nothing came of the matter, though the offer was *apparently* flattering, I shall fay no more about it.

While at Chatfworth my wife recovered for me what I had long mislaid, and had originally obtained through Triphook the bookfeller, viz., an unpublifhed poem by Pope : it is in his own handwriting, and it is interefting, not merely on that account, but because it fhows, that Pope cenfured and ridiculed in 1704, when he was only fixteen, what, when he was twenty-feven, *he actually did himfelf*, with the aid of his two friends Gay and Arbuthnot. In 1704 Vanburgh, Congreve, and Walfh produced at the Lincoln's Inn Theatre their "Squire Trelooby": Pope raifed a laugh at the trio ; and yet in 1717 he and his two coadjutors brought out at Drury Lane Theatre their "Three Hours after Marriage." "Squire Trelooby" was little more than a tranflation of Molière's *Monfieur de Pourccaugnac* ; and the following are Pope's lines, in 1704, ridiculing the refult of the combined authorfhip of Vanburgh, Congreve, and Walfh.

THE CONFEDERATE TRANSLATORS.

" Oft has Apollo with harmonious sounds,
    Oft has he strove with various antick rounds,
    To entertain y⁵ fair, yet now he sees

Nothing but sweet variety will please.
Tofts rosy bow'rs no more can raise y$_r$ Love,
Elford and Labbé unregarded move :
Purcell himself scarce gets a second smile,
Purcell the Orpheus of our Brittish Isle.
Since musick, then, nor dancing will go down,
Hee'l try some other way to please y^e town.
Without delay a generall court he kept
Of all who on Parnassus ever stept :
Thither in crowds the rhiming bards repair,
(For mount Parnassus is a fruitfull air).
One mov'd an Opera, one a Pastorall,
A masque the third, but were rejected all.
Congreve at last, assisted by Vanbrook
And Walsh, propos'd a farce : ye motion took.
Strait the triumviri of wit engage
To bring Pourceauniac on ye English stage,
From France the country put and quack must come,
Tho' we have much a better breed at home.
Vanbrook instructs ye doctor how to cant,
Congreve gives humour, wch ye others want,
For Walsh's Lines are Am'rous and Gallant.
The two Dramatick bards contend in wit,
Which still to Walsh's judgment they submit.
Such is the force of well-united thought,
In twice ten days ye mighty work is wrought ;
When drest in patch work by ye triple pen,
Moliere can't know his country put again."

The above is neatly written on both fides of a fheet of note-paper; and on recently fending it to Mr. John Wilfon Croker, he wrote back to me, "I have no doubt that the poem is Pope's autograph, though rather lefs free than his later hand. It is fingular enough that twenty [thirteen] years later Pope, with his friends Arbuthnot and Gay, fhould have been fatirifed as the Confederates in a farce."

June 27.—Nobody can at all fatisfactorily edit any work by Michael Drayton, unlefs he have all the old, as well as the new impreffions before him. For inftance, his "Tragicall Legend of Robert, Duke of Normandy, furnamed Short-thigh", was originally publifhed in 1596, after the firft appearance of his "Legends of Matilda and Piers Gavefton" in 1594. He tells us that, in the two laft, in confequence of foul play and "finifter dealing" of the printer, came out "as many faults as lines"; yet it does not at all follow that fome of the faults were not his own, becaufe he was never fatisfied, even with his own compofition. I have been led to this remark on comparing the earlieft ftanza of "The Duke of Normandy", as it was iffued in 1596, with the firft ftanza of the fame poem as Drayton altered it in 1605, when he put forth his own edition of "Poems by Michaell Drayton, Efquire", in 8vo. In 1596, it ftood exactly thus :

> " What time sleep's nurse, the silent night, begun
> To steal by minuts on the long-liv'd daies,
> The furious Dog-star chasing of the Sun,
> Whose scorching breath ads flame unto his raies,
>   At whose approch the angry lyon braies ;
> The earth, now warm'd in thys celestiall fire,
> To coole the heate, puts off her rich attire."

Without other "faults", it feems enough that Drayton fhould himfelf have reprefented the lion as *braying;* but he alfo faw other objections, and nine years afterwards he gave the ftanza as follows :

> " What time soft night had silently begunne
> To steale by minutes on the long-liv'd daies,
> The furious dogge pursuing of the sunne,

> Whose noysome breath addes fervor to his raies,
> That to the earth sends many a sad disease ;
> Which then inflam'd with his intemprate fires,
> Her selfe in light habiliments attires."

Allowing for the faulty rhyme (not then fo faulty) of
"raies" and "difeafe", there can be no doubt as to the improvement. I have been recently afked to fuperintend a
reprint of all Drayton, but I have declined on account of the
difficulty of the tafk : another queftion is whether, in any
new edition, we ought not to preferve the very words in
which the poet expreffed his earlieft ideas? I do not know
where a firft edition of the " Gavefton" is to be found ; but
the firft edition of the " Matilda" is in Sion College, where
I have feen it.

Malone fays that " Julius Cæfar" was not produced by
Shakefpeare until 1607. Drayton, every time he reprinted
a poem, made fome alterations, more or lefs important,
in it ; and I think it may be fhewn by one of the alterations in his " Barons' Wars", firft called " Mortimeriados" in
1596, that " Julius Cæfar" had been brought out at the Globe
Theatre before 1603. If ever I edit Shakefpeare, I fhall
enlarge and infift upon this point, adverting efpecially to
the paffage, clofe to the end of the tragedy, where Mark
Antony gives this character of Brutus :

> " He only, in a generous honest thought
> Of common good to all, made one of them :
> His life was gentle, and the elements
> So mix'd in him, that Nature might stand up
> And say to all the world, This was a man."

Now, without adverting to the very different appearance
of the following lines in 1596, and in 1603, furely we may

affert that before 1603 Drayton had feen acted, or had read, and governed himfelf by the above quotation from "Julius Cæfar": in 1603 it was that Drayton remodelled and reproduced his "Mortimeriados" of 1596 as "The Barons' Wars", and there we read (b. iii, ft. 40) precifely as here-under :

> " Such one he was, of him we boldely say,
>   In whose rich soule all soveraigne powres did sute,
>   In whome in peace th' elements all lay
>   So mixt, as none could soveraignty impute ;
>   As all did governe, yet did all obey :
>   ,   His lively temper was so absolute,
>   That 't seemde when heaven his modell first began
>   In him it shewd perfection in a man."

I contend that this ftanza was written by Drayton, in all probability, in confequence of having heard Shakefpeare's lines in "Julius Cæfar", and in imitation of them : the infer-tion of the words, "th' elements all lay, fo mixt", and " per-fection in a man", was not an accidental coincidence.   I owe this note to the recent purchafe of a copy of " Drayton's Poems", 8vo, 1603.

June 28.—Leigh Hunt, befides being a good poet, is alfo a good goffip, though not a very good talker; and the fub-ject of " The Beggars' Opera" being ftarted in company, he reminded us yefterday that, in fpite of its prodigious fuccefs, it was thought fuch a " touch-and-go" bufinefs on its firft production, that Quin had refufed to take the cha-racter of *Capt. Macheath*, and had faid that the piece was only faved by " Oh ponder well," etc., as sung by Mifs Fenton, afterwards Duchefs of Bolton.

Somebody in company remarked that her real name was

Lavinia Befwick, and that the marriage licenfe was in that name, and the façt feems to be fo. It may have been a ticklifh affair on the firft night, but certainly never afterwards ; and it fo happened that at the moment we were converfing, I had Rich's account-book in the houfe, ftating the receipts for thirty-two nights, when the firft run was interrupted by benefits. Here we faw alfo exaçtly what Gay was made *rich* by, and Rich was made *gay* by : Gay's nights were the third, fixth, ninth and fifteenth, producing refpeçtively the following fums : £162 : 12 : 6, £189 : 11 : 0, £165 : 12 : 0, and £175 : 18 : 0, or in the whole £695 : 13 : 6. If the King and Queen were hoftile to Gay, Rich informs us that they and the Princeffes were neverthelefs at the theatre (Lincoln's Inn) on the twenty-firft night, when the receipts were £163 : 14 : 6. The loweft amount taken at the doors during the run of "The Beggars' Opera" was £156 : 8 : 0, on the tenth night; while £183 : 4 : 0 and £185 : 8 : 6 were obtained on the thirty-firft and thirty-fecond nights. After the benefits the popularity of the opera increafed to £184 : 13 : 6 and £198 : 17 : 0. It feems remarkable that the heroine for her benefit, on the forty-eighth night, had only £155 : 4 : 0.

Thefe façts, which were new, were alfo very amufing and fatisfaçtory. "The Beggars' Opera", we find on the fame authority, was played fixty-three times in that feafon, agreeing with the ftatement in the note to the *Dunciad*, which has been improperly difputed.

I copy the following from the original in the large, plain hand-writing of Addifon. It was perhaps addreffed to Ambrofe Phillips, but the addrefs is wanting : it is not one of thofe I formerly mentioned as having been lent, and never returned. The date is only " March 10", but the year ought to be 1704, from what is faid of Dennis's tragedy.

" DEAR SIR,
        " By a letter I received from you about a week ago I find
that one I left for you at Harwich, to be put into the packet, did not
come to your hands.   I told you in it that your two pastorals, with the
translation of an ode of Horace by myself, did not come soon enough
to be inserted in Tonson's last Miscellany, which was published some
time before I came for England.   Your first pastoral is very much
esteemed by all I have shown it to, tho' the best judges are of opinion
you should only imitate Spencer in his beauties, and never in the
rhime of the verse ; for there they think it looks more like a bodge
than an imitation, as in that line—'Since changed to heaviness is all
my glee.'   I am wonderfully pleas'd with your little essay of pastoral
in your last, and think you very just in the theory as well as in the
practical part.   Our poetry in England at present runs all into lam-
poon, which has seldom anything of true satire in it besides rhime and
ill-nature.   Mr. Row has promis'd the town a farce this winter, but it
does not yet appear.   He has too on the stocks a tragedy on Penelope's
lovers, where Ulysses is to be the hero.   Mr. Dennis has a tragedy
that is now in the first run of acting.   It is called ' Liberty Asserted',
and has the Whigs for its patrons and supporters.   I am much obliged
to you for your sending my letters after me, and should be glad if you
could find out any way of making me serviceable to you here, who
should be very much pleased to let you see how much I am
                    " Your most affectionate humble Servant,
" Pray give my humble service to Mr.   " J. ADDISON."
Thompson and Mr. Poultney, if he is
still with you. Jacob Tonson told me he
should write to him speedily.
        " *March* 10, London."

Rowe's "Ulyffes" was printed in 1705. Perhaps the farce
was "The Biter", which was printed in 1705, the only comic
attempt of Rowe.

        I may take this opportunity of tranfcribing the following
from Sir R. Steele to Phillips, which fhews that in 1716 the
latter was a juftice of peace for Weftminfter: Steele's autographs are not common.

"DEAR SIR,

    "The bearer, Mr. John Cousins, is one whom I have known many years, and whom, as being a near kinsman of a deceased friend of mine, Mrs. Arabella Hunt, the lady who was famous for her voice, I have long endeavoured to serve.

"He tells me he is put to some molestation by reason of his being present one evening at the Mugg house, when a constable took offence at what passed there, and is this day to appear on that subject. Your favour and protection to him, within the rules of justice, is what I take the liberty to ask in his behalf; and herein you will very particularly oblige,   "Sir, your most obedient and

most humble Servant,

"RICHARD STEELE."

"*Sept.* 24, 1716, St. James's Street.

   "Mr. Phillips."

It feems ftrange that Steele and Phillips at this date fhould have been on fuch formal terms.

I accidentally met Moxon, the publifher, to-day : he is a very deferving man, and a pretty fonnetteer. He tells me, and he muft know, that Rogers has expended more than £7000 upon the illuftrations of his new edition. The old man wifely relies more upon his plates than upon his poetry : the beautiful engravings from Stothard and Turner cannot be forgotten.

FINIS.

T. RICHARDS, 37, GREAT QUEEN STREET.

Old Man's Diary.

FORTY YEARS AGO.

PART I.

AN OLD MAN'S DIARY,

FORTY YEARS AGO;

FOR THE LAST SIX MONTHS OF

1832.

Omne meum : nihil meum.

LONDON :
PRINTED BY THOMAS RICHARDS.
1871.

PREFACE.

WHAT follows is a fecond inftalment of egotifm for the year 1832, and I prefent it to my friends with the fame injunction of privacy that accompanied my Diary for the preceding fix months.

I muft repeat, with greater emphafis, what I formerly ftated on the queftion of precife dates ; becaufe an early friend of mine, by a note containing further details than I poffeffed, has convinced me, againft my will, that, in the former portion of this Diary, I have antedated an important tranfaction, in which the generous bounty of the Duke of Devonfhire towards Leigh Hunt was recorded. In what follows, I may, poffibly, have committed a fimilar error more than once, but it cannot in any way alter facts. My memoranda were ufually made in hafte, often on feparate flips of paper, and fometimes I accidentally omitted to put the year after the day of the month. In this way, confufion may now and then have arifen, and I may have mixed up incidents of a fomewhat earlier or later date, with those which ftrictly belong to 1832.

There is one perfon for whom I felt fincere refpect and attachment for many obligations, whom I
have not mentioned in any part of my "Diary". I
refer to the late John Walter, Esq., the maker,
though not the eftablifher, of the *Times*. He was
the firft perfon who difcovered any ability in me,
who employed it and rewarded it: how liberal he
was may be judged from the fact that he gave
me £50 for a few communications, and £100 for
getting the newfpaper out of a fcrape, in which I
myfelf had accidentally involved it. I was ufeful
to him for at leaft a dozen years, and I never fhould
have quitted him but for a difagreement with a leading perfon on his eftablishment. Mr. Walter himfelf
endeavoured fubfequently to arrange the affair, but
failed, as far as both parties were concerned; though
he ever afterwards kept up acquaintance and correfpondence with me, and to the laft vifited me at
Kenfington, just before I determined to retire into
the country, more than twenty years ago. In what
follows I have endeavoured, where I could conveniently do fo, to exclude my newfpaper-reminis-
cences, and hence my filence regarding a man to
whom I owed much, and the *Times* incalculably
more.

Maidenhead, September 1, 1871.   J. P. C.

OLD MAN'S DIARY,

FORTY YEARS AGO.

PART II.

July 2, 1832.—Six months ago I quoted a letter of Jonathan Swift's to Ambrofe Phillips ; I had not then an opportunity of extracting more than the firft paragraph from it relating to Addifon, but I can now copy the whole ; and, as it adverts to many topics of intereft, and as the Dean's autographs are rare, I will here infert it entire. It is addreffed "for Mr. Phillips," and was indorfed by him, "Jonathan Swift, 1708 : refpd. Sept. 29," meaning that he had anfwered it about a fortnight after its date. It runs precifely thus :—

"Lond., Sep^br 14, 1708.

"Nothing is a greater argument that I look on myfelf as one whose acquaintance is perfectly useless, than that I am not so constant or exact in writing to you as I should otherwise be ; and I am glad at heart to see Mr. Addison, who may live to be serviceable to you, so mindful in your absence. He has reproached me more than once for not frequently sending him a letter to conveigh to you. That man has worth enough to give reputation to an age, and all the merit I can hope for with regard to you will be my advice to cultivate his friendship to the utmost, and my assistance to do you all the good offices towards it in my power.

"I have not seen Ld Mark these three weeks, nor have heard anything of him, but his poetry, which a lady shewed me some time ago: it was some love verses, but I have forgot the motto and the subject, or rather the object, tho' I think they were to Mrs. Hales.

"I can fitt you with no fable at present, unless it should be of the man that rambled upon (*sic*) and down to look for Fortune, at length came home and saw her lying at a man's feet who was fast asleep and never stirred a step: this I reflected on tother day when my Ld Treas^r gave a young fellow, a friend of mine, an employment sinecure of £400 a year, added to one of £300 he had before. I hope, though you are not yet a Capt., Ld M. has so much consideration to provide you with pay suitable to the expense and trouble you are at, or else you are the greatest dupe, and he the greatest —— on earth ; and I wish you would tell me plainly how that matter passes. You say nothing of the fair one : I hope you are easier on that foot that when you left us, else I shall either wish her hanged, or you marryed, but whether to her or some Yorkshire lady with ten thousand pounds, I am somewhat in doubt. There is some comfort that you will learn your trade of a soldier in this expedition—at least, the most material part of it, long marches, ill diet, hard lodging, and scurvy company. I wish you would bring us home half-a-dozen Pastorals, though they were all made up of complaints of your mistress and of Fortune. Lady Betty Germain is upon all occasions stirring up Ld Dorset to shew you some marks of his favour, which, I hope, may one day be of good effect, or he is good for nothing. Ld Pembroke is going to be married to Lady Arundel. We are here crammed with hopes and fears about the siege of Lisle and the expectations of a battle ; but I believe you have little humour for public reflections. For my part, I think your best course is to try whether the Bp. of Durham will give you a niece and a golden prebend, unless you are so high a Whig that your principles, like your mistress, are at Geneva.

"I have never been a night from this town since you left, and could envy you, if your mind were in a condition to enjoy the pleasures of the country. But I hope you will begin to think of London, and not dream of wintering in the North, *Scoticas pati pruinas.*

"Here has been an Essay of Enthusiasm lately published that has run mightily, and is very well writ. All my friends will have me to be the author, *Sed ego non credulus illis.* By the free Whiggish thinking I should rather take it to be yours, but mine it is not; for tho' I am every day writing my speculations in my chamber, they are quite of another sort. I expect to see you return very fat with York-shire ale. Pray let us know when we are to expect you, and resolve this winter to be a man of levees, and be a man of hopes, and who knows what that may produce against spring. I am sure no man wishes you better, or would do more in his power to bring those wishes to effect, which, though they are expressions usually offered most freely by those that can do least, I hope you will do me the jus-tice to believe them, and myself to be entirely

"Your most faithful and most humble servant,

"J. SWIFT.

"I saw Dr. Englis to-day, who tells me Ld Mark has grace to con-sider you so far, as not to travel at your own charges."

By the bounty of a friend this autograph is now mine, as well as another from the same hand, which I have given to Dyce at his most earnest request. He tells me that he has placed it among his most valuable papers, but cannot now find it: I unluckily neglected to copy it.

July 3.—C. Kemble has put into my hands a theatrically interesting letter from John Philip Kemble (his brother), dated 13 Nov., 1790, which adverts to his performance of Charles Surface, for which part he had the strongest inclina-tion, but in which he was considered to have made a signal failure. It is a remarkable point in the biography of the great actor. J. P. Kemble returns thanks for some praise that had been bestowed on him, and then adds, "I will study to deserve more: your knowledge of the stage will

induce you to believe me, when I fay I was horribly
frightened, and will perfuade you to attribute fome of my
awkwardneffes of manner and defects of voice to my em-
barrafment. . . . I have much, very much, at ftake on my
fuccefs in this delightful comedy." He had previoufly
acted the part in the provinces, but never with fuccefs.

I am indebted to a theatrical collector for the fight
of a feries of Foote's letters when he was in Dublin in
1760. The payment he there received feems extraordinary,
if not extravagant, viz., £50 per night; and yet the engagement was fo profitable to all parties that it was renewed
on the fame terms. Foote tells his friend that he fhould
make £1200 by the trip; and he fubjoins a curious paragraph
about old Sheridan, father of Richard Brinfley, which is
worth quoting: "that piece of bufkin'd buckram (he fays)
has produced his quaint frigidity in the part of Cato to a
very poor houfe, fince which he has retired to plant cab-
bages in his native bog." Sheridan had firft played Cato
in England in 1744, but he never could render the tragedy
popular, let him perform it where he would.

Garrick's "Epitaph on General Wolfe" is hardly worth
quoting, though he was rather proud of it: it has not been
printed that I am aware, and I copy it from the original, in
his own handwriting, fubfcribed alfo with his initials.

> "The nation's glory is thy monument,
> Its ample base the Western Continent;
> The adamantine pillars public good:
> The epitaph is written in thy blood." D. G.

The above may have appeared before, but I cannot anywhere find it: my fources regarding the productions of

Garrick are not numerous. I have, however, " Lethe", with his lateſt alterations, in his own hand, before me.

July 7.—The Duke of Devonſhire, perhaps to teſt my Italian, yeſterday brought into the library where I ſat a copy of Arioſto, complaining that he had never yet ſeen ſatiſfactorily rendered the two famous ſtanzas in the firſt book of the *Orlando Furioſo, " La Verginella è ſimile à la roſa,"* etc., and aſked me if I had ever attempted to tranſlate them ? I anſwered at once in the negative, adding that the original was ſo beautiful that I had always ſhied them, paſſing them over in order that I might be more practiſed before I ventured on what muſt tax the beſt powers of any verſifier. Such was exactly the caſe. He then enquired if I had ſeen Hoole's verſion, and I told him that I was acquainted with no modern tranſlation ; but that Hoole, as far as I had heard, had employed couplets, a form, I . fancied, very ill-ſuited to the old romance. The Duke told me that he had ſeen no other, excepting one in French, and then he went on to ſpeak ſomewhat diſparagingly of the *Orlando Furioſo*, which I had always held in a ſort of adoration, more ſo than its rival-poem, Taſſo's *Geruſalemme Liberata*, which, perhaps, I undervalued. The Duke aſked what old Engliſh tranſlations of Arioſto there were, and I replied that I knew but one of the *Orlando Furioſo*, that of Sir John Harington, which had gone through three impreſſions, in 1591, 1607, and 1634. "Do not be too bibliographical with me (added he, ſmiling), but I ſhould like to ſee how the two ſtanzas were rendered about two hundred and fifty years ago." I anſwered that Harington's verſion was not, as far as I knew, in his Grace's London library.

but that, although rather a fcarce book, I was pretty fure it muft be at Chatfworth: as I had at home the editions of 1591 and 1634, I promifed to bring a tranfcript of the two ftanzas with me to-morrow.

Accordingly I produced them this morning, and they were in the mind (and, indeed, in the hand) of the Duke as foon as he faw me; which was when, as usual, he brought me my bread and wine at one o'clock. I had written them out plainly, and as he always likes to read anything to himfelf, he conned them over once or twice. They ran thus, but I do not infert the original Italian here becaufe anybody who has an Ariofto (and few have not) can refer to it: as they probably cannot refer to Sir J. Harington's tranflation, I give it :—

" Like to the rose I count the virgin pure,
  That grow'th on native stem in garden fair,
Which while it stands with walls environ'd sure,
  Where herdmen with their herds cannot repair,
To favour it it seemeth to allure
  The morning dew, the heat, the earth, the air.
Gallant young men and lovely dames delight
In their sweet scent, and in their pleasing sight.

" But when that once 'tis gathered and gone
  From proper stalk, where late before it grew,
The love, the liking little is or none ;
  Favour and grace, beauty and all, adieu.
So when a virgin grants to one alone
  The precious flower for which so many sue,
Well he that getteth it may love her best,
But she foregoes the love of all the rest."

I had transcribed it without the old fpelling, that it might appear lefs quaint to the Duke, and I added Sir John

Harington's marginal note, "This is taken out of Catullus, but greatly bettered; *ut flos in feptis fecretus nafcitur hortis,* etc." The Duke thought the verfion neither graceful nor literal, and remarked upon the defect that in the first line Harington fpeaks very properly of a rofe in the fingular, and afterwards alters it to the plural. I informed the Duke that, for the fake of comparifon, I had alfo brought with me another verfion of the fame ftanza of Ariofto, three years anterior to that of Harington, and of which no notice had ever been taken. I placed this alfo in the hands of the Duke, who read it; and I faw, by the expreffion of his countenance, that he did not like it; nor did I, efpecially the fecond ftanza: it was neither graceful, literal, nor grammatical.

> " The faire young virgin 's like the rose untainted
>   In garden faire, while tender stalk doth beare it;
> Sole and untouch'd, with no resort acquainted,
>   No shepherd nor his flock doth once come neare it.
> The aire full of sweetnes, the morning fresh depainted,
>   The earth, the waters, with their favors cheere it;
> Daintie young gallants, ladyes most desired,
> Delight to have therewith their heads attyred.

> " But not so soone from greene stocke where it growed
>   The same is pluckt, and from the branch removed,
> As lost is all from heaven and earth that flowed,
>   Both favour, grace, and beauty, best beloved.
> The virgin faire that hath the flowre bestowed,
>   Which more than life to guard it her behoved,
> Loseth her praise, and is no more desired
> Of those that late unto her love aspyred."

The Duke efpecially pointed out the " gouty line", as he termed it,

> " The aire full of sweetnes, the morning fresh depainted,"

and remarked upon the defect, that both ftanzas concluded
with the fame double rhymes. " As you do not (faid I) like
that quoted from *Mufica Tranfalpina*, 1588—and it is certainly ridiculoufly inferior to the original—I will venture
to fhew your Grace what was the refult of my own attempt
laft evening, when I fat hammering away, with our un-
malleable Englifh, for nearly two hours before I could work
my verfion into any decent fhape ; and now I feel almoft
afhamed of putting it into your hands, but here it is.

> "A virgin pure is like a lovely rofe,
>   In a fair garden on its native thorn ;
> In youthful beauty all fecure it blows,
>   Nor by their flocks, nor by rude fhepherds torn.
> Sweet air and morning's beam its leaves unclofe,
>   Both land and water greet it, newly born,
> While many a youth and many a loving maid
> With it their bofoms grace, their temples fhade.

> " But all fo foon as for its charms felected,
>   And reft from parent ftem where firft it fhone,
> By all who once admir'd it 'tis neglected ;
>   Its favour grace and beauty all are gone.
> So fhe who gives the flower (to be protected
>   Above or fight or life) to any one,
> Ev'n from that one fhe coldnefs foon difcovers,
> While quite forfaken by her earlier lovers."

" Well (faid the Duke) let me read it again"; and he read
it again, and a third time, before he returned it to me. " I
muft own (added he) that in fpirit, harmony, and literalnefs
you come nearer to Ariofto than either of the others, though
I do not find by any means full warrant in the Italian for
the laft line but one : ftill, it is quite in confiftency with
the meaning of the whole paffage in the original.   With

your leave, I fhall keep your manufcript." The Duke was walking away with it, when I called his attention to an unnoticed profe-verfion of the fame two ftanzas, which had been printed twenty-four years before Sir John Harington publifhed his verfe-verfion. I had brought the book with me, and as it was in black letter, with which the Duke was not familiar, I read the following paffage aloud to him from Geofrey Fenton's "Certaine Tragicall Difcourfes", 4to, 1567, where he is speaking of "the purity of a maid "—" whom (fays he) we may compare to the red rose, desired of every one, fo long as the morning dew maintaineth him in odoriferous fmell and pleafant colour; but when the force and heat of the fun hath mortified his orient hue, and converted his natural frefhnefs into a withered leaf, the defire to have it decayeth with the beauty of the thing : even fo fhe, that hath once mortgaged the flower of her virginity, is not only defpifed of him to whom fhe hath been fo prodigal of that which fhe ought to make a moft precious jewel, but alfo in common contempt with all men, what fhow of diffembled courtefy foever they prefent unto her."

"A very evident and not a very bad tranflation," faid the Duke, "and it looks like a grofs plagiarifm." Fenton, I added, profeffes here to tranflate a novel by Bandello, of "The Villany of an Abbot"; but the plagiarifm from Ariofto was not, of courfe, by Bandello, but by Fenton, who, recollecting the two ftanzas by Ariofto, thought he could appofitely introduce them in profe. In other places Fenton takes fimilar liberties : he had lived much abroad, and was well acquainted with the *Orlando Furiofo* long before it found its way into Englifh.

C

The Duke had liftened patiently to what I read and faid, and moreover thanked me for the information I had afforded. What he did with my tranflation of the two ftanzas by Ariofto I know not, but he took them away with him into his own room, and that was all I faw of him yefterday.

July 12.—I was taught fomething of German when a boy, and I fhould have learned a good deal more, if I had been as induftrious as my mafter (F. Shoberl, author of many works and tranflations) was painftaking and capable; but I never applied the little that I knew until I was above thirty, when I was afked to put into Englifh two ballads by Schiller, which had been illuftrated in outline by a famous German artift named Retfch. Subfequently I took the fame courfe, and for the fame reafon, with a ballad by another German poet, on the fuicide of the daughter of a clergyman. The ballads by Schiller were his "Fridolin," founded upon a ftory in the *Gesta Romanorum*, alfo narrated in Italian and in other languages, and his "Kampf mit dem Drachen." Thefe two laft were alfo publifhed in Englifh, with copies by Mofes of Retfch's beautiful defigns; but my verfion of the third ballad never appeared in England, but accompanied the German words when they were reprinted abroad. In all three inftances the German original and my tolerably literal tranflation were printed oppofite to each other, fo that my attempt was expofed to the fevere teft of inftant comparifon. Neverthelefs, I fucceeded fo well that even now, after the lapfe of fix or feven years, I am not afhamed of the verfes. It muft always be remembered that the prefence of the original neceffarily "cramped my genius," becaufe I was compelled to be fo literal that anybody learning German could eafily derive inftruction by comparifon. I was affifted here and there by H. C. Robinfon, always a great and kind encourager of German ftudies. I mention thefe ballads becaufe they were my firft printed effay of the kind: S. Prowett, of Bond Street, was the Englifh publifher. ,

As it has never been tranflated, that I am aware, I add here the tale, exactly as it ftands, rather confufedly, in the *Cento Novelle Antiche*, Novel. 68.

"How an Innocent Man was saved from the Malice of his Enemies.

"A rich man, having an only son, sent him, while he was yet a youth, to serve a king, that he might learn gentle and noble manners. As he was much beloved by the king, some of the courtiers, instigated by envy, corrupted one of the principal knights, by prayer and reward, to bring about the death of the youth in this way. One day the knight secretly called the young man to him, and told him that what he was going to say arose out of the great love he bore him; therefore he thus spake: 'My dearest son, the king esteems you beyond all his familiars, but, according to what he says, you offend him too much by your breath: by God, then, if you are wise, when you give him his drink, close your mouth and nose, and turn your face another way, that your breath may not offend him.' The youth did as he was told, whereby the king was greatly offended, and calling the knight who had taught him to do so, commanded that, if he knew the reason of it, he should instantly declare it. He, obeying the king, perverted the whole fact, for he said that the youth could not endure the breath of the king. Therefore, by the advice of this knight, the king sent for a Fornaciajo (kilnman), and commanded him that the first messenger he sent should be put into his burning furnace, and that if he did not do so, or revealed the matter to anybody, the king promised, on his oath, that he would cut off his head. The kilnman, undertaking to do everything, willingly made a fire in a great furnace, and waited anxiously for the arrival of the person who had merited this punishment. The next morning the innocent youth was sent to the kilnman to tell him to perform what the king had commanded. When he was near the furnace, the youth heard mass sounded, and, alighting from his horse, he tied him in the cloister of the church ; and, after hearing mass attentively, he went to the furnace and told the man as the king had commanded : to which the kilnman replied that he had already done everything ; because the principal in the malice, in order that there might be no delay, had gone there first, and inquired of the man if he had done the deed? He said that he had not yet completed the command of the king, but that he would do so quickly. Accordingly he seized him, and instantly put him into the burning furnace. The youth then returned to the king, and informed him that what he had ordered had been done. The king, marvelling at what he heard, prudently came to the knowledge of the truth. When he discovered it, he cut the envious people all to pieces who had falsely accused the innocent young man : he told him all that had happened, made him a knight, and sent him home to his own country with great riches."

July 17.—The Duke left London for Bolton Abbey soon after the paffing of the Reform Bill, and on his return he fent for me, and with rather a grave face told me that he had now no intereft at Knaresborough, for which, before the meafure paffed, he had been able to return fuch men as Tierney (who died in the beginning of 1830), and Sir James Mackintofh (who died very lately). The Duke expreffed himfelf highly fatisfied with the change, though it prevented him from being as ufeful as he wifhed to his party. I remarked that he had no doubt a great deal of influence left at Knaresborough, from perfonal liking as well as from his pofition and property ; but he affured me that he never intended to exercife it again, but to leave the electors to the difcharge of their duties according to their own unbiaffed fenfe of right and wrong.

I have a valuable MS. containing poems of the reigns of Elizabeth, James I, and Charles I, and among them thofe occafioned by the quarrel between Ben Jonson and Alexander Gill, which Gifford (vol. vi, p. 123) printed from, as he fuppofed, "the only copy in exiftence". My copies differ very materially from his, and fupply words and lines there wanting. It is not worth while to repeat, even with corrections, Gill's attack, but the name and claim of Ben Jonfon demand that whatever he wrote fhould be preferved in the moft accurate form, and for this reafon I tranfcribe exactly his brief and fcorching answer to Gill.

"To ALEXANDER GILL.

" Doth the prosperity of a pardon still
Secure thy railing rhymes, infamous Gill,
At libelling?   Shall no Star Chamber peers,
The pillory, the whip, nor loss of ears,
All which thou hast incurr'd deservedly,
Nor degradation from the ministry
Unto the den of thy own father's school,
Keep in thy bawling wit, thou bawling fool?
Thinking to stir me, thou hast lost thy end :
I laugh at thee, poor wretched tike !   Go send
Thy blatant Muse abroad, and teach it rather
A tune to drown the ballads of thy father ;
For thou hast nought in thee to cure his name
But tune and noise, the echo of his shame.
Oh! rogue by statute, censur'd to be whipt,
Cropt, branded, slit, neck-stockt : go, thou'rt stript.
                              " BEN JONSON."

The line, as given by Gifford,

    " *To be the Denis* of thy father's school,"

might have been intelligible in Pope's day, but could have

had no meaning in the time of Ben Jonſon : " the *den* of his father's ſchool" has a clear meaning as applied to both father and ſon—" old Gill, and young maſter Gill."

July 20.—There is a note in Moore's *Life of Byron* (1, p. 38, edit. 12mo) in which a tribute is very *judiciouſly* paid to Thomas Barnes, who has long been the oftenſible editor of the *Times*, the writing for the newſpaper being done by Stirling and others. Barnes, whom I have known for the laſt twenty years, is the ſon of a ſolicitor, who at one time was under-ſheriff of Kent, and died early. He had two ſons, John and Thomas : the latter was educated at the Blue-coat School with Leigh Hunt, Mitchell, and others, being junior to Coleridge and Lamb. They were all Grecians, and Barnes in due time went to Pembroke College, Cambridge, where he obtained a well-founded reputation for Latin compoſition, and took his degree. His father died before he quitted Cambridge, and left him, as the ſon told me, a few thouſands, which he contrived very ſoon to get through, having, however, paid part of the money as pupil to Chitty, then "a pleader under the bar", as the phraſe went. Barnes, at this date, intended to be called, but he never obtained the rank of barriſter; and after he had ſpent his patrimony, he took chambers at the very top of Lamb-buildings in the Inner Temple. There he lived when I firſt was introduced to him by Barron Field, who afterwards went out to Auſtralia as a judge, and ſubſequent to his return became head of the Admiralty Court at Gibraltar. Barnes, while he lived in Lamb-buildings had a long, ſerious illnefs, and I uſed to call upon him almoſt daily. Field was at this date theatrical critic to the *Times*;

and procured the place of parliamentary reporter for Barnes. It was at this time that Barnes wrote his "Parliamentary Portraits"; and was neverthelefs fo poor, and fo much in debt, that I conftantly ufed to lend him fmall fums: as he was intimate in my father's houfe, when Barnes had any friends in his chambers, he ufed to borrow bottles of wine out of my father's cellar for their entertainment. He was very capable and diligent, and after my father had declined the poft of oftenfible editor of the *Times* (an offer made to him on the death of Brownley, a very clever fellow and a capital after-dinner fpeaker) it was propofed by Mr. Walter that Barnes fhould take the office. He is a man of good addrefs, as well as of good education, and perhaps no better appointment could have been made. His falary was inftantly much advanced; but he never offered to pay me what he owed me, and the loan of £20 to him, in one fum, after I married, led to a difference between us, and to my relinquifhment of the fituation I then held on the *Times.* Barnes has never forgiven me the fmall obligation I laid him under: I cared little for the £20. He wrote no other work than his clever "Parliamentary Portraits", firft inferted in *The Examiner ;* but in 1814 he contributed a few articles to a "Lady's Magazine" which had but a short exiftence.

The following is not a bad Bacchanalian fong: it was written for a friend who wifhed to fet it to mufic : whether he did fo or no I never heard.

DRINKING SONG.

Fill full and be jovial, my lads !
To be happy can never be wrong :
'Tis a proverb we had from our dads,
A merry heart always lives long.

Our wine is the emblem of life ;
　For soon as its spirit is fled,
'Tis no longer worth trouble or strife,
　Both are fatally flat when they're dead.

Then, drink while wine's spirit remains,
　Life's spirit as quickly departs :
As long as wine lightens our brains,
　Care never can burden our hearts.

We must not too rigidly examine the morality or the logic of the fong, but drinking has little to do with either.

July 24.—I met my old friend Morton, father to Thomas, Maddifon, and Edward, at Lord's Cricket Ground. When young he was very fond of the game, but he owns that he never could play well: his fons do not care about it : Maddifon feems to me the cleverest of the three. The father was alfo a great fisherman, and to thefe outdoor employments he attributes the excellent health he enjoys at nearly feventy. How contrafted with his contemporary Frederick Reynolds, who, however, is Morton's fenior! Reynolds always drinks a bottle or more after dinner, two or three glaffes of brandy and water at night, and never goes to bed without a dofe of fifty drops of laudanum. Reynolds is the earlier dramatift of the two, for his "Werter" was brought out in 1786, while Morton's "Columbus" was not produced until 1791. Morton told me how he came to write it. He had been entered a ftudent of Lincoln's Inn, and was living a gay, idle fort of life, principally upon what his rich uncle allowed him, when his wine-merchant fent in a bill of £150, to difcharge which he was utterly unprepared. He therefore fet about writing "Columbus", fancying, as he faid, that he was nearly as capable as fome others of that day. It was brought out at Covent Garden in 1791-2, and had a confiderable run. It is fingular that Morton introduced me at Lord's, on the very fame day, to old Miller, the publifher of "Columbus", who had carried on bufinefs in Fleet Street, and finally fold it to Murray, who afterwards removed to Albemarle Street : *florcat !*

Morton makes it a boaft that he never did, and declares that he never will, write a line gratuitoufly, whether comedy, farce, play, even prologue or epilogue. His moft profitable piece was his "School of Reform", and he faid that he liked it better than anything elfe he had written; not excepting his "Cure for the Heartache", which had literally been a cure for the heartache to him.

Morton, notwithftanding his dramatic propenfity, was called to the bar, but never practifed. My mother-in-law knew him when he was a young man, flourifhing in fociety, efpecially at Bath, and fays that he was extremely handfome. He is fo ftill, making due allowance for his years. He was, and is, no common man.

He was nominally reader of plays, etc., fent in to Drury Lane laft year, but only nominally fo, efpecially towards the end of the feafon: the laft piece he faw in that capacity, before its production, was a comedy by Mrs. Gore, which he fent back for alteration, but which, when altered, he never read again. I think he faid that he did look over "Der Alchymift", but not until it was in courfe of preparation, when he tried to render it tolerable, but did not fucceed. He made up his mind that while reader to Drury Lane he would not write anything for that houfe, and yet would not permit his play on the ftory of Baron Trenck to be

D

produced at Covent Garden. He is not captious, but he feems to think that both houfes have in fome way ill-ufed him. He is excellent goffipping company.

July 27.—I dined yefterday in a company confifting mainly of literary men, including two or three profeffed poets, when Dryden's "Panegyric on Cromwell", came under difcuffion, and efpecially this ftanza :—

> " His grandeur he deriv'd from heaven alone,
>   For he was great ere fortune made him so ;
>   And wars, like mists that rise against the sun,
>   Made him but greater seem, not greater grow."

Some held that the fine thought was poorly conveyed, and that the rhymes were faulty : "alone" was a bad rhime to "fun", and "fo" a very weak rhyme to "grow". This fmall point few were difpofed to deny, but they infifted upon the unufual felicity of the expreffions to convey the writer's meaning. Leigh Hunt was pofitive that no improvement could be made ; but Campbell (who, by the way, was half-cocked) was fomewhat loud on the other fide. Amyot maintained that no one word could be altered without in-jury, and challenged Campbell to change even a fyllable with advantage. Campbell inftantly accepted the challenge, and, drolly enough, confented to go into an adjoining ftudy to compofe his fubftitution. In about a quarter of an hour (he took his wine-glafs with him) he returned, and read as follows :—

> " His greatness he from heaven alone had won,
>   For he was great ere greatness he could dream ;
>   And wars, like mists that rise against the sun,
>   Made him not greater grow, but greater seem."

The change was admitted to be ingenious, but it was

univerfally voted a failure, though Campbell, as well as he then could, *flood* up for it. Harnefs afked whether, if the " Panegyric" had been in Campbell's words, the homage would have been paid to it which it had received from the days of Dryden downwards ? One of the company infifted that every line had been fpoiled by Campbell, excepting the third, where no alteration had been attempted ; but two or three argued that "greatnefs" was better than "grandeur", and one gueft ftated that he had read an old copy where it ftood "greatnefs". Dyce, who is generally accurate, faid that he had never feen any fuch fubftitution, adding, as an objection to it, that "great" was in the very next line.

Somebody rather malicioufly threw in Campbell's teeth,

" And treacherous Scotland, to no interest true ;"

but though a little *winy*, and therefore rather irritable, he did not take up the cudgel; and Dyce, the only other Scot prefent, was never very eager to fight the battles of his country. Altogether it was a very pleafant party, and the cheerfulnefs of it was not diminifhed by the following droll parody, which was meditated by T. Hood while Campbell was out of the room : it had reference to the notorious red-nefs of brewer Cromwell's nofe and complexion :

" His redness he deriv'd from heaven alone,
  For he was red ere his beer made him so :
Tobacco fumes, like mists against the sun,
  Made him but redder seem, not redder grow."

This was voted very good for the extemporaneous attempt of a bafhful verfifyer, who fpoke fo low that he could not do juftice to his own performance. Hamilton Reynolds wrote it down, and read it aloud. We fat late.

July 30.—Some years ago I printed in the *London Maga-zine* (publiſhed by Taylor and Heſſey) a tranſlation of the introductory octave ſtanzas to Goethe's poems, and it was well liked by Goethe's friend, H. C. Robinſon. I am very far from a good German, but I have recently done Schiller a ſimilar dis-ſervice as regards ſome very elegant ſtanzas pre-ceding his poems. They form a ſpecies of allegory, charm-ingly worded; and though I cannot pretend to do it juſtice, I admire it ſo much that I have attempted a verſion of it in Engliſh : it muſt be regarded, however, as a mere experi-ment. Schiller heads it

THE MAIDEN FROM AFAR.

The humble shepherds of a valley
　　Saw a wondrous maid appear,
With the lark's first blithesome sally,
　　In the youth of every year.

Not born in those secluded places,
　　Whence she came could no one tell,
And they lost her faintest traces,
　　When the maiden bade farewell.

Where she mov'd she bore a blessing ;
　　Humble hearts at distance sigh,
Too much boldness still repressing
　　By her graceful majesty.

Fruits and flowers she yearly brought them,
　　Grown elsewhere, but sweeter none,
For a happier nature taught them
　　Ripen 'neath a brighter sun.

On each a gift bestow'd the maiden,
　　Fruits to these and flowers to more ;
Staff-propp'd age, and gay youth laden,
　　Home some joyful present bore.

> All were welcome that drew near her,
> But a pair whom Love had blest,
> Gain'd a boon far sweeter, dearer,
> Fairer flowers than all the rest.

I am fure that I am far below the delicate grace of the imaginative original, and I am not unlikely to have miffed fome of the refinements of the infpired author.   Yet much as I admire the above, I am delighted with the beautiful fimplicity of Goethe, in one of his minor poems :

> I sing like bird in greenwood tree
> Its notes of gladsome burden,
> The song it warbles blithe and free
> Is its own richest guerdon.

Or thus :

> I sing like bird in greenwood tree,
> Though no one e'er regards it :
> The song it carols blithe and free
> Rewards, and well rewards it.

Or thus, a third time :

> I sing like bird in greenwood tree,
> Though no one ever hears it :
> The song it warbles blithe and free
> Rewards as well as cheers it.

The fecond is, perhaps, the beft, and the third certainly the worft ; the word "guerdon" in the firft is hardly known to readers of our day.   The original runs thus :

> *Ich singe wie der Vogel singt,*
> *Der in den Zweigen wohnet;*
> *Das Lied das aus der Kehle dringt*
> *Ist Lohn der reichlich lohnet.*

The above I made the motto for my *Poet's Pilgrimage* when I printed it ten years ago.

Shewing my tranflation from Schiller to the Duke of
Devonfhire, and lamenting my deficiency in the niceties of
the language of the original, he was fo pleafed with it that
he declared, if ever he went to Germany again, he would
take me with him. I thanked him, but anfwered that a
brief vifit would not do me much good, adding that my
principal mafter (H. C. R.) had fpent fix years at Jena and
Weimar, and yet declared that he was fometimes puzzled.
I added that I had not yet dared to fhow H. C. R.
my verfion of "The Maiden from afar". "Then, why dare
you fhow it to me?" the Duke inquired.—"Becaufe I venture to think that I know nearly as much of German as
your Grace," was my reply; and he had too much fenfe to be
offended, but left the room, playfully fmiling, and faying,
"Then we fhall be upon pretty equal terms in Germany,
when we get there."

He was always cheerful, friendly, and encouraging, never
touchy with me; for, as he kindly faid, I knew how far I
ought to go, and he never feared, let him introduce me to
whom he would (and he one day prefented me to the Duke
of Wellington), that I fhould overftep the line. This, in
fact, was more praife than I deferved, for *gaucheries* have
feveral times got me into fcrapes in the courfe of my life.
Another point of praife which the Duke gave me had reference to his own partial deafnefs : he faid that he could
eafily hear me, becaufe I formed my words in fpeaking :
moft other people made no ufe of their lips, but mumbled
what they had to fay between the tongue, the teeth, and
the roof of the mouth : the lips, he juftly faid, ought to be
ufed in feparating and finifhing the words fpoken. I have
mentioned this before.

Auguſt 1.—A curious friend, that is, a friend who owns and is fond of curioſities, eſpecially in biography and letters, has given me the following copy of the petition of Lady Ruſſell to the Houſe of Lords, made from the original in her own handwriting. The faƈt of courſe is well known, but I do not find that the exaƈt words of the document, at all events on ſuch authority, have ever yet been given. She was one of the delicately-framed but ſtrong-minded women of her generation—a model and mirror of her sex for courage and affeƈtionate tendernefs.

"To the Right Honoᵇˡᵉ the Lords Spiritual and Temporal, in Parliament assembled.

"The humble Petition of Rachell Lady Russell, relict of Wm. Lord Russell.

"Whereas, their most gratious Majestyes and both Houses of Parliament have, with greate justice, reversed the barbarous attainder of her deare lord. And whereas this honoᵇˡᵉ House, with like regard of justice to him and others, have it now under consideration to enquire after the advisers and accessaries of those malitious proceedings, and to finde out the undue and irregular practice in the returne of the pannell of the jury :

"Your Petitioner finds herselfe under greate obligations of giveing her humble thanks to this honoᵇˡᵉ House for your just and honoᵇˡᵉ proceedings therein, and humbly petitions your Lpps. that you would be pleased effectually to pursue this just inquisition for blood, which you have soe honoᵇˡʸ begun.

"And your Petʳ shall ever pray.

"R. RUSSELL.."

The above document has no date, but it belongs to the tranſaƈtions of 1689.

In the biographies of Archbiſhop Grindall we are told that "at his death he became a conſiderable benefaƈtor to learning"—that he left £30 a year to the ſchool at St. Bees,

and £366 to various colleges in Cambridge; but the following extract from a letter preferved at Lambeth, written by
N. Fant to Anthony Bacon, gives a remarkable account on
6th May, 1583, of the conclufion of the Archbifhop's career.

" The good Archb. of Canterbury is presently to resign his place,
being now altogether blind in body, but most vigilant in mind to do
good so long as he liveth. And, therefore, having made good suite
to be removed, and to obtain license to found certain schools and
places of learning in the University, hath to that purpose discharged
his trayne, and employed all the profits he hath spared of his living,
besydes his ordinary expenses, reserving some little to maintaine him
and a few servants the rest of his life, which cannot be long. It is
thought that Whitgyft, now B. of Worcester, shall succeed him."

I met with a vexatious difappointment to-day. I was
paffing through Turnftile to Lincoln's-inn-Fields, and fo to
Somerfet Houfe, when I caft my eyes upon fome fhelves with
books, outfide a fhop kept by a man of the hiftorical name
of Cornifh. I faw one book that I much defired to poffefs,
viz., the Kilmarnock edition of the Poems of Burns, dated
1786. As I was going farther, and intended to return
directly, I put it back on the fhelf, making up my mind to
purchafe it on my way home : the price was only 1s. 6d., but
I knew that it would not be dear at a guinea ; and when I
returned by the fame way, I did not for a moment forget
my book—for I already confidered it *mine*. My mortifica-
tion, therefore, was not a little when, as I paffed the place
again, I found it gone—fold for 1s. 6d. to fomebody elfe.
I refolved from that time never to run fuch a rifk again.
It was uncut, and in the original boards : I have
never feen any fuch copy. ·Let cafuifts decide, whether to
have given the poor bookfeller only 1s. 6s. for a book worth
a guinea, would not have been impofing upon him ? No,

he obtained his profit out of the 1s. 6d., and I fhould only have availed myfelf of a little fuperior knowledge, which perhaps I had bought very dearly.

Aug. 2.—Nothing can more decidedly fhew the popularity of Dryden's "Abfalom and Achitophel", foon after his death, than the faƈt that both parts of it were printed and publifhed in 1709 at the price of one penny. I bought a copy of it on Saturday, but inftead of one penny, it coft me a whole fhilling. I have gone through it, and find many fewer mifprints than I expeƈted; the paper is very coarfc, and the type much worn, but, to fay the leaft of it, readable: the imprint is, "London: Printed and fold by H. Hill, in Black-fryars, near the Water-fide. 1709." I alfo bought, from the fame prefs, a penny edition of Rofcommon's "Effay on Tranflated Verfe:" likewife a copy of Sir John Mandeville's "Travels", with a fhip on the title-page, and his arms at the back of it, "Printed for M. Hotham, at the Black Boy, on London Bridge"; but this is in quarto, fills twelve leaves, and coft me ten fhillings.

I have in my poffeffion feveral printed and unprinted Prologues and Epilogues by Dryden, not included in any edition of his works to which I have accefs; but moft of them are fo broad in their expreffions, and fo improper in their allufions, that I cannot tranfcribe them. Killigrew's "Parfon's Wedding", a moft exceptionable comedy (included, however, in all the reprints of "Dodfley's Old Plays"), was aƈted entirely by women, whether the chaaraƈters were male or female, and muft have been extremely popular. How the parts were diftributed we have no means of knowing, but it appears from contemporary

authority that the prologue was fpoken by one of the Marfhalls, the reputed daughters of a Puritan minifter: it
was not printed with the comedy in 1663, nor is it known
by whom it was written: my copy may be faid to fettle
that point, and affigns it to Dryden. It begins unobjection-
ably, as follows :—

> " Women, like us, passing for men, you'll cry,
> Presume too much upon your secrecy :
> There's not a fop in town, but will pretend
> To know the cheat himself, or by his friend.
> Then, make no words on 't, gallants : 'tis e'en true ;
> We are condemn'd to look and strut like you.
> Since we thus freely our hard fate express,
> Accept us, these bad times, in any dress."

I can go no farther with any regard to decorum, and
Dryden himfelf feems to have been afhamed of his own
work, cutting the matter as fhort as poffible : the whole,
exclufive of the introduction above quoted, only confifts of
feven couplets. Still, even this, bad as it is, is not so
offenfive as the Epilogue (alfo omitted in the printed copy
of the comedy) addreffed to men, and fpoken by a girl of
between twelve and thirteen years old, in which fhe is
made to utter the moft offenfive double meanings. There
is no pofitive proof that this outrage was alfo committed
by Dryden.

Aug. 8.—I copied the following *literatim* from the original in Pope's handwriting ; on comparifon, it will be
found to contain fome not immaterial variations.

" On my Grotto.

> " O thou, who stop'st where Thames' translucent wave
> Shines a broad mirrour through yᵉ gloomy cave,

Where ling'ring drops through min'ral roofs distil,
And pointed chrystals break the sparkling rill ;
Unpolish'd gems no ray on pride bestow,
And latent metals innocently glow :
Approach, great Nature studiously behold,
And eye the mine without a wish for gold.
But enter awful the inspiring grot,
Where, nobly pensive, St. John sat and thought :
Here British groans from dying Wyndham stole,
And the bright flame was shot through Marchmont's soul.
Such, only such, shall tread the sacred floor,
Who dare to serve their country, and be poor."

I have already inferted the copy of an original letter from Swift to Ambrofe Phillips. The following is another from the fame to the fame, and like the firft, as far as I am aware, unprinted. It is fingular to find the Dean writing queer Englifh.

"London, July 10, 1708.

"I was very well pleased to hear you were so kind to remember me in your letter to Mr. Addison, but infinitely better to have a line from yourself. Your saying that you know nothing of your affairs, more than when you left us, puts me in mind of a passage in Don Quixote, where Sancho, upon his master's first adventure, comes and asks him for the island he had promised, and which he must certainly have won in that terrible combat. To which the knight replied in these memorable words : ' Look ye, Sancho ; all adventures are not adventures of islands ; but many of them of dry blows, and hunger, and hard lodging : however, take courage, for one day or other, all of a sudden, before you know where you are, an island will fall into my hands, as fit for you as a ring for the finger.' In the meantime, the adventures of my lord and you are likely to pass with less danger and with less hunger, so that you need less patience to stay till midwife Time will please to deliver this commission from your *womb of Fate.*

"I wish the victory we have got, and the scenes you pass through, would put you into humour of writing a pastoral, to celebrate the D. of Marlborough, who, I hope, will soon be your general.

" My lord and you may, perhaps, appear well enough to the York
ladies from the distance of a window, but you will both be deceived
if you venture any nearer.　They will dislike his lordship's manner
and conversation, as too southern by three degrees ; and, as for your
part, what notion have they of spleen or sighing for an absent mistress ?　I am not so good an astronomer to know whether Venus ever
cuts the arctic circle, or comes within the vortex of Ursa Major ; nor
can I conceive how love can ripen where gooseberries will not.

" The triumvirate of Mr. Addison, Steele, and me, come together as
seldom as the sun, moon, and earth.　I often see each of them, and
each of them me and each other ; and, when I am of the number, justice is done you as you would desire.

" I hope you have no intention of fixing for any time in the North.
Sed nec in Arcto sedem tibi figeris orbe ; but let my Lord Mark,
though he is your north star, guide you to the South.　I have always
had a natural antipathy to places that are famous for ale.　Wine is
the liquor of the gods, and ale of the Goths ; and thus I have luckily
found out the reason of the proverb, to have guts in one's brain—that
is, what a wise man eats and drinks rises upwards, and is the nourish-
ment of his head, where all is digested ; and, consequently, a fool's
brains are in his guts, where his beef and thoughts and ale descends.
Yet your hours would pass more agreeably if you could forget every
absent friend and mistress you have, because of that *impotens deside-
rium*, than which nothing is a more violent feeder of the spleen, and
there is nothing in life equal to recompense that.

" Pray tell my Lord Mark Kerr I humbly acknowledge the honour
of his remembrance, and am his most obedient servant : tell him I
love him as *un homme de bien, honneste, degagé, disintéressé, liberal,
et qui se connoit bien en hommes.*　As for you, I have nothing to wish
mended but your fortune, and in the meantime a little cheerfulness
added to your humour, because it is so necessary towards making
your court.　I will say nothing to all your kind expressions, but that
if I have deserved your friendship as much as I have endeavoured to
cultivate it ever since I knew you, I should have as fair pretensions
as any man could offer.　And if you are a person of so much wit and
invention as to be able to find out any use for my service, it will increase my good opinion, both of you and myself.

" St. James's Coffee House is grown a very dull place upon two accounts: first, by the loss of you ; and secondly, of everybody else. Mr. Addison's lameness goes off daily, and so does he, for I see him seldomer than formerly, and therefore cannot revenge myself of you by getting ground in your absence. Coll Froud is just as he was, very friendly and *grand rêveur et distrait.* He has brought his poems almost to perfection ; and I have great credit with him, because I can listen when he reads, which neither you nor the Addisons nor Steeles ever can. I am interrupted by a foolish old woman, and, besides, here is enough. Mr. Addison has promised to send this, for I know not where to direct, nor have you instructed me.

" I am ever your most faithful humble serv‘,

" J. SWIFT."

Aug. 12.—In a note on Byron's " Life", Moore remarks upon a coincidence between a paſſage in the " Two Noble Kinſmen," and another in " Childe Harold," where a man on horſeback is likened to a ſhip on the ocean. Poſſibly Lord Byron copied from a play by Chapman, called "Byron's Conſpiracy," printed firſt in 1608, to the reading of which he might be led by the coincidence of the name. It is a very noble paſſage in the old poet :

> " Your majesty hath miss'd a royal sight,
> The Duke Byron on his brave beast, Pastrana,
> Who sits him, like a full sail'd argosea
> Danc'd by a lofty billow, and as snug
> Plies to his bearer—both their motions mix'd," etc.

After all I doubt whether Lord Byron was indebted to either B. and F. or to Chapman, becauſe the ſimile might naturally occur to any poet. There is often nothing more abſurd than theſe accuſations of plagiarism.

In England the autographs of Voltaire are far from common, but I have a curious undated one, which ſerves to prove how deſirous he was of ſtanding well with readers in this country. The editor of *The Monthly Review* had praifed fome work by Voltaire, who haftened to exprefs his thankfulnefs in writing, and therefore fent the following, which devolved into my hands with fome other old papers belonging to my father : it has no date of place or time, but it is written moft carefully in a formal cramped hand, and is addreffed thus :

" *Pour faire rendre à Monsieur * * *, autheur du monthly review.*

"j do return the most sincere thanks to the generous author of the monthley review; he has told what j would be, rather than what j am.

"yet j must own j deserve the praise He was pleas'd to bestow upon me, when he said j am a lover of truth. my passion for truth and freedom has kindled the benevolence of a free writer, who gives letters of naturality to a frenchman.

"j am with a due gratitude

"his most humble s^t

"VOLTAIRE."

Voltaire was fond of being thought a proficient in our language and literature.

Aug. 14.—I fpent the evening at the Garrick Club in company with Theodore Hook, James Smith, the Rev. R. Barham, Poole, Dance, and two or three more. The converfation, as may be fuppofed, was rather free and very merry, and the eatables and drinkables excellent. James Smith afferted that he was the author of a certain riddle or conundrum, which has been going the round of fociety for fome weeks, viz., " If a man have the hydrophobia, why fhould he call out in the terms of an infcription often feen in the windows of confeⅽtioners ? Anfwer : Water Ices and Ice-creams, *i.e.*, *Water I fees and I fcreams.*" Smith's claim was not difputed, and Barham told the ftory, among other merriments, of the one-eyed husband, who, returning home unexpectedly, and late at night, furprifed his wife "and one more," and how fhe contrived the efcape of her lover. I told Barham that I could fhow him fuch a novel in profe (Queen of Navarre's *Novelle*, fo. 20, edit. 1560). He replied that he could fhow it me *in verfe.* "Do you mean in Englifh?" I afked. "Yes" (faid he) "in Englifh." "And printed?" I inquired. "No" (anfwered he), "but ready to be printed"; and putting his hand into his coat-pocket, he pulled out a sheet of paper and gave it to me. Several made a fnatch at it in fun, but I kept my hold, and when I got home I read it. Some fmall allowance muft here, of courfe, be made, but Barham, in his converfation, never deviates beyond drollery, at leaft in my hearing. What follows is fo well done, that I cannot refrain from copying it : I believe it to be Barham's, but not acknowledged :

"THE GLASS EYE.

" Once on a time, not very long ago,
   A Colonel, fomething past the prime of life,
   Took to himself a young and pretty wife :
'Twas not quite prudent, but men will do so.
One of his eyes, when he was young, the foe
   Depriv'd him of ; and as he wish'd to pass
   Still for a handsome man, an eye of glass
He had procur'd, like his good eye in show.

" Now, being oblig'd to join his regiment
   Abroad, he left his darling wife behind,
And she betray'd no little discontent
   To part with her dear husband semi-blind ;
   But overjoy'd at heart, as you will find.

" No sooner gone, but she call'd in a friend
   She lik'd a great deal better than her lord ;
And wondrous happy were they thus to spend

The time while the poor Colonel was abroad.
But it so happened that the war was over
Much sooner than the lady and her lover
  At all expected that their bliss would end.

" One night, when both upstairs, but not asleep,
  They heard a knock ; nor was it long before
The maid, entrusted with the secret deep,
  Rush'd in, and cried ' The Colonel 's at the door !'
The lady (like most ladies, with a head
For all emergencies) leap'd out of bed :
  ' Fear not', she cried, and then ran out to meet
  The Colonel, as he ent'red from the street.

" ' How glad I am to have you back so soon !
  I was in bed, and dreaming but of you.
I dream'd that, though you went away with one
  Poor seeing eye, yet you came back with two :
Do tell me, darling, if my dream be true ?
I hope it is—with all my heart I do.
  Is it a miracle from heaven above,
  Thus to reward my constancy and love ?'

" And then she kiss'd him, placing her soft hand
  Over his seeing eye. ' Now, tell me, dear,
If you can see : is that an eye of glass,
  Or with it can you see me plain and clear,
Or anything before you that may pass ?
  Tell me, dear husband, here as we both stand.'

" ' Alas !' he answer'd with a sigh and smile,
  ' Your dream but flatter'd : I can nothing see,
But I can feel your soft warm hand the while :
  Oh ! do not take it off ! sweet, let it be !
  It is the hand that gave yourself to me.'

" While this was passing, the affrighted lover
  Needed no hint of what he ought to do,
  But slipp'd away unseen, and unheard, too ;

> And the poor Colonel, failing to discover
>> How he was cheated, went to bed, right glad
>> To find how true and fond a wife he had."

I may mention here that on another occafion I had shown Barham my lines " On the Creation of Man"; and the next time I met him, he gave me the following, the original of which he faid he had found in an old foreign jeft-book.

MATRIMONY.

> " We're told by Aristophanes,
>> When man was first created
>> He had two heads, four legs, and these
>> To four arms were related.

> " But such rare gifts made him so proud,
>> His maker he derided ;
>> And Jove, descending in a cloud,
>> This double man divided.

> " One-half was woman, t'other man ;
>> And here we see the reason
>> They get together, when they can,
>> Both in and out of season."

Barham did not tell me his authority at the time, and I forgot to afk him afterwards : it was certainly not *Airy ftuff in eafe*, as Swift etymologifes the Greek name.

Aug. 24.—I give the following fpecimen of a converfation between the Duke and myfelf : it occurred this morning, after our return from Brighton.

D. I was reading nearly all Sunday one book : guefs what it was ?

C. The Bible, of courfe, as it was Sunday.

D. No : that was read to me twice at church. "Plutarch's Lives"—I accidentally took up a volume, and could not lay it down again.

F

C. Which of the biographies interefted you moft ?

D. The lives of Julius Cæfar, Mark Antony, and Coriolanus were thofe I read.

C. Three of Shakefpeare's heroes.

D. That was my main reafon. I wifhed to fee how far
our great poet had been indebted to Plutarch.

C What edition did you read ?

D. Langhorne's : is not that the beft ?

C. Not for your purpofe, at all events. I never looked
into any tranflation of Plutarch but that which Shakefpeare
muft have ufed, not only becaufe there was no other, but
becaufe he has in many places followed it verbally : thus,
look at the fpeech of Coriolanus to his mother, in act v, fc.
3, after Volumnia has prevailed :

> "You have won a happy victory to Rome,
> But for your son," etc.

What are the words as given in the old tranflation of Plutarch ? "O mother !" faid he, "you have won a happy
victory for your country, but mortal and unhappy for your
fon", etc.

D. That is very remarkable.

C. And there are many places in the three plays you
have mentioned where the verbal obligation is quite as
ftriking, if not more fo : therefore it is clear to what translation of Plutarch Shakefpeare reforted.

D. It was not clear to me, becaufe till now I did not
know. From what edition do you quote ?

C. From one which was firft printed in a large folio
volume, when Shakefpeare was in his 15th or 16th year, 1579.
It was made by Sir Thomas North, not from the original
Greek, but from a tranflation into French by a bifhop of

the name of Amyot. Still, it is a capital book, and contains fpecimens of fine unfrenchified Englifh.

D. Is there a copy of it in my library?

C. Not of that edition, I darefay, though I have it at home preferved among my Shakefpearean books: the oldeft impreffion is a rarity, and the copy I own is the more valuable becaufe it contains the only known autograph of John Offley, as the owner of it, to whom old Isaac Walton dedicated his "Complete Angler" in 1653. The Plutarch was printed in Black-friars by Vautrollier.

D. Now again, as the other day, you are getting too bibliographical; becaufe it can be of little confequence by whom it was printed : the question is, how, and to what extent, it was ufed by Shakefpeare.

C. I beg your pardon; the printer of it is a point of fome importance, for this reafon : it was printed by Vautrollier, to whom Richard Field was then an apprentice.

D. Do you mean the Field who was the author of two plays which you reprinted four or five years ago, and which you borrowed of me for the purpofe, "Woman is a Weathercock", and "Amends for Ladies"? I have the reprints, which you gave me.

C. That was Nathaniel Field, an actor of great merit and celebrity, who was a performer in Shakefpeare's day, and the fon of a noted Puritan divine, who had another fon of a very different character ; for, after he had written and publifhed fome poems in the year 1600, he was made a bifhop by James I. Thofe Fields were of a different family to that of the Richard Field who was apprenticed to Vautrollier, who printed North's "Plutarch": that Field was intimately connected with Shakefpeare, as both came from

Stratford-on-Avon ; Richard Field was the fon of a tanner at Stratford, who failed in bufinefs, and put his fon apprentice to Vautrollier.

D. Was Richard Field in any other way conne&ted with Shakefpeare than as his contemporary and townfman ?

C. Certainly : he married Vautrollier's daughter, when out of his time, fucceeded to the bufinefs, and was a&ually employed by Shakefpeare to print his "Venus and Adonis" in 1593, and his "Lucrece" in 1594. Befides, Richard Field worked in the Black-friars, clofe to one of the theatres where the plays of Shakefpeare were daily a&ed.

D. Aye. I now underftand. Shakefpeare is thus fhewn to have been a friend of the very apprentice who probably aided, when a boy, in printing North's tranflation of Plutarch in 1579.

C. That was about fix or feven years before we fuppofe Shakefpeare to have come to London.

D. And the employment of his townfman as a printer in the Black-friars might poffibly have fome connexion with the introdu&ion of Shakefpeare, as a&or and dramatift, to the company then occupying the Black-friars' playhoufe.

C. Precifely fo ; but as yet we are without proof upon the point : we only know that Richard Field was apprentice to Vautrollier, that Vautrollier printed the tranflation of Plutarch, and that after Field fucceeded to his mafter's bufinefs, having married his daughter, Field printed "Venus and Adonis" and "Lucrece".

D. Well, I wifh I knew more about fuch matters. If, as you fay, I have not North's "Plutarch" of 1579, I know that I have, bound up with my "Old Plays", Shakefpeare's early poems printed by Richard Field.

C. As to the ufe of the "Plutarch" of 1579 by Shakefpeare, Field's mafter being the printer of it, you are to
obferve that there was a fecond edition of the work in 1595,
and that may have been the impreffion which Shakefpeare
ufed for his three Roman tragedies. I could give you all
the dates connected with the two families of the name of
Field, but you would find it fo tedious that you might have
again to fay, " Do not be fo bibliographical." There is one
point I may juft mention : that as Nathaniel Field became
a player and dramatift (in fpite of his father's—John Field's
—puritanical preaching) early in the reign of James I, there
was a much more extraordinary inftance of a fimilar kind
juft after the Reftoration ; for the two Mifs Marfhalls, who
were about the firft women who ever appeared on our ftage,
were the daughters of another Puritanical minifter—as if
the feverity of the fystem, in both cafes, had driven the
young people into the very oppofite extreme.

Juft at this moment Lord Clare was announced, and the
Duke having, as he always did, introduced me to him, they
left for the Duke's ftudy. I have given the above as nearly
as poffible as it occurred ; and if it be thought that I was
too eafy with the Duke, I can only fay that of all things,
he diflikes to be *begraced*, *beduked*, and *belorded*.

Aug. 26.—Poole to-day at the Garrick told me of a droll
faying of his, when George Lamb left the bar, in order to
attend to his duties in the Houfe of Commons : Poole remarked upon the occafion that the right hon. gent. had
ceafed to be a *Baa*-lamb, and had become a *Houfe*-lamb.

He did not like Power, the actor, who had juft brought
out with much fuccefs a piece (founded upon an older drama)

called "Born to Good Luck": Poole being aſked, how Power wrote—with what force or vigour? replied, "He writes with a *onc-aſs power*."

. In the Chapter Houſe, Weſtminſter, yeſterday, were ſhewn me ſeven original letters from Sir W. Cavendiſh to Cromwell, Lord Privy Seal; they are without date of the year, but extend from the 5th March to 3rd December. By theſe it appears that Sir William was actively engaged by Cromwell in the work of the ſuppreſſion of the monaſteries. The firſt is from Dover, March 5th, when, in conjunction with his "friend and fellow John Anthony," he was by commiſſion ſurveying the religious houſes of Dover and Canterbury, the yearly rent of which amounted to five hundred marks. The next letter is from Little Marlow, June 23rd, ſtating that he had diſſolved the priory there, and had "diſcharged my lady and the religious perſons of the ſaid houſe." A third letter is dated "from my poor houſe at Northawe, the 5th day of September," and it ſolicits the auditorſhip of St. John, and the intereſt of Cromwell with "my lord of Saint John" to obtain it—"wherin ye ſhall no leſſe bynde me, then hereto-fore ye have, in provyding and preordinating the lyff that I now leade of a powr honest man." The fourth letter, from Buſhemede, the 8th September, ſhews that Sir William was then in Bedfordſhire as one of two Commiſſioners, "for the defacyng of all houſes diſſolved within the ſaid ſhire." By the fifth letter, from St. Alban's, 11th October, it appears that he was then making ſome demand of the monks there, to the royal advantage, with which they were moſt unwilling to comply. Sir William was at Northawe again on 11th October, from whence he dates his ſixth letter, an-nouncing that he had been appointed auditor by Lord Beauchamp. The laſt (the ſeventh) letter relates to his proceedings at Ely, from whence it is dated on the 3rd December, mentioning the difficulties he had met with there, from the obſtinacy of the prior, in the execution of his duty as "auditor and receptor" of the monaſtery. Sir William ſent to Cromwell by the ſame opportunity eleven pieces of plate, he had procured, no doubt, from the monks, weighing forty-eight ounces and a quarter.

In the ſame collection there are alſo four letters to Cromwell and Lord Suffolk, from a perſon ſigning himſelf Richard Caundyſlhe (query, if he be of the ſame family), two dated from Lubeck and Hamburgh, one without place, and a fourth from Norton. The three firſt relate to the affairs of England with the Hanſe towns, and the laſt (to Lord Suffolk) to the digging for gold at or near Norton, where it was ſuppoſed that it was to be found, from the ſhining of certain minerals on the ſurface.

Sir W. Cavendiſh was long ſuppoſed to be the author of the "Life of Wolſey," until the Rev. Mr. Hunter ſhewed that it was written by his elder brother, George Cavendiſh.

Auguſt 30.—Stephen Price, late American leſſee of Drury Lane, told me that during the three ſeaſons he held the theatre he loſt the following ſums :—In the firſt ſeaſon more than £3,000, in the ſecond more than £7,000, and in the third nearly £9,000. His bankruptcy was not, however, owing to his bad ſucceſs as manager, but to other circumſtances, viz., the acceptance of bills for (I think) Jobbling, a wine merchant in the Adelphi. He aſſerted that, if time had been allowed him, he ſhould have ſtill paid every ſhilling, and that fince his return from America he had acquitted himfelf of every demand.   All this *cum grano.*

I afked him what he faid to Kenney's claim on the fcore of *Mafaniello,* and his anfwer was this—that he had paid Kenney £300 in hard cafh for a play (the title he had forgotten) reprefented to be new, but which turned out to be very flightly altered from a comedy by Holcroft, which had been played feven nights, and printed about .1794.   Thus he infifted that Kenney was in his debt, and that *Mafaniello* was agreed between them to be taken at £100, in part liquidation of that debt.   *Cum grano.*

When Kenney's and Morton's *Peter the Great* was brought out by Price, it was fupported by Young at £25 per night, and by Lifton and Mifs Stephens at £15 per night each, and it never paid more than its expenfes.   *C. g.*

September 1.—I bought a copy of Horace Twifs's "Pofthumous Parodies", publifhed as long fince as 1814.   I have known him fince 1806 or 1807, when he ufed to be a frequent and lengthy fpeaker at the Academics, during their meetings at the Globe Tavern in Fleet Street.   It is faid that he fent copies of his "Pofthumous Parodies" to all the principal people mentioned in them, and unqueftionably I have feen two proofs of the fact.   When he dines out he is fond of fpeechifying, and I have heard him, in large companies, get up (at the requefted requeft of fomebody) and entertain his audience, by the hour together, with imitations of the ftyle of fpeaking of various parliamentary orators,— Pitt, Fox, Windham, Tierney, etc.   Moft people confidered it a bore to have converfation fo ftopped, but I muft own there was often great clevernefs in his attempts of the kind. I dined with him very lately at C. Kemble's (to whom he is nephew), but his talk was then unusually flat and flimfy. Sam Rogers was of the party; as well as Tom Campbell, looking very haggard in fpite of his fcratch-wig. Mrs. C. Kemble (who is rather ill-natured) afferts that fhe once came behind him, while he was gazing at himfelf in the glafs, when fhe heard him exclaim in his broad Scotch accent, as he turned away from the mirror in fome difguft, "Ah now, fee what it is to grow like an old cat!" He had, and yet has, a great deal of perfonal vanity, and twenty years ago he was confidered very handfome, as indeed he is reprefented in Sir T. Lawrence's portrait of him.

Mr. Morris, the proprietor of the Haymarket Theatre, is my authority for the fubfequent particulars of the prices he gave at various dates to O'Keefe and others for the following productions for his ftage :—

Son-in-Law	- -	- 1779	- £42
Dead Alive	- -	- 1780	- £42
Summer Amusement, a comedy	-	1780	- £64 10s.
Agreeable Surprise	-	- 1781	- £42
Young Quaker	- •	- 1782	- £102 12s.
Peeping Tom	- -	- 1784	- £50
Beggar on Horseback	-	- 1785	- £31 10s.

Morris defired by this enumeration to fhow that authorfhip was not by any means fo well paid then as now : he had recently given Poole £400 for "Paul Pry", and Kenney as much for "Sweethearts and Wives".

Colman, the prefent licenfer, obtained the then unprecedented fum of £1,000 for his "John Bull" at Covent Garden in 1803. The fame author's "Africans" afterwards (1808) produced him £1,500, but he was then one of the

G

proprietors of the Haymarket, where it was firft acted. When Colman received £500 upon it from the Haymarket Treafury, he faid drolly enough to Poole: "I have juft been paying myfelf £500 on account of the 'Africans', and upon my word I can very ill afford it." The play met with extraordinary fuccefs, fupported by Young, Lifton, Mrs. Gibbs, Mrs. Lifton, etc.

To fhew how the greateft actors were paid formerly, Morris ftates that when "The Mountaineers" was originally produced at the Haymarket in 1794 or 1795, John Kemble, then in the height of his reputation, engaged himfelf to play in it at only £12 a-week. There is not a vaft deal of difference between the value of money now and in 1795, and unqueftionably all performers, but efpecially thofe of the higheft grade, are paid too much. F. Kemble and his daughter, laft feafon and the feafon before, had each £30 a-week from beggared Covent Garden.

Jerrold says that his drama of "Black-eyed Susan" was played four hundred times in one year (often on the same night at different theatres), and yet he obtained no more than £50 for it from the Surrey Theatre, and he fold the copyright for only £10. Now, T. P. Cooke acknowledged that he had been paid £60 for playing William in it one week at Covent Garden. For "The Rent Day" Jerrold received £150 from Drury Lane, the laft payment being made on the twenty-fifth night.

September 2.—The late Mr. James Perry, the proprietor of the *Morning Chronicle*, and one of the leaders, as well as the public fupporter, of the Whig party, was a man who had feen great variety of life. Born in Scotland, he was in the

outfet of his career affiftant in a draper's fhop in Aberdeen ;
this I have from the Rev. A. Dyce, who is himfelf a native
of that town, whofe grandfather fent out various fuccefsful
fpeculations to India, and was able to buy, or obtain, com-
miffions in the army for one or more of his fons. They
have all done well.

Perry was of an enterprifing turn, and foon became weary
of the drapery bufinefs : he, therefore, took to the ftage, for
which he had fome talent, though his figure was not good :
in Scotland, and at different places in the north of England, he fucceeded tolerably, even in fome leading characters ; and he was once under the management of Tate
Wilkinfon. At this time he fell in love with a young actrefs, who, however, flighted him, and married an actor
much older than herfelf or Perry, of the name of Sparks.
My father and mother ufed to talk of Mrs. Sparks as an
actrefs of confiderable merit, who afterwards made her way
to London ; and I have fome recollection of having feen her
play an old woman's part in my boyhood, but of this I am
not certain : my notion is that fhe preceded Mrs. Davenport.

Perry quitted the ftage after his difappointment in love,
and came to London, where, in connexion with newfpapers,
he had good fuccefs, and was employed by Woodfall on the
Morning Chronicle, fometimes reporting debates in Parliament, and, as they phrafe it on the ftage, "making himfelf
generally ufeful." After a time, and when Woodfall became weary of the management of the newfpaper, it fell
into Perry's hands, who fubfequently obtained the pro-
prietorfhip of it, either in part or entirely : he had previoufly been alfo engaged on the *Gazetteer,* but in what
capacity I never heard. The fale of the *Morning Chronicle*

as Perry told me, was fo fmall then, that it only juft paid
its expenses, and that with the utmoft economy. To aid
him in his new undertaking, Perry invited two friends from
Scotland, of the name of Spankie, William and Robert, I
think : twenty years afterwards I was acquainted with
Robert, and they both ufed at times to visit at my father's
houfe. What became of William I never knew, but Robert
was called to the bar, became a sergeant, and, through the
intereft of the Whigs, was fent out to India in a judicial
capacity. He became tired of Bombay (I think it was),
returned to England, and with fome reputation began to
practife at the Old Bailey and in other minor courts, fhowing great confidence and great cleverness, but he never became a lawyer, or obtained any higher rank in the profeffion : his bufinefs, however, at one time, brought him (as he
told a friend of mine) between £3,000 and £4,000 a-year.
Before Robert Spankie went to India the fale of the
Morning Chronicle, by the exertion of Perry and his friends,
had rifen from 1,000 to 4,000 copies per day ; it was never
in Perry's time much higher than 7,000 copies per day, and
that was in 1810, when he defended himfelf in perfon againft
a profecution for libel, which he had merely copied from
another newfpaper (the *Examiner*). Perry acquitted himfelf fo well, that he was acquitted. I was prefent at the
trial with my father, who was then engaged on the *Times.*
Perry was always partial to me, and, before I married,
invited me to his table, where I met Erfkine, Tierney,
Adam, Ponfonby, and others of the Whig party. There,
too, I met old Zachary Macaulay, the father of Thomas
Babington : Zachary talked with a ftrong Scotch brogue.
During every debate on the Slave Trade, he was fure to be

found in the gallery of the Houfe of Commons. He had remarkably fmall quick eyes, and ftooped in the fhoulders.

There was a joke about Perry, and his connection with the Whigs, fome ten or twelve years ago. He was arguing a political point at a dinner-table, when his adverfary advanced fome rather Toryfied doctrine, on which Perry exclaimed, "Why, I thought you were a Whig!" "So I am," faid the other, coolly; "but not a *Perry-whig.*" This ftory was long current, and the more fo as it annoyed the fubject of it.

Sept. 3.—I have lately feen a good deal of Mrs. Munden, the widow of the famous old comedian : fhe is an extremely nice old lady, whofe maiden name was Butler. She was originally on the ftage, and had the diftinction of having delivered at Litchfield Mifs Seward's "Monody on the Death of Garrick," of which fhe fhowed me the authorefs's copy, in her own handwriting. She remembered Garrick perfectly, and had often acted with him in the provinces ; but had never feen him off the ftage until after his retirement, when fhe waited upon him, at his houfe on the Adelphi Terrace, with a tragedy a friend of hers had written, and which was recommended to his notice by George Garrick. She did not tell me the fubject of it; but faid that fhe was highly pleafed with the great-little man's reception of her, though he declined to interfere about the acceptance or performance of any piece, now he had relinquifhed the management of Drury Lane Theatre. She added that Garrick made himfelf look fo young and well on the ftage, that fhe was furprifed, and even fhocked, by the difference of his appearance off it : though vivacious, he looked very haggard, and his livelinefs was forced and *ftagy*. Mrs. Munden is herfelf the authorefs of feveral dramatic productions—one of them a verfion of "The Chimney-Sweeper of Madrid", on the fame foundation as Power's "Teddy the Tiler", and Cafti's celebrated Italian ftory, fo admirably verfified, and forming a main portion of his *Beretto Magico*.

As Garrick died three months afterwards, the following muft be one of the laft letters he wrote. How it came into my hands I do not remember.

"19 Oct., 1778.

"My dear Sʳ,—I shall think no pains I take for you disagreeable, and I shall be really happy to shew my regard and attachment to you. I wrote the article at Hampton, where I could not look into More's Fables, but I had made myself master of that matter before I had the pleasure of yʳ letter.

"I have spoken of Brooke as a good man. I wish you would cast your eye upon a note in the second volume of the 'Batchelor', which our friend Becket will send you; and, though I allow much to party resentment, yet sure there cannot be so open and dreadful an attack upon a man's character without some little foundation. The authors of that note are respectable men and wits : how far their last character have effected their first, I cannot tell : if you think any note necessary, pray insert it ; and I beg that you will never give yourself the trouble to send proofs of my stuff to me, unless you may have some doubts. I shall endeavor to do something better for your next : this article has, I fear, got a little of the weakness that troubled me at the time of writing it.

"I am, dʳ sʳ, most sincerely yours,

"D. GARRICK."

Thus it is evident that the writer was, almoft to the laft, interefting himfelf with literary matters. He longed to eftablifh a literary reputation.

This anecdote was narrated to me by a perfon who was prefent. When Wordfworth was laft in London, Quillinan (the author of "Dunluce Caftle", etc., and nearly related to Sir Egerton Brydges) read to him fome portions of Sotheby's tranflation of Homer; and coming to the line,

"Here are the horses saturate with corn,"

Wordfworth exclaimed,

"Here am I, Wordsworth, saturate with Sotheby,"

and would liften to no more of it. I have not Sotheby's Homer, and do not know in what part of his verfion the line is to be found.

Sept. 5.—The Duke faid to me this morning, "I have bufinefs for fome days at Chatfworth and Hardwicke, with my auditor, Mr. Currey : I do not afk you to go there with me, nor to expect any company; but if you can meet me there, fay on Saturday, it will give me pleafure. I fhall be engaged in the middle of the day, but not in the mornings and evenings, and it will be agreeable to me to have fomebody there that I can talk to, befides my chaplain and my man of bufinefs." As I was then pretty much at leifure, I thanked the Duke, and accepted his invitation at once : he moft confiderately added, "You muft do it at my expenfe, becaufe I cannot expect you to lay out your money for my perfonal convenience and pleafure." I anfwered that it would be for my own fincere pleafure alfo, and that I could not think of accepting remuneration for what many would be very glad to pay. "Never mind (added he), we fhall be able to fettle the matter between us;" and, fhaking me by the hand, he left me on the underftanding that I should meet him at Chatfworth on Saturday afternoon. In the evening, a blank envelope was fent to my houfe, containing a cheque for £25. The Duke was never to be outdone in generofity, taking the word in the fenfe of high-minded liberality, amounting, as in this cafe, almoft to profufenefs.

What happened during the five days I remained with the Duke is not of much confequence. I went down by coach to Bakewell, and took a fly from Bakewell to Chatsworth, where I found I was expected, and where my apartment (the View-room, with a lovely profpect to the fouthweft) had been duly prepared for me. I did not fee the mafter of the houfe until near dinner-time, and, although I was told no ladies were expected, I dreffed myfelf as for a party, and the Duke did nearly the fame : the only others at table were the auditor and the chaplain : we were thus merely four, the Duke at the top, the chaplain (who duly faid grace) at the bottom, Mr. Currey on the Duke's left hand, and myfelf on his right. The dinner was plain; no fifh, but foup and feveral made difhes, with a leg of mutton, which the chaplain carved, and a curried rabbit. The dinner was of the fame character every day I ftayed, excepting that one day we had fifh, and on another day Irifh ftew; for which laft the Duke apologifed, faying that it fmelled fo good, as he was croffing the hall at the dinner-time of the fervants, that he had ordered it alfo for his own table. We all liked it much, and the Duke remarked that we fhould be on equal terms as regarded the important in · gredient, onions. We fat rather long over our dinner and wine ; after which we ftrolled about the gardens until it was as dark as it ever is in this month, and after fome wine and water we went to bed.

Next morning the Duke and I breakfafted without more company than a fine Scotch terrier, which came to the window, and which was inftantly admitted by the Duke, who jumped up from his chair to open the window, ob-ferving playfully "I muft not keep him waiting: he is not ufed to it." Breakfaft ended, we walked to the fountains, which, however, were not playing. On returning to the houfe, the Duke faid, "You will not fee me again until the afternoon: go where you like, ftay as long as you like, and when you are tired you can amufe yourfelf with my books: they are in great diforder, upon temporary fhelves in fome of the fitting-rooms: you may like to vary your purfuits by going into the fculpture gallery, in the arrangement of which I was affifted by Sir F. Chantry and Allan Cunning-ham." I had feen it, in fact, before: then, the Duke took his leave for a time.

I haftened upftairs, and certainly I never faw fo many valuable books in fuch confufion: not a few of the moft coftly, which had been bought by the Duke for hundreds of pounds, were thruft into obfcure corners; but, by means of a pair of lofty fteps, I could get at any that I liked. The dramatic portion was, of courfe, in-London; but I routed out fome curious old poetry. Thefe books are quite feparate from the room where the Bishop of Ely's library is duly arranged. We dined and fpent the evening much as the day before; but the next day I was for feveral hours among the fculptures, the works of Canova, Skaddow, Thorwaldfen, Chantry, Weftmacot, etc.; and there was a ftrange gentleman at dinner, who, I think, was a relation of

II

the Arkwrights, to one of whom we paid a vifit the next day, for the Duke had told me that "he meant to make it a half-holiday."

We ftarted at about eleven o'clock, in a brougham drawn by four fmall greys, with the gardener on the box, and drove, as I underftood, for I did not know the country, towards Matlock, calling upon Mrs. Arkwright, the daughter of Stephen Kemble, a homely-looking dame ; and very un- like what I expected would be the appearance of the poetical compofer of Mrs. Hemans' fong, "What hid'ft thou in thy cavern'd rocks," etc.   She was playing at bil- liards with another old lady, who disappeared when we arrived, and fhe addreffed all her converfation to the Duke, to whom fhe was very obfequious.   We did not ftay long, and took luncheon at another houfe on our way back, but the Duke did not mention the name, and I did not think it neceffary to inquire.   We did not return to Chatfworth until late in the afternoon, and nothing more that is mate- rial occurred before bed-time.

Next day, the Duke was early at bufinefs with his au- ditor, and, I think, his folicitor ; but in the afternoon he led me into the kitchen-gardens, fhowed me the wall, warmed by pipes and hot water, for the production of grapes; and from thence we went to look once more at Robin Hood's Stone, and at the very ancient oaks which grow near it. Here he faid that I had made a very good tale out of fmall materials, and repeated the ftanza about Kate's fpinning.

He took a whole holiday, and drove with his four greys to Chefterfield, where we had poft-horfes to carry us to Hardwick Hall.   On the road the Duke told me of an odd adventure which he met with at the inn at Chefterfield,

which I fhall have fome difficulty in narrating with pro-
priety. It was early in the day, and he had very urgent
occafion to ftop for a few minutes : the fmall apartment to
which he wifhed to retire was on the ground-floor of the
inn, at the very end of a long wide paffage : it happened,
unluckily, that there was a wedding celebrated there
that morning : the Duke's arrival at the inn was foon
known, and when he emerged from his retirement at the
end of the long paffage, he found the bride, bridegroom,
bridesmaids, and their numerous friends, ranged on each
fide of the very path he muft take : he could not help himfelf, and, not only was he obliged to run the gauntlet of
the whole party, but a book was formally prefented to him
by a young girl, one of the bridefmaids, for his fignature
as a witnefs of the union. Of courfe, he made them a prefent; and although, while narrating the affair to me, he
laughed heartily, he faid that it was anything but a laughing matter to him at the time, for all muft have known from
whence he had come, and for what purpofe.

We took our luncheon at the fine old houfe of Hardwick Hall, whither the Duke had written the night before,
that they might prepare for us. The Duke's ftout agent there
fat very gravely and filently at the lower end of the table,
and feemed not at all at his eafe on the occafion. We
returned to Chatfworth to a late dinner.

I need not dwell longer upon this, my fecond, vifit this
year to Chatfworth, which the Duke rendered very agreeable. I returned to London with him, as before, fleeping
on the road. Thus, of the £25 fent to me by the Duke
before I ftarted, I only fpent about £5. My wife and I
debated whether I fhould filently return the remainder ;

but we decided againſt it on the ground of delicacy, and I
think we were right.   I may add, that the Duke aſked my
wife to accompany me, and he offered, if ſhe did, that we
ſhould have a ſeparate table and rooms to ourſelves ; but
as ſhe kept no lady's-maid, as one was indiſpenſable, and
as we could not extemporiſe our houſemaid into one, we
ran the riſk of declining.   Here, again, we were right.

Sept. 16.—At Dyce's chambers, I was introduced to his
firſt couſin, William Dyce, a very clever, but verſatile young
man : he is now collecting curious books, and I gave him a
ſpare copy of Biſhop Hall's "Satires", 1597.   He has alſo
a paſſion for painting, but I have yet ſeen nothing but ſome
very daſhing original water-colour drawings : if he live he
muſt gain diſtinction ; but he has only juſt begun oil-paint-
ing, and would ſhow nothing he had yet done in that
branch.   One thing he did ſhow me, and that is ſome
printed ſheets of an admirable reproduction (if he go on
with it) of the Prayer-book, as it exiſted, I apprehend, in
the reign of Edward VI, or earlier.   Every page has marginal arabeſque wood-cut borders, carved, as I underſtood,
by his own hand.   He is an excellent church muſician, and
the whole choral part of the ſervice is arranged by him ;
but it will be publiſhed by a Roman Catholic bookſeller,
and I can plainly ſee that his own tendencies are in that
direction, in ſpite of the mild remonſtrances, and not very
convincing arguments of his couſin the Rev. Alexander.
William Dyce is one of the moſt intereſting men of our
generation that I happen to have ſeen.

I have been able to reſcue the following important original letter, written by the famous Sir John Hawkins to Sir

Walter Mildmay in 1583. He was then employed to examine into and remedy great abufes and want of economy in the Navy—continued till our day.

It will be feen that at Chatham, from whence he dates, he had effected a saving of £3,231, much to the diffatisfaction of certain interefted parties. It is in fact a public document of importance in reference to the hiftory and condition of our Navy. I obferve the very spelling of the old flave-making sailor.

"Syns I wrote unto your honour I have had many occasyons to buseye my selfe, for syns Xmas was twelve monthe, that the offycers have taken corrage and hardynes to oppose them sellves against me, dyvers matters have byne omytted, delayed, and hynderyd by many subtyle practyses ; which now, with some travayle and dyllygence, I mynd, with God's favour, to put in order, and I hope wyll not requyre above xv dayes of my presence.

" I have brefflye, as my layser wold, scryblyd owt a note of the joynynge of thordynary and extraordynary together, which I send your honour to peruse; and, at your good pleasure and layser, to consyder whyther the same booke hath suffycient order to be presentyd to my lord Tresorer and my lord Admyrall : and, yf your honour shall have lykynge of yt, I wyll sett the same in order, and present yt ; for yt shall not only end all objections, make a saffe, sure, and proffytable service, but declare that there ys 3231*li.* charge yeerly sparyd of the expence in tyme past.

" The thowsand pouwnd which is to be sparyd yeerly for supplyes I do not speke of, for that yt ys another matter, which I wyll speke of hereafter.

" Some body from me shall attend upon your honour for your good pleasure to be sygnyfyed to me in this matter.   Humbly takyng my leve, from Chattham the 14 of Marche, 1583.

"Your Honours most bownden,

" JOHN HAWKYNS,

" The officers wyll hold this for a myracle at the first syght, for they wold have the sparynge of 1714*li.* gyven to the carpenters to perform thordynary, for they say all ys to lyttell.

> " To the R$_t$ yhonorable Sr Walter Myldmay, Knyght, one of her Maties privy counsell gyve these. In hast, hast, hast. For her Maties service."

Sept. 19.—It is ftrange .that it feems to have ftruck nobody, not even his laft and acute editor Gifford, that " The Tale of a Tub" muft have been one of Ben Jonfon's early plays, if not his earlieft. He mentions Queen Elizabeth in feveral places, noticing one of her predeceffors alfo, but never once fpeaking of her fucceffor: thus, in A. i, fc. 3, he makes Turf ask—

> " Does any wight present *her Majesty's person ?*"

On the next page he speaks of

> " King Edward, our late liege and sovereign lord."

Befides, the whole piece, its dialogue, and conftruction, are very much upon the model of the more ancient form of our drama : note, too, the old rhyming verfification ; thus Hannibal Puppy breaks out in Act iii, sc. 2—

> " Instead of bills with colstaves come, instead of spears with spits ;
> Your slices serve for slicing swords, to save me and my wits ;
> A lady and her woman here, their huisher by side,
> (But he stands mute) have plotted how your Puppy to divide."

Again, in the fame fcene we have a fpecimen of the fhorter ancient comic meafure, though the editors have not perceived it, and print the lines confecutively :—

> " No, lady gay,
> You shall not say
> That your Val Puppy
> Was so unlucky
> In speech to fail,
> As to name a tail,
> Be as he may be,
> Before a fair lady."

Then, the allusions are all old, and John Heywood, the dramatiſt, of the reign of Henry VIII, is mentioned by name, with the battle of St. Quintins, which happened in 1557, an old character aſſerting that he had then been a captain. Skelton and his "Elinor Running" are likewiſe ſpoken of, with "Tom Tiler" and other matters which would have been quite out of date if, as Gifford tells us, "The Tale of a Tub" had been the "laſt piece which Jon-ſon brought on the ſtage." Theſe points may serve to ſhow that the comedy was in fact written many years be-fore it was acted in 1633, and more than forty years before it was printed in the folio of 1640, poſterior to the death of the poet. I may be wrong, but the hint is worth following up by any new editor. We meet in the play with no notice of James I, nor of his son, though allu-sions to them might have been very eaſily and appropri-ately introduced. I should date the play at leaſt as early as 1595, when Ben Jonson was twenty-one years old.

I am convinced that the firſt ſcene, in which alone Antonio Balladino appears, was prefixed to Ben Jonſon's "Caſe is altered," ſoon after, but not until, Antony Munday had been called "our beſt plotter" by Francis Meres in his "Wits Treasury," 1598. This praiſe excited Ben Jonson's ire, and as his "Caſe is altered" was then about to be acted, he inſerted the firſt ſcene merely to ridicule Balladino, who, throughout has nothing more to do with the play or the characters: it was an ebullition of bile on the part of Ben Jonſon. Naſh speaks of the play when it was of eſtabliſhed reputation, but when it was, perhaps, without the introductory ſcene in ridicule of Munday. Ben Jonſon inſerted it on ſome revival of the piece, and ſo it was printed in the quarto of 1609. This is my notion of the manner and time of the introduction of the fcene. Gifford cenfures what he calls the "mountebank title" of the quarto, but the words "pleafant comedy" are the only ones used ; and it is clear that Gifford never faw that edition, for he afferts that it bears the name of Ben Jonfon—"Written by Ben Jonfon"—when it is not found on the title page. Gifford varies from the old quarto of 1609, in very many places to the omiffion of words neceffary to the fenfe, and mifprints one of the lines in act v, sc. 3, absurdly—

> "Without or touch or conscience of religion,"

which, of courfe, ought to run,

> "Without a touch of conscience or religion."

The introductory scene between Juniper, Onion, and Antonio Balladino, was no part of the original play as firft written, and acted at the Black-friars' theatre.

Sept. 20.—I bought yefterday an admirable old play for the collection at Devonfhire Houfe : I have full permiffion to give what price I like for fuch productions. It is called "The pleafant Comedy of Patient Griffill", on the famous ftory of Grifelda, which has been treated by many authors, both in profe and verfe. The main body of the piece is, of courfe, in blank verfe, but the excellent comic fcenes are in profe, and it was printed in 1603: it had three authors, of diftinction in their day, Thomas Dekker, William Haughton, and Henry Chettle, but it is impoffible to decide, with any certainty, which portion was by one and which by another. Dekker was the moft celebrated of the trio, and to him I would affign the charming opening, where the hero enters with a hunting party, all caparifoned for the chafe. I cannot help copying, in modern fpelling, the firft fpeech, which breathes the very air of frefhnefs, youth, and morning. The Marquis of Saluzzo fpeaks :

> " Look you so strange, my hearts, to see our limbs
> Thus suited in a hunter's livery ?
> O ! 'tis a lovely habit, when green youth,
> Like to the flowry blossom of the spring,
> Conforms his outward habit to his mind.
> Look how yon one-ey'd waggoner of heaven
> Hath, by his horses' fiery winged hoofs,
> Burst ope the melancholy jail of night,
> And with his gilt beam's cunning alchemy
> Turn'd all the clouds to gold ; who, with the winds,
> Upon their misty shoulders bring in day.
> Then, sully not the morning with foul looks,
> But teach your jocund spirits ply the chase,
> For hunting is a sport for emperors."

This is in the higheft fpirit of joy and jollity, and nearly the whole drama, in the feveral departments of poetry, is as good : I can hardly refrain from copying more of it. The Duke was delighted with my purchafe, though I gave £10 for it, and though he had previoufly an imperfect copy of the comedy on his fhelves, which imperfect copy he kindly gave to me : I fhall preferve it as a keepfake. Boccacio, I think, was the earlieft narrator of the ftory, having obtained it from Petrarch : our Chaucer acknowledges that he had heard Petrarch himfelf relate the incidents. I do not think them well adapted to the ftage, but the fkill and power of the old poets overcame important difficulties. Pepys, in his Diary, informs us that one of the fongs introduced into this play, " Beauty arife", was popular even down to the reign of James II. The compofer is not known.

I

Richard Jones is faid to have been the compofer of the muſic to " The Tempeſt", on its firſt produ&ion : no ſcrap of it has, I believe, come down to our day ; but I have before me a ſong by the very ſame muſician, in his own handwriting, and with very clever words : I do not ſuppoſe that he wrote the words as well as the muſic, but he put his name, " Ri. Jones", to the whole. I copy the ſtanzas as a relic of the time of Shakeſpeare : for aught we know, they may be his, but they read more like a fancy by Sir Walter Raleigh.

"The love of change hath chang'd the world throughout,
　　And naught is counted good but what is ſtrange :
New things wax olde, olde new, all turne abought,
　　And all things change, except the love of change.
Yet feel I not this love of change in mee,
But as I am, ſo will I allwaies bee.

"For who can change that likes his former choyce ?
　　Who better wiſh that knowes he hath the beſt ?
How can the heart in things unknown rejoyce,
　　Yf joy well tride can bring no certaine reſt ?
My choyce is made : change he that liſt for mee :
Such as I am, ſo will I alwaies bee."

There is no date either to words or muſic.

Sept. 26.—When I entered the long library at Devon-ſhire Houſe this morning, I found lying on the table, where I uſually ſat, a copy of Taſſo, in turning over the leaves of which I for ſome time amuſed myſelf, before I learned why it was placed there. The Duke then came into the room, and, pointing to the book, ſaid, " I am going to ſet you a taſk. A young female relative of mine has lately read with great pleaſure the " *Gerufalemme Liberata*", and, looking afterwards into the biography of Taffo, fhe faw there quoted an ode he had addreffed, while imprifoned, to Alfonfo Duke of Ferrara : the poet was then about in his thirty-fifth year ; and, as my coufin admired this ode greatly, fhe afked me to refer her to a good tranflation of it. It fo happens that I know of none ; and in my own mind I determined, when I next faw you, to put a queftion to you about it. Can you find me any Englifh verfion of it ?"

I replied that I was not well acquainted with tranflations from the Italian poets: indeed, the only verfion of the " *Gerufalemme*" that I had ever *read through* was that by Edward Fairfax, printed in 1600: that did not contain any ode ; but I added that I would inquire, and would let him know the refult to-morrow. All of a fudden the wicked thought came into my head that I would tranflate the ode myfelf, and, palming it upon the Duke as the tranflation of fomebody elfe, afk his opinion of it. In this fpirit I went home, and in the evening fet about my tafk; and I thus executed it in the meafure, and, as much as I could, in the manner, of the original.

TASSO'S SUPPLICATION TO ALPHONSO, FROM HIS PRISON,
IN 1579.

Noble, high-minded son
  Of glorious Hercules,
All thy paternal worth and deeds excelling ;
Who brought from exile one
  Who liv'd in splendid ease
Under the shadow of thy royal dwelling :
  Hear him, his sorrows telling
    From dungeon dark and deep ;
  Who turns his mind and eyes
  To thee, and as he cries

Kneels humbly ; nor can chuse but weep
  While thus his woes presenting,
With thee, and to thee, not of thee, lamenting.

  Oh ! bend on me one look.
    Behold me hopeless pine ;
Let woe and sickness now some pity waken,
  Compell'd all griefs to brook :
And I, who once was thine
Now lost to sight, of all but death forsaken !
By thousand woes o'ertaken,
  With hollow eyes and sad,
  With limbs by filth defil'd,
  Their former strength exiled,
Their vital moisture dried, in misery clad,
  While my lone anguish teaches
To envy any lot which sweet compassion reaches.

  Pity lives not for me,
    And courtesy is dead,
Unless to live with thee they be delighted.
  What troops of woes I see
    Countless around me spread ;
Ah ! how can I hope succour, thus despited ?
The cruel stars have blighted
  My hopes, nor will refuse,
    With those the earth who hold,
    In purple clad and gold,
To wage an endless war with my poor Muse :
  My prayers I have expended
On thousands ; and on thee, the most offended.

  Jove's anger, though so fierce,
    By vows is pacified,
And he lays by his bolts, to calm returning :
  So when thine arrows pierce
    My too-offending side,
With high disdain thy wrathful spirit burning,

What can I do, but turning
And bending low before thee,
  By vows in happy hour
  To sooth thine ireful power ;
And while as Jove or Phœbus I adore thee,
  Find all their virtues blossom,
And many more, within thy royal bosom.

But no : I must not dare
  With a presumptuous tongue,
In war or peace to offer thee my praises :
  My songs unworthy are
  Thy triumphs, which are rung
In arms and arts, for each thy glory raises.
  My humble zealous phrases
May haply but offend thee:
  Though I might hold them dear,
Or boast them, yet I fear,
Unhappy swan ! the thunders that attend thee,
  Though prompt to fly wherever
Thy nod commands, and faithful in endeavour.

  Go, song, without rebuke ;
And find the great unconquer'd Duke
  Between his sisters fair,
And thou wilt surely see pale pity with them there.

I placed the above in the hands of the Duke; but I
refolved not to play him the unworthy trick of pretending
that the tranflation was not my own : I only told him, as
the faƈt was, that among my books I had not been able to
find any printed verfion. He accepted what I gave him
with a thankful fmile, and carried it away with him : he
afterwards expreffed himfelf better pleafed with it than, I
own, I was. I am fure the Duke preferved it, for I faw it

afterwards on his table; and he told me that, when he had fhown it, he fhould put it among his papers.

Sept. 28.—I dined in a company confisting of "Pleafures of Hope," "Pleafures of Memory," "The Story of Rimini," "The Mermaid," "Rejected Addreffes," the author of "Wood-whittington," and fome more not yet diftinguifhed by the production of any work: in other words, T. Campbell, S. Rogers, Leigh Hunt, Hamilton Reynolds, James Smith, Theodore Hooke, Harnefs, Kenyon, Robinfon, and Talfourd. I had been in the fociety of Rogers two or three times before, but I had never been formally introduced to him: on this occafion, the mafter of the houfe, feeing I ftood apart from Rogers but near him, goodnaturedly said, "Mr. Rogers, you know Mr. Collier: Mr. Collier, of courfe, knows you, efpecially as I hear that you were an old friend to his father." Rogers made a fort of half bow, and afked, in his ufual fmall voice, "What name did you fay?" "Collier," replied our hoft; on which Rogers bowed again, and faid, "Yes, I recollect the name": then, addreffing himfelf to me, he coldly inquired, "Is your father alive?" I replied that he had been dead fome years, but that I had often heard him mention the name of Rogers. "Aye, aye," he added, "it is a long time ago: we knew each other when we were young; but I entirely loft fight of him for many years. He is dead, is he? And you are his fon"; and then he turned his back to fpeak to fomebody elfe. As our hoft fancied that I had made an acquaintance with an old friend of my father, he placed us together at table, but I obferved, or fancied, that Rogers was ftudioufly filent towards me; and under that im-

preffion I did not much exert myfelf to fecure his attention. Other people were difpofed to treat him deferentially,
and that seemed to gratify him, but I purpofely difregarded
him ; and it was not until after he was gone, about ten
o'clock, that the converfation became lively and interefting.
I took very little fhare in it, for I was in bad humour at
finding Rogers fo indifferent, not fo much to myfelf as to
my father, with whom I knew he had formerly been fo intimate, and for whom he had at one time *profeffed* fuch
warm friendfhip: witnefs the fubfequent note to him, which
I found among my father's old letters.

" 17 Feb., 1789.

" My dear Friend,—Your birthday; and I write to congratulate you.
You are enjoying all the blessings of matrimony, while I am, and am
likely to continue, an unhappy solitary : my main resource will be
your and your dear wife's friendship, which I hope long to partake, in
spite of my favourite Goldsmith's denunciation,

> "' For what is friendship but a name,
>   A charm that lulls to sleep ;
>   A shade which follows wealth or fame,
>   But leaves the wretch to weep.'

" As I have neither 'wealth' nor 'fame', I must be a 'wretch' who is
'left to weep'; and if I am 'lulled to sleep' it is, under my circumstances, the best I can anticipate. You are prosperous and happy,
with another 'little pledge', as you married folks call them, and the
picture is not likely to be reversed ; but without looking into the dusk,
or rather dark, of futurity, I shall always remain, my dear friend,

" Yours most assuredly,

"SAM. ROGERS."

The fact is that, after my father's misfortunes in 1793-4,
Rogers never took the slighteft notice of him ; and, in 1810,
as William Maltby (my father's coufin) told him, declined an

invitation to dinner, becaufe he heard that his "dear friend" of 1789 was to be one of the company.

Sept. 30.—My "Parliamentary experience", or, rather, experience of Parliament, is of fo early a date that I can recollect Addington, both as Speaker of the Houfe of Commons, and as Prime Minifter, after the refignation of Pitt. He was then a comparatively young man, with a fonorous voice. It was during Addington's adminis-tion; and Pitt did not take his place on the Oppofition benches, with Fox, Ponfonby, and Tierney, but below what was then called "the gangway" on the minifterial fide of the Houfe. I heard him fpeak only twice, and both times briefly; but I well remember the upright fteadinefs of his deportment, and the firmnefs of his voice and delivery: his tone was, I thought, rather dictatorial, as if he were condefcending to talk to inferiors. This muft have been previous to the vote of thanks to him in May 1802.

The earlieft fet fpeech I heard from Fox was, I think, on the French war with Pruffia: his ftyle was not fatisfactory to my ear, as he hefitated much, and feemed to be at a lofs fometimes for words: his voice, too, was not good—rather fcreeching when animated, and as if obftructed by the fat in his throat: I did not hear him in reply, which was faid to be his *forte.* Ponfonby was very unattractive, but argumentative: Tierney always delighted me, he was fo pungent in his expreffions, and fo clofe in his reafoning. Windham was clever, acute, and flowing, and I never fhall forget the roar of laughter when, fome years afterwards (1810), he likened the notion of a *coup de main* in the Scheldt to a *coup de main* in the Court of Chancery. This admirable fpeech never appeared in the newfpapers, in confequence of an affront Windham was fuppofed to have put upon the reporters : this was in March, and he died in April. Amyot could not obtain the fpeech.

The earlieft great harangue I remember by Brougham was in the fummer of the fame year (1810), on the Slave Trade, but I afterwards liftened to his famous feven-hours' oration on the Orders in Council : he fixed the attention of the Houfe during the whole time !

In connection with the proceedings of Parliament, I may mention that I was prefent when Bellingham fhot Mr. Perceval in the lobby of the Houfe of Commons in 1812 : I was not actually in the lobby, but juft above it, where there was a wide opening into the lobby below, and up this opening the fmoke of the piftol afcended : looking down, I beheld the dying man carried into the Speaker's refidence. I afterwards faw the affaffin tried and convicted at the Old Bailey. I could not fee a man hanged.

I have been prefent at many ftrange trials in my time, beginning with that of Governor Wall, in 1802, for flogging a foldier to death : next, at the trial of Peltier for a libel on Buonaparte, I heard Sir James Mackintofh for the defence : thirdly, I was prefent at nearly the whole of the proceeding on the impeachment of Lord Melville in 1805. This was followed in 1806 by the conviction of Patch for the murder of Mr. Blight, when I fat, with my father, exactly in front of the dock, and when the murderer's hand, to my young horror, touched my fhoulder.

The trial of General Picton, for torturing Louisa Calderon, occurred in the fame year, when my father gave evidence as to the Spanifh law on the fubject. Perry was

K

acquitted of a libel in 1810, in my hearing. Dr. Watfon and Thiftlewood were tried in 1817, and I fat it out nearly the whole of feveral days—I forget how many. I liftened, in the ftudents' box at Guildhall, to Hone's three trials for blafphemy in 1818. The Cato-ftreet confpirators followed in 1820; and the king-perfecuted Queen's trial in the Houfe of Lords in the fame year.

I miffed the trial of Thurtell and others for murder in 1824, becaufe it took place at Hertford; but it fo happened that I knew Weare, the victim, well, having played hundreds of games of billiards with him: he was a regular black-leg, and was content to do bufinefs in a fmall way, if he could get no larger prey: fo, as he was a good player when he liked, he ufed to earn a few fhillings from me, who never rifked more. I was devoted to the game, and, I am forry to confefs, fpent all my fpare money and time upon it. Another of my billiard-mafters, of the name of Bailey, was foon afterwards hanged for forgery: he was a moft gentlemanlike gambler, and dreffed to perfection: his tailor hanged him; and I might have hanged my tailor, who, in 1817, forged my handwriting to a bill of exchange —the only one on which my name, I am glad to fay, was ever feen. All this happened fome years before I was called to the bar. Owing to my many other and discordant avocations, and to an inimical feeling produced by one of my early publications, I did not affume the gown and wig till too late to give me any reafonable chance of fuccefs: Scarlet was always my enemy, though I had publicly lauded him even beyond his deferts:

> " To praife a man above his merits,
> No thankfulness, but hate inherits."

Oct. 1.—The Duke of Devonſhire gave me his portrait, drawn on ſtone by Wilkin—a good, though not a flattering, likeneſs—which I ſaw in progreſs in the hands of the artiſt while the Duke was ſitting for it. I do not think that it is yet publiſhed, if it be to be publiſhed at all. It is more manly than Landſeer's kit-cat in the Exhibition.

Through me, the Duke gave permiſſion to Jerdan for the engraving of the portrait of Lord Mulgrave, (my joint ſponſor at the Garrick), which is going to Chatſworth.

At Devonſhire Houſe, I ſaw, by deſire of the Duke, Mr. Dudley Coſtello, an ingenious young officer, who, being on half-pay and in Paris, copied, very nicely, ſome of the illuminations of MSS. in the *Bibliothèque du Roi.* He alſo made ſome fac-ſimiles of the writing of the works to which the illuminations belong. He wanted the Duke to buy his drawings, etc., but it was not thought worth while : they ſeemed to be in no ſeries, ſo as to illuſtrate the ſubject periodically, or ſyſtematically.

Oct. 4.—I learn, on the beſt authority, that Moore received, in the whole, £4,890 for his Life of Lord Byron ! Moore, though a charming verſifier, is too much of a toady and a tuft-hunter : the Life ſhews it.

Leigh Hunt tells me that his new poem, " The Battle of the Shift", is to be inſerted in the volume of his collected poems : it is in two cantos, and is founded upon the French *fabliau* of " The Three Knights and the Smock", in vol. ii of Way's Tranſlations. It was offered to the *Metropolitan Magazine,* but declined, as they objected to the title, and Hunt, rightly, would not alter it, to pleaſe the hyperſqueamiſhneſs of an editor.

EPIGRAM, BY C. LAMB, ON THE FAST DAY.

" To name a day for general prayer and fast
Is surely worse than of no sort of use ;
For you may see with grief, from first to last,
On *fast*-days people of all ranks are *loose*."

Oct. 5.—I bought this day, and for more money than I can well fpare, but ftill a bargain, one of the greateft literary curiofities I have ever had the good fortune to meet with: it is a poem by one of Shakefpeare's great contemporaries —I may almoft fay rivals—which till now has never been heard of. The fubject is (like " Venus and Adonis") mythological, viz., " Endymion and Phœbe"; and feems to have been written in couplets, in emulation of Marlowe's " Hero and Leander"; which, though not publifhed until 1598, was very well known in MS. before 1593, and was in all probability feen by Shakefpeare : it is, however, generally fuppofed that his " Venus and Adonis" was compofed before he quitted Stratford-on-Avon about 1586 or 1587. " Endymion and Phœbe," the title of the hitherto unknown poem I bought, is by no lefs a man than Michael Drayton, the author of " The Barons' Wars", and of " England's Heroical Epiftles", to fay nothing of his great and longer work, in fourteen-syllable lines, " Polyolbion." As " Endymion and Phœbe" is dated on the title-page 1594, it is older than any other production by the fame author, excepting his " Harmony of the Church", and his " Shepherd's Garland", which came out refpectively in 1591 and 1593. It is unqueftionably the greateft literary curiofity I poffefs, and it is befides of incalculable value as a relic by a poet only fecond in reputation to Shakefpeare. Yet what would not I, or any man, give for a fimilar *new and original compofition* by our

great dramatiſt? Why ſhould it be more unlikely to discover ſuch a work by the one, than by the other? I have not
yet made known my find, and I ſhall not do ſo until a fitting
opportunity. Meanwhile, for the ſake of recognition if any
other copy ſhould turn up, I give here the firſt and the laſt
lines of the produ&ion. It begins:

> " In *I-onia*, whence sprang old poets fame;"

a not very harmonious local line; and it ends

> " To whom all pens shall yearely sacrifice."

It fills in the whole twenty-five leaves, and it conſiſts
of about twelve hundred lines in ten-ſyllable meaſure.
Near the cloſe is a ſpecial addreſs to Spenſer, Daniel, and
Lodge, but without the ſlighteſt mention of or alluſion to
Shakeſpeare, whoſe earlieſt poem had appeared in the preceding year. I value it more as a great poem than as a
great rarity—it is both, and it is mine!

O&ober 14.—I have been ſuffering for the laſt week under
one of my ſevere quinzies, and have therefore kept my bed:
ſtill I could not " keep my pen from walking"; and as, juſt
before my illneſs, I had been reading with great pleaſure
Machiavelli's " *Aſino d'Oro*", I thought I would put one of
the beſt parts of it into Engliſh verſe of the ſame meaſure
and form, the *terza rima*, made famous by Dante. I dare-
ſay that I have tranſlated ſome thouſand lines of it, and I
have pleaſed myſelf ſo well that I tranſcribe the ſubſequent ſpecimen from the cloſe of the ſpeech of the Hog,
who had once been a man, but transformed by magic into a
beaſt: he refuſed to be reſtored again to human ſhape, and
human inferiority. Allowance muſt be made for the difficulty of the taſk of imitating the Italian meaſure.

At this conclusion I with ease arrive,
That man, who boasts so vainly, is indeed
More wretched far than any brute alive.
Kind Nature 's our best friend : the lives we lead
Shew that in us her virtues are display'd :
Where we have plenty, you would die for need.
In proof I call the senses to my aid,
And, though the contrary you may suppose,
Even you I can in a few words persuade.
The eagle's eye, the dog's fine ear and nose,
The taste of all is far more delicate ;
And if the touch we grant you out of those,
It was not given in honour to your state,
But merely to augment your amorous lust,
Whence spring 'mongst men such discord and debate.
We are born cloth'd, and to that clothing trust
To guard us from the cold, and it is worn
In every climate : Man alone is thrust
Defenceless into life, and naked born
Without a fleece to keep him warm or dry,
Bristles nor scales, but helpless and forlorn.
His life commences with a puling cry :
His every tone bespeaks his wants and woes,
A pitiable sight to every eye.
Nor is his lot much better as he grows,
And not to be compar'd, when old or young,
With any beast upon the earth that goes.
Nature, indeed, gives him both hand and tongue,
Ambition, too, and scraping avarice,
To balance the account ; and hence have sprung
Full many a sad infirmity and vice,
By Fortune foster'd for her votaries, when
She promises, though only to entice.
The pride, ambition, luxury, of men,
Have brought in leprosy, its war to wage
Against that life so prais'd by speech and pen :
There is no animal, I dare engage,

With frailer being, more desire of life,
More full of fear, or more unbridled rage.
If among beasts you sometimes hear of strife,
Men, only men, their fellow creatures burn,
Or crucify, or slay with sword or knife.
Think'st thou to human shape I would return,
While I am free from all the miseries which
I suffered while a man ? Thine aid I spurn.
If thou hereafter see a man that's high,
And who seems happy, know his joy is hollow,
For I am far more happy in this sty,
Where, free from thought and care, I lie and wallow.

Shewing the above afterwards to the Duke, he afked me
if I had-feen Macaulay's article upon Machiavelli, and upon
the chara&ter of his writings, in the *Edinburgh Review*, two
or three years ago ? I replied that I had ; and that I was
furprifed the critic faid fo little that was really informing,
and not a syllable upon Machiavelli's poetry. " His obje&t
(continued the Duke) was different ; what he wanted was to
vindicate Machiavelli from the imputations univerfally caft
upon his profe work, ' The Prince.' " " That (I observed) he
has done pretty succefsfully ; but furely he might have faid
fomething about his '*Afino d'Oro*', more especially as the
nature and purpofe of it falls in with, and fupports Macaulay's views, fince there is no word there that favours the
duplicity and cruelty he recommended to his patron." "As
to the magical transformation of men into beafts, and
their preference of the latter condition (the Duke fubjoined)
he took very much the line of argument adopted by the
clever Italian tailor, Baptifta Gelli, in his ' Circe', which,
however, came out, I believe, many years after Machiavelli
wrote : Lucian and Apuleius, of course, preceded both."

"Spenfer (I added) refers to it at the very conclufion of the fecond book of his 'Fairy Queen', where the Palmer exclaims, 'Let Grill be Grill, and have his hoggish mind.'"
"As to Spenfer (refumed the Duke) in your 'Hiftory of our Drama', I am forry to fay you clearly prove the fad imputation upon Lord Burghley, that he effectually oppofed himfelf to the Queen's intended bounty to the great poet." "Perhaps (said I) there never exifted a man with fo little of the poetical and imaginative in his compofition as Elizabeth's Lord Treafurer : he was the very oppofite, and the ftrongeft contraft to his ward, the impulfive Effex." "Remember in fairnefs (the Duke concluded), that he was an old man and Effex a young one, and that the old man was dead a year or two before the young man was executed. If Burghley had lived, Effex would never have rebelled, and never would have been beheaded."

Oct. 17.—The following unprinted proclamation refers to one of the moft melancholy events in Englifh hiftory juft above alluded to. I copy it from the original MS. We can eafily underftand why it was not publifhed.

"BY THE QUEENE.

"Wheras the Earle of Essex, accompanied with the Earles of Rutland and Southampton, and divers other their complices, gentlemen of birth and qualitie, knowinge them selves to be discovered in divers treasonable actions, into which they have heretofore entred, as well in our realme of Irelande, where some of them had laid plots with the traitoure Tirone, as in this our realme of England, did upon Sundaye, beinge the eight of this moneth, in the morninge, not onely imprison our Keeper of our Great Seale of England, our Chiefe Justice of Englande, and others, both of our nobilitie and counsell, that were sent in our name to his house to perswade the saide Earle to lay open any his petitions or complaintes, with promise (iff he woulde desperse his disordered company in his house) that all his just requests should be hard and gratiously considered ; but also did (after strait order given by him to murder our said counsellers and others, whensoever they should offer to stirre out of that place) traiterously issue into the City of London in armes, with great numbers, and theare breaking out into open action of rebellion, devised and divulged base and foolish lies, that their lives were sought ; spreading out divers strange and seditious inventions to have drawen the people to their party, with purpose to attempt traitourous actions, both against our person and state, and so to expose (as it nowe appeareth) our cytie and people, with their goods, to the spoyle of a number of needy and desperate persons, their adherents, continuing still in armes, and killing divers of our subjectes after many proclamations of rebellion made by our kinge of heralds.

For asmuch as notwithstandinge (God be thanked) they have found them selves deceived of their expectation (beinge nowe all apprehended and within our towre of London, as well the three principall traitours, Earles of Essex, Rutland, and Southampton, as divers others of the principall gentlemen, theire confederates) our good subjectes of our cytie, and elsewhere, having shewed them selves so constant and unmoveable from theire duties towards us, as not any one of them of any note (that we can yet heare of) did offer to assist the said carle and his associates, we have bene contented, in regard of the comfort that we take to find by so notorious evidence the loyall disposition of our people (wherof we never doubted) not onely to make knowen to all our saide subjectes of our cytie, and else where, in how thankefull parte we doe accept both their loyall persisting in their dutie, and stay from following the false perswasions of the traitours, but to promisse on our parte, that whensoever we shall have cause to shewe it they shall finde us more carefull over them then for our selves. And hereby also, in regarde of our gratious meaning towardes our good people, to admonish them that, seeing this open acte was so sudden, as it cannot yet be throughly looked into, howe farre it stretched, and how many hartes it hath corrupted, but that it is to be presumed, by the comon example of the maner of proceeding of all rebells in like actions, that it was not without instrumentes and ministers, dispersed in divers places to provoke the mindes of our people to like of theire

L.

attemptes, with calumniating our government and our principall servants and ministers thereof, That they shall doe well (and so we
charge them) to give dilligent heede in all places to the conversation
of persons not well knowen for their good behaviour, and to the
speeches of any that shall give out slanderous and undutifull wordes
or rumours against us and our government. And they that be in
authority to laye holde on such spreaders of rumours ; and such as
be not in authoritie to advertise those thereof that have authoritie, to the
ende that, by the apprehension of such dangerous instrumentes, both
the drifts and purpose of evill minded persons may be discovered,
theire designes prevented and our people conserved, in such peace and
tranquillitie as heretofore, by God's favour, we have maintained, and
doe hope still to continewe, amongst them. Given at our Palace of
Westminster, the ninth of Februarie, 1600, in the three and fortieth
yeere of our raigne.

" God save the Queene."

October 20.—I have lately renewed my search in the parish
registers of St. Giles', Cripplegate, and have met with some
curious early notices of Richard Hathaway, or Hathway (the dramatist, contemporary with Shakespeare), who
seems to have had a daughter named, as if after Shakespeare's wife, Anne, who on July 28, 1605, was married to
John Harris—"John Harris to Anne Hathaway." In one
entry Richard Hathaway is designated, most unusually, as
"poett": this was when his son Edmund was christened on
21 March, 1601 ; but at a considerably earlier date, 1586,
he is called in terms, "Master of Arts", and then his
daughter Dionica was baptised. Afterwards, on 22 November, 1589, another daughter, called Margaret, was christened,
and in the entry we are told that Richard Hathaway was at
that time a "schoolmaster". The probability is that he
occupied his vacant time by dramatic composition, and the
result was five dramas; but as none of them was printed,

we may doubt how far they were popular, and we know of no manuscript copies of them. It has not been at all ascertained whether he was in any way related to Shakespeare's wife, but the fact that he had a daughter, *Anne* Hathaway, seems to make it not improbable ; and her marriage with John Harris may have produced the John Harris, who after the Restoration was so famous as Wolsey. The point deserves farther investigation, but I do not know to what source to resort : we have no evidence ; but this Richard Hathway, poet at one time, and schoolmaster at another, may himself have come from Stratford, and may, by possibility, have been the brother of Shakespeare's wife. The example of Shakespeare may have made him a " poet", but there is nothing, that I am aware of, to show that he was at any time an actor.

What fine lines and sentences we sometimes meet with in unlikely places of our old drama ! I have before me an anonymous play, printed in 1620, called " Swetnam, the Woman-hater accused by Women", in which this noble couplet occurs, with reference to the punishment of an offender :

> " Justice, like lightning, ever should appear
> To few men's ruin, but to all men's fear."

This, I presume to say, is superior to the vaunted and often quoted couplet by Webster,

> " Glories, like glow-worms, shine afar off bright,
> But, look'd to near, have neither heat nor light."

It is not true that glow-worms give no light when they are closely examined : on the contrary, I have seen several shining at once in my hand as I looked at them. Taking

up an old play, even one of the worft, is fomewhat like
diamond-digging : one jewel is difcovered in a large quantity of rubbifh, but when found it is worth all the trouble
of fearching, wafhing, and fifting.

Oct. 24.—Brougham coming, not long fince, from abroad,
told a man whom I knew that he wifhed to fee me, and
when I called upon him in a ftreet near Eaton-fquare, he
feized me by the hand, and kiffed me on both cheeks. I
was in hopes he wifhed to do fomething important for me,
but, when I wrote, he referred me to his fecretary. This
reminds me of what Simeoni tells us of Leo X and Ariofto :
the Pope "preffed the poet's hand and *kiffed him on both
cheeks*," but did nothing for him but grant him a patent
for the fale of the *Orlando Furiofo*. This does not quite
tally with what the fame author fays elfewhere, that his
holinefs contributed *piu centinaja fcudi per fornire il fuo
libro.* When Brougham was in office he was peftered
for places, and I might then, *poffibly*, have fucceeded ; but
I did not take either the right way or the right time :
to mutual friends he always expreffed the beft opinion
of me. As I was quiet, he let me remain fo.

I think I rendered the following from a quotation in
Burton's "Anatomy of Melancholy", but I cannot now light
upon the place : it might properly have gone with the other
light fancies about " The Creation of Man" (p. 52, pt. I)
and " Matrimony".

> " If we of Plato's dogma may be sure,
>   There are two Venuses, and Cupids also :
> These are immortal, unbegotten, pure,
>   Ruling the pious, or what people call so ;
> Not naughty livers, like to me or you.

The other Venus doth the world subdue,
And with her Cupid leads men all astray,
To her own wanton, wasteful, wicked way."

Oct. 27.—Henry Crabb Robinfon is the fon of a tanner at Bury St. Edmonds, and was at firft educated at the grammar fchool there, but lived with his aunt at Bungay after his father's fecond marriage. He was two or three years younger than my mother, and, when he refided with us, they ufed to joke each other as to confequent fuperiority or difadvantages. He was articled to an attorney at Witham, and Amyot was a clerk in the fame office. Robinfon entered a folicitor's office in London about the year 1793, and was very fond of frequenting forums, Coachmakers' Hall, and other debating places and focieties, whither my father and mother alfo frequently went : my father was a popular fpeaker there, and they often admired Robinfon for the excellence of his harangues. This led to an acquaintance that foon ripened into intimacy ; but on the death of his father, when Robinfon came into fome property, he refolved to go to Germany, and fixed his abode at the Univerfity of Jena, where he formed a warm and lafting friendfhip with Goethe, Richter, and other poets and authors. Here he made himfelf a mafter of German, and ufed to fend over to my father, who was then editor of a magazine (the *Monthly Regifter*), various fpecimens of tranflation, moft of them in the claffical meafures of the originals. He returned to England in the year 1805 or 1806, and took up his refidence as one of our family, where he continued feven or eight years. His claffical education not having been attended to, he felt the want of it in fociety; and, as I was at that period hard at Greek and Latin, he joined me in my leſſons : we eſpecially laboured at, and competed in a work on Greek roots. Even thus early I had a taſte for poetical compoſition ; and he and I had a *fliting*, as the Scotch call it, on a not very delicate ſubject, in which, I muſt own, H. C. R., who was ten or or a dozen years my ſenior, had the beſt of it : I beat him, however, in trans-lations, eſpecially from Horace, and he took copies of ſeveral of my eſſays, whether original or tranſlated : he eſpecially liked my verſion of " *Quis multa gracilis te puer in roſa,*" etc., which he ſhewed me some years afterwards, when I had forgotten it. When Robinſon began ſeriouſly to ſtudy for the bar, he quitted my father's houſe, and be-came a pupil to Littledale (afterwards a judge). He was called to the bar, I think, about the year 1819 or 1820, and went the Norfolk Circuit, with very little ſucceſs at the out-ſet ; but he ſoon became rather a favourite, and was eſpe-cially proud of a verdict of acquittal for ſome, as he knew, guilty ſheep-ſtealers. While ſtill reſiding with us he trans-lated "Amatonda", and ſome tracts on phrenology from the German. He is now purſuing a ſucceſsful career as a barriſter, and is much liked on and off the circuit. He has always been moſt kind and affectionate to me and to all my family, and promoted my vain call to the Bar in 1829 : I never could *ſtudy* the law.

Oct. 28.—I do not recollect to have ſeen the following any-where reprinted : it firſt appeared in Thomás Jordan's "Jewels of Ingenuity", publiſhed without date ; but the event occurred at the ſiege of Cheſter, in 1645, when Wil-liam Lawes was ſhot, it is ſaid accidentally, fighting, of courſe, on the king's ſide : it is headed

"An Epitaph on Mr. Will. Lawes, Bachelor in Musick,
who was mortally shot at the Siege of
Westchester.

> "Concord is conquerd ! In this urne there lies
> The master of great Musick's mysteries ;
> And in it is a riddle like the cause :
> Will. Lawes was slain by such when Wills were Laws."

He was not of the eminence, nor merit, of his brother
Henry, the compofer of " Comus".

Oct. 29.—Through his brother-in-law, Mr. Charles Greville, I have obtained an introduction to Lord Francis
L. Gower, fecond fon to the Marquis of Stafford : his
deportment is moft courteous, kindly, and confidential :
as a body, I muft do the Tories the juftice to fay that their
manners are far more agreeable than thofe of the Whigs,
always excepting my exalted friend (for fo he calls himfelf, and allows me to confider him), the Duke of Devonfhire. The Whigs, efpecially the underlings of the party,
are fo curfedly condefcending, juft as if they were doing you
a great favour by taking notice of you at all : the Tories
confer a favour with the grace of receiving one, and fuch
is exactly the cafe with Lord Francis L. Gower, who, after
a comparatively fhort acquaintance, has given me his keys,
and has put all his valuable, I may fay invaluable, books
and manufcripts at my difpofal : he has made no referves,
even as to family papers ; and I am at liberty to felect
and to print any that feem to me of hiftorical or biogra-
phical importance. He knows of my connection with the
Duke of Devonfhire, and of the nature of my other employments, fo that I have no difficulty in going to his houfe

at any period of the day, to continue my refearches. I have, of my own, a very interefting MS. of the Effays of Lord Bacon, who was, as it were, patronifed by the firft Baron Ellefmere ; and in the outfet I have directed my inquiries to Lord Bacon's hiftory. Almoft the earlieft document I found related to him perfonally, and to the accufations brought againft him : it has no date, but clearly belongs to the year 1621, when he was under trial. The moft important part of it is in the handwriting of John Earl of Bridgewater, who was fo created in 1617, and who died in 1649. It is entitled, " Corruptions charged upon the Lo. Chancellor"; and it contains a fpecification of all the accufations againft him, preceded by the following, in the handwriting of Lord Bridgewater, as taken down, pof-fibly, from the mouth of Lord Bacon, then under charge before the Houfe of Lords :

" My Lo. Chancellor will make no manner of defence to the charge.

" But meaneth to acknowledge corruption, and to make a particular confeffion to every point, and, after that, an humble fubmiffion.

" But humbly craves liberty that, where the charge is more full than he findes the truthe of the fact, he may make declaration of the truthe in such particulars, the charge being briefe, and contayning not all circumftances."

This is fucceeded by twenty-feven feparate accufations of corruption in the execution of his office, with the fums of money, or prefents, he received. They begin with £500 from Sir Rowland Egerton, in a caufe between him and Edw. Egerton ; and in the margin is written, " Guilty : no defence"; and it is followed by the imputation that Lord Bacon had alfo been paid £400 by the other fide, to which this note is appended : " When he firft received the Seale : for

favours paft and not for favours to come." It is needlefs
to go into all the charges, but Bacon admits that in the
caufe of Kennedy and Vanlore, he accepted a cabinet faid
to be worth eight hundred pounds, but which the Lord
Chancellor afferted was over-valued, while he admitted that
he had been paid a thoufand pounds by the oppofite fide.
Pendente lite, he had five hundred pounds from Sir Ralph
Hausby, and in another cafe two hundred pounds, and a
diamond ring valued (overvalued, faid Bacon) at fix hundred pounds ; but in thefe, and in feveral other cafes, it was
after the decree had been pronounced in favour of the party.
I only felect thefe as fpecimens, and in the end Lord Bacon
adds that " he confeffeth it was a great fault that he looked
no better to his fervants," who received large gratuities,
which never reached his hands.

I hope to obtain from this fource much important information, but I have yet had time only to inspect a very
few of thefe original hiftorical documents.

Nov. 1.—The Duke has recently fpoken much of a
new projeft, on which he is difpofed to fpend a large fum
of money—the ereftion of a fpacious glafs Confervatory.
While indulging this fancy, he has appeared to me to ne-
gleft the purpofe he formerly entertained of completing his
noble colleftion of Englifh Plays of all dates. In order to
make him acquainted with my fears on the fubjeft, and if
poffible, to recal his attention to his earlier purfuit, I ventured to write, and to forward to him, the following poem, in
which he is reprefented as dreaming both of his new Confervatory and of his Old Plays. He received it moft kindly,

M

not taking it as a reproof, but merely as a playful exercise of invention on my part. I entitled it

THE DUKE'S DREAM.

Fatigued with ducal duties of the day,
   Numberless, noisome, nameless, and some needless,
I threw me on a couch to read a play
   Within my library— of all else heedless.

While thus with my old dramas rang'd around,
   A gently soothing drowsiness came o'er me ;
And, while I lay asleep, methought I found
   Our ancient English dramatists before me.

Shakespeare I saw, with ample forehead high,
   And look all careless of his future glory ;
Ben Jonson, with rough face and piercing eye,
   And Chapman (Homer's bard) serene and hoary.

Old Kyd still bore in age a youthful look,
   While Lily mov'd about with pace affected ;
Greene, who had written many a pleasant book,
   Then too much priz'd, and now too much neglected.

Marlowe, precursor of fair Avon's bard,
   The first who scorn'd the use of rhyming jingle ;
Peele, who with poverty long struggled hard ;
   Bold Marston, keeping far aloof and single.

Webster the nervous, Nash severe and free,
   The vigorous Drayton, Heywood the prolific,
The ready Dekker, Fletcher full of glee,
   Rare Massinger, and Shirley the pacific.

All these, and others more, I saw the while,
   And each had of their chiefest works a number,
Of which upon the floor they made a pile,
   Heaping them up like so much worthless lumber.

Each then, methought, took from a fire a brand,
  And made a blaze of all the heap together,
While they went round it, joining hand in hand,
  Watching the flaming paper, scorching leather.

And, by degrees, as the old books consum'd,
  I dream'd the figures of the authors faded,
Till all their plays were in black ash entomb'd,
  And I, entranc'd, could not prevent what *they* did.

Oh, grief! my " Hamlet", sixteen hundred three ;
  My " Old Wives' Tale", my " Of a Shrew the Taming";
" Queen Dido" burnt once more on pile I see ;
  And hundreds more, for very woe past naming.

And far aloof I mark'd a hapless wight
  In agony of sorrow, grizzle headed,
Who turn'd him weeping from the woful sight :
  To poetry and plays he had been wedded.

I stirr'd not when all left me in the lurch,
  But kept mine eyes still fix'd upon the ashes :
" Parson and clerk were quickly out of church";
  Behold ! I cried, where all my ill-spent cash is !

And now I heard a distant strain and high,
  Full of deep grief, while voices voices follow :
It seem'd the Muses' nine-fold elegy,
  While his sad lyre was stricken by Apollo.

But still mine eyes were on the ashes fix'd,
  And, as I watch'd them, they appear'd in motion :
With lively green I saw their blackness mix'd,
  But what had caus'd the change I had no notion,

Until I saw some leaves and buds arise,
  Then, tapering stems adorn'd with varied flowers ;
Some grew up into trees of goodly size,
  With spreading arms, and building leafy bowers.

All my whole library was sudden chang'd
 Into a mighty Stove to raise exotics :
From plays and poets now I seem'd estrang'd ;
 Or I look'd on them merely as narcotics.

The trees, shrubs, plants, increas'd on every side :
 I could imagine nothing more delightful ;
Bread-fruit and Norfolk Island pines I spied,
 And pitcher-plants that made the building quite full.

Instead of poets, whom I late had seen
 Burning their plays, once priz'd by me so dearly,
A troop of gardeners, in coats of green,
 And Paxton at their head : I saw them clearly.

I saw them rake the ashes, black and dun,
 And into wheel-barrows they careless threw them :
They serv'd but as manure, and better none,
 For their exotics ; they from ashes grew them.

While I was joying in the sight and smell,
 Gazing on all with pleasure and blank wonder,
Methought a storm of hail on sudden fell,
 And with it forked lightning and loud thunder.

It struck remorseless through the roof of glass,
 And every pane and every plant it shatter'd,
Save Bay and Laurel, which all trees surpass,
 And are by lightning ever vainly batter'd.

Then, all at once, a heavenly splendour broke,
 And clear'd away whate'er the storm demolish'd ;
And instantly, as if an angel spoke,
 A grove of Laurel rose, all brightly polish'd.

No leaf but bore some goodly poet's name
 In golden characters, once fondly cherish'd,
Whose works, methought, amid th' unrighteous flame
 Had sunk erewhile, and all their glory perish'd.

I woke astounded : in mine ears there rung
 The sweetest sounds of joy, can nought come near them ;
Apollo and the Lady Muses sung ;
 No wonder if long time I seem'd to hear them.

Mine ears were quicken'd by th' immortal sound,
 And mine eyes dwelt upon each heavenly feature,
While flowers celestial starting from the ground,
 I read the very poetry of nature.

Soon I beheld the Muses, with the Graces,
 Busily moving 'mong the trees and bowers,
Restoring the dear volumes to their places,
 Uniting heavenly poetry and flowers.

And be it ever so ! I cried ; for Heaven
 Itself decrees that they shall be united :
And never be the barbarous hand forgiven
 By which or books are burnt, or flowers are blighted.

At this time the Duke had accidentally hurt his knee, which confined him to his bed-room and to the houfe. His medical advifers apprehended a white-fwelling, and the Duke thought it poffible he might lofe his leg. I had fent him the preceding ftanzas before I knew of the accident, and I did not fee him for fome time afterwards. When I was again admitted, it was to his dreffing-room, and he was comparatively well. The firft thing he djd, after welcoming me, was to thank me for my poem ; and to fhew how much he liked it, and how kindly he took the hint it conveyed, he recited to me all the ftanzas defcriptive of the old dramatifts, faying he liked that part beft, and the introductory quatrain leaft ; for he knew of no " ducal *duties*" that were not agreeable, efpecially thofe in which I was at all interefted. He faid, too, as if in his own vindication, that flowers, whether home-grown or exotic, were but another form of poetry ; and that, in this fenfe, he meant his new Confervatory to be an affemblage of the floral poetry of all the world. To this I could of courfe object nothing ; and he added that his zeal for our early drama, I fhould find, was undiminifhed, and that the more plays I bought for him, to complete his feries, the better he fhould be pleafed. In the meantime I had been unwell, and I was, on this account, glad that he had not needed my fmall fervices. I only wifh that they were greater, and that I might be more clofely and permanently connected with fuch a truly noble man.

Nov. 15.—I cannot afcertain the date of the following note from the famous Sir Charles Sedley to an unknown peer; but we may prefume that when he wrote it he was somewhat fteadier (the writing too indicates it) than when he was wild enough to expofe his perfon *in puris naturalibus* in the balcony of a tavern in Bow Street, Covent Garden— the Bond Street of that day. It is from a rare autograph :

"My Lord,—I am sorry to give you the least trouble ; but my brother, Sᵣ William Sedley, having made the Lord Hallyfax a trustee for a lease of 98 yeares, which my lord afterwards did conveigh to Mr. Savage and others, it hapens that some small parcell of land was left out, and by reason of your lordships being executor to my lord [your] father, remains now in your sett. My request is, that you would bee pleased, according to advice of your own councill, to convey it to me, or such others as I shall name : the gentleman I send with this will inform your lordship more in the particulars.

"Your own faithfull and humble servant,

"CHARLES SEDLEY."

Katherine Sedley was the ugly miftrefs to James II.
Supped at Kenney's. He told me that on the death

of Nelſon, one of the houſe of Longman and Rees called upon him, and propoſed to him to write a " Life of Nelſon", not to be publiſhed by them, but by ſome inferior bookſeller. He was to prepare it, being furniſhed with all the neceſſary books, newſpapers, etc. He ſet about it, and by the next evening he had corrected the proofs of a pamphlet occupying about a hundred and twenty pages, all which he had written, or ſciſſored, in twenty-four hours, allowing himſelf but little ſleep. This flimſy piece of biography ſold rapidly, and produced him a hundred pounds clear of all expenſes, with which, of courſe, he had no concern. It was publiſhed under the pretence of having been written by a Captain of the Royal Navy. He gave me alſo the following.

THE THRICE-MARRIED WIDOW.

A woman had three husbands, and all of them had died :
At the funeral of the third she went to church, and cried
So bitterly and long, that her neighbours, all for fear
It might endanger life, bade her be of better cheer.
She only wept the more, and when they press'd for reason,
She answer'd that her grief could not be out of season,
Considering her great loss : three husbands she had buried,
And could hardly hope again a fourth time to be married :
Till now she'd had a chance to be again a mother,
But, after her three husbands, where could she find another ?
This was a grief of griefs : she knew that men must die,
But for a fourth good husband 'twas almost vain to try.
Still she would do her best, and, though her eyes were tearful,
If her friends could find the man, she promis'd to be cheerful."

Kenney had married Holcroft's charming widow.

Nov. 16.—The Duke aſked me whether I had ever ſeen his houſe and gardens at Chiſwick ? My anſwer was that I had formerly lived for four years within a ſtone's-throw of them, but that I had never been infide the houfe, or over the grounds. "When was that?" he inquired; and my reply was, "Five years after I married; in a houfe with a garden down to the river, at the end of what was called Hammerfmith Terrace." "You muft have lived clofe to Mrs. Mountain, then." "Yes, within fifty yards." "What a charming finger fhe was!" added the Duke. "Indeed fhe was: the laft time I heard her (faid I) was in 'No Song, no Supper,' with Jack Bannifter as Robin: her finging of 'With lowly fuit and plaintive ditty' was delicious—I never fhall forget it." My deafnefs (added the Duke) is againft my doing juftice to a delicate voice and refined mufic; but I ufed, neverthelefs, to be delighted with Mrs. Bland, formerly Miss Romanzini, a little Jewefs." "Did you ever hear her (afked I) fing 'Wapping Old Stairs?'" "Yes (anfwered the Duke), often, and never too often: it was exquifite of its kind."—"That fong (I obferved) was compofed by my mother's old mufic-mafter, Percy, who alfo compofed 'O, Nanny, wilt thou gang with me.'" —"Indeed! (cried the Duke) I have heard it difputed who was the compofer of that beautiful ballad."—"My mother was taught it by him (faid I), and fhe knew that he was the compofer of it. If it be ever again difputed in your Grace's company, you may boldly fay that it was compofed by old Percy, also the author of 'Wapping Old Stairs', which my mother likewife learned to fing from him. She had a fweet voice, of courfe not equal to, but fomething like Mrs. Bland's."—"Aye, aye (rejoined the Duke), that is one reafon, perhaps, why your voice is fo pleafing to my ears (*fit venia*); you have it from her; but, befides, as I have often told you, your enunciation is fo diftinct and clear. But, dropping that, as you

fay you have never feen my Chifwick watchbox, I fhall
have occafion to go there to-morrow, and, if you like, I
will take you with me. It is worth feeing, though fome
people formerly laughed at it. We will ftart at eleven ;
half an hour will take us there, and we shall have ample
time to fee the place, and to lunch there."

"Why do you call it your *watchbox?*" I afked.—" Becaufe (faid he) Horace Walpole, I think, faid that it was
too fmall for a houfe, and yet too large to hang as a
bauble to one's watch-chain. Therefore I call it my
watchbox."

Accordingly we went there yefterday in a brougham,
and entered by the long avenue from the high-road. I was
pleafed, but not furprifed : everything was upon a fmall
fcale compared with Chatfworth, but in excellent tafte, excepting the houfe, which certainly was not a good dwelling-
place, the rooms, as in many houfes, being facrificed to the
hall and lobbies, out of which they opened : there were
many fine pictures, but one or two of them, as I told the
Duke, mifnamed ;—for inftance, Vandyke's Belifarius had
the name of Marino at the bottom of the frame. The Duke
fhewed me the drawing-room and dining-room, but left me
to wander through the billiard-room and fome other apartments. I found no library, properly fo-called, but feveral
ftands and tables which had books upon, and under them,
turning round fo as to enable a reader to take any he liked.
After the Duke had gone through the little bufinefs with
his head-gardener for which he came, he returned to me,
and led me into a room on the fame floor as the drawing-
and dining-rooms, handfomely, though heavily furnifhed,
but a bed-room. " In this apartment (faid he) two of the

N

greateſt men of our day died, viz., my old early friend Charles
James Fox, and my younger and later friend, George Canning."—"I remember them both (I obſerved). I heard Fox
ſpeak, and ſaw him go to Court as Foreign Miniſter in
1806 ; and Canning, beſides hearing him ſpeak very often,
I dined with in the year 1824, when he was reſiding in a
houſe belonging to Lord Harrington in Brompton."—
"They occupied the only ſpare room of any conſequence in
this watchbox (continued the Duke) for we are badly off
here in that reſpect; there I put all my gueſts—and they
have been many ſince it ſaw the laſt of thoſe two diſtin-
guiſhed orators. I was only fifteen or ſixteen when Fox
died, but conſiderably above thirty when Canning died.
Fox was very playful with me when I was a boy, and he
was a frequent gueſt in my father's time."

The Duke inſiſted on my playing a rubber at billiards with
him, which I won eaſily, as he is far from a good player.
It is impoſſible for any man to play well, unleſs he ſee good
play, such as is exhibited in public rooms by profeſſors—
and that the nobility never see, unleſs now and then a
match be made up for their amuſement by men whose buſineſs it is to play ſkilfully : even then they learn nothing
practically. The Duke uſed to have Kentfield, the beſt
player of his day, down to Chatſworth, or in London, to in-
ſtruct and amuſe his gueſts: amuſe them he might, but
they could not learn anything of the real art of the game.
The Duke never did, and never could play well, becauſe he
really took little intereſt in the game, and knew nothing of
the power and peculiarity of the ſide-ſtroke. He propoſed
the rubber to fill up the time with me, while we were at
Chiſwick : I did not want to play, but he, knowing my

paffion, thought I did. Books, beauty, and billiards were
my chief purfuits until I married, and then the only one I
left off was the fecond ; for my wife, though a very charming, well-educated, and accomplished woman, is not a
beauty: fhe is a great deal better. The Duke, after luncheon, returned to London by four o'clock.

I dined in company with Thomas Taylor, the Platonist,
on all accounts a remarkable man—for the peculiarity of
his polytheiftical faith, for the extent of his learning in that
direction, and for his perfonal appearence. His face is
as rugged and rough as Ben Jonfon's, and he ftrongly reminded me of the poet. He is full of egotifm, but of the
fimpleft and least offenfive kind: he recited fome of his
own poetry, efpecially an Ode to Venus, beginning rather
queerly,

" Before I enter on this great affair," etc.

He was very violent in his abufe of a German profeffor
(I think of Drefden) who had charged him with ignorance
and literary difhonefty in what he had publifhed regarding
the Chaldean Oracles; and he read an article he had written
in reply, which ended with a fentence that he gave with
peculiar emphafis, ftating that he anfwered " not becaufe
he had received any injury, but becaufe the Profeffor had
done one."

He alfo bitterly complained of old D'Ifraeli, with whom
he had been on terms of intimacy forty years ago ; and who,
in the firft edition of his " Cur. of Lit.", had afferted that
Taylor was a fit fubject for St. Luke's ; in the next edition
had given him extravagant praife for his learning and
talents ; and in the third edition had abufed him, and ridiculed him for believing that Jupiter was the father and

creator of the world, that Venus was the Virgin Mary,
Cupid Chrift, etc. I may add here the following.

DISPUTE AND DECISION.

A.

I hate all men,
Dull, envious, ignorant, and blind.

B.

I love all men,
Wise, virtuous, generous, and kind.

C.

Within ourselves the error lies,
  That thus we still dispute :
We see not with the self-same eyes ;
  So let us ev'n be mute,
And think that God has fashioned man
Upon his own eternal plan,
That he may worship, and not scan.

Nov. 8.—A friend, upon whofe veracity I can rely, a few
days ago, was fhown a very extraordinary MS.—"The
Life of Lady Caroline Lamb", written by herfelf. It was
contained in forty fides of notepaper, and entered into
many curious particulars, without the flighteft referve. It
fet out with ftating that the original memoir had been of
greater length, with copies of correfpondence, verfes, etc.,
but that "William" (meaning the Rt. Hon. William Lamb,
Lord Melbourne) had obtained poffeffion of it, and had
burnt it : in confequence, Lady Caroline fat down, when
fhe wrote this MS., to fupply the deficiency, as well as fhe
could, from memory.

It commenced from her refidence in the family of the
Duke of Devonfhire, where fhe firft faw the Hon. W.
Lamb, and where he fell in love with her, though fhe never

much liked him, as he was heavy and indolent. After
going over many fmall particulars, the MS. went on to
mention her earlieft acquaintance with Lord Byron ; who
came to call upon her in company with Samuel Rogers,
who produced fome verfes, and Lord Byron alfo fhewed
her one of his own poems. Lady Caroline admitted that
fhe foon felt the ftrongeft paffion for Byron, and, in very
plain terms, confeffed her *faux-pas*. It feems to have
made fome confufion in the family ; for fhe related that,
when her lady's-maid faw Lord Byron for the firft time, fhe
expreffed her aftonifhment to her miftrefs, that a man who
was lame, and fo comparatively infignificant in appearance,
had caufed fuch a rumpus. After this date, they would
have dealt with her as infane; but fhe would not fubmit to
any fuch treatment, and ufed threats of felf-deftruction if
they attempted coercion. From this period fhe made no
fecret of her attachment to Lord Byron, though he feems,
after a time, to have returned her paffion rather coldly, which
of courfe filled the lady with rage and defpair. It was
at this juncture that fhe wounded herfelf in the arm while
at an entertainment at Devonshire Houfe, in order to draw
Lord Byron's attention to her there. She went on to fpeak
in violent terms of an actrefs, who was a rival of hers with
Lord Byron, but fhe did not name Mifs Booth, who was under
the fofa. One fingular circumftance we may take for true
or falfe on fuch authority : Lord Byron died on April 18,
1824, and Lady Caroline Lamb afferted that on that very
night fhe faw him ; that he diftinctly appeared to her ; and
that she woke her husband, who was fleeping by her fide,
and faid, " William, I fee Lord Byron": he laughed at her,
could fee nothing, and went to fleep. Afterwards she be-

held a long funeral proceſſion.   The MS. then detailed a
number of particulars of little value relating to the publication of Lady Caroline Lamb's "Glenarvon."   My friend
was well acquainted with her handwriting, and diſtinctly
aſſured me that the whole was of her penmanship. Where
or how he had ſeen it, he declined to tell, but I fully believe
in its exiſtence.

Nov. 11.—I have found, among ſome old papers belonging to my father, ſeveral copies of ſmall poems by Samuel
Rogers : I think that they have all been printed by the
author, excepting one on the death of his father in 1793;
and the two earlieſt quatrains of that, I feel ſure, I have
read ſomewhere in type : the third has not hitherto been
added to the poem ; and, as it is certainly one of the beſt,
if not the very beſt, I ſubjoin the whole here. The third
quatrain ſeems to anticipate the recovery of the old gentleman, and as the complaint under which he was ſuffering
ended fatally, perhaps it was ſtruck out on that account: at
all events, the poem is incomplete without it.

" Within that bed, so closely curtain'd round,
    Worn to a shade, and pale with slow decay,
A father sleeps.   Oh ! hush'd be every sound.
    Soft let us breathe the midnight hours away.

" He stirs, yet still he sleeps.   May heavenly dreams
    Above his smooth'd and settled pillow rise ;
Nor fade till daylight through the window streams,
    And on the hearth the flickering rushlight dies.

" Touch not the curtain ! leave him to repose ;
    'Tis Heaven's will he calmly sleep awhile,
And if again his aged eyes unclose,
    Both he and morning may upon us smile."

While my father was in Spain, before his marriage, he and young Rogers were frequent correſpondents; and I well remember, in my youth, to have ſeen ſeveral letters from the latter, written in the neateſt clerk-like hand : this muſt have been at leaſt thirty years ago ; and what became of them I know not. I ſhould not wonder if my mother had burned them, after Rogers had put an end to all former and friendly intercourſe. I have an in-diſtinct recollection of having once ſeen him in my father's houſe at Leeds, when Rogers was on ſome journey of plea-ſure, and that muſt have been when I was not more than three years old : it was, I apprehend, the laſt time Rogers was ever within my father's doors ; for when our family was living at Thames Ditton, in narrow circumſtances, he never came near the house ; nor did he ever, I believe, ſpeak to my father afterwards.

Nov. 15.—I hope the following ſong is worth preſerving, becauſe I wrote it, though very many years ago.

THE RESOLVED LOVER.

Sorrow hath pierced deep my sad heart's core,
And joyful days I never shall see more :
The cause of all my woe is beauty's charm.
Ah ! why should beauty ever work men harm ?

· Woe worth the hour I first was beauty's thrall !
    The gilded cage did dazzle my weak eyes.
With such a bait I could not choose but fall,
    And at all times the wisest are not wise.

The sage and silly in this well agree,
That both must yield to beauty's power like me ;
But this the difference that them doth sever,
The sage may profit, but the silly never.

> In this the wise man I will imitate,
> And be myself my own deliverer :
> A good deed never can be done too late,
> And freedom never can be bought too dear.

The enſuing dialogue is in the ſame predicament : let it be read as if it were two hundred and fifty years old.

THE FORSAKEN SHEPHERDESS.

Chloris.   Cheer thee, sweet shepherdess, for thou art young,
            And fair as loving shepherd ever sung.

Daphne.   Ah ! what avail my fairness or my youth,
            When they are prey to spoiler-man's untruth?

C.   Trust not to man, since he is so unjust.

D.   Alas ! the day that I did ever trust !

C.   Once having trusted, never more rely
     On man ; for man is all inconstancy.

D.   Though he be false, and I his falsehood prove,
     Still must I love him, and none other love.

C.   After such falsehood, can such love be given ?

D.   Love will controlment bear, no, not from Heaven.

C.   Not such the falsehood of the shepherd swains,
     When I was young, and fed these grassy plains.

D.   Falsehood like his was never known before,
     And love like mine will never be known more.

C.   Time will recure thee in his rolling years.

D.   Time will roll ever on, and so my tears.

C.   Love is but folly, pleasure bought with grief,
     And like all pleasures vanishing and brief.

D.   True love, they say, doth come of heavenly seed,
     But slighted love is misery indeed.

C.   But she that loves must on man's faith rely.

D.   Forsaken by him, left by him to die !

C.   These youngling hearts too easily are won ;
     They melt like snow beneath a moment's sun.

D.   The sun is true, returning day by day ;
     But man is false, born only to betray.

C. Thou find'st men false, but all too late, I trow.

D. It never is too late to find them so.

C. Search all the fields, and where is found a swain
Worth the endurance of a moment's pain ?

D. I hold him worth, though his untruth I rue ;
How worthy, then, if I had found him true !

C. But let some other swain thy thoughts employ.

D. To think of him, though false, is all my joy.

C. But what avail of tears this ceaseless shower?
They but bewray thy love, and prove his power.

D. Flow on for ever then, my tearful eyes,
Still let me fill his thoughts, though he despise.

C. Where is the pride in female hearts oft found ?

D. Pride breaks the heart, but never cures the wound.

C. Farewell, lost maid : to reason is but vaine
Against the sway fond love is known to gain.

D. The winds may hear thee and obedient prove,
But reason ever was the slave of love.

Rather of the namby-pamby fchool.

Nov. 17.—I was at the Garrick Club, where Walfh (the finging mafter) told the following ftory of Mrs. Siddons, afferting that he had it from her own lips. On her return to the ftage in London (after her failure in 1776), fhe had to play, as her probative part, *Ifabella* (I think). She had rehearfed it feveral times with the Drury Lane company, and, on the day when fhe was to re-appear, a rehearfal was appointed at ten in the morning. She went to bed late, fatigued, agitated, and anxious, but could not get to sleep. At laft fhe flept foundly—fo foundly, that when it was time next morning to go to the rehearfal, her mother found her ftill faft afleep. She confulted with the father, and they agreed not to wake her : ten, eleven, twelve o'clock came, and ftill fhe flept. At one fhe awoke, alarmed and vexed at having miffed the rehearfal. She rofe, and dreffed herfelf in fome perturbation, and began to be very nervous about her fuccefs, when fuddenly the fun broke forth from the clouds, and fhone brightly into her apartment. She took this for a good omen, and told her mother and old Roger, that fhe now felt confident that fhe could not fail, and fhe went to the theatre in that full affurance.

I faw to-day the Old Bailey Seffions-paper of 1735, containing the whole trial of Macklin for the wilful murder of Thomas Hallam, the actor. At the end, is a circumftance not noticed, I think, by the biographers of Macklin: it occurs where all the prifoners are brought up for fentence; and, after thofe who were ordered to be hanged, come the names of thofe ordered to be branded, or burnt in the hand; where occurs that of Charles Mechlin, for fo his name is fpelt, both in that place and in the commencement of the trial. Poffibly the fentence was commuted, or not carried into execution; but I have not fince had time to inquire into the matter.

Mathews, with all his popularity and notoriety, is conftantly fancying that he is neglected and unknown. His laft entertainment did not attract quite fo well as fome of the others; and one day at the Garrick, out of forts, he was ftanding before his own bill, hung up over the fire-place, and exclaiming that people fcarcely knew of his exiftence, when Lord Fife unluckily came in with " Ah, Mathews! I am very glad to fee you. Where have you been all this while? one never hears of you now." Mathews, as may be fuppofed, looked very black and blank, and filently pointed to the bill of his performance, which was then in the middle of its feafon. I have been led to remember this incident by reading a letter to-day from Mathews to Yates, written from fome place in the West of England, where Mathews had been exhibiting without any great fuccefs. It complained that he was entirely forgotten, and expreffed his deep regret that his name could not have ftood in the bill of Drury Lane, even among thofe of the fupernumeraries employed in the proceffion "in honour of Sir Walter Scott." "There (faid Mathews) I faw Mr. Bartley, Mr. Evans, Mr. Brown, Mr. Green, Mr. White, etc., and everybody but Mr. Mathews. Nobody now miffes *me.*"

He fays that his recent accident, in addition to his old calamity, has totally difabled him from walking, and that he has, befides, fprained his wrift : yet he was to perform at Portsmouth on Saturday—two days after the date of his letter to Yates.

Douglas Jerrold, very much out of heart, tells me that he has very recently had two new pieces rejected by the manager of Drury Lane : one he called by the very attractive title of " Hearts and Diamonds". He wifhes he had adhered to his profeffion of the Navy, where he was a midfhipman until he was turned adrift by the peace. He is now above thirty, and talks of going on the ftage, where his father was an actor ; but his face has not fufficient power of expreffion, and his figure is fmall, though not bad.

Coleridge, who did not at all like Fufeli, did not fcruple to tell this ftory of him with great glee : I heard him tell it once. Fufeli (who was, I think, a Pruffian) went to Liverpool, where he expected to be a lion ; and fo he was, to a certain extent, but found that he had a rival in the town, a countryman of his own, who was exhibiting extraordinary feats of eating, to the aftonifhment of the inhabi-

tants : fo much fo, that he was the fubjeƈt of univerfal converfation, and wherever Fufeli went he was fure to hear a
vaft deal about his wonderful countryman. One day, in a
large company, he was thus addreffed by an elderly lady :
" Well, Mr. Fufeli (Coleridge, out of ridicule, ufed to pronounce it Fuzzeli), your countryman outdid himfelf this
day, for what do you think he did ?"—" I cannot guefs,
madam."—" Why, he atc up a cat."—" Indeed !"—" It was
a horrible fight."—" I dare fay, madam."—" Mr. Fufeli, you
are great at the horrible, they fay—a horrible painter—and
I cannot help thinking that your countryman, in the aƈt of
devouring a live cat, would be a fine fubjeƈt for your
pencil. It was horrible, and would exaƈtly fuit your
horrible ftyle."—" You mean my terrible ftyle—terrible—
you mean terrible—if (*afide*) a foolifh woman could mean
anything." Unworthy of Coleridge !

Southey divides his day thus, and gets through a great
quantity of work. He rifes at half-paft feven ; writes and
reads till nine ; breakfafts ; reads and writes again till two ;
then takes a walk till four, when he dines : he remains with
his family until after tea, which is brought at fix ; retires to
his ftudy until ten ; rejoins his family, and goes to bed.
Thus, he reads and writes for more than eight hours a day.
He is of a moft tranquil temper, but fanguine, and exces-
fively fond of his children.

Nov. 19.—I have no edition of Rabelais, excepting the
earlieft, and no tranflation of any part of his " Garagantua";
but, reading it this morning, I fell upon the fubfequent fancy,
which I could not refrain from putting into verfe (Book iii,
ch. 31).

CUPID AND THE MUSES.

Little Cupid one day by his mother was ask'd
  Why constantly still he refuses,
However by gods or by goddesses task'd,
  To assail any one of the Muses?

Dear mother (he answer'd), I often have tried,
  I swear by your doves and your sparrows,
To make an impression, but me they defied,
  And turn'd all the points of my arrows.

How can that be? (quoth Venus) your weapons, I thought,
  From us deities take no denial.
Excepting from them (replied Cupid) and, taught
  By experience, I gave up the trial.

I found them so busy whenever I went,
  They hardly had leisure to look up ;
Or, if ever they did, back my arrows were sent
  By their holding some thick stupid book up.

Let mortals by study but strengthen the mind,
  I can place on my darts no reliance ;
But, pray, keep my council, or people will find
  'Tis easy to bid me defiance.

The Duke generally fpends the dull, dreary month of
November at Brighton, where he has a corner-houfe looking to the fea and to Kemp-town Square : my brother-in-
law lives not a ftone's-throw diftant. I and my family were
ftaying with my hofpitable relation, and the Duke, knowing
it, conftantly fent my wife prefents of fruit and flowers. I
dine with him fometimes, but he fees little company
generally, giving, however, two or three fmart parties : he
afked my wife and me, two days ago, but we declined for
various good reafons. About a fortnight fince, before my

family arrived in Brighton, he invited me down, and I flept
at his houfe until my wife and children came to ftay with
my brother-in-law.   This was, I think, the only occafion on
which I felt time hang heavy on my hands in the Duke's
fociety—perhaps becaufe I was expecting my family, with
whom, of courfe, I was generally merry and lively.   The
Duke took me feveral drives, and behaved moft hofpitably :
among other places, we went to Sompting and Weft Grin-
ftead, both of which churches have interefting Anglo-Saxon
and Norman remains.   We alfo went to Worthing, where
I had not been fince I was four or five years old, when my
father and mother lodged in a houfe with a large garden,
both now abolifhed by new buildings, and I did not recog-
nife a fingle place or object.   Broadwater Church and Old
and New Shoreham Churches attracted our attention.   I
did not then underftand much about architecture, efpecially
ecclefiaftical ; but I found the Duke better inftructed, and
I did not fcruple to avow my ignorance, and to avail myfelf of his greater knowledge.   He was impreffed particularly by the fine horfefhoe arch in Broadwater Church,
which, however, looked infecure, from a fault occafioned by
a finking of the foundation.   I was almoft afhamed to
confefs that I had never feen the ruins of Kirkftall or
Fountains Abbeys.   "Well (faid the Duke), you fhall fee
them when you come to ftay with me at Bolton Abbey,
which itfelf is worth the journey."

I muft take care, while refiding in the Duke's houfe, not
to make myfelf a nuifance, like the hedgehog in the following little apologue, which I picked up, I do not know
where, but in fome foreign book, perhaps Yriarte : it may
be in Englifh, but I do not know it.

A hedgehog thus bespake a rabbit,
  The weather being very cold :
" Good friend, permit me to inhabit
  Your burrow with you ; two 'twill hold."
The rabbit answer'd, " Keep your distance,
And I will offer no resistance."

The burrow was so very narrow,
  That neither could well turn him round :
Hedgehog prick'd rabbit like an arrow,
  Inflicting many a painful wound.
The hedgehog car'd not ; rabbit smarted,
And wish'd he had been harder hearted.

" My friend," said hedgehog, " you're uneasy."—
  " Your spikes into my side you run."—
" I'm really sorry to displease you ;
  If you don't like it, pray begone.
I can't help being prickly, so
'Tis your own fault, if you don't go."

Nov. 23.—I have lately, while from home, tranflated feveral Italian fonnets ; and I think fo well of them, that I tranfcribe them in this Diary. The firft is by Petrarch, in anfwer to one by Ortenfia di Guglielmo, and it is to be found in Buttura's Collection (i, 213).*

Lust, greedy luxury, and lazy sleep,
  From the wide world have banish'd ancient worth :
  Nature is driven from her seat on earth,
Beneath low artifices buried deep.
  Heaven's light benignant, that once bless'd our eyes
And human life inform'd, is spent and gone ;
  And vulgar fingers point with huge surprise
At him who brings fresh streams from Helicon.
Where is the laurel's beauty, myrtle's grace ?—

" Philosophy may wander, naked, poor,"
The crowd exclaims, intent on all that's base :
    Their friends are few the loftier path who take.
    Thee, gentle spirit, I beseech the more
Thy noble purpose never to forsake.

The next is by Gabriello Simeoni, a Florentine; and is
fuppofed to be addreffed to the foul of Dante, who was
buried, and had a monument, at Ravenna, from whence the
repentant citizens of Florence afterwards attempted in vain
to obtain the great poet's bones. Simeoni had himfelf been
banished from Florence.

Spirit divine ! whose worth at length we see,
    Fair Florence gladly own, that held as vile
    Thy splendid name and subtle work erewhile,
Her glory, and thine immortality,
Look down on one thus far resembling thee,
    In seeking a new land, another style.
    Envy must still the noblest souls revile,
And hunt them till they die in misery.
    Mourn we together : thou in lofty seat,
And I who fall on times of grief and rage,
    That it were better I had ne'er been born :
We must rely upon a future age.
    Thy bones are here : I lead a life forlorn :
Virtue at home will ne'er its guerdon meet.

This is neither fo good a fonnet, nor fo good a tranflation
as the preceding one : the next, by Taffo, is, I hope, better
in both refpects: it has reference, in fact, to the ode inferted on page 59 of this Diary, and is addreffed
to the foul of Hercules II, Duke of Ferrara ; the poet
having previoufly in vain made his appeal to his fucceffor,
Alphonfo, for releafe from his difmal imprifonment.

Oh ! great Alcides' soul ! thou view'st, I know,
  The cruel rigor of thy royal seed,
  Who by unwonted arts, by word and deed,
Strives to draw from me whence his wrath may grow :
From milky way, above the stars that glow,
  Above the sun, whose beams so far exceed,
  Thy messenger of pity flies at need,
A human spirit to inspire below,
  And sound upon his heart, "Ah ! why this wrong,
My blood degenerate ? And where the worth,
  The generous valour of thy lofty line ?
Thou just and merciful ? To the divine
  Envoys from heaven, when they descend to earth,
Thine ears are deaf, and to the swan's sweet song.

I laid thefe before the Duke, who liked the fecond better
than I did : he afked me to give him copies of all three,
and this, I believe, not in mere compliment : he owned,
at the fame time, that, as a form of poetry, he did not
prefer the fonnet. I hope yet to make him a convert,
though not by my own attempts in that kind : my original
fonnets are, I fear, not good.

Nov. 28.—Returning to London, I have lately met with
two or three documents illuftrative of the life of Roger
Afcham ; and, among other points, I find that, although a
Proteftant, he was allowed, under Queen Mary, not £10
a-year penfion, but £26 : 13 : 4, as *Secretarius in linguâ
Latinâ.* In the year that he died, 1569, he had a fon
chriftened Thomas at Cripplegate Church ; and his widow,
at a date not mentioned, was remarried to a perfon of the
name of Rampfton : fhe is called Margaret, *nuper uxor
Rogeri Afcham defuncti.* On June 20, 1579, fhe obtained a
grant of the parfonage of Whittleford, Cambridge, giving

P

Afcham's two fons, Giles and Thomas, an intereft in it to the extent of £18 : 16 : 2 per annum. On May 13, 1590, this rent-charge was transferred to Dudley Afcham, "youngeft fon of the faid Roger Afcham", for term of life; fo that we may prefume that at this date Thomas Afcham, baptifed in 1569, was dead. Thefe particulars, though trifling, are entirely new.

Bifhop Bale was not only one of the founders of Proteftantifm, but the author of our very earlieft femi-hiftorical play. Before the Reformation, he was the parish-prieft of Thorndon, Suffolk ; but, having changed his faith, he complains bitterly, in an undated letter to Cromwell (therefore prior to 1540), that he had been expofed, "at the inftigation of the Earl of Suffolk", to every kind of annoyance and fuffering : when he wrote he was in prifon, having been arrefted by the Bailiff of Thorndon, and compelled to endure "vilenefs, ftink, penury, cold, and other incommodities." He adds that fome of the witneffes had been threatened with the lofs of their copyholds if they did not appear againft him. He concludes thus, and, as far as I have been able to afcertain, although Bale's original letter is in the British Mufeum (MSS. Cleop. E. iv), it has never been noticed : "My confcyence giveth me that I have nother offendyd God nor my prince in that I have done ; yet am I not fo fure but I may be dyffeyved. Wherefore I defire your gracyofe goodnes, if I have offended more than I can perfeyve in my felf, gracyoflye to bere with myne ignorant blyndnes, and I shall not only endevoure my felf to amend that is paft, but alfo applye to my utmoft power from henceforth to ferve God and my prince with more fobernes." It is fubfcribed "Your contynuall orator and bedefmen, John Bale, pryft."

The " femi-hiftorical play" above-mentioned I have recently bought for the Duke's dramatic library : its foundation is the reign of King John, and the bafe fubmiffion of
that monarch to the Pope and Cardinal Pandulph : it is
partly allegorical, like an old myftery or morality, and
partly founded upon facts, illuftrated by the characters
engaged in them ; and, as far as refearch has yet gone, it
has no parallel in our language. Bale, the author, was
anxious by it to forward the Reformation ; and no mercy
is fhown to the Roman Catholics of his day, who had pro-
voked him by the cruelties they had inflicted upon him.
There can be no doubt that, in point of date, it belongs to
the reign of Edward VI : I have not yet been able to trace
the hiftory of the MS., but there is reafon to believe that
it came out of the corporation cheft of Ipfwich, in which
town it was performed before Mary came to the throne. It
is the more valuable and remarkable, becaufe half of it is
in the handwriting of Bale himfelf, while the reft was copied
by a fcribe, and throughout corrected by the author. I know
of no more interefting dramatic relic ; but, unluckily, I did
not know of its exiftence when I wrote my three volumes
on the hiftory of our old plays and theatres.

Dec. 1.—I was shown, by earneft requeft, a note, very carefully written by J. P. Kemble, in anfwer to a perfon of the
name of Kempe, who, in 1817, when Kemble retired from the
ftage in Coriolanus, fent him an addrefs in verfe to be then
fpoken. Kemble's note returned the lines, as he ftated,
unread, not out of difrefpect, but becaufe he had made up
his mind not to take leave in verfe ; and because, if he had
permitted himfelf the pleafure of reading Mr. Kempe's addrefs, he feared it might make him waver in his determin-

ation. Upcot would not allow me to take a copy of Kemble's courtier-like note.

The following advertifement I copy from the *Mercurius Reformatus* of June 11, 1690: it is worth preferving.

" Mr. John Bunyan, author of the ' Pilgrim's Progress', and many other excellent books that have found good acceptance, hath left behind him ten manuscripts, prepared by himself for the press before his death. His widow is desired to print them (with some other of his works which have been already printed, but are at present not to be had), which will make together a book of 10s. in sheets in fol. All persons, who desire so great and good a work should be performed with speed, are desired to send in 5s., for their first payment, to Dorman Newman, at the King's Arms, in the Poultry, London ; who is empowered to give receipts for the same."

The book was published in 1692. Bunyan had died, at the age of fixty, two years before the appearance of the above advertifement.

Dec. 2.—I went to the veftry of St. Clement's Danes, in order to fee if Cunningham were quite correct in ftating to me that the regifter there contained an entry of the baptifm of " Florence, daughter of Edmund Spenfer", under the date of August 16, 1587 ; if fo, and if the daughter were legitimate, Spenfer muft have been married twice, viz., before 1587 and in 1594. I found that entry, but no other regarding Spenfer ; but looking earlier, I met among the baptifms with two entries of Lord Burghley's sons :

" 23 April, 1561, Master William Cecill."
"6 June, 1563, Master Robert Cecill, the sonne of the Lord High Treasurer of England."

The laft, of courfe, was the afterwards famous Earl of Salisbury, fecretary to Queen Elizabeth and King James I. Thomas Cecill, who fucceeded to the title of Lord Burghley and Earl of Exeter, was older than either of the above, and the offspring of a firſt wife. In Chalmers' "Biograp. Dict." it is ſaid that Robert Cecill was born about 1550 : the regiſter eſtabliſhes that he was not ſo old by thirteen years, ſo that when he became Secretary to Elizabeth in 1596, he was in his thirty-third year. This makes a very material difference as regards him ; and the entry farther ſhews that as early as 1563 his father filled the office of "Lord High Treaſurer of England." Is not this a miſtake, becauſe in the biographies of Lord Burghley it is ſtated that he was not made "Lord High Treaſurer" until the death of the Marquis of Wincheſter in 1573, and not in 1563 ?

Dec. 3.—A letter preſerved at Lambeth, from A. Standen to Anthony Bacon, dated Kingſton, Feb., 1594, contains the following charaĉteriſtic anecdote of Queen Elizabeth : "The remove from this place is quite conformable to the ſpeech of the carter, that three tymes had been at Windſor with his cart to carry away (upon ſummons of a remove) ſome part of the ſtuff of her Majeſty's wardrobe ; and when he had repaired thither once, twice, and a third time, and that they of the wardrobe had told him, the third time, that the remove held not, clapping his hand on his thigh, ſaid theſe words : 'Now I ſee (quoth the carter) that the queen is a woman as well as my wife!' Which words being overheard by her Majeſty, who then ſtood at the window (ſhe) ſaid, 'What a villain knave is this!' and ſo ſent him three angels to ſtop his mouth."

James Kenney, author of "Raiſing the Wind", "Sweet-hearts and Wives", etc., brought me his tragedy on the Sicilian Veſpers in MS. He avowed it to be mainly translated from the French, and I promiſed to give him my opinion of it—not a pleaſant duty for an old friend. He married, as I have elſewhere ſtated, Holcroft's widow, a charming French woman, whoſe maiden name was Mercier. Holcroft was a remarkable man, very ugly, very clever, but juſt not clever enough : he wrote his own biography from the time that he followed a travelling tinker's donkey to the time when he became a literary man, going through the not very congenial intermediate ſtages of ſtable-boy and Newmarket jockey. He married, I think, three times, and had children by each of his wives. His " Road to Ruin" was his most ſuccefsful play, but he wrote many others. He was a frequent viſitor at my father's houſe when I was a boy, but was not very agreeable company.

Dec. 14.—I have been ſo unwell for more than a week that I have hardly been able to move. The Duke ſent to inquire after me, and called himſelf. He has made up his mind to have a *fac-ſimile* prepared in lithography of a very valuable MS. book he has in his library of drawings and ſketches by Inigo Jones, particularly while this great architeᴄt and artiſt was in Italy. It bears date at Rome in 1614, and the ſignature of Inigo Jones is preceded by this line :

<blockquote>" Altro diletto che imparar non trovo."</blockquote>

Many of the ſketches are from ſtatues, and others from pictures which the author admired during his travels. I was talking with the Duke on the improvements in lithography, when all of a ſudden, as if ſomething had juſt come into his head, he jumped up from his chair, ran out of the room, and returned with a parchment-covered little 8vo volume in his hand. I highly applauded his intention of having it copied in *fac-fimile*, and the Duke agreed to have it done at once, and directed me to make inquiries on the fubject as to the beft artift and the probable expenfe. There is a good deal of MS. interfperfed explanatory of the different fubjects, and in many inftances with the names of the feveral artifts. The Duke was kind enough to give me two or three original fcraps, which I fhall preferve with great care.

Dec. 16.—Where is it faid, in what life of Judge Jeffreys, that when in the weft he tried a rebel, and ordered him to be hanged next morning, the poor fellow befought him for a longer day, and the Judge replied that the morrow was St. Barnabas' Day, the longeft in the year?

In "Polly Peacham's Jests," 1728, and I darefay in older authorities, we are told that Sir Thomas More made the fame joke; but that was in a civil fuit, and not where a poor wretch's life was at ftake :—"Sir Thomas More, when on one occafion the counfel of the party preffed him for a longer day to perform a decree, faid, 'Take St. Barnabas Day, which is the longest in the year'; and happened to be in the next week."

I have looked into all the old jest books to which I have access, extending from about 1560 to 1760, and I have not met with any fuch anecdote of More.

The following is from one of thefe jest-books, at least two hundred and fifty years old; it is in profe, but it ran into verfe almost as I read it :

THE NEW-MADE KNIGHT.

A new made knight, who always wore
  His badge outside, to show it,
Stopp'd an old friend upon the way,
  That he might see and know it.

The friend was mounted on a horse
  Not easy to be guided,
And ere he parted from the knight,
  It back'd and rear'd and sided ;

And would not pass the new-made knight,
  Who ask'd his friend the reason?
The jade, he answer'd, will not pass
  An inn at any season.

" Am I an inn ?" inquired the knight.—
  "Why, no," said he ; " but, look you,
With that thing dangling at your neck,
  For a sign-post it mistook you."

Planché, the author of " Oberon," and of various dramatic pieces of merit, was apprenticed to Murton the book-
binder, as the latter informed me.   I was at a dinner given
by John Murray soon after my " History of English Dramatic Poetry and the Stage" came out : there were at least
twenty authors and authorlings prefent, and Planché, quitting his place at table, favoured us with fome very good
imitations of popular performers : I am not by any means
fure that he has not fomewhere given them in public.   I
have heard worfe from profeffors.

Dec. 21.—A day or two ago, I bought a book which,
though not what bibliographers call rare, is uncommon : at
leaft, I have been in fearch of it for a year or two ; viz.,
" The Crafty Courtier ; or, the Fable of Reinard the Fox,
etc."—London, 1706. Even before I married, H. C. Robinfon often urged me to attempt an English tranflation, not
of the original Saxon work, but of Goethe's " Reineke
Fuchs", in twelve *gefangen*, as he calls them ; and, for that

purpofe, H. C. R. gave me a copy of it : but I found that the twelve fongs were in hexameters, which may read very well in German, but which do not fuit my ears in English. I tried, but could make nothing of them to fatisfy me : H. C. R. alfo tried, and, I think, did equally ill. However, after I had finished, and indeed printed, my " Poets' Pilgrimage", I thought I would make the experiment, not in hexameters, but in English Hudibraftic eight-fyllable couplets. I adopted for my text " Reineke de Vofs", as published in 1798 (with a gloffary of the *olden Saffifchen Worde*), the foundation of all our English profe verfions from the time of Caxton to the year 1701, when, I apprehend, the lateft impreffion of "that moft delectable Hiftory of Reynard the Fox" appeared.

" The Crafty Courtier", 1706, I found to be merely a modernifation, with names and applications belonging to the reigns of James II, William III, and Anne ; but I determined that my verfion should be fimply a humorous narration of the chief incidents of the droll-wife ftory, as far as decency would allow ; and I perfevered with it at intervals until I had written more than a thoufand lines, when I was informed that Samuel Naylor, another friend of H. C. R.'s, had fet himfelf the fame tafk, and was already approaching the completion of it. I therefore fufpended my undertaking; and I was the more ready to do fo, becaufe I heard that Naylor had printed a fpecimen of his verfion (in eight-fyllable lines like mine), and intended, chiefly at his own coft, to make it a beautiful book. I did not burn what I had done, and it remains now among my difcarded papers. H. C. R. fpeaks well of what he had feen of Naylor's work : I grew weary of mine.

Q

I wrote the following, as may be supposed, when I was very young; but it has passion in it.

SONG.

Her breath 's not like the rose ;
　Such similes I discard :
Her hand none will suppose
　To be, like ivory, hard :
I love it that I find it soft,
When she permits me kiss it oft.

Her eyes are not so blue
　As is the summer sky ;
But they are clear and true,
　And I will tell you why ;
Because her eyes are both so bright,
They drive all cloudy doubts from sight.

I cannot choose but own
　She 's far above my praise :
I love her—her alone—
　And will do all my days.
Her lips not rubies, teeth not pearl,
But she 's the loveliest English girl.

When I say that, 'tis all,
　I'm sure, that need be told :
She 's not too short or tall ;
　She 's not too young or old.
I'm truly glad she 's not divine,
But real flesh and blood—and mine !

Dec. 25.—I may mention here that, some years ago, I wrote a small dramatic entertainment, somewhat in the form of a masque for Christmas. It was all in rhyme, with appropriate songs, and required only five or six

actors. The Duke read and liked it, and propofed to
have it got up and reprefented at Chatfworth; but the
want of two female performers, who could fing, prevented
the execution of his purpofe. I call it " The Contention
of the Seafons", reprefenting that one had encroached upon
the other, and calling for the interpofition of Apollo to re-
ftore the balance of power.

I copy one of the lyrics belonging to it, upon a theme
which has borne many better productions of the kind,
though I am fond of my own.

THE SONG OF SPRING.

What 's sweeter than the spring,
   At morning's earliest hour,
When the lark, with quivering wing,
   Mounts to her airy tower ;
O'er the horizon peering,
To see the daylight nearing?

What's sweeter than the eve
   Of spring, when toil is over,
When the hare will covert leave,
   To feed on the fresh green clover ;
When light is slowly sinking,
And the waking stars are winking?

The other fongs were equally *feafonable.*

Dec. 30.—I have already mentioned that the Duke does
not very well like the form of poetry to which the fonnet
belongs. I copied out and fent him the following, and he
muft have received it at a favourable moment, becaufe he
acknowledged that it pleafed him much.

THE CONSOLATION.

If I am wrong, and if my song be nought,
　I have myself, and but myself, to blame,
　That ere the style of manhood I could claim,
The favour of the Muses only sought,
And to obtain it bent my toil and thought,
　Though with it poverty and kindred shame.—
Thus far I know my muse not vainly sings ;
　For I have learn'd my single heart to frame,
So that I draw my bliss from other things
　Than those which many highest blessings name :
And if I cannot soar upon the wings
　Of fancy, as some use, I may rejoice,
Where'er I go, that endless pleasure springs
　From Nature's various face, and Nature's cheerful voice.

The Duke approved highly of the alexandrine at the
clofe, but he expreffed his doubts whether, ftrictly fpeaking,
it was regular to employ it. I agreed that it was not, according to the beft practice of the Italian poets ; but I
affured him that I could produce many good examples of
it in Englifh. I obferved that my fpecimen was altogether out of the regular courfe as regarded the fucceffion
of the rhymes; and that Wordfworth, our beft modern fonnetteer, ufually divided the fourteen lines into two portions,
not fo much diftinct in thought, as diftinct in verfification.
The Duke liked it better than any other fonnet that he had
feen—of mine. "Perhaps," added he, " one reafon why I
like it the better is, that it is not a regular fonnet : it is,
at all events, a fonnet without its formality and ftiffnefs.
Some people who write fonnets, in their effort to make
them feem original, only arrive at the unintelligible." This
I confider a juft piece of criticifm.

My "friend" (fo venturing for once to call him) has a

keen fenfe of the beauties of Nature; and, when walking out, he will not unfrequently touch me on the fhoulder, in order to direct my attention to fome profpect or object he fancies I had not noted. His liking for poetry depends much upon its naturalnefs: he fees fmall merit in the clever turns and conceited trifles of the time of Charles II, while he is enthufiaftic in his admiration of fentiments and language which proceed, without apparent effort, from the heart: he cares little for what he aptly calls *head-poetry*: "there is *heart* in that," he will fometimes fay, almoft with tears in his eyes—and quite in mine.

He likes the fubfequent fcrap, and fo do I:

ON READING WHILE WALKING.

I pity much the man, whose looks,
While wandering by the fields and brooks,
  Can ne'er his page forsake ;
For God has made far better books
  Than man can ever make.

I conclude with the following: it does not, in truth, belong to the fame period as all that precedes it :—

ON RETIREMENT.

If an author, arriv'd at his life's chill December,
  Retire to the country, that nothing may fret him,
He knows, though one friend may not chance to remember,
  An enemy certainly will not forget him :
And this his advantage, whate'er they pretend,
To be sure of his foes, if he have not a friend.

I fay nothing of my foefhips: I hope I have outlived fome of them ; but I have not been fortunate, or perhaps judicious, in my friendfhips. My firft and deareft went blind at thirty, and died before he was forty. My fecond took to habits of intoxication, and killed himfelf down the well of his own ftaircafe; a third expired in a hofpital, having been wounded in a fcuffle; a fourth and a fifth died in a madhoufe, and in a workhoufe; a fixth entered into lofing fpeculations, and deftroyed himfelf; a feventh was found dead in his bed; an eighth lived to more advanced age, but was at laft brought to the end of his career by mortifica-tion and difappointment; a ninth, who really had the gift of tongues and was a mafter of fix modern languages, became an irredeemable beggar; a tenth took a wife and poifon in the fame year; but an eleventh is ftill living and profperous, who was as intimate as a brother, but whom I have not feen for five and forty years, becaufe I declined, in breach of my duty, to infert a puff-paragraph for him in a newfpaper with which I was connected. All thefe were "friends", more or less intimate; but among thofe to whom, owing to accidental pofition, however infignificant, I was perfonally known, I can name no fewer than four fuicides— Calcraft, Romilly, Castlereagh, and Whitbread. I faw Per-ceval fhot, Canning when he was dying, and Sheridan dead —drunk in Drury Lane.

FINIS.

's Diary.

ARS AGO.

III

AN OLD MAN'S DIARY,

FORTY YEARS AGO;

FOR THE FIRST SIX MONTHS OF

1833.

Omne meum : nihil meum.

FOR STRICTLY PRIVATE CIRCULATION.

LONDON :
PRINTED BY THOMAS RICHARDS.
1872.

PREFACE.

A PREFACE feems fcarcely needed to this third part of "an Old Man's" *private* "Diary": it includes the firft fix months of the year 1833. I fhall endeavour to follow it by fimilar memoranda belonging to the later half of the fame year : I can carry it no farther, becaufe, after the clofe of 1833, I kept my entries in a much fmaller compafs, feldom taking the trouble to copy documents and letters, making only brief notes, etc., regarding them.

In preceding portions of this work I have quoted fome letters by Swift, which came into my hands in 1831 : thefe were feen by a gentleman in North Wales, a ftranger to me, who informed me that he was in poffeffion of other communications by the fame pen ; and he favoured me with· the tranfcript of one of them, perfonally of great intereft, dated much later in the Dean's career; viz., December 1736, when he was confined to his bed in Dublin. If it had come into my poffeffion forty years ago, I fhould certainly have quoted it at length in thefe pages; but, as I only obtained it very recently, I do well fee how I can avail myfelf of it, and of other letters which appear to be in the hands of the fame obliging poffeffor. My advice is that, if hitherto unknown, he fhould print them feparately, and, if I can be of the flighteft ufe to him in fo doing, he may depend upon my beft fervices.

An error on p. 41, where I incautioufly fix the date of the old actor Tarlton's death in 1584, is of fome confequence: he was buried, in fact, on Sept. 3rd, 1588, under the name of Richard Torrelton, as I afcertain from the original regifter at Shoreditch, where he died. This miftake may make fome difference in the argument upon the fubject of *extempore* reprefentations upon the ftage before the time of Shakefpeare, and I therefore mention it. Minor errors of dates, if any, may perhaps be left to correct themfelves.

I know of but two or three perfons now alive, who were " in the flefh" at the time to which this portion of the Diary applies.

J. P. C.

Maidenhead, Jan. 11, 1872.

OLD MAN'S DIARY,

PART III.

Jan. 1, 1833.—Owing to the dangerous illnefs of my wife, who keeps her bed with rheumatic fever, we have had none of the jollity ufual with us and our family at this cold but merry feafon. I have before mentioned my intended Chriftmas Entertainment which was to have been got up and reprefented at Chatfworth, had we not wanted female fingers, and had not the Duke, very ftrongly and properly, objected to the admixture of profeffionals, hired for the occafion. Its title, as I have before ftated, was "The Contention of the Seafons," arifing out of the extraordinary intrufion of fome of them on the province of each other, efpecially of Winter, who arrived before his time, interfering with the period ordinarily affigned to Autumn. I have already inferted the Song of Spring, and here that which was affigned to Old Winter will not be out of place: it was, like the others, fet to mufic at the expenfe of the Duke, but by what compofer I do not know: the chief merit of my lyric is its appropriatenefs.

B

THE SONG OF WINTER.

Though the woods are all bare,
　And the fields are all white,
Yet has Winter to spare
　Both of love and delight :
　　And travellers through snow,
　　When they see the blaze glow,
With frosted cheeks smile, and rub hands at the sight.

Then in hall and in bower
　The jovial song rings,
And pleasure has power
　To give Winter wings.
　　The lone pilgrim there
　　Of the feast has his share,
And thanks the brave Lord for the blessing he brings.

The whole performance would not have occupied an
hour; and as Apollo's decifion of the ftrife is, in my
opinion, the beft of the fpeeches (all fhort), I almoft feel inclined to tranfcribe it here, but juft now I am too bufy.

Jan. 3.—Thomas Campbell ("Pleafures of Hope") having
agreed with a publifher for a " Life of Mrs. Siddons," for
which he is to be paid £400, applied to me in the firft
inftance for fuch materials as were in my poffeffion.   I faid
that I had not much information about her, and referred him
to Winfton, Secretary of the Garrick Club : Campbell faw
him, and came away diffatisfied, becaufe, as he faid, nearly
all that Winfton knew had been derived from the very queftionable fource of Mrs. Hatton, commonly known as "Anne
of Swanfea," who had been on the ftage, had always been
on bad terms with her fifter Mrs. Siddons, and had written
againft her : her unfupported teftimony was therefore far
from reliable.

After a time Campbell came back to me with a diſtinct offer that he and I ſhould compoſe the biography in concert. I, rather reluctantly, at firſt conſented ; and aſking what remuneration I was to have, Campbell ſaid that, before he anſwered, he wiſhed me to ſee what he had already done. I accordingly went to his lodgings in Duke Street, St. James's, and there found a vaſt maſs, or rather vaſt maſſes, of unarranged materials, partly in Campbell's own formal handwriting, and partly ſcribbled by others, but all confuſed and undigeſted—not even ſorted into years or ſubjects. I ſaw therefore very plainly that, if I agreed to join Campbell, I ſhould have all the work to do ; and when I put a queſtion again to him about payment, he heſitated, and at laſt named £100. I at once civilly declined, obſerving that, even ſuppoſing he worked as hard as I did, he would obtain three-quarters of the whole ſum offered by the publiſher, while I was required to be ſatiſfied with one-fourth. The matter was thus broken off; but without any ill-will on either part, for I afterwards ſaw Campbell ſeveral times during the progreſs of his undertaking, and never refuſed to give him hints as he proceeded. I did not, however, feel myſelf at all bound to ſupply him with my materials, among which was the following intereſting letter from Mrs. Siddons to ſome near and confidential friend, relating to her performance of Belvidera on the 31ſt October, 1805.

" 1 Nov. 1805.

"To ſpeak ſincerely, and as it were to myſelf, making my own confeſſion, I never played more to my own ſatisfaction than laſt night in Belvidera : if I may ſo ſay, it was hardly acting, it ſeemed to me, and I believe to the audience, almoſt reality; and I can aſſure you that, in one of my ſcenes with my brother John, who was the Jaffier of the night (a part by the way of which he is not very fond), the real tears 'coursed one another down my innocent nose' so abundantly, that my handkerchief was quite wet with them when I got off the stage.

"I do not like to play Belvidera to John's Jaffier so well as I shall when Charles has the part: John is too cold—too formal, and does not seem to put himself into the character: his sensibilities are not as acute as they ought to be for the part of a lover: Charles, in other characters far inferior to John, will play better in Jaffier—I mean to my liking. We have rehearsed it.

"The Pierre was a Mr. Snow (a banker's nephew), whose stage-name is Hargrave: he is a sort of professional amateur, with a good figure, and may do better hereafter; but at present he is hard and dry: the wheels of his passion want oiling, and his voice is harsh; though that is not of so much consequence in Pierre. He wants to play Othello, but I fear it will not do: he would be more fit for Iago with a little practice.

"To return to myself, I never was more applauded in Belvidera certainly; though, of course, as a piece of mere acting, it is not at all equal to my 'Lady.' Belvidera, I assure you again, was hardly acting last night: I felt every word as if I were the real person, and not the representative. Excuse all this about

' Yours most affectionately,
"S. Siddons."

C. Kemble played Jaffier firſt on November 7th, 1805.

T. Campbell had told me that the letters of Mrs. Siddons were generally very inſipid and worthleſs, but the above, at leaſt, does not deſerve that character. Hargrave had come from Dublin under that name, but met with little ſucceſs, having played Henry VI to Cooke's Richard III, Banquo to Kemble's Macbeth, Dumont in *Jane Shore*, etc.; but after his Pierre, I am not aware that he was ever again heard of in London. Winſton gave me the copy of the preceding letter, obſerving that Campbell had fo pooh-poohed his information that he had withheld it and others. As I have faid elfewhere, Winfton is the fon of an old actor, has trodden the boards himfelf in his youth, and is now Secretary to the Garrick Club: he knew all the Kembles.

Jan. 8.—I have juft been lucky enough to obtain another very rare old play for the dramatic library at Devonfhire Houfe. The exiftence of it has been long known; but as there are probably not more than three copies of it extant, comparatively little has been faid about it. I quote here, with the utmoft accuracy, the old title-page: the body of the piece is (like the "Grifelda" which I purchafed a fhort time ago) in the black-letter, which fo long continued more popular than the Roman type, that ballads, etc., were printed in it after the Reftoration, and almoft down to the reign of Anne. The old rare drama is called— "A moft pleafant and merie new Comedie, intituled a *Knacke to Knowe a Knave.* Newlie fet foorth, as it hath fundrie tymes bene played by Ed. Allen and his Companie. With Kemps applauded Merrimentes of the men of Gote- ham, in receiving the King into Gotcham.—Imprinted at London by Richard Jones etc. 1594."

Alleyn here mentioned was the founder of Dulwich College, and Kemp was afterwards a famous actor in Shakefpeare's plays. It may be concluded that the comedy was older than the period when our great dramatift began to write for the ftage, and it was performed by Henflowe's Com- pany at the Rofe Theatre in June 1592, two or three years, therefore, before the Globe was built on the Bank- fide. I did not hefitate to give £15 for it, and, as I have already ftated, the Duke is always fatisfied, and leaves price entirely to my difcretion. "A Knack to know a Knave" is the more curious, becaufe it is one of the tranfition-performances of the reign of Elizabeth, forming a late, but clear link between Morality, as it exifted even as early as the reign of Henry VI, and Hiftory and Comedy, as we find them from the hands of Shakefpeare and his contemporaries. The main plot relates to King Edgar, Elfrida, and Bifhop Dunfton ; and what are called on the title-page "Kemp's applauded Merriments" are fcenes of mere clownage and low buffoonery. The Duke has given me leave to reprint any of his plays, and if I ever do fo, this will be one of the firft I fhall felect. It contains a good deal illuftrative of the manners of the times : take, for example, what a fenfible old Farmer fays to the complaints of a poor out-at-elbows Knight :—

> " Truly, sir, I am sorry you are fallen into decay,
> In that you want to maintain household charge ;
> And whereof comes this want ? I will tell you, sir :
> 'Tis only through your great housekeeping.
> Be ruled by me, and do as I advise you :
> You must learn to leave your great train of men,
> And keep no more than needs of force you must ;
> And those you keep, let them be simple men,
> For they will be content with simple fare.
> Keep but a boy or two within your house,
> To run of errands, and to wait on you ;
> And for your kitchen, keep a woman cook,
> One that will serve for thirty shillings a year ;
> And by that means you save two liveries." Etc.

The verfification here is irregular, as, indeed, it ought fometimes to be ; but now and then it is fo good as clearly to have been the work of no common poet, though we nowhere have the flighteft hint by whom the comedy was written. The comic portions are, of course, in mere profe, as well as fome of the fpeeches of inferior characters.

Jan. 10.—Since the appearance of the flavering Life of Byron, by T. Moore, for which he received from Murray nearly £5000, I have amufed myfelf by writing "Arguments", or introductory ftanzas, to the sixteen cantos of "Don Juan": I copy them here as not, I think, bad fpecimens of that half ferious and half jocofe kind of compofition to which "Don Juan" belongs. Let me note, in the beginning, that A. de Anguillara was the author of the "arguments" to Ariofto's *Orlando Furiofo;* that Dominichi had performed the fame office for Boiardo's *Orlando Innamorato;* that Orazio Ariofto contributed the arguments to Taffo's *Gerufalemme Liberata;* that the Abbate Berifono did the fame for Taffoni's *Secchia Rapita;* that Antonio Malatefta wrote the arguments to Lippi's *Malmantile Racquiftata;* Sanvitale those to Marino's *Adone;* and, finally, Petrofellini thofe to Fortiguerra's *Ricciardetto.* Who may have performed a fimilar office for any, if any, of our Englifh poets, I do not recollect; but the following are my preliminary octave ftanzas to Byron's "Don Juan"—claiming indulgence, in the fecond, for a falfe quantity, rendered neceffary by the rhyme: my fixteen ftanzas contain, in brief, the whole fubject and progrefs of the uncompleted ftory.

CANTO I. Juan's birth, parentage, and education :
His mother is defcrib'd, as well as father.
His earlieft crime, and beauty's firft temptation :

Fair Julia's fall and frailty; who had rather
Too old a husband for her : his vexation,
    And shrewd suspicion, which ere long went farther.
Juan found out, the mystery unravels :
His mother sends him off upon his travels.

II.   Juan, to please his mother, not the ladies,
        Embarks for Leghorn.   After going through
Gibraltar's Straits (he had set out from Cadiz),
        A storm makes havoc of his ship and crew.
Juan is cast on one of the Cyclādes,
        Having been well nigh drown'd, and famish'd too,
And there is succour'd by a Grecian lady,
Whom some may call Haydĕe, and others Haydĕ.

III.   Lambro, the father of the lovely Greek,
        A sea-attorney, that's to say, a pirate,
Reported kill'd, returns his home to seek,
        And finds his people feasting at a high rate.
Juan with Haydĕ had spent many a week
        In love's delight : her father don't admire it;
But, undiscover'd, marks what he is sorry at,
And listens to the song of Juan's laureat.

IV.   Lambro surprises Juan and his daughter
        Asleep together, when they least expected.
She saves her lover from her father's slaughter,
        Then bursts an artery, and dies dejected :
After, Don Juan is sent off by water,
        With other slaves the pirate had collected
For Turkish marts : poor Juan has a bad head.
A short description of the slaves is added.

V.   At the Sublime Port Juan soon is sold,
        With a new friend (who afterwards is parted
From him): they're led, through windings manifold,
        To a great palace, and so rich, they started

The splendour of the chambers to behold.
  Juan, in female dress, and heavy-hearted,
Is introduc'd to the Sultana's highness,
Whom he offends by showing too much shyness.

VI.   The Sultan's presence disappoints the scheme
        Which his Sultana would have fain concerted. ·
      Juan retires among the maids, who deem
        Him a maid too, or with him might have flirted :
      He sleeps with fair Dudu, who had a dream
        About a bee and apple, she asserted.
      Gullayaz, when inform'd, is on the rack,
      And threatens both the parties with the sack.

VII. Great works are undertaken, for the capture
        Of Ismael, under the renown'd Suwarrow ;
      And, toward the brief conclusion of the chapter,
        Juan and Johnson join ; who, without sorrow,
      Or, I should say, with military rapture,
        Agree to lead the hope forlorn to-morrow.
      Two ladies and a eunuch from the harem
      Are with them, but the martial tidings scare 'em.

VIII. Juan and Johnson are among the first
        To mount the breach, despite the Turkish foemen ;
      And Juan saves from Cossacks' greedy thirst
        A female child, found 'mid the slaughter'd women.
      Into the city's heart the Russians burst,
        Destroying all *sans* pity ; leaving no men,
      Or very few alive, for blood their trade is ;
      But treat with great forbearance all the ladies.

IX.   Juan is chosen to convey dispatches
        To Catherine of the taking of the place ;
      Is introduc'd, and pleases so, that matches
        Might well be lighted at the Empress' face :

Her character is given by hints and snatches,
  Not in detail, though not for want of space.
She sought our hero's love, and Juan gave her it,
And supersedes at once the reigning favourite.

X.   After residing in the Russian capital
        Some time, poor Juan's taken ill ; indeed,
      So ill, he cannot eat, and scarce can lap at all.
        For health to England order'd to proceed,
      He leaves his vacant office to the happy tall
        Who filled it ere he came ; and then with speed
      Travels with little Leila (such the name
      Of her he sav'd) till he to England came.

XI.   Juan, employ'd on mission from the Court
        Of Russia, is assail'd, descending Shooter's
      Hill, by some pads who make it their resort:
        He kills with pistol one of the freebooters.
      In London his arrival makes some sport
        Among the West-end ladies, who are suitors
      To gain the favours of the handsome stranger,
      Maids, wives, and widows, sharing in the danger.

XII.   A short debate ; wherein the author mixes
        Some novel thoughts on female reputation,
      Which, as it well might do, long time perplexes
        Don Juan in this highly moral nation.
      On Lady Pinchbeck's care at last he fixes,
        To keep strict watch o'er Leila's education.
      Our hero's notions upon English beauty,
      And manners, offer something that is new t' ye.

XIII.   The Lady Adeline Amundeville,
        In this and other places, we hear much of ;
      And of her husband's, the Lord Henry's, skill
        In politics we also have a touch of.

Descriptions of their Norman abbey fill
　　Some pages ; and the author speaks of such of
The guests as suit him.　Juan will to hunt try,
And relishes the pleasures of the country.

XIV.　More of Don Juan's hunting : after that
　　　　We find a duchess looks on him with favour,
Fitz-fulke her name, full-blown and rather fat :
　　　　Her former lover sighs like any pavior.
The Lady Adeline sees what she's at,
　　　　And does not much approve of her behaviour,
As for the sake of Juan's morals merely ;
But this point does not seem establish'd clearly.

XV.　The Lady Adeline, in her great care
　　　　For Juan's morals, recommends a marriage,
And points out several ladies who are there,
　　　　All of most unexceptionable carriage.
Aurora Raby Juan hints is fair,
　　　　And her alone the lady's words disparage.
Juan sits next Aurora fair at dinner,
And says soft things that are design'd to win her.

XVI.　Don Juan sees the ghost of the black friar,
　　　　And what to make of it he can't divine.
The Lady Adeline, to harp or lyre,
　　　　(Harp suits the fact, and lyre suits the line)
Sings of him in a ballad.　Knight and squire,
　　　　On public day, with the Lord Henry dine.
Juan sees it again at night, and clutches
To catch the ghost, but catches the fat duchess.

Jan. 11.—My birthday, which, in confequence of my
wife's fuffering, was paffed over very quietly.　I add the
following, which I wrote at night, when in a refleƈtive or
refleƈting mood : I entitled it

HEAVEN'S JUSTICE.

The will of God forbear to blame,
Though cares o'ercast thy scene :
The face of Heaven is still the same,
Though clouds may come between—
Clouds, that only have their birth
In the dull atmosphere of earth.

Jan. 13.—"Which (said the Duke to me yesterday, as he seated himself just opposite at my writing-table) is the oldest play in our language?" I answered, that it was impossible, in the present state of information, to decide, as there were several collections of manuscript religious dramas, performed in very early times, on the comparative antiquity of which nobody can speak with even tolerable accuracy.

"I do not mean (he added) manuscript, but printed plays. Tell me which is the oldest printed play known in our language ?"

C. The oldest known printed play is, I apprehend, a dramatic piece which came from the press of Wynkin de Word ; as you know, our second earliest printer, not to mention Lettou and Machlinia. Wynkin de Word was, as it were, apprentice, or assistant, to Caxton, our first printer; and, about 1493, after the death of his master, worked upon his own account, and, among other books, put forth *our earliest printed play.*

D. At what date, and what is its name ? You will smile at my ignorance, after reading your book on the history of our drama and stage ; but I do not readily and steadily carry dates in my head.

That (said I) is the best part of my memory : I have a

good head for dates, but not fo good a head for remembering the precife order and fucceffion of words. The name of the play (fo to call it, for it is properly what was then termed a "morality" or "moral play") is "Hick Scorner"; which feems to have enjoyed fuch great popularity, that "Hick Scorner's Jefts" became a proverbial expreffion, in ufe, perhaps, long after the origin of it had been quite forgotten.

D. Well, the earlieft printed play being "Hick Scorner", what is its date?

C. I ought firft to fay, that it is not quite certain that the earlieft printed play was "Hick Scorner"; becaufe, I underftand, there has recently been difcovered in Holland a flyleaf of a book, apparently printed by Caxton (fo, at leaft, I am told), which is the fragment of a "moral play", where the allegorical reprefentations of Charity, Temperance, Juftice, Hope, and Prudence, are engaged in converfation. If this be fo, it is important, and may deprive Wynkin de Word of the claim of being the firft printer of a play in Englifh. The type of the fly-leaf, I am farther informed, is certainly Englifh ; but I have not feen it.

D. I fuppofe that there is no date to that fly-leaf.

C. Certainly not ; nor is there any precife date to "Hick Scorner": it came from the prefs of Wynkin de Word without any ; but, as he put forth no work after 1535, and began printing on his own account in 1493, it muft have been iffued in fome intermediate year.

D. Have I "Hick Scorner" in my collection?

C. Yes, in one or more reprint ; but there is only a fingle copy of that piece extant, as it came from the hands of Wynkin de Word ; and that is in the Garrick Collection, now in the Britifh Mufeum.

D. I am not worthy of my own collection, I am forry to fay ; and I want you, as far as you can, to make me more worthy of it by informing my ignorance.

C. Still, it is not clear that you are not the poffeffor of the earlieft printed play in our language. Suppofing "Hick Scorner" to have been publifhed in, or fhortly before 1535 (and Wynkin de Word made his will, and probably died at the very close of 1534), you have in your cafes a play, which I bought for you at a great price, dated 1533; and that *poffibly* may be older, as regards the year of publication, than "Hick Scorner."

D. Indeed! I am glad to hear it. When did you buy it, and what is the name of it ?

C. I purchafed it only a month or two after you gave me licenfe to buy, at what I thought reafonable, any play deficient in your dramatic collection : the title of it is, "A Merry Play between the Pardoner, and the Friar, the Curate and Neighbour Pratt." It was printed by William Raftell in 1533 : he began printing in 1531, and ceafed to print, I think, in 1535.

D. And who was the author of it ?

C. A very celebrated man, a poet and a musician, retained in the houfehold of Henry VIII ; who, as you are aware, died thirteen years after the date of John Heywood's play, for Heywood was the writer of the production.

D. Did he write any other dramas ?

C. Yes, five or fix ; all with odd titles, and different from any other dramatic performances that went before them or came after them : he was an original genius, to whom juftice has never yet been done. In my book I dwell upon his undoubted merits.

D. That I can refer to, and I am efpecially rejoiced that you procured me that original fpecimen of his abilities. I fuppofe that you give fome account of the particular play the title of which you have mentioned?

C. I do—And here is the piece itfelf; but it looks uncouth in the old and fomewhat rude black letter. After a very little praćtice, you would be able to read it pretty fluently; but ftill the old fpelling might make you fmile occafionally.

[Here our converfation was interrupted by the entrance of a fervant with a letter for the Duke, which he read, threw into the fire, and ordered his carriage to be ready in half an hour.]

D. I wifh I had time to continue our converfation, but we can revive the fubjećt another day; for I want you to give me information, not only about our old dramas, but about our old aćtors.

C. We have very little information about our old aćtors, until nearly the time of Shakefpeare; when our plays affumed a more regular form, and were divided into aćts and fcenes, which was not ufually the cafe until after Queen Elizabeth came to the throne. Hiftorical plays, and plays femi-hiftorical, formed partly out of real events and partly out of invented allegorical materials, came up next to the "interludes", as they were commonly called, of John Heywood; and our earlieft attempt at a hiftorical drama was made by Bifhop Bale, one of whofe remarkable performances, in his original manufcript, I had the good fortune to add to the Collećtion foon after I obtained my firft introdućtion to your dramatic library.

D. Which was that?

C. A drama, partly founded on hiſtory and partly allegorical invention, on the reign of King John. Bale was at
one time Biſhop of Oſſory, and, early in life, wiſhing to
forward the Reformation in a popular way, he wrote this
play, in order to bring odium on the Roman Catholics for
their treatment of King John by Stephen Langton and
Cardinal Pandulph, the performance being concluded by
the poiſoning of the ſovereign by a monk. It is a moſt remarkable piece in connexion with the hiſtory and progreſs
of our drama ; for it is neither pure hiſtory nor mere allegory, but both at once; and I know of no other ſo ancient
ſpecimen of the kind.

D. I muſt now go out; but we will renew the ſubject
either to-morrow or ſome early day, when you are here and
I am diſengaged. I conſider this as my firſt leſſon, bringing
me acquainted with my own ſtores of information : I ſhall
afterwards better know how to value them.

So ſaying, wiſhing me good morning, the Duke left the
room, giving charge to the ſervant not to forget my bread
and wine, which, when at home at luncheon time, he invariably brings himſelf.

Jan. 16.—Being at the Garrick Club, I aſked the Rev.
R. Barham whether the Barham of Telſon, mentioned in a
bond I had met with among the old papers belonging to Lord
F. L. Gower, were any relation or anceſtor of his? He anſwered that he knew that a branch of his family had been
ſettled in Kent; but I inſert a copy of it here mainly becauſe
it is the only document I have found ſigned by Dr. Donne,
then a young man, and acting as ſecretary to Sir Thomas
Egerton, Keeper of the Great Seal to Queen Elizabeth,

and afterwards Lord Chancellor to James I. It is indorfed by the Lord Keeper, "The bonde for Mary Barham's apparance", followed by the words,

"Sealed and delivered, to the use of the Queenes Majestie, in the presence of

"J. DONNE.
"JOHN PHILLIPS."

The bond was given by Thomas Antrobus, of Lincoln's Inn, and Thomas Barham, of Telfon, Kent. After omitting the Latin formal introduction to the inftrument, it proceeds as follows, in equally formal Englifh :

"The condition of this obligation is such, that if Marie Barham, daughter of the above-named Thomas Barham, shall personally appear before the L. Chancelor, or the L. Keeper of the Great Seale for that tyme beinge, within eight daies next after warning in that behalf given, at the now dwelling house of the said Thomas Barham, in Scroop Court, in Holbourne, by writing subscribed with the hand of the said L. Chancelor or L. Keeper ; and shall not, before such apparance, marry or contract her self with any person, or doe any other acte wherby she may be disabled to perform such sentence as is given against her in the Court of the Arches, that this present obligation shalbe voyde and of none effect, or els to stand and be in full force and virtue."

Donne was at this date [1599] intending to ftudy the law ; but he publifhed fome poems in 1611, entered into holy orders in 1614, and became Dean of St. Paul's in 1620. His wife had died in 1617 ; and in the regifter of St. Leonard's, Shoreditch, under the date of May 11th, 1619, there is an entry of a marriage between John Donne and Dorothy Gale: this may have been, and probably was, a different man ; though a Mr. Gale, a folicitor whom I knew many years ago, claimed, he did not pretend to know how, to have been related to the old Dean of St. Paul's.

Jan. 17.—In looking for one quotation to-day, I found another, which I have been long in fearch of, and which, I am almoft afhamed to fay, I could not find, though by fo popular an author as Pope : had he been lefs popular, I might poffibly have found it more readily.

I can remember Whitbread, and his fomewhat drayman-like appearance, as well as I can recollect any public man of about twenty years ago : he was not tall, but rather ftout, and with a fort of Cromwellian rednefs of face. He was haughty in his manner, and required to be treated deferentially, even by his fuperiors : he was evidently mortified that he did, not belong to the ariftocracy, like the Greys, Grenvilles, and Hollands, of his party. Perry introduced me perfonally to him foon after the trial of 1810 ; but he was cold and referved, even to Perry, who, I fancied, was always difpofed to treat the leaders of the Whigs with fubfervient refpect. He never quite loft his retail manner, acquired in the draper's fhop at Aberdeen. Whitbread deftroyed himfelf from difappointed ambition ; and I feel fure that he never entirely got over the ridicule caft upon him by Perceval, when Prime Minifter, who, replying to him, and adverting to Whitbread's repeated failures in attempts to affail him, quoted Pope's couplet, likening him to a crawling fpider :

> " Deftroy his web of sophistry in vain,
> The *creature's* at his *dirty work* again."
>
> (*Epistle to Arbuthnot.*)

Here Perceval foftened the point a little, for the original is, " Deftroy his *fib or* fophiftry", being unwilling to render it more perfonally offenfive. This, I think, occurred in or about 1812, and Whitbread cut his throat in 1815 ; but in

the three years neither Whitbread nor his friends had forgotten the injury, and efpecially the word " creature." It
was inflicted rather late in the debate, and, though prefent, I do not bear in mind what either Whitbread or any
others said in reply : the effect on the Houfe was fudden
and wonderful. I do not mean to fay that Whitbread died
of Perceval's quotation, but I am fure it weighed upon his
mind, and among other things tended to derange it : the
verdict of the jury was temporary infanity. About 1813
and 1814, I ufed to fee Whitbread not very unfrequently,
becaufe he was chairman of a Committee, with the proceedings of which I had fomething to do : he always
treated me, as I thought, fomewhat as an inferior, and fo,
of courfe, I was in pofition. He was neverthelefs a warm-
hearted man to thofe whom he could ferve.

Perceval was never a good fpeech-maker in introducing
a fubject ; but he was a capital debater, and the excellence
of fome of his replies could not be difputed : here nobody,
in my opinion, was a match for him. When firft I recollect
him, I do not think he had even a filk gown, and practifed
at the Chancery bar. Lord Eldon was his friend.

Jan. 23.—Having fome leifure, in confequence of the
abfence from London of the perfon who generally engages
much of my attention, and often cheerfully occupies my time,
I have been trying my hand at familiar, or rather comic, verfification, fomething in the ftyle of a moft charming Italian,
and comparatively modern poet ; whom I am afraid to
name, not merely becaufe it may lead friends to expect a
better commodity than I can fupply, but becaufe his name
is not generally affociated with what, in this country, is

looked upon as ſtrictly decorous. There is, however, nothing objectionable in what follows on that ſcore ; and, as I have the opportunity, I go through the drudgery of copying here my own rough ſlips.

A Cure for the Toothache.

The Marquis of Ferrara had a jester,
    A monstrous clever fellow in his way,
Who us'd all courtiers there to jeer and pester,
    Because he had a privilege to say,
And do whate'er he pleas'd : a motley vesture
    Made him not only seem extremely gay,
But it distinguish'd him and his retort
From other fools, of a far different sort.

What is the reason that in former times,
    When courts and princes were the most despotic,
And punished by their own mere will all crimes,
    That they encouraged such a strange exotic ?
As, when we're making punch, we mingle limes
    By way of contrast to the sweet narcotic,
So in all states most absolute in power,
To relish sweets they also had their sour.

Thus, in the midst of falsehood, vice, and pride,
    Where men are all alike, and sing one tune,
The honest truth was suffer'd to abide
    But in the person of a mere buffoon ;
As if to show that all at Court should hide
    Those qualities, but fools.   That custom soon
Was banish'd, too, from courts ; and that's the reason
Virtue and truth are never there in season.

Jesters were then admitted to the table
    Of all the great and in their known capacity,
And not as now, disguised, as some are able,
    Like gentlemen of learning and sagacity ;

Small poets, too, who, give them line and cable,
　Run glibly on with vulgarest audacity,
Admitted but as rhymers, punsters, jokers,
To entertain the gourmands and the soakers.

One day at banquet, in a pleasant mood,
　The conversation turn'd on what profession
Was largest in the State: the Marquis stood
　Out for the lawyers, who, at every Session,
Made so much noise and did so little good.
　Another noble spoke of the possession
Own'd by the Church within Ferrara's borders,
Which led so many to take holy orders.

A third upon the army's claim insisted,
　Contending it was most in point of number.
When 'twas Gonella's turn, who'd only listed
　In what is sometimes call'd a fox's slumber,
He said at once, as not to be resisted,
　"The Doctors most of all our land encumber:
You stare, and think I've gone beyond my tether ;
They're more than all the others put together."

"Impossible !" cried several, all at once;
　" Nonsense !" cried others ; "what can the fool mean?"
" I mean but what I say, and I'm a dunce
　If I don't prove it too, as shall be seen,
Or freely pay the forfeit of my sconce."—
　" Then be prepar'd to have it cut off clean,"
Observed the Marquis, " for we've only two
In all our city, and not one too few."—

"I mean by Doctors," said the Fool at ease,
　"All sorts who will prescribe for the afflicted :
Quacks you may call a number, if you please,
　But by good manners I must be restricted.

I call those Doctors, who can cure disease,
　Or boast they can, but often make the sick dead.
They're thousands, as I'll prove at any hazard,
And bet against that golden cup my mazzard."

"That is no wager," said a Courtier near,
　"Your head is of no value were it sold,
While that large cup has cost the Marquis dear:
　There's no resemblance 'twixt your head and gold."—
"Now," said Gonella, drinking off the cheer
　The cup contained, "to say I may be bold,
Your head and it are very near allied,
For both are empty—are you satisfied?"—

"Now for your proof, your proof!" exclaimed each guest;
　"The trial only the bold bet secures."
"Proofs" (said Gonella) "are not like a jest,
　Ex-tempore—my Lord, I don't mean yours.
Give me three days—'tis all that I request
　To bring you a long list of names and cures."
The time was granted; and 'twas fixed to meet
　At three days' end, to witness his defeat.

Next morn the citizens beheld Gonella
　At the Cathedral Gate, his head upbound
In rags and flannels: for a witty fellow
　All the town knew him, for he was renown'd
Through Italy: his dress of red and yellow
　He wore, and still his head his coxcomb crown'd.
He took his seat just where all ranks must pass
To hear the celebration of High Mass.

He sway'd his body slowly to and fro,
　As if in utmost pain, and held his jaws,
Groaning aloud to let the people know
　How much he felt, that they might ask the cause.

All marvell'd greatly to behold him so,
　And fail'd not on their road to make a pause
To ask in pity what his bound up jaw meant,
　And what occasion'd him such cruel torment?

" This cursed, cursed tooth !" was all he said
　Time after time to every kind inquiry :
They thought as much, believing in his head
　He really had a pain acute and fiery.
Some author says " a raging tooth, instead
　Of pity, gains but ridicule"—a liar ! he
Never in all his lifetime could have felt it,
Or, if he'd had a heart, 'twould almost melt it.

The Fool found all compassionate, be sure:
　At least the passengers declar'd their pity
That he should such a horrid pain endure;
　And most of those who came out of the city
Prescribed a different, tho' a certain, cure.
　Male, female, old and young, the plain and pretty,
All named the remedies which they expected,
Or rather knew, would ease the part affected.

The rogue, pretending pain, was well enough
　Of many names to make a memorandum,
As well as of the sorts of doctor's stuff
　He was to use—when he could understand 'em.
Of course he took them only in the rough,
　Intending, when he'd copied them, to hand 'em
Up to the Marquis, when at table seated :
But yet Gonella's list was not completed.

He had indeed of names at least two hundred
　Of doctors who could cure, as they profess'd,
The pain he felt, altho' perhaps he blunder'd
　In setting down the med'cine that was best.

At his success himself he almost wonder'd;
  But as he meant to make a final test,
He went from the Cathedral to the Court,
To swell his list, and thus increase the sport.

It soon was thought that he was in a state
  Which render'd it impossible to win,
And many griev'd at his unlucky fate
  On seeing how he'd swath'd his jaws and chin:
Not that they fear'd his Lord would meditate
  The forfeit of the pledge the fool put in,
But that they wanted him to gain the suit,
And pitied him the pain he felt, to boot.

Doubly desirous therefore to remove
  His suffering, which of course must have prevented
His having time the point in doubt to prove,
  Many prescribed, and not a few presented
Their remedies; or undertook to move
  The Marquis, who most willingly consented,
To grant a further day, and put his hand to it:
Gonella still refused, and vow'd he'd stand to it.

The Marquis even, who from early youth
  Had suffered toothache, furnish'd his receipt
To cure his pitied jester's raging tooth.
  Gonella now believ'd his list complete,
And writing it out fair, soon made the truth
  Apparent, and secured his Lord's defeat. ·
The Marquis' name stood first, and in degrees
Follow'd the rest—all Doctors without fees.

To the surprise of all at the fix'd hour
  Gonella with his proof was quite prepar'd:
The Courtiers laughed, until they lost all power
  To read their own names; and the Marquis star'd

To read his title first. A golden shower
  Became ere long the witty fool's reward,
Besides the cup, for proof as true as humorous,
That Doctors (alias quacks) were far most numerous.

Jan. 26.—Kenney reminded me, by a note, that I have
ftill in my hands his MS. of his " Sicilian Vefpers", and
that I undertook to give him my opinion, whether it was
or was not likely to fucceed on the ftage. I am forry to
fay that, in my opinion, in its prefent ftate it will not do,
and fo I muft tell him, however unwillingly: there is
hardly incident enough, and fome of the fpeeches, *à la
mode Françaife* (it is, in the main, a tranflation from the
French) are too long, and want force and vigour. Kenney
can write a comedy or farce, but he is not equal to tragedy
—who is ?—befides, in these days, our audiences do not
like tragedies—experimental tragedies, leaft of all. Even
ferious dramas, though good, are only tolerated. Kenney's
blank verfe is not amifs; it is fmooth and flowing—too
fmooth and flowing: it wants variety and backbone: the
hero and heroine are good parts for good performers, but
the reft are fo fo. I am afraid he will be disappointed
by my verdict; but it is my verdict—the ftrict truth, and
my honeft judgment. I believe that it is in accordance with
the opinion of C. Kemble; but I would not give much for
his decision on a literary queftion, though it is worth fomething as regards ftage-management, and what would be
acceptable to the public.

I do not think that anything depends upon it, as the piece
has been refufed, and a publifher will feldom give money for
a play until it has been acted. The only modern inftance
to the contrary, that I remember, was in the case of Fanny

E

Kemble's play, which, even if not acted, would have been
sure of a certain sale. I hear that Murray advanced £200
upon it. I must write Kenney a kind note, and let him
down as easily as I can ; but I cannot say that his "Sicilian
Vespers" would have any chance of prosperity : he has one
or two good similes, but they stop the progress, and do not
illustrate character. If action be everything in oratory, it
is more than everything in a play at one of our great
theatres, where all is seen and little heard. It is almost a
fault in a drama now, that it reads well in a sitting-
room. I read all the main scenes again last night, in order
to be sure that I am not doing injustice to a very clever,
and far from a rich man. I remember that, among Larpent's MSS., I have a play on the story of the "Sicilian Vespers", by Mrs. Hemans. I doubt if it were ever offered to
either theatre ; yet, then, how came it into Larpent's hands?

Jan. 29.—We had another conversation to-day about
our early stage and our old actors ; and it began by my
informing the Duke (who again called himself my pupil), in a
very general way, that our most ancient plays were nothing
more than representations of scenes and incidents in
Scripture History : afterwards, for variety's sake, and for
the amusement of auditors and spectators, buffoonery was
introduced, generally in connection with the Vice or Clown,
and the Devil, who was always made a butt and a laugh-
ing-stock. To these scriptural dramas succeeded what were
called morals, or moralities, in which vices and virtues were
personified, sometimes in relation to real or supposed human
beings ; as in "Hick Scorner", who figures in the same
scenes with Free-will, Contemplation, Pity, Imagination,

etc. Another piece of precifely the fame clafs was called "Lufty Juventus", a hero expofed to all the temptations that affail youth and vanity : it was written and printed in the reign of Edward VI, and is one of our earlieft ftage productions of a purely proteftant tendency. Comedy of a more regular conftruction came next, under the titles of "Ralph Roifter Doifter" and "Gammer Gurton's Needle", the firft relating to life in London, and the fecond to life in the country, acted, I think, before Queen Elizabeth came to the throne. John Heywood's humorous farces in the reign of Henry VIII, I had noticed already, as well as Bale's attempt at a hiftorical drama depending upon incidents in the time of King John : it was, in fact, a hiftorical tragedy, but with the introduction of matter belonging to the period of the prevalence of moralities.

The Duke liftened very attentively to this fomewhat tedious detail, only interpofing a queftion now and then regarding a date or a name, and afking whether fuch-and-fuch a play were in his collection ? I was obliged often to difappoint him, becaufe J. P. Kemble, from whom he obtained the bulk of the volumes, had not begun to make his affemblage until after Garrick, Steevens, and Malone had fecured nearly all the rareft and moft valuable productions. I confoled him, however, by telling him, that he was the owner of a complete fet of the firft editions of the works of Shakefpeare, including now the original "Hamlet" of 1603, and "The Merry Wives of Windfor" of 1602. Thefe two, I believed, exifted only in his library.

"Now", faid the Duke, "you have given me fome general notion of the character of the performances, I want you to fupply me with a little information regarding the actors in them. I find, from your book, I think, that it then often happened (though feldom feen in our day) that the writers of plays were ufually alfo actors in them : fuch was the cafe with Shakefpeare, Ben Jonfon, and feveral more."

We do not know (I interpofed) of any play in which Jonfon acted : he probably grew too fat, early in his career, for many parts, but he certainly began as an actor.

D. It would have been a great treat to have feen the jolly old fellow in fuch a character as Falftaff : he might have taken that part, if no other, and, like Stephen Kemble, perhaps without ftuffing.

C. He might, but he did not, as far as we are informed ; and, in fpite of Gifford's vindication of him, it is certain that he was a little envious of the fuccefs of rivals in his art : he fell foul of a fuccefsful playwright named Anthony Munday, becaufe a contemporary critic had called him "the beft plotter" of the day, meaning that he laid out the fcheme and ftory of a play with more fkill than others. Munday was part-author of two excellent and moft rare plays, which I am glad to fay are in your cafes, on the ftory of Robin Hood. Jonfon wrote againft him on account of his fuccefs, and crammed a fcene into the "Cafe is Altered" for no other purpofe but to ridicule Munday.

D. Yet Shakefpeare, we know, acted in Ben Jonfon's "Scjanus", and probably in other plays. He is, I think, fuppofed to have had fomething to do with the composition of that Roman play in its original fhape.

C. And yet how different, in all refpects, is the character and conftruction of "Sejanus" to any one of the three Roman plays of Shakefpeare. However, if you pleafe, we will not now enter upon that queftion, but confine ourfelves to the actors in dramas of that time, and fomewhat earlier. Even in the reign of Henry VIII, fome of the authors of dramatic productions were actors in them: we know that John Heywood was; and that he was the inftructor of a company of boys, who took minor characters, while their mafter had the leading part. The fame, I apprehend, was the cafe with Mulcafter (a fchoolmafter), if not with Hunnis (a religious poet), who both, during the reign of Elizabeth, were at the head of the boys of the Chapel, or the boys of the Revels, and poffibly of other juvenile affociations who used to exhibit at Court.

D. But in the time of Shakefpeare was it not common for authors of plays to be themfelves performers in them? Shakefpeare, we are told, played the Ghoft in his own " Hamlet", and Adam in " As You Like It."

C. I have no doubt that he acted alfo in other, and perhaps fmaller parts; but when we recollect that he wrote at leaft fix-and-thirty plays, and that he was not much above twenty years connected with the ftage, it is to me wonderful that he had any time at all for acting. His memory and his rapidity of compofition muft have been aftonifhing; for if a dramatift of our day produce a good five-act play once in every two years, we are furprifed at the fecundity of his mufe.

D. Befides, if I underftand rightly, Shakefpeare mended at leaft as many plays as he wrote; and, although he may have contributed a fcene, a fpeech, or only a few lines to them, the work muft have occupied time.

C. There was at that date what we may call a profligacy, a prodigality of poetry, efpecially of dramatic poetry; and Thomas Heywood (who muft not be confounded with

John Heywood, who wrote more than fifty years earlier) one of Shakefpeare's contemporaries, and a hired daily performer on the ftage, tells us himfelf that he had written, or helped in writing, no fewer than, I think, two hundred and forty dramas. He left not a few behind him, fuch as the fine hiftorical play of "Edward the Fourth", the comedy of "The Englifh Traveller", and, above all, the tragedy of "A Woman killed with Kindnefs", as true and pathetic a drama as was ever put upon the ftage : it is purely fimple and merely domeftic.

D. I hope I have thofe.

C. You have, and many more by him, perhaps, in fome refpects, equally good.

D. You muft look me out fome of them, efpecially the laft you mentioned.

C. That you can read in the reprint in Dodfley's Old Plays, of which I lent a hand to an edition fome feven or eight years ago. This will fave you from being offended by the rough paper, the old coarfe type, and the uncouth fpelling.

D. They are at firft forbidding, but I can eafily overcome thofe objections, if the black-letter be not ufed.

C. That, I believe, you would foon learn even to like, as I do, from mere habit, and from the pleafure I have derived from books and poems printed in it. Such a play as Heywood's "Edward the Fourth", you may fee in both ftates ; for the older editions (and there were at leaft four) are in black-letter, while the later ones are in Roman type. There is ftill a clafs of dramatic compofitions of that period of which we have faid nothing, but it is well worth notice —I mean *ex-tempore* plays.

" That" (faid the Duke) " we muſt referve for a future occaſion : for the prefent, I muſt unwillingly break off here."

Feb. 1.—Harnefs (the Rev. W.) called while I was out, and left a pretty little poem for me, which he has juſt privately printed. He is an agreeable talker, not by any means firſt rate, and a very good preacher, but ſtill not firſt rate : he was at College, I think, with Dyce, who introduced me to him a year or two ago, and we have been rather intimate ever ſince. He is, I hear, the ſon of a phyſician, who uſed to reſide in the Fulham Road. I have met " Fazio" Milman at his houſe, and they are faſt friends; they were both, I believe, at Harrow. Harnefs has a brother, a ſcientific ſoldier, and a ſiſter, who keeps his houſe for him ; ſhe is rather milk-and-watery, but kind and uſeful in the neighbourhood, and the brothers are juſtly fond of her. W. Harnefs is very modeſt as to his poetical claims; and his privately printed trifle is pretty, but the thought rather commonplace. As he has put it forward in a permanent ſhape, though only for his friends, there can be no reaſon why I ſhould not tranfcribe it here. At firſt it was without the two concluding ſtanzas, and ſo he printed it a year ago ; but he lately added them, and reprinted the whole, calling it

THE WISDOM OF AGE.

The April morn was bright and mild,
  And the sunbeams danc'd on the dewy moor,
As an aged man and little child
  Thus talk'd beside their cottage-door.

" Look, grandfather ! what joy ! what joy !
  'Twill be a fine sunshiny day ;
In cowslip-fields," exclaimed the boy,
  " I'll pass the happy hours away."

"'Twill rain ere noon," the old man replied ;
  " And when you have liv'd as long as I,
You will know better than confide
  In this soft air and glowing sky."

" Oh !" cried the boy, " if this is all
  We gain by growing gray like you—
To learn that showers at noon will fall,
  While yet the morning heavens arc blue,

" I'd rather know, as I do now,
  Nothing about the coming hours,
And while it's fair, with careless brow,
  Enjoy the sun and gather flowers."

" Ay, but, my boy, as we grow old,"
  Sigh'd that aged man, " we learn much more ;
Truths which in youth we're often told,
  But never feel as truths before ;

" That love is but a feverish dream ;
  That friendships die as soon as born ;
That pleasures which the young esteem
  Are only worthy of our scorn ;

" That what the world desires as good,
  Riches and power, rank and praise,
When sought, and won, and understood,
  But disappoint the hopes they raise ;

" That life is like this April day,
  A scene of fitful light and gloom ;
And that our only hope and stay
  Centre in realms beyond the tomb."

Thus wisely spoke that gray-hair'd man,
  But little fruit such wisdom yields ;
Off, while he talk'd, the urchin ran
  To gather cowslips in the fields.

And sure in nature's instinct sage,
  The child those withering lessons fled,
Conn'd from the worn and blotted page
  Of the world's book perversely read.

For soon he reach'd those fields so fair,
  Murmur'd his songs and wreath'd his flowers ;
While, laughing, 'neath the hawthorns there,
  He crouch'd for shelter from the showers.

This is pretty, but the laſt two ſtanzas are not wanted, and rather weaken the effeɕt of the reſt : they are like the "moreover" or "yet again" in ſome ſermons, when all that need be underſtood has been ſaid : it ſeems written in ſome ſort as an imitation of Wordſworth ; but he would not have uſed ſuch words as "confide", "eſteem", and "fitful", in a dialogue between the old peaſant and the boy.

Feb. 7.—I have been for ſeveral days moſt intereſtingly engaged at Devonſhire Houſe, in looking over two large boxes or caſes containing an aſſemblage of relics, either by Inigo Jones or relating immediately to him and his works. They belong to different dates in his career, from the earlier part of the reign of James I to the middle of the reign of Charles I, and they were accumulated by the Earl of Burlington, who, as is well known, was a great admirer of Inigo Jones, and of his ſtyle of architecture.

When examining the regiſters of St. Bartholomew-the-Leſs, in Smithfield, I found that Inigo Jones was born in 1573, and that his father was a "clothworker" in that pariſh. Thus, Inigo Jones was juſt a year younger than Ben Jonſon, whoſe maſques and court entertainments were

F

mainly got up, furnifhed, and decorated by Inigo. The
two boxes contain original fketches of the great artift
for this purpofe: the fmall defigns were to be worked out
on canvas of much larger dimenfions, and they are actually
in many inftances fplafhed by the diftemper ufed in various
colours. It would not be difficult to affign fome of them
to their original purpofe; and the freedom and rapidity of
the hand of Inigo is borne witnefs to by all thefe remains.
Not a few were architectural fketches and elevations; and,
among others, as well as I could make out, the original
defign for the water-gate to Buckingham Houfe, which ftill
exifts at the bottom of Buckingham Street, in the Strand.
I did not obferve any applicable to Inigo's great work, the
Banqueting Houfe in Whitehall.

It is impoffible for me to give a notion of the wealth of
this collection; but the Duke had the boxes brought from
Chifwick for my ufe; and when I entered the library on
Thurfday laft I was furprifed by the fight of them, for the
Duke had not led me to expect to fee them for fome weeks:
in fact, I do not think that he knew for certain where they
were depofited, whether at Chifwick or Chatfworth. They
were found in one of the lower rooms at the former, and I
do not think the boxes had been opened for many years:
the keys (which were laid on the table for my ufe) and the
locks were rufty.

If I am ever able to fuperintend a new edition of my
book, where I treat of the Court Entertainments, thefe
curious and authentic relics cannot fail to be of moft effen-
tial fervice.

Feb. 13.—Dr. Todd has favoured me with a tranfcript of

a remarkable MS. exifting, I believe, in the library of the Univerfity of Dublin. It is a miracle-play, intended to enforce the doctrine of the Sacrament and Real Prefence. It fuppofes five Jews to have furreptitioufly poffeffed themfelves of the Hoft, and to have expofed it to deftruction by fire, water, force, etc., without avail : it miraculoufly refifts all their efforts ; and, finally, being put into an oven, it burfts it, and the Saviour rifes from the flames, and at once overcomes all the doubts of the Jews, who are converted upon the fpot. It is not eafy to fix the earlieft date when it was reprefented ; but it certainly carries us back to the time of Wickliff and Lollardifm. It would have been of great ufe to me two or three years ago.

It was prefented, as we are told by the prologue-fpeakers (for there are two of them), at Croxton, A.D. 1461 ; and fo ignorant was the author on the fubject, that he reprefents the Jews as worfhippers of Mahomet, and the firft line of the firft fpeech is,

" Now, almighty Maehomet, marke in thy majesty," etc.

It is unufually long, but full of variety; and an attempt is made to give it lightnefs and vivacity by the introduction of a quack-doctor, who feems intended to be the Vice of the reprefentation : the name of Brundzele is given to him, and he has a fervant called Coll, who adds to the amufement by his praifes and treatment of his mafter. At the end is a list of the characters, thus tranflated :

> Jesus.
> A Bishop.
> Aristorius, a Merchant.
> A Clergyman.

Jonathan,
Jason,
Jasden,
Musphat,   } Jews.
Malchus,
Mr. Doctor.
Coll, his servant.

It is added that the fcenes are fo contrived that "four may play the peace with eafe." It is undoubtedly a great dramatic curiofity; but it comes, I am forry to fay, too late to be of ufe to me.

Feb. 15.—A tolerably bold undertaking for any man to write a fonnet in "imitation of Milton"; yet Dr. John Hoadly did fo in 1743. I have his original copy before me, figned and dated by him October 30th in that year. The title refers to the oratorio he had produced, which had been compofed by Dr. Greene.

"SONNET IN IMITATION OF MILTON.

" To Mrs. Bowes, with ' The Force of Truth', an Oratorio,
set to Musick by Dr. Greene.

" O Florimel, whose tuneful skill once gave
    To verse of mine such harmony and grace,
    With innocence of mind and voice and face,
Mixing my rill with the Castalian wave ;
Now that your virgin hand you given have
    To your Myrtillo in that holy place,
    Let artfull Fuges renew th' harmonious chace,
And Musick's every charm his heart inslave :
Of verse and harmony the Muses join'd
    Shall teach him (knowledge seen but of a few)
Great in his works the God of Truth to find,
    And praise that greatness greatly shewn in you :
There see the nobler temple of the mind,
And own *The Force of Truth* and *Beauty* too.
                    " J. HOADLY, Oct. 30, 1743."

Nothing can furely be more unlike Milton either in fenfe or found : Milton's ear could never have allowed fuch a bungling line as "Now that your virgin hand you given have"; and what but the want of a rhyme could have driven Hoadly to talk of the "harmonious chace." I have among my books his copy of Dodfley's Collection of Poems, where his own verfes are corrected by his own hand ; and a new ftanza in MS. is fubftituted for the printed one in his tranflation from Anacreon, "In the dead of the night," etc. : when a boy, I heard Mrs. Jordan fing it with a double *encore*. Hoadly's fubftituted ftanza is this :

> " In compassion I straight struck a light with all speed,
> Let him in ; and behold a child, little indeed,
> A mere chit, with a bow and with arrows equipp'd,
> On his shoulders had wings, and the rain from them dripp'd."

This was only making bad worfe, as may be feen on com-parifon. Hoadly alfo corrected there his poem called "Vaca-tion", but the changes, any more than the original, are not worth mentioning.

Feb. 16.—At Lambeth to-day, among the MSS., I met with the following interefting letter about Mary Queen of Scots, which has not, I think, been publifhed : it is dated June 15, 1570, and was written by his fteward, Knyveton, in London, to the Earl of Shrewsbury, at his houfe in the country.

> "There was great hope of some good conclusions betwixt the Queenes Majestie and the Queene of Scottes ; but the setting up of the bull upon the Bishop of London his gate, and the departing of the Lord Morley and such lyke, are hinderance thereunto. The Erle of Southampton was sent for to the Courte, and is now at Kingston under commandement, which is certenly thought to be, for that the

Bishop of Rosse and he were knowen to be in consultation very late in the night, and knowen by the watch coming over the water from Southwarke. Sir Thomas Cornwallis is not yet commytted to the Tower, for that he desyred a tyme of conference for the better [satisfaction] of his conscyence in relygion, and so remayneth under the kepinge of a scolemaister at Westminster."

Feb. 20.—Where I dined (at Dyce's) there was a good deal of pleafant converfation between Mitford, Harnefs, and young W. Dyce, on old poets and poetry, but nothing very new. Sandby was there alfo, and referred to the time when he and Dyce were curates together fomewhere in Cornwall, and when they, with the affiftance of a few others whom they did not name, got up private theatricals, Dyce having once taken the part of Othello, and Sandby that of Iago. Harnefs did not deny his fondnefs for the ftage; and we endeavoured to perfuade him to read us a fcene or two from his drama, yet far from finifhed, on a Flemifh ftory, the principal charaöters refiding at Antwerp. We could not prevail. The converfation then turned upon flcep, and the quantity it was neceffary for human beings to indulge in. I quoted Chaucer's "Shipman's Tale", where thefe lines occur:

> " Nece (qd. he) it ought ynough suffise
> Fyve hours for to slepen on a nyght,
> But it were for an olde palsed wyght,
> As ben these olde wedded men." Etc.

I expreffed my doubts whether the monk kept to his own rule; and Mitford reminded us of what is faid on the fubjeöt in "January and May": this led to the queftion whether, in the time of Chaucer, people ufually flept without night-clothes? The point was held doubtful, becaufe when May laid herfelf down by January, he had required her to get into bed and lie down by him *in puris naturali-bus*, as if it were not then ufual to do fo :

> " Who ftudieth nowe but faire freshe May,
> And adown by January she lay,
> That slept tyll the coughe hath him awaked." Etc.

The next line or two are not quotable in thefe days, but it is clear that, whether it were or were not ufual, the young lady did as fhe was defired. Harnefs adverted to a text in Exodus, which feems to make it clear that the Ifraelites flept with fome covering on their bodies besides the bed-clothes (ch. xxii, v. 26, 27).

> " If thou at all take thy neighbour's raiment to pledge, thou fhalt deliver it unto him by that the sun goeth down ; for that it is his covering only ; it is his raiment for his skin ; *wherein fhall he fleep ?*"

Hence another queftion arofe in reference to Chaucer ; viz., whether he was more grofs than his age ? and it was, I think, voted in the affirmative ; but I was difpofed, I now think wrongly, to exprefs an oppofite opinion.

Feb. 23.—I have lately met, in the State Paper Office, with the following very interesting notices of Ben Jonfon's comedy, " Every Man in his Humour": the firft fhows that it was extremely fuccefsful at Midfummer 1597, and is an extract of a letter from that recorder of town-goffip, John Chamberlain, to Sir Dudley Carlton, dated " London, this longeft day of June, 1597."

> " We have here a new play of *Humours* in very great request, and I was drawn alonge to it by the common applause ; but my opinion of it is (as the fellowe sayde of the shearing of hogges) that there was a great crie for so little wolle."

The next extract proves that the fame comedy continued attractive in the autumn of the next year: a letter from Tobie Mathew to Sir Dudley Carlton, dated " 20 Sept. 1598", mentions that " an Almaine had loft his purfe and 300 crownes at the theatre, the play being *Every Man's Humour."*

Why have we no fuch notices of any of the plays of Shakefpeare : moft of his productions muft have been more popular than thofe of Ben Jonfon, and yet no letter, that I am aware of, has yet turned up with the bare mention of any one of them. " Twelfth Night" is only fpoken of in an old extant diary ; and the performance of " Hamlet" on board fhip by the failors in 1607 or 1608 has been fimilarly recorded. We fee above that two writers of News-letters, without connection, fpeak of " Every Man in his Humour"; but the dramas of Shakefpeare, whether comedy, hiftory, or tragedy, are paffed over in utter filence, as far as has yet been difcovered.

Feb. 28.—" I dare fay you think me very frivolous, as well as verfatile, in my reading and purfuits" (faid the Duke to me yefterday) ; " but how can I avoid it, confidering the fort of life I am compelled by my pofition to lead ? You do not know how little time I really have to myfelf—how much vifiting I have to do, and how much I am vifited. Then, as to my reading ; going into fociety as I am obliged to do, I feel myfelf at a lofs if I have not feen fomething of the laft fafhionable book or novel that is come out : whereas, in your cafe, it fignifies little whether you have, or have not looked at a page, or even at the outfide of fuch a foolifh work. You are only put to a difficulty, if you have not feen fome work of real value, hiftory, fiction, voyage, or defcription ; when it really does not matter one ftraw, among moft of my acquaintances, whether I have feen it or not. I can hardly come to talk to you for half an hour without, as you know, being broken in upon by fome caller, whom I fhould be loth to fend away without fhowing him the civility that is due to him, and from me. I have been trying for feveral mornings to renew our conversations on old plays and players, but, time after time, I have been prevented."

"Let us hope for better luck now," I interpofed.—"I remember that I was about to fay a few words regarding fome performances on our old ftage, on which little has been written ; and for the beft of all reafons, becaufe very little is known—I mean *extempore* plays, of which the plot was fketched out and laid down beforehand, with fome fort of hint as to the characters, and that was all."

D. I remember reading—I think in Tirabofchi—of fuch productions on the Italian ftage ; and the peculiar readinefs at unpremeditated verfification by the Italians made it very poffible for them ; but I did not know that the thing had ever at any time been attempted in Englifh, and by Englifh performers.

C. In Malone's Shakefpeare by Bofwell, and indeed in my book, fpecimens of the kind are given, from which we may gather the general fcheme of fuch performances, and we know that they are alluded to by fome contemporary, as well as by later authorities. There was in early times—that is, before 1584 when he died—an actor of much celebrity, who was famous for his extempore fallies, and he feems to have been the firft, or one of the firft, who rifked the experiment : his name was Richard Tarlton, and he left behind him a plot, or platform, of "The Seven Deadly Sins", confifting partly of action, partly of dumb fhow, and partly, as we may conjecture, of unpremeditated dialogue.

D. That, you fay, was previous to 1584, or not very long before Shakefpeare came to London, according to the ordinary belief. In 1584, Shakefpeare muft have been about twenty.

C. Juft fo ; and how much Shakefpeare may have done, even in that way, we cannot at all determine : I do not know that it has even been fpeculated upon ; but we may be fure that his genius muft have produced fome of his dramas almoft without premeditation, when we know that he wrote and procured to be acted, between about the year 1592 and 1612—that is, in twenty years—no fewer than thirty-fix or thirty-feven tragedies, comedies, and hiftories, which would be at the rate of more than a play and a half a year, befides acting himfelf in many, both of his own works, and in thofe of other dramatifts.

D. He was moft wonderfully prolific, certainly; for, as I faid before, if a dramatift of our day produce one five-act drama in two, or even three years, it is quite as much as could be expected. I have heard that the authorfhip of "Paul Pry" coft Poole not lefs than three years' labour.

C. So ready, and fo rapid was Shakefpeare's pen, that we have it, on the authority of Ben Jonfon, that he rarely blotted a line : the fame contemporary laments that Shakefpeare had not blotted a thoufand ; but how bleft we ought to confider ourfelves, that Shakefpeare was not half fo book-learned, while he was twenty times as man-learned, as his rival : Shakefpeare well knew what was in man, while he knew comparatively little of what was in books. Yet, when he wanted information, as to hiftory or manners, we faw, not very long ago, how carefully he reforted to the beft authorities, fuch as Plutarch, and with what fkill he applied all he acquired from them. See what Ben Jonfon made of the ftory of " Sejanus" when left to himfelf ; for he is fuppofed to have cut out of the edition of 1605 what Shakefpeare poffibly contributed, who had acted in the tragedy.

D. But are we not wandering a little from the extemporaneous plays, the particular fubject of inquiry ?

C. True ; but, as you ftated the other day, befides his own thirty-fix or thirty-feven plays, it is known that, in the outfet of his career efpecially, he employed himfelf in altering, amending, and adding to the plays of others, which he either found in the poffeffion of the Players of the Lord Chamberlain, or which were fent in by other poets : how much of this kind of work he went through we have no means of knowing. His fecundity was unbounded, and his refources infinite. However, this is a point on which you are as well informed as I can be ; and, with regard to extemporaneous performances, you have only to look at the variorum Shakefpeare to fee that there were feveral other dramas, and efpecially one upon the events of the reign of Tamerlane, which probably were never written down. This confideration may, in fome degree, account for the extremely imperfect ftate in which not a few old plays have defcended to us : portions may, and perhaps were, compofed, got by heart, and recited, while inferior portions were perhaps left to the invention and difcretion of the performers.

D. I apprehend that this is a new way of accounting for the grofs and obvious inequality of fome parts of old plays, as compared with other parts of the fame plays.

C. The comic bufinefs is often peculiarly lawlefs and un-licenfed : I take it that it was not unfrequently left to the invention of the actor. Thus, in a play I purchafed for your dramatic library a week or two ago, " A Knack to Know a Knave", printed in 1594, comic fcenes were intro-duced expreffly for the purpofe of affording room, as I fufpect, for the off-hand drolleries of Will Kemp (a famous comedian, who played Peter in " Romeo and Juliet", etc.), and three or four more of his merry fellows, no part of which may have been written down before it was delivered. It perhaps varied more or lefs upon every occafion, fimply for the amufement of the lower orders.

D. And hence, poffibly, Shakefpeare's denunciation in " Hamlet" of the practice of clowns to deliver "more than was fet down for them."

C. That is not unlikely : his own comic bufinefs, with his Dogberry and Gravediggers, was of a very different fort : it had points relating to the purpofe of the play, and was befides fo humorous, that he could not endure the fubftitu-tion of anything that might come into the head of even the beft comedian of that day. The fpeeches of fuch Clowns and Fools as Shakefpeare introduced into his " Lear" or " Twelfth Night" were not fuch as an actor could produce on the fudden. This point might be further illuftrated by reference to many dramas of that day : Marlowe, who was Shakefpeare's predeceffor as well as contemporary, feems, in his " Tamburlaine the Great", to have relied too much upon the comic talents of thofe who played inferior parts ; and what they contributed was fo bad, that the firft printer of that tragedy in 1590 omitted it all, as unworthy of the reft of the reprefentation. I fhould have liked to have feen it, bad as it might be.

D. Then you are of opinion that it was not an unufual practice for poets of that day to entruft fcenes, intended only to excite merriment, to the actors engaged in them.

C. I think the point capable of fome proof, although the proof may not be by any means conclufive : it is a matter I am engaged in inveftigating ; and when I find fuch a comedian as Kemp travelling, as he did, in Italy for the pur-pofe of making himfelf better acquainted with the Italian *improvifatori* on the ftage there, it gives fome fupport to my notion. John Singer was another celebrated comedian of that period engaged in the fame line of bufinefs, and he exprefsly wrote a drama, the title of which, " The Volun-tary", leads to the belief that it was, in the main, an un-written performance. Robert Armin was a third farce-actor, as we now call them, who unqueftionably helped himfelf at times by his own ready invention, and who wrote a piece called " The Italian Tailor and his Boy", which was meant as a fort of imitation of the transalpine practice : Armin had, in fact, been a pupil of the famous Tarlton. It was then a well-known cuftom at our theatres for auditors to fling what were called "themes" upon the ftage, confifting of odd or puzzling queftions, in order that a favourite comic performer might, on the inftant, humoroufly reply to them, whether in verfe or profe, as beft fuited his ready talent

D. That, of courfe, would be an exercife for his extem-poraneous powers. Are any of these "themes" preferved ?

C. Yes, and the anſwers to them ; but this is a point of ſtage hiſtory not yet ſufficiently illuſtrated, and the materials are not ſo ſcanty as may be imagined.

Thus our converſation ended for this day ; and the Duke, on leaving, thanked me, and expreſſed his hope that I ſhould not find him a diſcreditable ſcholar. " All you have ſaid" (he added) " ſhews me, more and more, how well worthy our ancient drama is of the moſt patient ſtudy."

March 1.—I was ſhown an original diary kept by Lord Sandwich, when ſent to Spain in 1666 ; but, on going through it, I found very few particulars of any intereſt. I was allowed to copy from it the following liſt of pictures his lordſhip then ſaw in the Eſcurial ; and it may be amuſing now to trace the preſent abodes of ſome of them after the viciſſitudes to which they have been expoſed. I know of no other authority of this date on the ſubject : it is obviouſly incomplete.

" The Queen of France's picture, in the little square room where the old statue is by the garden.

" Paulo Veronese, in the south gallery ; Venus and Adonis—6 foot high, 5 broad.

" Titian : Story of Diana detecting Calista being with child, below in the Boredadol Titiano.

" Hannibal Caracci : a picture over the door of the great room, where [are] the two great statues.

" Van Dyke, of King Charles II of England, when a boy, in armour: in the same room as the former.

" Van Dyke, of King Charles I of England, in armour, in the same room.

" Leonard da Vinci his Proserpina, on the stairs.

" Rubens, en las Borredas del Verano, of Nymphs and Satires, adjoining to a glass partition.

" Queen Christina, in small, to the west in the Boredas.

" Leonard da Vinci, of our Lady, our Saviour, St. John—3 foot long and 2½ broad.

" Raphael, the same and St. Anne—2 foot and ½ long and 2 foot wide.

" Paulo Veronese, Story of Moses : these three in the Dormitorio of the Quarto Baxo.

"Corregio, a Cupid, in the room where the late King's writing-table stands.

" Two of Van Dyke in the same room, one over the other, about 4 feet broad and 3 long, and the other 5 long and 4 broad."

Thefe are followed by a lift of fome of the reliques pre-ferved in the Cathedral, which Lord Sandwich inferts with obvious reverence, never hinting a doubt of their genuine-nefs : among them are thefe two fingular ones—" the cup prefented to our Saviour by the three kings ; the pot in which water was turned into wine at the marriage in Canaan."

March 2.—At the Garrick, Bartley, the actor (fon of a cook in Dublin Caftle, who came out as Hamlet, and is now the acknowledged reprefentative of Falftaff) told me that he was once prefent at a dinner where two of the company were Sir John Doyle and Captain Morris, the famous comic fong writer : it muft be obferved that, after leading a moft irregular life, and writing moft profane and indecent fongs, Morris turned very pious and repentant : Sir J. Doyle, on the contrary, though nearly as old as Morris, was what was called " a good fellow" to the laft, and was reckoned a very capital finger, not caring whether his fongs were broad or narrow, loofe or tight. Doyle was called upon to fing, and he complied readily by giving one of Morris's moft popular fongs, which drew down great applaufe. Morris was obferved to fit quite filent, until Doyle thus addreffed him.

Doyle. How do you like that fong, Morris?

Morris. Not at all.

D. Why, it is one of your own, and one of your beft.

M. That may be; but I diflike it, and I hope I fhall never hear it again.

D. Why fo? Perhaps you did not like my mode of finging it.

M. Not that fo much as that I difapprove of the fong. I diflike it entirely, and I diflike you for finging it, when you know I am averfe to fuch things.

D. I am very forry, but I meant to pleafe you.

M. That may be, but you difpleafed me extremely. I am difgufted.

D. What, with your own fong? And you fee everybody elfe liked it.

M. Such fongs do not become your age, nor mine—nor any age. I am forry I ever wrote it—that the Devil ever put it into my head. I am utterly afhamed of its impiety and indecency.

D. Why, I have heard you fing it yourfelf.

M. That, too, may be; but I did not fing it as you fang it. If you muft fing it, though I hope you never will again, you had better fing it rightly. It is fhocking to my ears.

D. Aye; fhocking to hear it fung badly, you mean.

M. No; fhocking from its immoral tendency: befides, you fpoiled it: you fhould have fung it as I wrote it.

D. I do not remember how you wrote it: I fang it as it is printed.

M. Very likely; but when they printed it, they fpoiled my fong.

D. We fhall be glad to hear how you wrote it.

M. You fpoiled the whole fpirit of it.

D. Well, I will fing it better next time, if you will enable me.

M. Mind, I do not ftand up for the decency of the fong, but only for the goodnefs of it, and the goodnefs of the writing.

And then, changed as he was, he rattled out one of the very worft of the verfes, with at leaft all its original coarfenefs, to the infinite delight of the hearers, and amidft loud fhouts of laughter.

Morris was a great friend (as fuch friendfhips go) of the late Duke of Norfolk (Jockey), who was a monftrous eater, drinker, and lover of what was called "good company." Morris lived near Dorking, in a houfe, I am told, belonging to the Duke, for which he paid no rent. When Jockey died, Morris hoped that, if he did not leave him a large legacy, he would at leaft give him the place he lived in ; but he was disappointed. When the new Duke fucceeded to the title and eftates, he wrote to Morris faying that, by fome miftake, nothing was found in the will about the houfe at Dorking ; adding that, neverthelefs, Morris might live in it as long as he wifhed, rent free. Morris was defperately angry, refufed the ·offer, but fubjoined that, if the Duke would put a price upon the property, he would buy it. Morris, at this time, had not a fhilling, and the Duke knew it ; but he wrote kindly to the old fongfter, naming what could only be confidered the nominal value : that trifle Morris's friends raifed, and there he lived and died.

Bartley had known Morris for years, I believe, in Dublin as well as in London ; and this narrative, befides the fore-going dialogue, I had from him.

March 4.—I mifs a book from my fhelves, and I do not know how to account for its, difappearance, unlefs the author, or rather editor, of it have (which I do not believe) refumed poffeffion of it. I refer to Dyce's "Specimens of Englifh Poeteffes", which he publifhed five years ago, before I knew him, and of which he has lately often told me he is really much afhamed. The truth is, that it is a very imperfect and incomplete work, and he has more than once afked me to return the gift to him. I never had much faith in lady-poets, from Sappho downwards, and efpecially in the Mifs Sewards, Mifs Smiths, etc. ; and I believe that Dyce has come very much to my opinion. I fhall not afk him whether he have really taken it away, and he knows that I never read ten pages of it; Lady Winchelfea being almoft the only contributor to the volume worth naming. " Sidney's fifter, Pembroke's mother", although flatteringly praifed by Ben Jonfon, did not leave a line behind her worth re-perufal. Poffibly, I ought to except Mrs. Thrale's " Three Warnings", but in that fhe had powerful affiftance : Mrs. Barbauld, too, has left behind her a few fhort pieces that young people, and perhaps old, ought to remember.

If he have filently refumed his gift, the act would be by no means unprecedented or inexcufable : inftances of the fort have come within my own knowledge ; and it is only faying, or as much as faying, "I repent that I ever edited fuch a book, or gave copies of it away": it cannot generally be afferted that the taker poffeffed himfelf of anything really valuable.

John Philip Kemble, in 1780, at York, and from the prefs of a printer whom I knew thirty years afterwards, publifhed a fmall thin volume of poems, called "Fugitive

Pieces". I had a copy of it; and, although I did not know him, a friend of mine did; and begged of me to give him the book that he might prefent it to the author, who was very anxious to fupprefs it, and, by hook or by crook, and fomewhat unfcrupuloufly, got poffeffion of every copy that came in his way. In confequence of competition, J. P. Kemble's " Fugitive Pieces" has brought ftrange prices at auction—from £15 to £2 : 12 : 6; but lately, fince the death of the writer, it has come down to what auctioneers call " a lower figure." Excepting as a curiofity, it is worth nothing. J. P. K. openly confeffed, and even warned people, that he made himfelf mafter of every copy he could lay his hands upon; and, after his deceafe, befides thofe he had burned, no fewer than feven copies, I am told, were found in his book-cafes. The wonder is, that he did not burn them all; they were the moft namby-pamby things imaginable. The Duke has no copy—at leaft, in London.

March 10.—The Duke fhewed me a packet of letters, and copies of letters, and afked me to guefs by whom and from whom they were written? Of courfe, I made no attempt to guefs, but waited until he fhould farther explain himfelf. He told me that they were from and to a friend of whofe intimacy he was rather vain than proud— the Emperor Nicholas of Ruffia—whom he always, by defire, addreffed as his " dear friend", and was anfwered in the fame terms. The Duke admitted his " weaknefs" in this refpect, but he added that the Emperor was fo kind to him, when he went to St. Petersburg on a vifit of ceremony, that what might be called an intimacy had been eftablifhed between them, and they had kept up a correfpondence ever fince. Thefe were the letters—moft of them originals, in the handwriting of Nicholas I, and fome of them copies of the Duke's anfwers. He faid that the whole (I fuppofe there might be nearly a hundred of them) wanted arrange-ment, and he promifed that, at fome time when I was ftaying with him at Chatfworth, I fhould look over the whole, and put them into "datified order." He repeated that he knew ·he was weak upon the point, but he really was fomewhat vain of the terms on which he ftood with the Emperor of all the Ruffias. Of courfe, I told the Duke that I would accomplifh his wifhes, as far as I was able, at any con-venient time. The correfpondence, as I underftood, was entirely in French.

March 14.—Dyce has juft printed, and given to me, a pretty little fquare 12mo volume, entitled "Specimens of Englifh Sonnets", and has appropriately dedicated it to Wordfworth, unqueftionably the fineft fonnet-writer of our day, if not of any day. I prefented a copy of it to my noble "friend", as he kindly choofes *to call himfelf*, and I introduced it to his notice by a fonnet of my own—a grofs piece of prefumption, confidering that the two hundred pages contain fimilar firft-rate productions of all dates, from the Earl of Surrey, in the reign of Henry VIII, to Keats, in the reign of William IV.

With unaffected diffidence, I fubjoin my trifle ; and I will follow it by a brief notice of certain omiffions of fon-netteers, whofe effufions of the fame kind might properly have been included in this collection, but are not found there. I wrote what follows on the fly-leaf of the copy I fent to the Duke.

Behold, my lord, within this little tome,
  The flower of our sweet English poesy,
Which challenges the works of Greece and Rome,
  Of France and Spain, Almain and Italy:
Perennial blossoms in one posy bound ;
  Or like thine own ancestral diadem,
  Beset with many a bright and matchless gem,
United in a perfect glittering round.
  Be these thy model : let each chosen friend,
Like these, be all bright, excellent, and pure ;
  A coronet wherein all virtues blend,
Rich without pride, and worthy, though obscure.
If one there be more lowly than the rest,
Thy smile can raise him equal with the best.

It is rather fingular that Dyce includes no fonnet by
Lord Surrey's contemporary, Sir Thomas Wyatt, who has
left us feveral of great excellence. I tranfcribed, and have
inferted, four of them in their proper place, both in my
own copy and in that of the Duke. Then, Dyce has not
given one by Lodge, although feveral moderate fonnets by
Daniel and Drayton are reprinted : here I inferted two in
Dyce's volume, as well as two more by the famous Robert
Greene, the original author of the ftory of " As You Like
It." Barnfield's are not good : therefore, I do not complain,
though he was a poet who, in fome of his lyrics, was miftaken
for Shakefpeare. Barnes might well have been paffed over
in filence, to make room for the great poet Chapman, who
has not a line. Dyce has given unufual and undue pro-
minence to Drummond, a comparatively poor verfifyer, becaufe he happened to be born north of the Tweed. Mifs
Seward and Mifs Smith do not at all deferve the fpace they
occupy ; while Sir Egerton Brydges, who afferts that he

has compofed more than two thoufand fonnets, has but one, but that one is capital. Southey has alfo only one ; while from Wordfworth's pen we have thirteen, and all excellent. In juftice to the genius of poor Robert Greene, who is here entirely neglected by the editor of his plays, I fubjoin a fonnet by him : he wrote but little in that form of poetry, but the following is dated in 1592.

> What meant the poets in invective verse
>   To sing Medea's shame and Scylla's pride,
>   Calypso's charms, by which so many died?
> Only for this ; their vices to rehearse,
> That curious wits, that in the world converse,
>   May shun the dangers and enticing shows
>   Of such false Syrens ; those home-breeding foes
> That from their eyes the venom do disperse.
>   So soon kills not the basilisk with sight,
> The viper's tooth is not so venomous,
> The adder's tongue is not so dangerous
>   As they that bear the shadow of delight ;
> Who chain blind youth in trammels of their hair,
> Till waste brings woe, and sorrow hastes despair.

Of courfe, here, as well as in all the older portion of Dyce's volume, allowance muft be made for a certain antiquated quaintnefs, which to my ear, from habit, is agreeable. In the whole, the editor of this little volume has omitted at leaft twenty fonnets that ought to have been inferted, and has inferted as many that his undoubted good tafte ought to have rejected. The fonnets of Ruffell and Edwards I am very glad to fee there, as, of late years, nobody has done juftice to their grace and originality.

March 19.—I was not aware until yefterday that my birthday (January 11th) was celebrated·in 1642 by the triumphant return to their feats of the five members of the Houfe of Commons, whom Charles I. had wifhed to arreft. The year in which I was born (1789) was remarkable for various events of importance, fuch as the capture of the Baftille in Paris, the trial of Haftings ; the deaths of Dr. - Price (my grandmother's coufin) and John Howard ; the mutiny of the *Bounty*, and the conviction of the father of the prefent proprietor of *The Times* for libels. I have among my queer books the Correfpondence between the Prince of Wales and Mrs. Fitzherbert, " Printed at the Logographic Prefs, and fold by J. Walter, Printing Houfe Square, Blackfriars"; but without any date of the year. It was not until 1804 that my father had anything to do with the *Times.* In 1808, he wrote a " Life of Abraham Newland", the cafhier of the Bank, without a fcrap of information fupplied to him : yet it only took one week to compofe and another to print it, though it formed a refpectable and creditable 8vo volume of nearly two hundred pages. Hilton, then a youth, afterwards the famous hiftorical artift, made the drawing for the portrait from a picture by Drummond. I went with him to the Bank, that he might examine, and afterwards borrow the painting from the directors, who readily entrufted it to him. Crosby was the publifher.

March 20.—In his fecond fatire, addreffed to Molière, Boileau abufes George de Scuderi feverely, and with more reafon than he had to abufe the unfortunate Quinault, whofe name, by bad luck, rhymed with *défaut*, and other words of difparaging import. However, it muft be owned that De Scuderi not only wrote with facility, but, in fome of his lighter pieces, with felicity. The following, " To a

Lady who Cried with Laughter", is rather an imitation than a tranflation from him, and it is in his jigging meafure. I forget where I met with the original.

> What a mixture confus'd every feature deranges !
>   Sweet Phillis, explain what it means, if you will.
> You laugh, yet you weep : do these wonderful changes
>   Presage to your lover good fortune or ill ?
>
> A calm and a storm I behold in one moment,
>   Stars that are adverse and planets most kind.
> Oh, tell me the secret ! without such a comment,
>   The more I endeavour less reason I find.
>
> Cruel maid ! thou art nothing but one contradiction ;
>   I know it too late—let my anguish be brief.
> When 'tis o'er I shall die in the certain conviction,
>   That you weep at my joy, and but laugh at my grief.

March 23.—I was fitting at the Garrick Club yefterday, reading the newfpaper clofe to the window, when a large family-carriage, drawn by two fine horfes, drove up to the fteps of the door : it was about eleven o'clock, and it fo happened, though a rarity, that there was nobody in the room but myfelf. I went on with my newfpaper, when a queer-looking gentleman, in a fort of boat hat, very loofe light coat, and loofer trowfers, twifted in fome odd way round the leg and diminifhing towards the foot and ankles, entered. He looked round, and feeing nobody there but myfelf, he faid, " I fuppofe there is no objection to my bringing a lady to fee the rooms, is there ?" I replied, " Not the leaft, that I am aware of"; and he went out again to fetch the faid lady. I gueffed that it was Lord Harrington, and, looking out at the window, I faw him handing a lady from the carriage, two footmen, in long brown coats and with gold-headed canes, ftanding one on each fide. The lady wore a veil, but as fhe entered the room fhe put it up, and I inftantly recognifed the *ci-devant* Mifs Foote, of "Foote and Hayne" notoriety, who in 1824 had recovered £3000 damages for a breach of promife. She was ftill very pretty, but, as I thought, with rather a ftage-worn look; and, while fhe was languifhing about the room, leaning on his lordfhip's arm, Winfton, the Secretary of the Club, entered: as he knew them both, he bowed to Lord Harrington rather obfequioufly, and to Lady Harrington a little more familiarly, as if they had been previoufly acquainted. A few words paffed between them, which I did not hear, and, after another fhort furvey of the room and furniture, they went away, leaving me with Winfton.

I had not moved from my chair, nor put down my newspaper; and, as foon as the vifitors had gone, Winfton came up to me, and afked me if I knew them. I faid "Yes, but not perfonally." Winfton obferved: "Who would have thought fhe would ever have become a peerefs! Why, I knew her when fhe was a little dirty, untidy girl about the Plymouth Theatre, when her father, Sam Foote, was manager of it, and her mother an actrefs of no repute, who was faid to be the daughter of a gentleman in the neighbourhood. Lady Harrington, then little Maria Foote, fome ten or twelve years old, ufed to take fmall children's parts, and to dance. I have acted with her fifty times. She was always very pretty and engaging, and became a great favourite with fuch audiences as they ufually have at Plymouth. Old Foote, who, I believe, had been a paymafter in the army, and his wife were very proud of their daughter; and fhe continued extremely attractive until ftories became

I

current about her early lovers and amours. She was born in 1798, fo that fhe was only fixteen or feventeen when fhe firft came to London, and played Amanthis, in ' The Child of Nature', about 1814. You perhaps remember it."—"I do not (faid I), but I heard her performance very well fpoken of."—"And very ill fpoken of (continued Winfton) ; for, firft of all, it was afferted that, as fhe was a natural child, fhe ought to play well in ' The Child of Nature'; while others, more ill-natured ftill, maintained that fhe herfelf had had a child of nature. At all events, if it were fo, the piece, as far as regards the title, was ill chofen, but not as regards her acting ; for I can fay it was excellent, and I had feen her in the part more than once before fhe came to London. However, now, to the furprife of everybody, fhe is a coun-tefs, after having had it proved in open court that fhe had lived with Lord Segrave, and had had two children by him. This was in 1824."—"I well remember the trial (faid I), for I was prefent at it ; but I do not remember any diftinct proof as to Mifs Foote's two children by Lord Segrave : it may be fo, neverthelefs."—"It was fo, I know (added Win-fton), and her career has been extraordinary ; but now fhe may be faid to have been fet up for life by her marriage with Lord Harrington two or three years ago."

" There is another peerefs of our time (I continued) taken from the ftage."—" Aye, two or three (faid Winfton) : what do you fay to Lady Thurlow, who was Mifs Bolton, a finger ?"—" The lady to whom I refer (added I) was a finger alfo, Lady Effex. Young, the actor, at one time, was very fond of her; but fhe naturally (I mean naturally for a woman) preferred a lord. I can remember Mifs Stephens, in her fix-teenth year, finging in the libraries and public rooms at

Margate, when fhe was very carefully attended by her
mother, who kept at a diftance the prefumptuous admirers
of the very pretty and moft promifing vocalift."—"She was
fome years younger than Maria Foote (faid Winfton), and
Lord Effex, as might be expected, died foon after he
married her. You mentioned Young, the actor : did you
know his brother George, the furgeon ?"—" Extremely well
(I anfwered) : he ufed to attend my mother, but confined
his practice much to the city, living, when I called upon
him, in Bucklersbury. He was a moft agreeable man at a
dinner-table ; but I fancied that he never liked to talk
about his brother Charles, who went on the ftage, as I was
informed, in oppofition to the wifhes of his family."

Other members of the Club here entered, and our
theatrical goffip ended for that day.

April 20.—I have been ill, and nearly confined to my
room for three weeks, during which time I have not made
a fingle entry in my Diary. Still, I was not unemployed.
A converted Jew friend of mine, fome years ago, directed
my notice to Burton's cenfure of Boccaccio's novel of " The
Three Rings," complaining that it had been entirely
misunderftood as a flight upon Chriftianity. From that
day to this, from one caufe or another, I have not looked
at it ; but during my illnefs I have amufed myfelf with
the works of the old Italian, comparing them with the
Englifh tranflation publifhed in 1620 ; for until then they
were only known in our language through Painter's
"Palace of Pleafure" and Fenton's "Tragical Difcourfes",
in feparate novels. I found that there was no valid reafon
for condemning "The Three Rings"; if there had been, I

should certainly not have attempted to put it into verse, even for my own private amusement : all that can be said against it is, that the old Jew did not exalt Christianity above Judaism; and surely it was something in his favour that, instead of inveighing against it, he put it on a level with his own belief, which even Christians do not dispute. To Saladin he might have denounced Christianity not only without offence, but with approbation : he did not do so, but left the Mahomedan monarch without the power of drawing even an inference. Nobody can refuse to admire the astuteness of the old usurer in avoiding a direct answer, and thus saving his money ; and that, in truth, is all that Boccaccio intended to illustrate. I thought that my version would run best in the old English ballad-measure, due allowance being made for the imitative simplicity of the style : I am not aware that the *novella* has ever yet been versified in any form.

THE THREE RINGS.

Fam'd Saladin of Babylon,
　Whose valour was so great,
As, from a subject, to become
　A mighty potentate ;

Who made the haughty Pagans rue,
　And to his valour yield ;
And Christians conquer'd not a few,
　In many a foughten field ;

Had spent at last his treasures vast
　In wars and pleasures free,
And knew not where to look for more
　In all his empery.

At length, he thought him, that a Jew
  In Alexandria dwelt,
Who had large heaps of ready gold,
  And in vile usury dealt.

Full well he knew this cunning Jew
  Lov'd money to his heart,
Yet was he loth', by force or oath,
  To make him with it part.

The Sultan's wants brook'd no delay,
  Supplies he must procure ;
And soon he call'd to mind a way
  To make his purpose sure.

For him he sent, as well content,
  And when the Hebrew came,
He thus bespake Melchisedeck,
  For so the Jew had name.

" Most worthy man, I oft have heard
  That you are wise indeed,
And in the things that touch God's word
  All others you exceed.

" I therefore sent for thee to learn
  Which faith you hold most true,
The Christian or Mahomedan,
  Or yours, who are a Jew ?"

The Jew, right wise, without surprise,
  Heard what the Sultan saith ;
But saw his purpose to entrap
  And punish for his faith.

He, therefore, held that it was best
  To neither to incline ;
To praise not one above the rest,
  And cheat the close design.

He set his ready wits to work,
   An answer so to frame,
As to defeat the royal Turk,
   And quit himself from blame.

He said, " My liege, the question sage
   Doth merit well reply,
And might the learned heads engage
   Of wiser men than I :

" But, since you bid me answer straight,
   To make my meaning clear,
You must await while I relate
   The tale you now shall hear.

" Most mighty prince, there liv'd long since
   A man with wealth to spare,
Who, among other jewels, own'd
   A precious ring and rare.

" Its price and beauty made him wish
   This ring should still descend
To his remote posterity,
   Whene'er his life should end.

" He, therefore, did by will declare,
   When he was under ground,
That son should be his only heir
   With whom the ring was found :

" That he who should the ring obtain
   Should make the same bequest,
That to the last it might remain
   By his own house possest.

" When this was done, from sire to son
   The ring for centuries past,
Until it came into the hands
   Of a good man at last ;

" To whom three noble sons were sent
   Who equally deserv'd ;
All fair alike, obedient,
   And ne'er from faith had swerv'd.

" He lov'd them, therefore, equally,
   And wish'd they all could share;
While each one hoped to have the ring
   And be his father's heir.

" He knew not which he should enrich,
   To whom the ring should fall ;
Till the old man devis'd this plan
   To satisfy them all.

" He to a goldsmith went with speed,
   Who made him other two
Like the first ring : so like, indeed,
   None could discern the true.

" Death now approach'd ; with secret care
   To each a ring he gave,
That each might think himself the heir
   When he lay in his grave.

" When he was dead, each own'd, he said,
   The real ancient ring,
And each son, to confirm his claim,
   Produc'd the precious thing.

" 'Twas found the rings were so alike,
   None could the true one say,
And which son is the heir by right
   Is question'd to this day.

" Such is the answer you require
   To question strange and new—
Which of three faiths our heavenly Sire
   Has giv'n us be the true ?

" Each one believes his own is right,
  And each his proof can bring,
But no one knows, by touch or sight,
  Which is the one true ring."

When Saladin thus heard him say,
  He knew all art was vain ;
And took another, plainer way,
  His purpose to obtain.

He told Melchisedeck his need :
  The Jew his wants supplied ;
And they remain'd firm friends indeed
  Until the Hebrew died.

It deferves a note to ftate that, although Boccaccio has always had the credit of this invention, it does not, in truth, belong to him: in whatever way we take it, the tale is found in the ancient colleftion of *Cento Novelle Antiche* (Nov. 72), and is even included among the religious ftories of the *Gefta Romanorum.* Properly viewed it may be faid to fupport the truth of Chriftianity, fince the old Jew could find nothing to fay againft it, even to Saladin, who would have been glad to hear it impugned.

Apr. 24.—I had the following anecdote from a friend of the *Pope*-ifh poet, W. L. Bowles. Not far from Bowles's parfonage, at Calne, there is a gentle hill and a turnpike: Bowles, a moft abfent man, is in the habit of walking up the hill, allowing his fteady old horfe to go on before him ; and the keeper of the toll-gate ufed to let the horfe go through, knowing that his owner was behind, and would pay by filently dropping three-halfpence into the man's hand. One day, Bowles was about to drop his money as ufual, when

the gate-keeper remarked to him that his horfe had not
gone on before him : " Oh, dear, no ! (faid Bowles, waking
up) I forgot that I did not ride to-day"; and returned the
money to his pocket. The words were hardly fpoken, when
the tollman faw the horfe quietly plodding up the hill after
his mafter : he mentioned it to Bowles, who, again waking
up, exclaimed, " Oh, dear, aye ! I remember now that I did
come out on horfeback." He was then paffing on without
paying the toll, as if the gate-keeper would obtain it from
the horfe, till his attention was called by the man to the
faét, that the horse had probably no money about him.

April 28.—The Rev. W. Harnefs is an excellent man—
excellent in many ways, but, as I have faid elfewhere, in no
way fuper-excellent : he is a good man, a good preacher,
a good talker, a good poet. I have already copied a little
privately printed apologue (we may call it) by him, which
contains an admirable moral, but nothing very new ; and,
as far as I know it, we may fay the fame of a drama that
he has in hand, having completed three aéts after Fanny
Kemble had commenced her theatrical career, having then
laid it by, and having now taken it up again ; and, as Dyce
thinks, is difpofed to finifh it. He was with me at Dyce's
laft evening, and was perfuaded, after a good deal of en-
treaty, to read to us an early fcene or two, and fome dis-
jeéted paffages, that were extremely creditable, and reminded us of the ftyle of thought and expreffion, not
certainly of the firft, but of the fecond-rate dramatifts of the
beft age of our ftage poetry,—the reigns of Elizabeth and
James. He allowed me, in my avowed admiration, to copy
the following, for which, as far as I underftood, he had yet

K

fixed upon no precife place, but which he intended to introduce into his play.

> " They, sure, who lead
> A country life must be more pure and holy
> Than in the crowded city : there the heart,
> Dwelling in solitude so profitable,
> Holds frequent commune with itself alone ;
> Or, which is still more sweet, may meditate
> Amid the endless melodies of nature ;
> The murmuring sound of bees upon the wing,
> The song of birds, the flow and fall of waters,
> Which calm the soul, and fit it for good thoughts
> Better than silence.   On the works of God
> The eye delights to rest, and there it meets
> No intervening obstacle to exclude
> The notice of his ever springing bounties
> Upon the earth.   Oh ! in the country
> We stand, as 'twere, in the Creator's presence,
> Surrounded by the wonders of his hand
> To charm and bless us, while land, sea, and sky,
> Are open all before us, and our hearts
> Receive an elevation and a purity
> From the deep sentiment they seem to breathe."

Surely, this is good thinking, good Englifh, and good
blank verfe, and almoft touches the verge of *fine poetry.*
Here and there I thought Harnefs had fpoiled a line by
redundant fyllables, as, very early, where a male chara&er
tells a female (I forget the names),

> " To you I owe my knowledge of these things :
> You taught me how to discriminate between them."   Etc.

Here Dyce and I both thought that the infertion of "how"
was quite needlefs, and fpoiled the meafure : at the fame
time neither he nor I wifhed to make the verfification too

ftrict and formal; to do fo would be inconfiftent with the
practice of our beft early poets. However, the whole play is
yet a mere embryo : I doubt if Harnefs have yet touched
the laft two acts. He does not say so, but I am sure he
wishes Fanny K. to play in it.

May 1.—The following was related to me by John
Stuart, Q.C., and M.P. for Newark, once a reporter on the
Morning Poft. Ellenborough being on the bench at *Nifi
Prius*, a witnefs, in a blue coat and gilt buttons, ftepped into
the witnefs-box, but when the New Teftament was put into his
hand he refufed to be fworn. " Why do you object to take
the oath, fir ?" afked the gruff Chief Juftice. " Becaufe I am
one of the Society of Friends", was the mild anfwer. " Then,
fir," faid the Chief Juftice, with loud emphafis, " if you are a
Quaker, why do you come here in the difguife of a rational
man ?"

May 2.—At the Garrick, I was fhewn a letter from
Alfred Bunn, manager of Drury Lane Theatre, to Lord
Segrave, refigning to him all right and title to Mrs. Bunn
(late Mifs Somerville), for as long a period as his lordfhip
chofe, at the price of five guineas a week, or £250 per
annum. At first I thought it only a bad joke.

May 7.—I dined with a fmall party ; Harnefs, Kenyon,
Campbell, and Hunt, being four of them. I was fomewhat
furprifed by the coarfeness of Campbell's conversation, and
Harnefs pofitively reproved him. Campbell was efpecially
abufive of the Countefs Guiccioli : he did not fpare her in
any particular, and infifted (a point on which he obtained
fome fupport) that Lord Byron, who had kept her, and
whom fhe affected to adore, was by no means a handfome

man. "Befides, he was full of affectation and pretence," added Campbell: "the firft time I dined with him was at Rogers's, where he would condefcend to eat nothing but vegetables, and drink nothing but water, in order that he might be talked about. After the party broke up, I happened to go into the Thatched Houfe Tavern, and whom fhould I fee there but my lord, eating a hearty fupper of folid meat and drinking a bottle of claret! I was difgufted by his affectation; and I took care to fpeak to him, that he might fee that I knew what an impoftor he was."

This anecdote was readily believed; and Kenyon faid that he had witneffed the fame thing as regarded vegetable diet: Byron's object was to keep himfelf interefting and pale. "Then he fhould have drunk nothing but *pale* ale (faid Hunt playfully), not 'rofy wine'." "When he dined with me and Milman (faid Harnefs), I obferved no particular abftemioufnefs about him: however, he was certainly not free from affectation, and wifhed to be thought to look high-blooded, but not high-coloured—pale, and like a poet.

> " Pale as the moon,
>   But not so placid :
> Still out of tune,
>   And sharply acid."

"He muft have been in one of his moft acid humours (remarked another of the company), when he wrote the fatire on his *friend* Rogers,

> " Wrinkles that would puzzle Cocker,
> Visage that would shame a knocker." Etc.

"You have not the correct text (faid Harnefs); and, befides, you have tranfpofed the lines, which run,

> " Face that would disgrace a knocker,
>   Wrinkles that would puzzle Cocker."

"I like the other reading better (faid the firft quoter) ; but I diflike the whole poem, and I am glad to fee a difpofition, almoft everywhere, to fupprefs it, and to deny that it is Byron's."

"The ingratitude of it is abominable (faid Campbell) ; for I know that Rogers was one of Byron's firft and beft friends, and ufed to talk him up as fuperior to any other poet of the day but himfelf. As to denying the fatire, that is impoffible ; and much of it was deferved."

This was a fore place with Campbell, who was by no means free from envy, and who often fpoke ill of Rogers, defignating what he wrote as mawkifh and namby-pamby; nothing better than Goldfmith, with the addition of milk-and-water, and a little fugar and butter for the rich and powerful. There was, in truth, nothing original in anything Rogers had produced and printed, with fuch pretty pictures in order to make his poems fell.

"Of courfe (faid Hunt), I do not mean now to compare the two poems, but, at all events, you borrowed your title, 'The Pleafures of Hope', from his title 'The Pleafures of Memory', and you have engravings, too."

"My title ! (exclaimed Campbell) what's in a title? There is not a line in my poem"—

Our hoft, feeing the turn the fubject was taking, adroitly diverted the converfation to other topics, and we parted late, all friends.

May 12.—An acquaintance has fent me an old newfpaper of Jan. 17, 1736, where I read the following :

"On Saturday last died, at his house in Bloomsbury, Mr. John Bannister, about 74 years of age. He was one of the gentlemen of his Majesty's Musick, and for many years esteemed a most excellent master of the violin."

This was the grandfather of old Charles Bannister, the bafs-finger and actor; who, in 1789, had been committed with Palmer as a vagrant, for acting plays without a licenfe, and who died in 1804; and the great-grandfather of Bannister, jun., or Jack Bannister, as he ufed to be called, who retired from the ftage on June 1ft, 1816. He had come out as a tragedian (having, it is faid, been inftructed by Garrick) in 1772; and, in my youth, I knew a gentleman who faw him attempt Shylock; but with fo little fuccefs that he never repeated the part, ultimately gave himfelf up to comedy and farce, and was the delight of my boyhood. After "Jack" quitted the ftage, he refided for fome years in Gower Street; and the laft time I faw him he was, with a ftick and the aid of the area-railings, making flow and painful way towards Bedford Square. He was fadly disappointed in his gouty old age by the death of Mr. Bridge (of the famous houfe of Rundell and Bridge), who died enormoufly rich, and from whom Bannister hoped for a large legacy. When Bridge was comparatively poor, Bannister had lent him £1400, at four per cent. intereft: the intereft was regularly paid, but no more, in fpite of Bridge's acknowledged obligations; and when he died he left Bannister only an inconfiderable annuity. It was after his disappointment that I faw him, in great pain, and looking very ill and unhappy; still, his eye was bright.

May 14.—A clergyman, who was prefent, told me the following anecdote of Sidney Smith. He (Smith) had invited friends to breakfaſt, and among them was a young curate juſt ordained, who affeĉted to be ſo familiar and intimate with his hoſt as always to call him merely "Smith", —"What do you ſay, Smith"; "I don't agree with you, Smith", etc. Smith took all in good part; but when the young "pulpit-prig" (as Smith called him to my informant) was going away, he took care to tell Smith that he was going by invitation to call on the Archbiſhop of Canterbury: "I hope he will give you a good living (ſaid Smith), but I adviſe you not to call him 'Howley'."

May 20.—We conſtantly at preſent laugh at the French for dignifying all rich Engliſh travellers as *mylords*. It ſeems to have been the ſame more than three hundred years ago, for Dr. Wotton thus wrote to Edward VI, from Paris, on Feb. 12, 1553:

"Pleaseth your Highness to understand, that knowing Sir Peter Carew to be here, and hearing it bruited abroad that there was *a great my-lord* (for so they call him here) come hither to require succour and aid against your Highness, I thought it meet for me to speak to the King and with Monsieur le Connetable of it."

Afterwards Wotton ſtates that another Engliſhman, who had no title, was termed "*un grand mylord.*" S. P. O.

May 23.—It is not always eaſy for me, with my large family and my ſmall means, to muſter ſuch a ſum as £25 to buy a ſingle poetical traĉt; but I have done ſo: it is highly curious becauſe it is the ſole exiſting copy, and moſt intereſting becauſe it has direĉt reference to Shakeſpeare and to "The Paſſionate Pilgrim." It is entitled "The Paſſionate Shepherd"; the word "ſhepherd" being, in this inftance, and at that date, univerfally ufed for *poct :* therefore, "Paffionate Shepherd" means *Paffionate Poct ;* and the tract (of only forty pages) is filled entirely by productions in verfe, many of them in direct imitation of others in "The Paffionate Pilgrim". I purchafed it ten days ago, and in the interval I have fearched in every direction, looked over every catalogue containing kindred works, and inquired of every old bookfeller and bookifh friend, without finding the fainteft trace of it. Therefore, I fay it is unique in itfelf, and nearly unexampled in its contents ; for thefe reafons I have put myfelf to fome inconvenience in order to poffefs it. It came out of a volume of tracts, with none of which it had any relation, and the feller of it afked me £30 for it ; but I obtained it for £5 lefs.

The date of it is 1604, and it was "imprinted by E. Allde for John Tappe", in fmall 4to : we are farther told on the title-page, that it contains "many excellent conceited Poems and pleafant Sonnets, fit for young heads to pafs away idle hours." The preliminary addrefs is fubfcribed "your poore Shephard *Bonerto";* and, in an old hand-writing, we are told that Bonerto means Bretono, or Breton, a moft noted verfifyer of that day, confirmed by his Chriftan name, Nicholas, being written preceding it. To the firft poem the following introduction is given : "Paftoral Verfes written by the Shepheard Bonerto to his beloved Shepheardefs Aglaia"; and the very firft fpecimen is precifely in the fame meafure as feveral of the pieces in "The Paffionate Pilgrim"; *e.g.,*

> " Tell me, ye shepherd swains,
> On Minerva's mountain plains,
> Ye that only sit and keep

Flocks, but of the fairest sheep,
Did you see, this blessed day,
Fair Aglaia walk this way." Etc.

There are twenty or thirty poems in the tract, all good, if not of the highest clafs, and all in various lyrical meafures. I am fo happy in my purchafe, in fpite of its high price, that I rejoicingly record it here.

May 26.—The Duke always hears and converfes beft in a carriage : he carried me with him this morning (I had not expected to go), when he went to the ftudio of Edwin Landfeer. He had danced the night before at a ball, where he met two famous ornaments of the ftage in different departments, Mifs O'Neil and Mifs M. Tree, one now mar-. ried to Mr. Wrixon Becher, and the other to a wealthy young tea-merchant of the name of Bradfhaw. The Duke danced with both, and infinitely prefers the laft, not only for her beauty, but for her genuine fimplicity—not ftage-fimplicity, that very common and offenfive fubftitute. He fays that Mrs. Becher (O'Neil) *is not*, and that Mrs. Brad-fhaw *is*, a natural character ; and he gave me the following contrafted anecdotes of them. He was dining in a company where they both were prefent, and it was propofed that on a future day they fhould all go to the theatre together. Mrs. Becher, who had been many years on the ftage, both in England and Ireland, was always anxious to fink her profeffion, affected not even to know at what hour the performances began, and, when fomebody in company recited a few lines from one of her moft popular parts, fhe went so far as to pretend not to know from whence the quotation came. On the other

L.

hand, Mrs. Bradſhaw (the *Tea* Tree), who is fond of talking of acting, and of her profeſſional triumphs, and never conſiders herſelf above them, when croſſing the ſtage from a private box, in front of the audience, but behind the curtain, exclaimed to the Duke, who was leading her, " How I do love the ſmell of thoſe dear, delightful foot-lamps! I never ſhall be happier than when I was gaining a living for myſelf and our family by having them conſtantly under my noſe." One of the ſiſters had been a *Columbine.*

The Duke told me that after Miſs Farren became Counteſs of Derby, ſhe was too much like Miſs O'Neil, and too little like Mrs. Bradſhaw.

May 30.—When George Daniel, the book and print collector, went to look over the gallery and dramatic curioſities of Mathews, at Highgate, almoſt every time the actor ſhewed him any remarkable and, as he thought, unique volume or engraving, Daniel uſed to ſay, " Aye, aye ; very rare, very valuable, etc., but I have a duplicate of it in my library." At laſt, Mathews got quite out of patience, and exclaimed, " Why, d— you, you have got duplicates of everything I have—excepting my lame leg ; I wiſh you had *that* with all my heart." This is Mathews's account of the interview : I heard it from him.

Daniel is a great pretender, talks bad Engliſh and miſpronounces it, and has no real knowledge of the inſide of books, but goſſips with great confidence about them, and their contents. He buys books, etc., to ſell again.

June 1.—I have obtained, by exchange and the addition of a conſiderable ſum of money, ſome very curious hiſtorical letters, three of them originals, by Cardinal Pole to Crom-

well, and two others from Thomas Starkey, chaplain to
Henry VIII, together with two copies of letters from Pole to
the Lord Privy Seal and the King, the firſt being that which
accompanied Pole's book on the Supremacy of the Pope,
when it was prefented to the King. An eighth letter is a
copy of one fent by a near relative of Pole (not named),
earneſtly diffuading him from repairing to Rome when he
was fummoned thither by the Pope, and ſtrongly cenfuring
the book which Pole had written, the contents of which the
writer had heard from Henry VIII himfelf. Of thefe I
ſhall perhaps make an article for the Antiquarian Society.
Pole's letters are very curious as containing, among other
things, a vindication of his miffion as legate into Flanders,
and repeated declarations of his fidelity and attachment to
the King, his relative. Whence did they come ?

June 2.—At the Garrick to-day they were very merry
over the following anecdote derived from old Conſt, the
barriſter, for many years the chairman of the Middlefex
Seffions. I did not think it fo good as fome others thought
it. J. P. Kemble had to fing a fong, or part of a fong, in
"Richard Cœur de Lion", produced at Drury Lane in 1786.
He had no great ſkill nor ear, and, when it was over, he
appealed to the leader, "Well, Mr. ——, how did I get
through my verfe to Blondell ?"—"Why, I muſt fay, Mr.
Kemble, that you *murdered* time."—"At all events, you
fet me the example (replied J. P. K.), for you *beat* him."

Theodore Hook laid claim to a riddle, or conundrum
now very current in fociety, efpecially among young ladies,
"What is the difference between the deaths of a fculptor
and of a hair-dreffer ? *Anfwer:* A fculptor *makes faces* and

busts, while a hairdresser *curls up* and *dyes*." This seems hardly worth recording ; but it was voted good by the hearers.

June 4.—I was asked to spend a night at Chiswick, and the Duke carried me there in his brougham. We met, on our arrival, his cousin, Lord Morpeth, afterwards co-trustee with me of Shakespeare's house at Stratford-on-Avon : he is a very pleasant, well-informed, and conversible man, and has some pretensions to be considered a poet—in a small way. The last time I had seen him, to speak to, was when we dined in company with the corporation of Stratford to celebrate our great dramatist's birthday. Lady Carlisle, the sister of the Duke, was also at Chiswick, and two gentlemen, with a lady whom I did not know : one of the gentlemen played pretty well at billiards, and beat me, though not easily : the Duke backed me for a trifle, and I happened to win for him. We dined at eight, and sat and had music in the drawing-room till half-past ten, when I retired to my room—the same, in fact, in which Fox and Canning had died. Before I had undressed, the Duke visited me, and we had a long conversation upon a favourite subject with us, our old actors, going back even to the time of Burbadge, Field and Taylor, who had played the principal parts in many of Shakespeare's dramas. The Duke did not leave me until nearly, or quite, midnight.

Among other things, the Duke expressed his surprise that it was not known that there was a single representative living of any one of the famous old dramatists, or of the celebrated actors in the best period of our stage. I added that even of the reign of Charles II, or later, I had heard of none ; or, if there were an exception, it was only in the cafe of Dryden : he was about the only dramatic poet of his day who had now any known living reprefentative ; for Mr. Shadwell, Q.C., as I underftood, had repeatedly difclaimed defcent from the voluminous and excellent playwright of the fame name, whom Dryden had fatirifed in the line,

" To talk like Doeg, and *to write like thee.*"

"Aye (faid the Duke), even the name of Garrick feems now unknown."—" Although (added I) he was only of yesterday, for my father faw him quit the ftage in 1776. We may fay the fame of his predeceffor Betterton, notwithftanding Mrs. Glover adopted it as her ftage-name before fhe married."—" There are now no Kembles left (obferved the Duke) but Charles and his daughter : what has become of the name of perhaps the greateft tragic aftrefs that ever lived, Mrs. Siddons ?"—" I have lately feen (I interpofed) a very interefting book which once was hers : I mean a firft folio of Shakefpeare, that was given to her by Garrick, with his handwriting on the fly-leaf as the donor, and hers, ' Sarah Siddons', as the recipient."—" Indeed ! (cried the Duke) that muft be a highly interefting memorial of both : is it to be purchafed ?"—I anfwered in the negative ; and expreffed my wonder how it had been allowed to efcape from the poffeffion of the family.—" I think (faid the Duke) there are ftill fome Siddonfes in the Eaft Indies : I have heard fo, but none of them upon the ftage ; and when once a family has feparated itfelf from that profeffion, it is generally inclined to difown the connection."—" Mrs. Abingdon (I obferved), whom I have feen at parties more than once, was always fond of talking of her theatrical triumphs : fo, we know from Walpole's Letters, was Mrs.

Clive."—" They (remarked the Duke) were the *triumphers ;*
but, if players leave any children' or relations behind them,
it feldom happens that they like to be reminded of their
origin.　Colley Cibber never could endure people to fay
that he was a better actor than poet."—" And Mrs. Cibber,
the wife of Theophilus (faid I), the fweeteft and tendereft
actrefs of her time, was more proud of her maiden name,
Arne (the daughter of an upholfterer), than of that fhe had
created by her own abilities."—" Yes, but remember (faid
the Duke) fhe naturally and properly defpifed her husband.
Still, all this does not fully explain why we have among us fo
few defcendants of performers of either fex : there feems almoft a fatality about the profeffion, and moft of the ladies of
the ftage, who have married well, have no children.　I do not
mention Lord Derby and Mifs Farren, becaufe he was old
when he took her off the boards."—" I faw her (faid I) as
late as 1820, driven down to the Queen's trial by Lord
Derby in a gay phaeton : fhe was then much wrinkled."
—The Duke left me by referring to the famous paffage in
" Macbeth", where the brief " hour" of a player's glory is
recorded.　My laft remark was, that thofe words, having
paffed into a proverb, had partly led to their own verification.

He brought me to London after breakfaft next day: the
other guefts had, I think, departed overnight.

June 6.—I have the following from a gentleman of the
higheft refpectability, who afferts that he obtained the information from Kean himfelf : ftill, we may doubt as to the
truth of the matter, although it is in the actor's own words :

" I was born in the year 1787 ; and, if anybody ask you who was
my mother, say Miss Tidswell, the actress : my father was the late

Duke of Norfolk, whom they called Jockey. I know that I am ille-
gitimate, but what of that? who knows whether he is legitimate or
not? It is a wise child, they say, that knows its own father; but I
know mine, as far as the assertion of my mother may go. I am not
the son of Moses Kean, the mimic, nor of his brother, as some people
are pleased to assert, though I bear the same name. I had the
honour of being brought up at Arundel Castle till I was seven years
old; and there they sometimes, I do not know why, called me Dun-
can. After I quitted Arundel Castle, I was soon put upon the stage
by my mother, and I will tell you the very first part in which I appeared: it was the robbers' boy in the 'Iron Chest', when it was
originally brought out at Drury Lane in 1796, so that I was then only
about nine years old: Kemble was Sir E. Mortimer, a character I
have often played since, and not the least like Kemble: he did not
understand the part, but I do not pretend that I thought so then: I
think so now—indeed, I am sure of it. I did little till I was sixteen
or seventeen, when, strange to say, I had an old man's part in 'Who
Wants a Guinea', at the Haymarket. Fawcet was at the wing, and
when I got off the stage applauded me, and said I was a clever young
fellow. That is my early history as far as the stage is concerned. I
tell you what, sir, as to my real paternity: I was at Arundel Castle a
few years ago; and, as I showed to the people who had charge of it, I
knew every room, passage, winding, and turning in it. In one of the
large apartments hung a picture of the old Duke of Norfolk, and the
man who was with me said, turning first to me and then to the portrait, 'You are very like the old Duke, sir.' And well he might say
so, for the reason I have given you: I am his son."

I inquired of the gentleman who. told me this ſtory,
whether Kean was quite ſober at the time? He anſwered
that, although it was after dinner, the narrator had taken
little wine. I do not remember the parts of the Boy or of
the Old Man. Kean always repudiated the idea that he
was the ſon of Saville Carey.

June 8.—A friend has given me a few old newſpapers,

with fome curious paragraphs in them : what follows is from *The Daily Poft*, of Sept. 19, 1723.

"His Royal Highness the Prince of Wales [afterwards George II], with several persons of quality of both sexes, went on Monday night last to Mr. Pankithman's, the famous comedian's, Booth in South-wark Fair; where his celebrated droll of *Jane Shore*, his surprising *Picture of the Royal Family*, and the wonderful performances of his *Tumblers*, gave his Royal Highness and the rest of the company entire satisfaction."

June 11.—Southey and Coleridge, as is well known, married two fifters of the name of Fricker : I never faw either of them, but a third fifter fettled as a mantua-maker in London, and for fome years fhe worked for my mother and her daughters. She was an intelligent woman, but by no means above her bufinefs, though fhe was fond of talk-ing of her two poet-married relations. She was intro-duced to my mother by the following note from Mary Lamb, who always fpoke of my fifters as *her* girls.

"DEAR MRS. C.,—This note will be given to you by a young friend of mine, whom I wish you would employ : she has commenced busi-ness as a mantua-maker, and, if you and my girls would try her, I think she could fit you all three, and it will be doing her an essential service. She is, I think, very deserving, and if you procure work for her among your friends and acquaintances, so much the better. My best love to you and my girls. We are both well.

"Yours affectionately,
"MARY LAMB."

The note had no date, but it was long kept by my mother : the refult was the employment of Mifs Fricker for at leaft feven years; and then, if I remember rightly, fhe returned to her family in Briftol.

The finding of a copy of this note relating to Coleridge's

fifter-in-law (the fifter of his wife), puts me in mind of an incident related, when I was one of the company, by the Rev. H. J. Rofe, head of King's College, London, whither I fend my two boys to fchool. The incident, as I well re-collect, was this.

Coleridge came to Rofe one day early, obvioufly in great trouble : he fat down without faying a word, and tears even began to flow down his cheeks. Rofe inquired earneftly what was the matter—what was weighing upon his mind ? but for fome time he could get no anfwer. At laft, Cole-ridge told him that he was come to confult him about fomething relating to the conduct of his wife. Rofe was ftartled, yet he could not think that fhe had been guilty of any ferious mifconduct, and told him fo. Coleridge an-fwered that what fhe had done, if he yielded to it, would embitter the reft of his life. Rofe was alarmed, and be-fought Coleridge to tranquillife himfelf, and to tell him what had happened : he hinted a hope that it was nothing affecting her moral character as a wife.—" Oh, no (faid Coleridge), nothing of that kind, but it is fomething that I cannot think of without the deepeft pain."—" Well (faid Rofe), let us hear it : perhaps it is not fo bad as you at this moment confider it."—" I came to you (added Coleridge), as a friend and a clergyman, to afk. you what I ought under the circumftances to do ?"—" Let me hear the cir-cumftances (rejoined Rofe), and then I may be better able to judge. Calm yourfelf."

Again Coleridge wiped his " large gray eyes", and went on to apologife for the trouble he was giving. Rofe affured him that his main trouble was to fee a friend fo unhappy ; and, after beating about the bufh for fome time

M

longer, Coleridge declared that he could never live with his wife again, if fhe were not brought to her fenfes. Rofe here began to fear that Mrs. Coleridge had literally gone out of her mind; but Coleridge reaffured him upon that head, adding, however, that a fane woman could hardly have required of her husband what fhe had expected from him; viz., that on the coldeft mornings, even when the fnow was on the ground, and icicles hanging from the eves of their cottage, fhe compelled him to get out of bed in his night-fhirt, and light the fire, before fhe began to drefs herfelf and the baby (I fuppofe H. N. C.).

Rofe could hardly reftrain himfelf from a burft of laughter at this woeful difclofure; but what took place afterwards he did not explain, farther than by faying that he at laft relieved Coleridge's mind fo effectually, that he went away comparatively cheerful. I had heard fomething of this ftory before, with greater or lefs exaggeration: H. C. Robinfon had mentioned it at my father's; but here I had it from one of the parties to the interview. Even as Rofe related it, it appeared to be more invention than reality. Neverthelefs it was quite true. Whether Mrs. Coleridge was fubfequently induced to relax a little the feverity of her rule, I do not know. My notion is, that Coleridge was abroad at the time this ftory was current.

June 13.—The following may have already been translated, and it deferves it, though I do not recollect to have feen any attempt of the kind: I take it from the *Faccetiæ* of Poggio, p. 127 of the edition of 1564.

> A man with melancholy mien,
> Paffing along the ftreet was feen.
> " What ails you?" afk'd a friend.—

> The other answer'd, " I'm in debt,
> And cannot pay."—" How can you let
> Such grov'ling thoughts your spirit fret ?
> Leave them to such as lend."

Theodore Hook was at the Garrick Club late laft night, with James Smith (author of " Rejected Addreffes," etc.), and fome others. I joined the merry gin-punch drinking party, while I flowly confumed a fingle glafs of the fame beverage. One principal topic of converfation was a fmall femi-ferious burlefque production, which Hook (as was afferted, and he did not deny it) had put forth in 1820, about the time of the Queen's trial, in ridicule of Sir Mathew Wood, Lord Mayor of London, under the pretence that it was the hiftory of Whittington, and called " *Ten-tamen,* or an Effay towards the Hiftory of Whittington," with a likenefs of Wood upon the title-page. It fills nearly a hundred fmall octavo pages, and is by no means deficient in drollery, fatire, and ability, but ftill it is too long for a joke. Hook did not fay a word in defence of it, and I have never feen any lift of his works that contains it. The mock dedication of it to the Duke of Suffex is not one of the worft parts of it, efpecially where he charges the Duke with having been the patron of fome thirty or forty charities, without having given one penny to any of them. If the trifle have been mentioned anywhere, I have not happened to fee it : it was printed by the printer and at the office of the *John Bull* newfpaper.

The following joke was talked about on the fame evening, by James Smith. After the death of George III, a clergyman preached at the Savoy on the acceffion of George IV, choofing his text from I Kings, xv, 24 : " And

Afa flept with his fathers, and was buried with his fathers, in the city of David his father, and Jehofafat (viz., *Geo*, or George, *fo fat*) reigned in his ftead." George IV, at this time, weighed nearly twenty ftone, and the new King, being told of the undefigned joke, took it in good part, and anfwered merrily and appofitely, that it was better to be *Geo-fo-fat*, than Jehofabad (*Geo-fo-bad*). *Ben Trovato* is the real author of many jokes, and this may be one of his.

June 14.—I was lucky enough this morning to meet again with an old friend—a book that I have miffed for a good many years: it was one of my earlieft purchafes of the kind—Roger Biefton's " Bayte and Snare of Fortune", printed by Wayland before the Reformation. It is a very thin folio, and it had flipped behind fome other books. It is a very clever difcuffion on the value and ufes of money, the refult being that money is admitted to be fuperior to everything elfe : it is a dialogue between Man and Money. Man throughout has the beft of the argument, but Money at the clofe the beft of the bargain. This Biefton, or Bee-fton, was the father or grandfather of the men of the fame name, who were connected with our old theatres before and after the time of Shakefpeare. Thomas Nafh, in 1592, dedicated to a Beefton one of his anfwers to G. Harvey.

Some weeks ago, I purchafed the third edition of Jofhua Sylvefter's fo-called " tranflation" of Du Bartas. The work has always been treated as a mere tranflation, a tame ver-fion from French into Englifh ; but it is by no means that, or anything like it : people who have written about it have never read it, or they would have feen that not much lefs than a quarter of it is *an original poem*, in which Sylvefter

not only fpeaks of himfelf, but of his contemporary, and
even earlier poets : thus, in one place he mentions " Chaucer and his Donnington"; and elfewhere, Spenfer, Sydney,
Daniel, Drayton, and nearly all the diftinguifhed poets of
the day, *excepting Shakefpeare.* In other places, he
fketches his own hiftory ; how he was born at Lambourn,
in Kent ; and how he had been toffed about by fortune,
both at home and abroad, until he fet himfelf down to the
tafk of giving a fort of anglicifed Du Bartas, introducing
many pages of original matter. Surely, for inftance, the following defcription of London in the reigns of Elizabeth
and James I is curious, and deferves efpecial notice : Sylvefter fuppofes a boor to fee London for the firft time.

> " When afterward he happens to behold
> Our welthy London's wonders manifold,
> The silly peasant thinks himself to be
> In a new world ; and gazing greedily,
> One while he, artlesse, all the arts admires,
> Then the faire temples and their topless spires,
> Their firm foundations, and the massie pride
> Of all their sacred ornaments beside.
> Anon he wonders at the different graces,
> Tongues, gests, attires, the fashions, the faces
> Of busie buzzing swarms, which still he meets,
> Ebbing and flowing over all the streets :
> Then at the signes, the shops, the waights, the measures,
> The handy-crafts, the rumors, trades, and treasures.
> But of all sights none seems to him more strange
> Than the rare, beautious, statly, rich Exchange.
> Another while he marvails at the Thames,
> Which seems to bear huge mountains on her streames :
> Then at the fair built bridge, which he doth judge
> More like a tradefull city than a bridge ;
> And glancing thence along the northern shoar,
> That princely prospect doth amaze him more."

June 15.—Canning died in the fummer of 1827, and R. Terry, now, I believe, Attorney-General in New South Wales, gave me his Memoir of the orator when it was publifhed. I think I have already mentioned dining, by invitation, with Canning in 1826, when he was living in Brompton, in a houfe the property of Lord Harrington. He was then ill, almoft unable to prefide at his own table ; and, early in the evening, his place was fupplied by Sir J. Mackintofh, who had alfo taken fome fort of fancy to me. Mr. Robert Gordon, then M.P. for Cricklade, was alfo prefent, and him I confidered my particular friend : he had carried me thither with him. I may here note, I hope without undue vanity, that Gordon fhewed me a letter from Canning to him, in which the minifter fpoke of me in much handfomer terms than I merited : he told Gordon "to keep an eye upon me, for he believed that fome day I fhould gain diftinction"; referring alfo generoufly to my conduct at the bar of the Houfe of Commons, when I was placed there for an injury I had unconfcioufly done to him. Had Canning lived, and remained in office, he might, and I think would, have aided me in obtaining fome public fituation in connection with my profeffion : he was as good as his word with others, whom he importantly ferved, but they were earlier in the field. When I afterwards afked Canning's fucceffors in power, to affift me, they either made me hollow profeffions of good-will, or offered me fomething that they knew I could not, with my family, accept. I mention no names, but I foon gave up afking. One of the propofals made to me was, that I fhould take a *puifné* judgefhip in one of the unhealthieft of our Weft India Iflands. Canning had given a poor deferving barrifter-friend of mine a place worth £1500 a year.

The Duke lately took me with him to Holland Houfe, and introduced me to the mafter and miftrefs : his lordfhip was eafy and gentlemanly, but my lady, the *divorcée* of Sir Godfrey Webfter, was evidently on her hind legs. I do not wonder that fhe ran away with Lord Holland, a moft engaging man ; but I do wonder that he ran away with her, a coarfe, overweening woman. There were plenty of literary celebrities there, from Moore and Campbell down to R., but we did not ftay long : it was quite obvious that " my lady" required a good deal of homage, but I kept out of her way, and fo, I thought, did the Duke, after he had paid his firft attention to her. She was fond of having a deferential circle round her, while Lord Holland moved about, and made himfelf agreeable to everybody. She is ftated to be arrogant and felf-willed, and does not fcruple to intrude herfelf where fhe likes : I am credibly informed that when there is a meeting of the truftees of the Britifh Mufeum, though fhe has no more right to be there than any woman out of the ftreet, fhe expects not only to be allowed to be prefent, but to offer her opinion upon any queftion, literary or fcientific. I faid to Sir Henry Ellis (Chief Librarian) one day, " Whofe chair is that upon wheels ?" —" That is Lady Holland's feat (he replied), and fhe is wheeled into the truftees' room upon it, and always placed on the left hand of the prefident." I laughed at the notion ; but he added that it was her cuftom, when in London, and that no truftee feemed difpofed to difpute her right. The Duke was one of the firft to leave Holland Houfe, and he took me back with him to Devonfhire Houfe, from whence, after a glafs of wine and water, I went home.

June 16.—Nobody, as far as I have feen, has done juftice

to Goethe's fong of fun and jollity in his "Fauft": fome have not attempted to put it into rhyme, but have left it in bald profe : others have tried to give the merriment in verfe of one kind or another, but not at all, as it feems to me, in the fpirit, or with anything like the fpirit, of the original.   It ought to be read as part of the noify, mirthful ruftic fcene, and, feparated from it, it will not go fo well ; but I have infolently attempted it in correfponding meafure, and what follows is the refult : we are to fancy the vociferous party dancing round a tree.

> For dancing now is dight the clown,
> With ribbon'd jacket, garland-crown,
>   So smart, head, heels, and middle :
> The ring is full around the tree,
> All dance right mad and merrily.
>   Huzza ! huzza !
>   Fol de rol lol la !
>   To the scraping of the fiddle.
>
> Into the throng one made a rush,
> And gave a buxom lass a push,
>   With elbow, rudely rather :
> She turn'd her round with angry brow,
> And cried, " Don't be so stupid now."
>   Huzza ! huzza !
>   Fol de rol lol la !
>   " I wish you had been farther."
>
> But nimbly went the circle still,
> And right and left they danc'd, until
>   The kirtles all were flying :
> The men and maids grew red and warm,
> And rested breathless arm in arm,
>   Huzza ! huzza !
>   Fol de rol lol la !
>   Hip against elbow lying.

Have done ! don't be so impudent.
How many a lass had need repent
  The breach of troth here plighted !
But soon he coax'd the maid aside,
While from the lime-tree sounded wide.
    Huzza ! huzza !
    Fol de rol lol la !
  Music and shouts united. .

June 14.—In the prologue to " Fame's Sacrifice", 1686 (which, by the way, was never acted), I find the following impudent plagiarifm by Nahum Tate.   He is fpeaking of Milton :

" While each rich thought of yours, each massy line,
  Drawn to French wire, shall thro' whole volumes shine."

It ftands thus in Rofcommon's famous " Effay on Trans-lated Verfe":

" The weighty bullion of one sterling line,
  Drawn to French wire, would thro' whole pages shine."

All that Tate did was, by exaggerating, to fpoil.   Ros-common died fome years before "The Sacrifice" was printed, and he could not have had the thought from Tate.

The following lines are from a prologue by Oldmixon to Gildon's alteration of "Meafure for Meafure", 1700; which alludes to Dryden's " McFlecknoe", and reminds us, at the clofe, of the opening of Pope's " Dunciad":

" Good sense was well receiv'd from honest Ben,
  While none would suffer Flecknoe's Irish pen :
  Yet in his *son* [the] sleeping monarch reigns,
  And dreadful war with wit and sense maintains.
  Study the Smithfield bards and him with care ;
  Like those write nonsense, and like these you'll fare."

N

June 18.—" We have already had a good deal of pleafant talk about our old dramatifts, their plays, and actors,
and you have mentioned to me fome of the names both of
their productions and their authors, with which I was not till
then acquainted. I want you now to give me, as far as you
conveniently can, fome notion of their different character-
iftics—I mean particularly of our old dramatifts."

Thefe are the words with which the Duke began a converfation with me yefterday ; and I will endeavour, as
nearly as poffible (and my memory is good), to write down
what paffed between us.

C. Nothing could give me greater pleafure than to be
able to comply with your requeft ; but, even if I were fully
competent to do fo, it would occupy more time than I
apprehend you have at difpofal.

D. You have already done fomething of the kind I want
in the poem you have called my "Dream", where you fay of
Shakefpeare,

> " Him there I saw with ample forehead high,
> And look all careless of his future glory."

C. And perhaps I may be pardoned for faying, that I
have there fuccefsfully touched both his perfonal and
profeffional character : the lines are a picture both of the
man and of his mind ; and there is, in my opinion, no
ftronger, or ftranger feature of Shakefpeare's faculties, than
his utter disregard of what might be his reputation after
death : when he got back to his native town, at about the
age of only fifty, he feems to have cared no more for his
immortal plays than for the duft upon his fhoes.

D. That is certainly moft extraordinary—as if he had
gone to London merely to fell a commodity, and returned

to Stratford to fpend the profit of the tranfaction, and enjoy tranquilly the remainder of his retired life. Jonfon, we know, took pains to collect and print his "laboured fcenes"; while Shakefpeare left his productions, like waifs upon the wide ocean, to take their chance of perifhing or prefervation.

C. And this has always feemed to me one of the moft inexplicable points of Shakefpeare's character—juft as if he thought all he had done, whether as plays or poems, not worth a moment's regard, or even recollection.

D. This, however, is going a little out of the courfe I now wifh to follow. I want to know, in as brief a form as you can put it, what were the broader and more obvious peculiarities of his dramatic contemporaries. I got by heart, as you know, the earlier ftanzas of my "Dream", as you call it; and there fome of the epithets you apply to various poets, fuch as "ferene" to Chapman, "bold" to Marfton, "ready" to Dekker, "prolific" to Heywood, and fo on, partly fupply what I want, but only partly. I defire more information.

C. You fet me no eafy tafk, recollecting their numbers and their efpecial characters as poets. Befides, where fhall I begin? If in point of date, there are feveral—I may fay many—who were contemporaneous, and whofe feparate claims it is very difficult to decide upon. You will, perhaps, give me leave to pafs over fuch notorious names as Ben Jonfon and Beaumont and Fletcher.

D Is it known, in the cafe of Beaumont and Fletcher, which of the plays, in the large folio of 1640, were by the one and by the other?

C. Generally it is; and, as Beaumont (an anceftor, as I

underftood, of a family I remember meeting at Chatfworth)
died rather early, not a few of the plays muft belong to
Fletcher alone, who had a much more lively and fanciful
genius than his grave partner. I will pafs over them as well
known; and the fame may now be faid of Ford, Maffinger,
and Shirley, whofe works have been edited by Gifford with
undoubted ability, though with too much reliance on his
own knowledge and powers, and two little refpect for the
attainments and information of his predeceffors.

D. He was an arrogant cobbler—the fon of a fhoemaker,
I believe, but learned and clever.

C. Indifputably. Chriftopher Marlowe deferves a place
next to Shakefpeare—indeed, before him in this important
refpect : he was the originator of the ufe of blank-verfe on
the ftage, and his firft drama of the kind, "Tamburlaine
the Great", was printed in 1590, feven years before the appearance from the prefs of Shakefpeare's earlieft play.
Shakefpeare, no doubt, had written for the ftage before
1592; but in "Love's Labour's Loft", as well as in
"Titus Andronicus", rhyme fometimes prevails; for even
Shakefpeare, the year before Marlowe's death, had not
freed himfelf from the fhackle of rhyme. Marlowe was a
genius of a high order; but, although he wrote our oldeft
ftrictly hiftorical play, "Edward the Second", he did not
live to complete his own defign.

D. In his "Edward the Second" did Marlowe, befides
difcarding rhyme, difcard alfo the unities of time, place,
and action ?

C. He did; but he was not the firft to do fo, in all probability, as even Bifhop Bale had fet the unities at defiance
in his drama of "King John", the original MS. of which,
you may remember, I bought for your library.

D. Whom do you place after Marlowe ?

C. Poffibly Thomas Kyd, the author of two plays, of very oppofite character, which are printed in Dodfley's Collection, " Cornelia" and " The Spanifh Tragedy": in the laft the rhyme is occafional, but in the firft whole fpeeches, and even fcenes, are in jingling meafure. Kyd was a powerful writer, but his imagination was not lofty nor various. After Kyd, poffibly before him, we ought to mention Lily, but he only wrote plays in profe, and that affectedly. Then comes Robert Greene, who has the merit of having furnifhed the charming novel on which Shakefpeare founded his " Winter's Tale"; while Lodge, another early dramatift, who ftill adhered chiefly to rhyme on the ftage, produced the happy narrative which Shakefpeare ufed in " As You Like It." Greene, who was more a man of fancy than of imagination, wrote moft of his dramas without rhyme, and one of the beft of them is contained in the laft edition of Dodfley's Old Plays in 1825 : to that impreffion I added five of the rareft dramas by Greene, Peele (who wrote a hiftorical tragedy on the events of the reign of Edward I, in blank verfe), and Lodge, a heavy play-poet, who penned blank verfe with much of the monotony of our earlier rhymers : Lodge was a charming lyrical poet, but a fomewhat wearifome dramatift. All thefe may be confidered Shakefpeare's early contemporaries, when he was trying the ftrength of his wing. He foon diftanced all rivals, both in height, ftrength, and fpeed.

D. Who followed thefe ?

C. A crowd of competing poets, who never afcended to the loftieft flights, but who now and then wrote admirable poetry, and conftructed excellent dramas : of thefe, Heywood and Dekker may claim to be firft named.

D. Since you lately pointed them out to me, I have read the two plays by Heywood, "Edward the Fourth" and the "Woman Killed with Kindnefs": I like parts, and even whole fcenes, of the firft, efpecially thofe in which Jane Shore is engaged ; but I was charmed by the fimplicity and pathos of the laft.

C. I am glad of it : it deferves all your admiration, for it is full of truth and tendernefs. Charles Lamb called Heywood "a profe Shakefpeare", and that gives his true character in an epithet. Dekker was not equal to Heywood in any refpect but facility. I ought not to omit the names of Munday, Webfter, Middleton, Rowley, Day, with many others ; and I can affure you that, though hundreds of old plays have come down to us in a moft mutilated ftate, from various caufes, there is hardly one of them that does not contain fomething excellent. I call to mind at this moment an old anonymous drama, which may be faid to prefent only one couplet that is remarkable, but it is fuch a couplet as might have proceeded from the pen of Shakefpeare himfelf without derogation. I have noted the fimile in my memorandum-book for its wonderful fenfe, compreffion, and novelty : it is this :

> " Justice, like lightning, ever should appear
> To few men's ruin, but to all men's fear."

D. Admirable!—furely, when we ponder upon it, nothing can well be finer in its fententioufnefs, its originality, and in its exact applicability.

C. If time allowed, I could point out innumerable proofs of the fame kind : hear thefe four lines, which I cannot forget, though I do not remember the name of the play they belong to :

> " Vain the ambition of kings,
>   Who seek by trophies and vain things
>   To leave a living name behind,
>   And weave but nets to catch the wind."

Or this, ftill fhorter, but moft pregnant of meaning :

> " Though in our miseries fortune have a part,
>   Yet in our noble sufferings she hath none."

This laft is from a fine tragedy, and by a man in what rank of life ?—Only a parifh-clerk, John Webfter.

D. You delight me. What is the name of his tragedy ?

C. "The Duchefs of Malfi." I hope that my friend Mr. Dyce will foon prefent us with an edition of his works. This is not the occafion for entering on the fubject, but I feel certain that many of the prodigious inequalities we perceive in our old tragedies and comedies arife out of the fact, not only that they were imperfectly taken down in fhorthand, but that fome, and perhaps confiderable portions of them were dictated from the memory of a perfon fent to the theatre, in order that a publifher, or a rival company of players, might benefit by a popular piece : ftriking fentences were remembered, and the reft was filled up according to the fkill of the perfon fo employed. This is my conjecture, but capable of fome proof, and it will account for feveral fuppofed errors, even in Shakespeare.

D. I grieve that we cannot go further now, but we muft break off here at prefent : another day I fhall be moft happy to renew our converfation on this highly interefting, and to me inftructive, fubject.

C. I can affure you, your time will not be wafted ; and, for myfelf, I am never weary of talking of our old ftage and its literary ornaments : my hope is, that I fhall not weary *you*.

D. Never fear that. Farewell for to-day.

June 19.—Having been ftruck in my youth by reading fome of the adventurous incidents in the lives of the early difcoverers of America, I thought that Vafco Nunez de Bilbao would not make a bad hero for a poem ; but I am not aware how far Barlow has availed himfelf of the circum- ftances attending the extraordinary career of this great and difinterefted victim. I began my work, and proceeded with it for fome hundred ftanzas, and the two following are the earlieft of them, juft after the poor but brave Vafco has been difcovered on board the fhip of Fernando, the com- mander of the expedition. I thus plunged at once into the ftory, adopting the octave ftanza as my vehicle.

> " Bring him before us !" said Fernando loud.
>   They brought him, clad in weeds of humbleft kind,
> But looking like a Spaniard, bold and proud,
>   As if within him stirr'd a haughty mind.
> He stood erect : his head he slightly bowed,
>   Perchance to prove his manners were refined
> Above his weeds ; and, with a steady eye
> Look'd on Fernando ; not insultingly,
>
> But as a man who was above all guilt,
>   Though not, indeed, above all sufferance ;
> Who in adventure blood had often spilt,
>   And pass'd through many a hardship and mischance.
> On his own worth he far too firmly built
>   To quail before th' Alcaldé's angry glance.
> Fernando cried, biting his pallid lip,
> " Villain ! how dar'st thou come on board my ship ?"

Such was the introduction of my hero; and, after another ſtanza, Vaſco thus anſwered :

> " I come to seek adventure, take my share
>   In all the perils of the sea or land :
> I ask no favour, nor beseech you spare
>   The vengeance you may threaten and command.
> Cast me on shore; you have one less to dare
>   The dangers that beset you on each hand.
> I say no more : do as you deem most fit.
> Your's is the power—mine courage to submit."

The commander of the expedition, thus aſſured, placed confidence in the ſtranger ; and Vaſco, having ſailed before in thoſe unknown ſeas, ſteered the veſſel ſafely into Darien, and ere long he became, in faĉt, the leader of the party. My heroine was to have been a truſtful and truthful Indian girl, but ſhe was not to come upon the ſcene for ſome time. The catastrophe was to be the ſelf-devoted execution of Vaſco, in the official robes of white which, according to hiſtory, he wore. One more ſtanza, regarding Vaſco and his early ſervices, is all that I ſhall extraĉt :

> But Vasco had an open generous nature,
>   Above all malice for past injuries :
> His mind, in truth, was noble as his stature,
>   And bent alone on gallant enterprise.—
> The wind was fair, and soon the sea-borne creature,
>   The ship, had won the port where Darien lies :
> They came to anchor in a spacious river,
> And the glad crew was bound to him for ever.

I had not proceeded very far in the ſtory before a ſit of ſelf-diſtruſt ſeized my pen, and, laying it down, I never took it up again.

O

June 21.—I have met with a very curious, and, as I think, unknown, printed broadfide, relating to the players at the Red Bull Theatre in the fummer of 1661 : it is headed "Boca-linus Junior, or News from Pernaffus", in which the Actors are reprefented as addreffing Apollo, to whom they could get no better introduction than a Beadle, a Broom-man, and an Orange-girl, fuch as Nell Gwin had been. The principal prayer is, that the god would take pity upon their poverty, and pay the rent of their houfe, obferving that their three plays, " Tu Quoque", "Young Admiral" (mifprinted *Admir-able*), and "Poor Man's Comfort", proved unproductive. "Tu Quoque" was, of courfe, the popular comedy by John Cooke ; " The Young Admiral" was by James Shirley ; and " The Poor Man's Comfort", by Robert Daiborne.   All three had been attractive in their day, but they had been fuper-feded by Sir W. Davenant's " Siege of Rhodes", which is particularly mentioned as then having a long run at the Blackfriars Theatre.   The date, 1661, was the period of the transformation of our drama from Englifh to French.

June 22.—I know not precifely how many years ago the following fong was written, but I remember to whom it was addreffed, and how it was received.   I quote it, though boyifh, with more confidence than ufual—perhaps becaufe it is boyifh.

THE YOUNG LOVER'S OLD SONG.

My lady sweet, you have my heart,
  And, having that, my all :
From thee it never can depart,
  'Tis such a joyous thrall :
For night and day I think and say,
Thou art my Love, my Lady May.

Say, shall I prove my constancy
  In ways till now untried?
Oh ! tell me how, and I will fly,
  Though far from thy dear side.
Go where I will, I see thee still,
The sum of all my good or ill.

Shall I go seek the Indian coast,
  To bring thee gems and gold?
Ah, no ! for thou thyself can boast
  More jewels manifold !
Thou art a gem worth all of them :
Dull diamonds thou may'st well contemn.

Shall I invade the realms of ice,
  Far in the frosty north?
Say, and 'tis done : there is no price
  That I not hold thee worth !
Thou art my sun, and winter none,
When I remember thou art won !

The heat and cold I both despise,
  So I have thy good will :
The climate that the farthest lies
  Remindeth of thee still :
When far away I'd smile and say,
Thou art my own, my Lady May.

Now, set the task : what need I care,
  I will not from it turn ;
Be it on earth, in sea or air,
  To freeze, to drown, to burn.
Whate'er I do shall prove me true,
To love, to live, to die for you !

June 23.—Although it is now nearly twenty years fince,
I diftinctly recollect the firft time I faw Coleridge and
Lamb together : they came to my father's ; he then living
in Hatton Garden, but was not at home : H. C. R. was

was there to receive them; and the converfation turning upon the finenefs of the day, my mother faid that the fun had almoft put out her eyes. "Yes," faid Coleridge, quoting a line from "Love's Labour's Loft",

> "Light seeking light doth light of light beguile."

I did not then know from whence the line came, but I knew it was verfe, not only from the meafure, but from the peculiar, rather fing-fong way in which Coleridge pronounced the paffage. Lamb made another quotation from the very fame play on the fame day; for my mother was employed upon painting a rofe, and Lamb, obferving it, faid,

> "At Christmas I no more desire a rose,
> Than wish a snow in May's new-fangled shows."

But how he applied it I do not remember, becaufe it it was now midfummer, not winter. They both made themfelves very agreeable, and even my young mind was ftruck by the pleafant way in which they treated the familiar topics of converfation; while Coleridge, as I thought, efpecially endeavoured to adapt his remarks to the younger children. I was then about fixteen or feventeen, and was in the middle of Spenfer's "Fairy Queen", out of which, not very long afterwards, grew my "Poet's Pilgrimage". I felt vaft reverence for Coleridge, and was a moft greedy liftener. They did not ftay long, but went away with Robinfon.

June 24.—Seeing thefe lines in Dryden's "Effay upon Satire", as printed among "State Poems", I, 179,

> "So cat, transform'd, sat gravely and demure,
> Till mouse appear'd, and thought himself secure;
> But soon the lady had him in her eye,
> And from her friend did just as oddly fly",

I called to mind that, when firft I went to Paris, while the Allied Forces were ftill there, I faw a famous *comédienne* act the part of the transformed cat moft admirably, ftill reminding the audience of all her feline pro-penfities, turning round to play with her tail, or fcratching her ear with her paw, all the time fhe was alfo fustaining her human part in the afterpiece, as though unable to get completely rid of her natural habits. I cannot call to mind her name, nor that of the author of the *vaudeville*, but the whole was moft cleverly done, efpecially by the actrefs. I am afhamed of my forgetfulnefs.

On my next vifit to the French capital, I had the advantage of again feeing Talma, the great French tragedian, in "Mithridates." He had not, as I have elfewhere faid, a good figure, too fquat and round, and his face not very expreffive, but his voice was fine and full, and gave the utmoft effect to Racine's lines. It was a Racine night, for "Mithridates" was followed by "*Les Plaideurs*", which I muft fay, I did not enjoy, nor, as it feemed to me, did the audience The heroine of the tragedy was Madlle. Georges, a fine large woman, but a mouthing actrefs. I had not an opportunity of feeing Madame Duchesnois, and I am the more forry, as, while I was once in Paris, fhe played Lady Macbeth in a French verfion of that tragedy. On a fubfequent vifit, a few years later, I faw Madlle. Mars in one of Molière's comedies, " L'Ecole des Femmes", and was highly gratified.

June 25.—The following documents, regarding Dr. B. Hoadly's admirable comedy, " The Sufpicious Husband", I think, quite new, and worth the trouble of copying. It fhould feem that Hoadly had prefented the piece to Garrick under the title of " The Rake", and had allowed him to use it in any way that appeared to him most advantageous; whether by representation, or by selling the copyright, when printed for some publisher. It had been originally brought out at Covent Garden, as " The Suspicious Husband", on Feb. 12th, 1747, when Garrick acted Ranger; but on Dec. 4th, in the same year, it was removed to Drury Lane, Garrick still playing the hero, but supported by Macklin, Yates, Mrs. Pritchard, etc. The following is in Garrick's handwriting; and the documents, in relation to a comedy so celebrated, are worth giving, from the originals just lent to me.

" In consideration of £80, which I am to receive from Mr. Rich, I shall give up half the profits to him of the third, sixth, and ninth nights, arising from the new comedy called " The Rake"; and am to allow Mr. Rich £60 each of the said nights for the charges of his house.

" Witness my hand,

" D. GARRICK.

" 27th December, 1746.

" N.B.—The copy of the play is my own, and the profit arising from the printing it."

On the back is the following receipt:

" Feb. 11th, 1746.

" Received of Mr. Rich, by Mr. White, eighty pounds in full for the agreement on the other side.

" £80. " DAVID GARRICK.

" N.B.—The title of " The Rake" was altered to " The Suspicious Husband."

June 28.—The Duke took me with him to Sir John Soane's Museum in Lincoln's Inn Fields. It is worth inspection, not only from the works of *vertu* and the curioſities and antiquities it contains, but for the ſmall compaſs into which they are all compreſſed. The Duke had ſent word that he was coming, and the old gentleman was full dreſſed, and very garulous and amuſing, though he often did not talk loud enough for the Duke to hear him. He was particularly anxious that the Duke ſhould ſee the contrivance he had introduced into what is uſually (and too often) the ſmalleſt apartment in the houſe: the Duke, laughing heartily, was led into it by the conceited old architect; but I did not think it neceſſary to follow them, and remained behind looking at the admirable Hogarths, the ſeries of the Rake's Progreſs, and the Election: to save room on the ſurface of the walls they were let in, one behind another, in the depth of the walls, very ingeniouſly, so that when a ſpectator had done with one picture, he turned it back on hinges, and expoſed another and another. Sir John took infinite pains to be facetious and agreeable, and to make the Duke ſenſible of the value of his aſſemblage of nick-nacks. He was eſpecially vain of one relic—the walking-cane of Sir Chriſtopher Wren, having a compaſs at the head, a caſe of inſtruments in the handle, and a five-foot rule encloſed in the lower part of the ſtick. I had never ſeen the Hogarths before, and they infinitely gratified me: ſo they did the Duke, who had alſo never ſeen the originals.

June 30.—I was at Lambeth yeſterday, and had an opportunity of copying a very valuable hiſtorical letter belonging to the year 1554, from Francis More to his maſter, the Earl of Shrewsbury, but without any ſtatement of the place where his lordſhip was then reſiding. It is ignorantly written and ſpelt, but it enters into many highly curious particulars of public and private events of that important time. I quote it *litcratim*, for to attempt to amend it would probably in fome places obfcure and alter, inftead of explaining and preferving the meaning of the writer. As far as my knowledge goes, it (like many others there) has never been printed : the mention of Sir Thomas Wyat and his accomplices is moft curious.

"Pleseth yt your lordshep to be adverteysed that, thanks be unto god, it is good quyetnes here; and the quene taques her jorney the nexte weke to Wensor, and ther tary tell after Ester halledeys, and then to Oxforthe, by the gras of god : the harbengyrs hath ben there, and they sey ther is logeng playce : more hors meyt ys the worste to come by. I have spoken with mester Tempell, and he well make the provigion that may be possible for your lordshep.

"If ytt shell pleys your lordshep forther, at my forste commeng I spoke to meyster Pcylestar concernyng the leytor your lordshep seynd to the quene, and how your lordshep was in dowte wether it came to the quenc or nowe, be case you hade no prevate answer of it. Mary, quoth he, let me alone for that, and take your lordsheps frend. With in thre deys after he spoke with the quene, and asked her henes when she reysseved anie letorys frome your lordshep ? and her heneys said, Not thes good wylle. Your heneys rescyved a prevate letor from hem : ded you not wryte a nother to heme ? and she sayd, Noe, the Consell ded wryte to hem, bote I knew not wen they send to hem, for I [am] sure I wolde a wreten a letor of my none hand to hem, or, if you colde get on conveyed, yet I wold wryte. Mary, sethe he, her ys a roffe servand of ys in the towne even nowe. Then I wez commanded to tary, for I sholde have a leytor even forth with ; and so I have ben promessed yt every dey these viii or ix days from dey to dey : and yesternight I was commanded by meyster Ryse, of the preve chamber, from the quene, that I sholde not departe, for her heyneys hade soche besenys, that she had no leysor to despatche me note as yet, for her heness would be the roberatory her selfe to your lordshep.

"Me lord, oppon fryday laste, the cownty Degmonde and the

cownte de Horne came in frome the hemprower, and came to the corte vppone saterday ; and, as I herde by a frend of myne, they broght a good sowme of Frenge crowne with them frome the hemprowre to the quene.

And, forther, yf yt shall ples your lordshep, sense meystor Savvile wente from London, there hath ben letyl exequsson abowte London, bote uppon fryday laste ther went to exequsson into Kente vj or vij gentelmen, that wer the too Kneveyttes, too mantellys, on Sowgheron, on more, on other I know not; and sense I came hether ther ys gone to the Towre, firste Lorde Thomas Grey and rogaryster gawanbarowe, and on gebes and on sentlowe, my lade Elsabethe mane. She lyeth in the corte, and letel talkeng of her nowe. Ser Wellyam Pekeryng ys in Franse : ser Artor Hopton, that wer kneght marshall, I can not lern wat ys be come of hem. Wyhote ys note araigned as yet, nore a gret mene moo of them, bote yt ys thoght they shall be these weke, Wyhote araned and other moo of them.

" My lorde, I have send your lordshep her with the partecular soome the awdetor of styrton rentts that ys be hind unpeyd within your offes in Walse to the quene; and wer, as they knowe, not the names of your lordsheps offacyrs they have left a spas for them to be pute in, and they requier your lordshep that you wyll send streyt commandement to them that they wyll answer the rentts at the nexte awedet, or else your lordshep can not be answerable your selfe. And thes I beseche Jhu preserve your lordshep longe in helthe, with moche increse of honore to god's plesor. From Coldeharbor the forthe day of marche,   " By your lordshep servande,

" FRANCYS MORE."

A few days ago, and for a comparatively fmall fum, I bought an unknown edition of Thomas Heywood's historical play, founded upon events in the reign of Queen Elizabeth, entitled "If you Know not me you Know Nobody", 4to, 1609: the Duke had already in his library the earlieft impreffion of it in 1605, but the copy of 1609 was quite a novelty in the old-book world ; and he was fo glad of my find, that he read the drama, and told me he was highly pleafed with it : he was alfo, I may here venture to add, fo highly pleafed with me, that, when I faw him next morning, he faid, the firft thing, that I was fo ufeful to him that he was afhamed of the little annuity he paid me for my fervices, and that he would double it. I thanked him heartily for his kind intention, but obferved that, as there were two words to every bargain, I pofitively would not accept any addition to the falary he allowed me as his Librarian. At the fame time, I thanked the Duke moft warmly but refpectfully; and he, feeing my determination, both in my countenance and words, then faid no more upon the fubject, but fhook me by the hand, and propofed that I fhould once more accompany him to Edwin Landfeer's.

We went there accordingly, but it feemed to me that on the way the Duke was unufually grave and filent ; when we arrived, they withdrew immediately into an inner room beyond the ftudio, and left me to examine the ufual furniture of fuch a place ; viz., old armour, old chairs, old cafts, etc. When they came back, the Duke looked more than ufually cheerful!; and, after a little general converfation, we came away, and drove to Calcott's houfe at Kenfington Gravel-pits, where we did not fee him, but Mrs. Calcott, who, againft the Duke's will, came out to the carriage : fhe was the author of, I think, a " Life of Pouffin", and of a moft pleafing and popular book, " Letters from the Mountains": I had read neither.

On our way home, the Duke afked me if I knew Edwin Landfeer's brothers ; and I anfwered that I had feen two of them, Thomas and Charles, both very clever artifts, and that I had played billiards with Thomas Landfeer. I added that I had not unfrequently feen their father, an excellent engraver, who lived in a large houfe in Lindfey Row, Chelfea, where my mother's uncle alfo refided. I informed the Duke that I had once attended a feries of Lectures on Art, which Landfeer fenior had delivered, either at the Royal or Ruffell Inftitution, I had forgotten which. The Duke was rather difpofed to laugh at me for not knowing more of John Landfeer's " Sabæan Refearches", which contained moft of the matter embraced by thofe lectures, adding a fact, of which till then I knew nothing, that as early as 1807 old Landfeer had delivered, at the Royal Inftitution, a courfe of lectures efpecially upon the art of engraving. The Duke afked me if I had ever feen Edwin Landfeer's " Monkeyana", to which I was obliged to reply in the negative, and he promifed to fhew it to me when we got back to Piccadilly : he forgot to do fo, but I faw the work afterwards in another library : it came out in 1827.

I have found the following among my loofe papers : it is obvioufly by fome poor, namelefs, difappointed rhymer (calling himfelf *poet*), but is worth a place.

THE POET AND THE PUBLISHER.

I took my Poem to a thriving tradesman,
　To ask if he would publish it—a trifle?
Though the confession, much I fear, degrades man,
　The real truth I'll not attempt to stifle :
To read it o'er to him I condescended,
And thus the man bespake me, when I ended.

" Your poem, sir, no doubt 's extremely good,
　Your subject also with some skill you chose ;
But would it not be better understood,
　If it were treated plainly—as mere prose ?
In prose the lesson you enforce would tell well,
And rhyme, I'm sorry to confess, don't sell well.

" Your work has some good sense ; and that, you know,
  Your real poets very seldom deal in.
Try it in prose : my judgment's but so so
  In matters of this sort, but I have feeling
For you, good sir : with us this rule's the test,—
That's the best poetry that pays the best.

" You author-folks write too much poetry.
  You think yours fine : perhaps it is : excuse me ;
I mean not to disparage, or decry
  What you have read : it really did amuse me.
Try it in prose, good sir ; I recommend it ;
And bring it to me when you have re-penn'd it."

Ah ! how could I endure to hear him prate,
  Affecting reverence for the genuine poet?
Ah ! how I scorn'd myself and curs'd my fate,
  That, having written, I had stoop'd to shew it
To such a drudge, without a soul or sense,
Who weigh'd the worth of Poetry by pence !

I brought it on myself, and I submitted.—
  For efforts labour'd by the failing oil,
I by a bookseller at last was pitied,
  And told that I had misapplied my toil ;
That my best verse I must reduce to prose,
To suit the taste of creatures such as those.

Shall I not rive my pen up to the back ?
  And rive my heart, if it were so indeed !
But why ? because I courted the attack
  Of such a drudge?   No : I will still proceed.
If one of real judgment told me so,
'Twere surely worse, for he, alas ! must know.

But he had been too delicate, too kind,
   And too considerate of that tender feeling,
So exquisite, wherein is left behind
   A wound that oft defies all power of healing.
The truly humble are the truly great :
" They also serve who only watch and wait."

What I would wish to be I not deny ;
   All I have written, all have ever done,
Has been to look, if not to reach, so high :
   Nor will I say, that hope to me is none
Yet to do something worthy, in the sequel,
To make me Muses' servant—far unequal.

A Poet is a being between heaven
   And lower earth created—as it were
A mortal angel, and to whom 'tis given
   To wander unconfin'd earth, sea, and air.
Poets, like clouds that gild the sky at even,
Are full of glorious light, and near to heaven :

Yet have they still so much of earth about them,
   They are attracted by it, like the skies :
The world were but mere barrenness without them ;
   They make it beautiful—they fertilise.—
I am no Poet :—if not far aloof,
I had despis'd this bookseller's reproof.

Ah, verse ! sweet verse ! ah, much deluding verse !
   How have I lov'd thee ! how I love thee still !
The blessing of my life—my heaviest curse,
   Cause of my poverty—my children's ill.
Ah ! self-reproach is worse than hell to damn,
Seeing what I might be, and what I am !

Why did I thwart my father's wise intent
  In giving me a lucrative profession,
Where powers of speech, which some call'd eloquent,
  Perhaps had led ere now to wealth's possession?
I shipwreck'd all friends' hopes by strength of weakness,
And if I now submit, 'tis not in meekness,

But in the agony of heart's despair ;
  For am I not outstripp'd by all my friends?
Some have ascended the judicial chair,
  And most have wealth which industry attends ;
While I, poor wretch! mistaken in my aim,
Have but myself, my selfish self, to blame.

Nought could excuse the folly of my course
  But great success ; and now what have I done?
Nothing, in truth : if anything, 'tis worse
  Than very nothing. Now my life is run,
I have no other prospect but to die,
And leave my children all my poverty.

What right had I occasion to neglect,
  Knowing the claims of those that me surrounded?
What right had I good fortune to expect,
  When to a few poor rhymes my toils were bounded?
But farewell, verse ! for ever farewell, verses !
I bless'd you once ; now take my latest curses.   1821.

The above ſtanzas would ſeem to have been written
many years ſince, and might refer to ſome high-flown imaginative work, ſuch as it would, perhaps, be unreaſonable
to expeƈt any mere publiſher to be able to eſtimate, or even
to comprehend; but, among other trifles, of a compara-

tively recent date, I have lighted upon the following lines, compofed in a different and in a much more healthy fpirit : in the MS. they are only headed

EPIGRAM.

Am I a poet ?   Then, no mortal power
  Can make me more ; nor can it make me less.
Am I no poet ?   I've well spent my hour :
  To love the Muse has been my happiness !
Nor of that happiness can Fate deprive me,
Though not one syllable I wrote survive me.

Let who will have been the writer of the preceding lines, he was probably much fuch an unhappy verfifyer as is thus defcribed in the *Poet's Pilgrimage* (canto i, ft. 46), compofed between years 1808 and 1814, and privately printed exactly half a century ago.

" If me thou would deter, such course forsake,
  And back recal some miserable wight,
    Who his ambition did for power mistake,
  And thought, because he long'd to reach the height,
  That he had strength of wing for such a perilous flight."

FINIS.

Old Man's Diary,

FORTY YEARS AGO

PART IV

AN OLD MAN'S DIARY,

FORTY YEARS AGO;

FOR THE LAST SIX MONTHS OF

1833.

Omne meum : nihil meum.

LONDON :
PRINTED BY THOMAS RICHARDS.
1872.

PREFACE.

I HAVE already explained (fee Preface to Part III) why I can carry this Diary no farther : in 1834 I began to make the entries much fewer, and fo brief that they are of comparatively little intereft. A man who undertakes to furnifh a popular and party newfpaper with leading articles, founded upon clofely watched public and private events, at the rate of fome fifty columns every three months, and for feveral years together, cannot have much time to apply to literary purfuits. At the date to which I am now referring, the fale of the undertaking on which I was engaged was daily increafing (as one of the well-fatisfied proprietors fhowed me from their account-books) from 4600 copies to 7100 copies ; and during that period I was a contributor to it in the way I have mentioned. Then followed the appointment of a

Commiffion on the Britifh Mufeum; and as I was nominated Secretary to it, I was obliged to relinquifh all other employments; but not, I am forry to fay, until, from the free character of my own writings, and of others falfely imputed to me, I had made not a few perfonal enemies. Moft of thefe I have outlived, excepting in one or two inftances, where offence feems to have been hereditary. But "Peace to all fuch!" I may well fay at an age almoft nearer ninety than fourfcore. I muft be excufed for adding, as a mere matter of fact, that after I quitted the newspaper, the fale of it gradually decreafed : it changed proprietors, continued to fall, and became extinct.

Some perfons to whom I fent Part III of this "Old Man's Diary" feem to have thought that any fequel to it would be needlefs; and they have not even let me know that what I forwarded by poft had reached their hands : thefe filent recipients I have not troubled on the prefent occafion ; but if I have accidently omitted others, and they will let me know their wifh to have this conclufion, they fhall be duly, and with pleafure, fupplied with it, as far as my limited impreffion will allow.

As to precife dates, my friends muft, as before,

make liberal allowances : each entry in my Diary was made at, or near the time fpecified; but here and there, when copying an extract, I may have added from memory one or two fmall explanatory particulars, which will generally be obvious. The whole, as previoufly ftated, is intended merely for *private* perufal, and in no inftance for publication.

I have mentioned hereafter the trifling part I took in the appointment to a reporterfhip on the *Morning Chronicle* of one of the greateft wits and novelifts of our age. He fubfequently fent me a kind note of acknowledgment, which I fear I deftroyed, not guefling the eminence at which the writer afterwards arrived. When he relinquifhed that reporterfhip — in the year 1837 I think — fome difference arofe between him and the proprietors refpecting a notice of his intended retirement; and, being then intimate with Dickens, and ftanding well with the proprietors of the newspaper, he got me to explain the matter to them. As his name will never die in our comic literature, and as his letter to me on the occafion is characteriftic, I venture to add it here as a fmall contribution to his biography.

"Furnival's Inn, Friday morning.

" MY DEAR COLLIER,—I feel very much obliged to you
for the trouble you have taken in my behalf. Nobody, I
affure you, is more fincerely defirous to ftand well with
every one than I am; but I cannot write to thank Mr.
Eafthope for the notice, fince I cannot retract one fyllable
of the letter of which he complains. It is odd that, in the
correfpondence which paffed between us, he complains before this letter was written or thought of; the real and
only ground of complaint feeming to be, that I fhould ever
have contemplated the poffibility of having anything better
to do than reporting for the *Chronicle.*

"At fome pecuniary lofs I gave my notice a long time
before I need have done fo. I knew that I could by no
poffibility have anything to do for fome time to come ; but
I was unwilling to take advantage of the fyftem the proprietors had eftablifhed, and fo gave my notice at once. I
acted with great fairnefs by them, and have nothing to
atone or explain.

" I am very anxious that you fhould now fee the letter
Mr. Eafthope complains of, and the epiftle which produced
it. I am chained to *Mr. Pickwick* juft now, and cannot
get away ; but on Tuefday morning I hope to be at
liberty, and fhall take the chance of finding you at home.

"I may add that, in writing to you about the ‘ Mifcellany’, I had not the moft diftant intention or idea of afking for any notice out of the ordinary courfe—much lefs
had I any notion of afking a favour at Mr. Eafthope's
hands, knowing the difficulty of having any notice in the
paper, when half-a-dozen proprietors and agents are pulling
different ways, each for himfelf. I appealed to your kind-

nefs and friendfhip to fee they did not negleſt what, after all, I am ſtrongly difpofed to think they would have done with the firſt number of a new periodical of Bentley's, had Powell himfelf been the editor. Believe me, my dear Collier,

"Moſt faithfully yours,

"CHARLES DICKENS."

Powell, at this date, was aſting as fub-editor of the *Morning Chronicle*, and was properly unwilling to take any ſtep about announcing the conneſtion of Dickens with "Bentley's Mifcellany", without authority from thofe above him. In 1839, Maclife had painted a portrait of Dickens; and on Oſtober 1st it was iſfued as a private plate, engraved by Finden : on the 9th of that month, Dickens prefented me with a proof of it, and fent it with the following note.

"Doughty Street, Saturday, Oſtober 9th.

"MY DEAR COLLIER,—I fend you the beſt proof I have —bad is the beſt, I fear ; but I have the confolation of believing that, bad as it is, you could not buy fo good a one, from a moſt excellent and moſt mangled piſture. Always believe me,

"Moſt truly yours,

"CHARLES DICKENS.

"John Payne Collier, Efq., 24, Brompton Square."

Of courfe I have the engraving ftill, but, as Dickens fays, it does not do juftice either to the fubject or to the artift. It ought to be re-engraved for both their fakes.

I may add here, that John Dickens, the father of Charles, a moft amiable, worthy, but by no means talented man, never belonged to the corps of the *Morning Chronicle*, but to that of the *Herald*. I was one day ftrolling with him under the piazzas of Covent Garden, when, noting the eminence at which his fon had arrived, I afked him if Charles had ever exhibited in boyhood any premonitory fymptoms of his after diftinction? His anfwer was, "Never: we none of us gueffed at it; and when we heard that he had become a reporter for the *Morning Chronicle*, my brother-in-law Barrow, Culliford, and other relations, anticipated a failure." I have mentioned this anecdote to feveral of the early friends of Charles Dickens.

J. P. C.

Maidenhead, June 30, 1872.

OLD MAN'S DIARY,

FORTY YEARS AGO.

PART IV.

July 1, 1833.—I never tranflate fo eafily, and, as I venture to think, fo well, as from the Italian, whether the original be ancient or modern : witnefs the following canzone by Dante, which, I apprehend, has never before appeared in an Englifh drefs. The authorifed quaintnefs of "weet" for *wit*, *i.e.*, know, muft be permitted, and to my ear it founds agreeably, efpecially recollecting the early date at which Dante wrote. It is from his *Vita Nova*, and may be feen, among other places, in the *Schelta di Sonetti*, 8vo, 1709, fo. 16.

CANZON.

All ye that travel upon Love's highway,
  Oh ! pause a while, and say
If any grief be hard as mine to bear ?
To stay and hear is all that I entreat ;
  Then shall you truly weet,
If I am not the dwelling-place of care.

B

Love, for no goodness that he found in me,
　His own nobility,
Once life on me bestow'd so blest and sweet,
That oft I cried, reflecting how it came,
　What worth of mine could claim
A joy of heart so perfect and complete?

Now, all the confidence I did possess
　Thro' wealth of love, is fled ;
　I am so poor instead,
I even fear to tell my wretchedness.

Thus I am now constrain'd to do like those
　Their want for shame who hide :
　I keep a gay outside,
And in my heart I stifle all my woes.

I hope that the fame may be faid of the fubfequent
graceful produdion : it is alfo by Dante ; but I have
omitted to record where I found it printed.　My notion is
that I met with it alfo in his *Vita Nova.*

SONNET.

Love sits within my gentle lady's eyes :
　Whate'er she sees partakes her gentleness ;
　Where'er she moves their homage men express,
And all hearts tremble at her courtesies.
Their pallid looks to earth they bend, and sighs
　Break forth to think their own unworthiness :
　Wrath, pride, forsake the place that she doth bless !—
Oh, ladies, how to honour her advise !
　All sweetness, all humility of thought
　Spring in the hearts of those who hear her speak :
At the first view they utter only praise ;
But what she seems when she a smile displays
　Cannot be thought, and speech is far too weak :
A new and gentle miracle is wrought !

July 5.—In confequence of a difcovery I have lately made, I am forry that Dyce's edition of the works of Robert Greene came out fo early : it is no fault of his, unlefs it were that he did not make sufficiently diligent fearch for all the productions of his author. I find one that is entirely omitted, but it is alfo one of which no bibliographer has yet taken any notice ; and yet it is one of the earliest that came from the pen of its prolific author, and in celebration of an important public event—the death of Sir Chriftopher Hatton in the year 1591. I met with it the other day in Lambeth Library, where it is under the care of my very kind friend, Dr. Maitland; but he was not aware of its rarity and value. I have never feen nor heard of another copy, and I think it probable that this one was fent to the Archbifhop for approbation, and that for fome reafon or other it was not licenfed. I give the title of it *totidem verbis et litteris.*

"A Maidens Dreame. Upon the death of the Right Honorable Sir Christopher Hatton, Knight, late Lord Chancelor of England. By Robert Green, Master of Arts.—Imprinted at London by Thomas Scarlet for Thomas Nelson. 1591." 4to.

If Dyce's " Greene's Works" come to a fecond edition, he will be fure to include this poem, which, although compofed in obvious hafte (Sir C. Hatton having died Nov. 20th, 1591—not Sept. 20th in that year), is in very good verfe of feven-line ftanzas, fuch as was called the Englifh meafure. The dedication is to Lady Hatton, wife of Sir Chriftopher's nephew, the fame rich lady who was fubfequently married to Sir Edward Coke, and led him fuch a woeful life. I quote one defcriptive ftanza from the introduction, where Greene defcribes the feven cardinal virtues,

and two others, Bounty and Hofpitality, lamenting over
the public lofs.

> " Elbow on knee and head upon their hand,
>   As mourners sit, so sat these ladies all :
> Garlands of ebon boughs, whereon did stand
>   A golden crown : their mantles were of pall,
>   And from their watery eyes warm tears did fall.
> With wringing hands they sat and sigh'd, like those
> That had more grief than they could well disclose."

It would not furprife me if this production of fo popular
an author had never been really publifhed, but forbidden
by the Archbifhop of Canterbury. Sir Chriftopher Hatton
died in debt and difgrace with the Queen; and from official
papers at Bridgewater Houfe, under the hands of Lord
Chancellor Ellefmere, Chief Juftice Popham, and others, it
appears that Hatton owed the Queen no lefs a fum than
£64,817 ; which, reckoning money then to be worth five
times its prefent value (the ufual calculation), would make
an enormous amount ; but from it are to be deducted fums
paid, and for lands and houfes fold (including Ely Place)
which reduced the Queen's claim to about £18,000: after
that was difcharged, Lady Hatton had remaining a very
large jointure, which, in fact, was the bait that caught Lord
Coke. The jewels that had belonged to Sir Chriftopher
were eftimated at £7168, and the plate at £7662, which do
not seem extravagant : his apparel was valued at £1335,
and his mufical inftruments at only £61. Before his death
he was paying annually £6830 as intereft upon money
borrowed of private individuals. All thefe facts are ftated
in documents at Bridgewater Houfe, with much more detail
than I have patience to insert.

July 10.—Charles Lamb has given me a copy of his friend White's "Falſtaff's Letters", publiſhed ſome years ago, and not eaſily met with. Till now I only knew them from a gift-book to H. C. R.; but, though I am glad of them, I own that I cannot ſee the drollery and refined humour in them that C. L. diſcovers. White was a ſchool-fellow of Lamb's at Chriſt's Hoſpital, and is now the keeper of an office in Fleet Street for the collection of advertiſe-ments for country newſpapers, and to my thinking rather a common-place ſort of perſon.

There is much more humour in an octavo which I have recently bought by another *wight*, who ſpells his name not White but Wight. It is called "Mornings at Bow Street", and conſiſts of reports from police offices, made for the *Morning Herald.* It has ſome wonderful illuſtrations by G. Cruikſhank, and their excellence, whether comic or ſerious, cannot be exceeded. The introductory etching of Cupid, in three ſtates, I do not much care for; but the wood-cut on the title-page repreſenting "Petticoat Govern-ment", and indeed all the wood-cuts, never were furpaſſed —never, I think, equalled: there are twenty-one of them, and that of the poor ſoldier waſhing the linen of his orphan children is moſt pathetic. My copy is of the ſecond edition in 1825, but the wood-cuts (by Thompſon, and firſt-rate in that branch of art) ſeem better, and more cleanly and deli-cately worked, than in the firſt edition. The "Cool Con-trivance" is in the higheſt and beſt ſtyle of humour : Cruik-ſhank has never done anything elſe ſo good. The letter-preſs is inferior, but ſtill droll and clever : I have no ac-quaintance with the inventive author.

July 14.—Having recently come upon the following

among fome of my old papers, I think it worth the trouble of tranfcribing, and therefore infert it here : it was written, of courfe, before I was married in Auguft 1816, at Putney Church. The date I affign to my rhymes is about 1809 or 1810, when I was pretty well acquainted with the character of our older lyrical poetry, and was fond of imitating it; and with this fort of preface what follows must be read.

A Bachelor's Lyric of Life.

Fields, fields, the green fields,
With all the country yields,
And trees to lie under at leifure :
Birds, birds, joyous birds,
And the lowing of the herds,
That fill all the welkin with pleafure.

Sun, sun, the bright sun,
Hot 'twixt twelve and one,
Shining with his noontide of power :
Clouds, clouds, fleecy clouds,
And now and then in crowds
To frefhen the earth with a shower.

Books, books, pleasant books,
In summer by the brooks,
In warm cozy nooks all the winter.
Girls, girls, bonny girls,
With cataracts of curls,
And not a single eye that's a squinter.

Songs, songs, cheerful songs,
And all thereto belongs,
But without any colds or pretences :
And certainly my choice is
For the sweeteft female voices ;
Then, 'tis music to all the five senses.

An Old Man's Diary.

Dance, dance, a lively dance,
  Got up as if by chance,
And not a stiff prance, cold and formal ;
  When steps that are elastic,
  And dainty figures plastic
Take the eyes of the gazers by storm all.

Friends, friends, honest friends,
  With talk that never tends
To anything that looks toward malice ;
  Wealth, wealth, easy wealth,
  But not too much for health,
And distant from any great palace.

Jokes, jokes, sprightly jokes,
  For young, or older folks,
And no nasty pokes that will hurt you ;
  But all in merry glee,
  As innocent as free,
And not the least offensive to virtue.

A cot, a well-built cot,
  With something in the pot,
And viands always hot and in plenty ;
  With no loud squalling brats,
  But a dog and purring cats,
And cheerfulness still to content ye.

Wine, wine, rosy wine,
  A little and that fine ;
No cellar of mine will I brick up :
  But of all the cups that flow
  The very worst I know
Is that curst diabolical hic-*cup*.

Wife, wife, a pretty wife ?—
  No, no, upon my life ;
And yet I would not be too lonely :

I so dote on all the sex,
That the rest I would not vex
By living but for one, and one only.

July 15.—Having not long fince become a member of
the Society of Antiquaries, I was looking over fome of
their MSS., when I met with the following interefting and
unprinted letter from the Earl of Effex, Queen Elizabeth's
favourite, to Anthony Bacon, elder brother of Francis. It
is dated Windfor, October 29th, without the year, but
clearly 1597, as the firft paragraph refers to the exertions
of the Earl to procure the office of Solicitor-General for
Francis Bacon, who, after fome delay, was inftalled in
it : in that capacity he was one of the counsel againft his
benefactor, fhortly previous to the facrifice of the life of the
latter on the block at the Tower. The addrefs is, " To my
very affured frend Anthonie Bacon, Efquire".

" Sir,—Yf I omitt any thing in dealing for your brother thatt my
witt and power can reach unto, think me unworthy of my frend.

" The Q. doth so much apprehend the danger of Scotland, as she
wold have me begin to entertayne thoughts a new, but I will have a
care of mine own creditt as of her service. You may, if you think
good, write to Dr. Morison whatt commission I have, but I forbeare
to use yt for these causes : First, because I think that Huntly is so
well allready, as he can nott accommodate himself by the Q.'s meanes
better then he is.

Secondly, because I see th' erle cold, and I hold yt unfitt, since he
hath honor, once to renew this negociation ; for in these thinges the
proposer hath the disadvantage.

" And lastly, because I know not what suddeyn countermand I may
have, as the last tyme ; but I woud have him write his opinion
whether they wold incline to any new mercy. Allso I would heare
from him, whether the Scottish Q. be with child, and, yf she be, how
neere yt is thought of her delivery. And you shall entreat what are

the umors that are sturred. I desire to know how yt standeth be-
tweene the K. and Q. Of these things, yf you will make a dispatch,
send yt me ; I will send yt away. And so, wishing to you as to myself, I rest your most assured frend "ESSEX.

"Windsor, 29th Octob.

> "I pray you tell Dr. Morison in your letter that my steward,
> who hath taken order with the merchants, is not returned
> from Dover, butt within 2 dayes he shall have the acquitt-
> ances sent him."

We never can forgive Bacon for the part he took on the
trial againſt the very man who had procured for him the
appointment which had enabled him to aid in the deſtruc-
tion of his beſt and nobleſt patron. The preceding letter
has never been anywhere publiſhed, and the exiſtence of it
was not known until I routed it from a heap of antiquated
documents. I cannot ſay the fame of the first portion of
the ſucceeding letter from the unfortunate Earl to the
Queen, when he was, on Auguſt 30th, 1598, at Ardbracken,
in Ireland, fulfilling the loathſome duties which ultimately
brought him to the ſcaffold : it is one of the Harleian
MSS., but hitherto moſt careleſſly and incorrectly printed
without the concluding ſtanza, which is now to be added to
the few ſpecimens we poſſefs of the poetical powers of the
Earl : it is highly intereſting, and I rejoice to have refcued
it. We muſt bear in mind that the Queen always called
Eſſex her *Robin :* it is headed

"A LETTER WRITTEN BY ROBERT DEVERUX, EARLE OF ESSEX,
TO QUEENE ELIZABETH, UPON HIS COMMAUND TO GOE
FOR IRELAND.

"From a mind delitinge in sowrow, from sperites wasted with
passion, from a heart torne in peeces with care, greefe, and travale,
from a man that hateth himselfe, and all thinges clse that keepeth

C

him alive, what service can your Matie expecte, since my service past deserves no more then banishment and proscription into the cursedst of all other countreyes? Nay, nay; it is your rebelles pride and successe that must give me leave to ransom my life out of this hatefull prison of my loathed bodie, which, if it happen so, your Matie shall have no cause to mislike the fashion of my death, since the course of my life could never please you.

> " Happie were he could finish forth his fate
> in some unhaunted desart, most obscure :
> From all society, from love, from hate,
> of worldly folke, then should he sleep secure,
> Then wake againe, and yeild god ever praise :
> content with hips and hawes and bramble berry,
> In contemplation passing still his daise,
> and change of holy thoughtes to make him merry ;
> Who where he dies his tombe may be a bush,
> Where harm[l]es Robin dwelles with gentle Thrush."
>
> " Your Maties exiled servant,
>
> " Ro. Essex.'

July 16.—There has been among bibliographers some apparent confusion about the " Life of Herbert" by Izaac Walton : they call it a 12mo volume, when it is an 8vo, and they say that it includes Herbert's Letters, when it does not contain one of them. I bought the first edition of it yesterday, and, as it is the work of so estimable a man regarding so admirable a divine, I will describe it here minutely. The fact seems to be that there were two impressions of Walton's " Life of Herbert" in 1670 ; the first in 8vo without the Letters, and the second in 12mo with the Letters: the 8vo without the Letters has the best and earliest impressions of the portrait by R. White : the book itself is there called merely " The Life of Mr. George Herbert", and the imprint is "London, Printed by Tho. Newcomb, for Richard Marriott, fold by moſt Bookſellers. M.DC.LXX." At the back of the title is the *Imprimatur*, dated April 21, 1670, followed by the commendatory verſes of Sam. Woodforde, dated Benſted, April 3, 1670. Then comes the "Introduction", where Walton mentions his biographies of Donne and Wotton, ending in theſe words, "For theſe reaſons I have undertaken it, and if I have prevented any abler perſon, I beg pardon of him and my reader". Then begins "The Life", ſo headed, commencing on p. 9 and ending on p. 80, with "*finis*" at the bottom of the page. On p. 81 begins a ſort of poſtſcript, or afterthought, regarding Mrs. Herbert and her grief and admiration, but adding : "Thus ſhe continued mourning, till time and converſation had ſo moderated her ſorrows that ſhe became the happy wife of Sir Robert Cook, of Higham in the county of Glouceſter, Knight". She lived nine years after her ſecond marriage, which continued eight years, and ſhe was buried at Higham in 1663, her firſt husband having died in 1632. Walton's Poſtſcript fills two pages, so that the book ends on p. 82.

It may be worth a note that Walton winds up his "Life of Herbert" by an erroneous quotation from a lyric by Shirley : no doubt, he thus adapted the words to the place from memory :

> "All must to the cold graves ;
> But the religious actions of the just
> Smell sweet in death, and blossom in the dust."

Shirley's words are theſe, in Scene iii of his "Contention of Ajax and Ulyſſes":

> " Your heads must come
>   To the cold tomb ;
> Only the actions of the just
> Smell sweet, and blossom in the dust."

My whole note is almoſt too drily bibliographical, but the names of Walton and Herbert muſt excuſe it.

July 24.—Mr. John Barrow, who is engaged on the *Times*, where there is no vacancy, told me that he has a clever nephew, named Charles Dickens, who has been employed, I believe, on the *True Sun*, and for whom he is anxious to obtain a ſituation on the *Morning Chronicle*. Barrow wants me to give him a letter to the proprietor of the *Morning Chronicle*, and I hope, from what I hear, that his application will be ſuccefsful. I do not often interfere in this way, the only other inſtances I can recollect being in favour of Douglas Jerrold and William Thackeray, when they were at one time ſadly in want of literary work. Barrow I have been acquainted with for the laſt five or ſix years— indeed, ever ſince he preſented me with a copy of his poem, I think, on the battle of Talavera, written in obvious imitation of Walter Scott.

I aſked Barrow where his nephew had been educated, but he could not exactly tell me, ſaying that he was the ſon of a clerk in the naval department at Portſmouth, who had been ſuperſeded on a reconſtruction of the office, and who had ſeveral other children. I inquired his nephew's qualifications, and the reply was that he was extremely clever, and that he (Barrow) had taught him Gurney's ſhort-hand, which he wrote well, as had been proved on the *True Sun*, a newſpaper which, ſtrange to ſay, I had feldom feen : his nephew wifhed of all things to become one of the parliamentary reporters of the *Morning Chronicle.*

I afked how old he was, and how he had been employed before he had connected himfelf with the *True Sun ?* The anfwer was rather ambiguous : the uncle only knew that his father's family diftreffes had driven Charles Dickens to exert himfelf in any way that would earn a living; and that at one time he had affifted Warren, the blacking-man, in the conduct of his extenfive bufinefs, and, among other things, had written puff-verfes for him. In this way, as well as in others, he had fhown ability ; and Barrow referred me jocofely to the rhymes (poffibly his) which accompanied the wood-cut advertifements of Warren's blacking, containing the figure of a dove, which, looking at a polifhed boot, and miftaking the reflection of itfelf for the real appearance of its mate, had gone on thus, in the perfon of the writer and suppofed fpectator of the amorous, but difappointed interview :

> " I pitied the dove, for my bosom was tender ;
>   I pitied the sigh that she gave to the wind ;
> But I ne'er shall forget the superlative splendour
>   Of Warren's Jet Blacking, the pride of mankind."

I did not fee precifely how, or why, a figh was to be pitied, though difappointment might produce it in the dove, as well as compaffion in the fpectator; but I thought the lines very laughable and clever for the purpofe—quite a match for fome other blacking-maker's device, of a cock fighting its own fhadow in a boot. The bold tranfition, or apoftrophe, from the dove to the blacking is fublime, and, if not pindaric, is at leaft Peter-pindaric. However, I was of opinion that I ought to fee more of the young man, and of

his doings, before I committed myfelf by recommending
him to a newfpaper as a competent reporter; and, at Barrow's inftance, I agreed to meet Dickens at dinner, his
uncle alfo informing me that he was cheerful company
and a good finger of a comic fong.

July 27.—I dined with C. Dickens, his uncle Barrow,
and that uncle's uncle (Culleford), Seymour Huffham,
their relation, and one or two more; and had reafon to like
the firft-named fo extremely, and to think fo very well of
his abilities (he was fo young that he had no veftige of
beard or whifkers), that I had little hefitation in recommending him to the proprietor of the *Morning Chronicle.* At
this dinner, I may mention that many comic fongs were
fung, moft of them by Culleford, who was excellent in that
way, and two by Dickens, who would not make the attempt
until late in the evening, and after a good deal of preffing.
One of them was called " The Dandy Dog's-meat Man,"
then much in vogue with the lower claffes, and the other
an effufion by Dickens himfelf, of which the firft verse (I
remember no more, though he fang it twice) ran nearly, or
quite, as follows :

> " Sweet Betsy Ogle,
>   In her bird's-eye fogle,
> Is round my heart-strings twined and twisted :
>   No voice is clearer ;
>   If you should hear her,
>   Pray, don't go near her ;
> Her looks can never be resisted."

The reft related to the love of a Barber for a Milk-
maid, whom he faw carrying her yoke and pails, when he

went out in the morning to fhave an old early-rifing citizen. We were all very merry, if not very wife, unlefs merriment be taken as another fort of wifdom. C. D. has not been taken on the newfpaper by my recommendation, for fome more influential perfon, whofe name I heard, had alfo fpoken in his behalf. I may here add, that foon afterwards I obferved a great difference in C. D.'s appearance and drefs; for he had bought a new hat and a very handfome blue cloak, with black velvet facings, the corner of which he threw over his fhoulder *à l'Efpagnol*. I overtook him in the Adelphi, and we walked together through Hungerford Market, where we followed a coal-heaver, who carried his little rofy but grimy child looking over his fhoulder; and C. D. bought a halfpenny worth of cherries, and, as we went along, he gave them one by one to the little fellow without the knowledge of the father. C. D. seemed quite as much pleafed as the child. He informed me, as we walked through it, that he knew *Hungcr*ford Market well, laying unufual strefs on the two firft fyllables. He did not affect to conceal the difficulties he and his family had had to contend againft.

July 30.—Since you gave me (faid the Duke, yefterday) the *fecond part* of "If you Know not̄ me, you Know Nobody" (4to, 1609), I have read the *firft part* of the fame play; and, comparing the two, I have been difappointed. It is very inferior to the fecond part.

It undoubtedly is (I replied) in the shape that it has come down to us; but as the fubject was really better, it feems probable that, in its true and original fhape, the firft part ought to be fuperior to the fecond part. The fuccefs of the firft part authorifed the fecond.

How fo, and why fo? (inquired the Duke.)

You may remember (I added) that I formerly explained why, in my opinion, many of our old plays have reached us in fo imperfect and mutilated a fhape. They were not fo written by their authors, nor fo acted by the performers; but when a new drama was efpecially popular, rival Companies and rival bookfellers, or printers, endeavoured to procure fomething like it, that would anfwer the purpofe of reprefentation or publication,—that would draw audiences and attract purchafers. I could not, perhaps, in the whole range of our old drama pick out two plays that would better illuftrate the point to which I refer. Thomas Heywood wrote his firft part relating, as the title-page exprefles it, to "the troubles of Queen Elizabeth", and there is no doubt that it became extremely popular on the ftage. There were, perhaps, half-a-dozen different Companies playing in London at the time, and more than as many bookfellers anxious to procure fomething which they could fell as the drama then fo attractive: they therefore sent a perfon, who could write fhort-hand and had a good memory, to Henflowe's Theatre, where the firft part was then represented, and he compounded, from what he could write down, recollect, and defcribe, a play which he called by the fame name as the genuine popular drama by Heywood. Thus the interefts of the dramatift and of the company might be, and no doubt were, injured; and when Heywood found that he could not adequately counteract the fraud, after he had compofed his *fecond part*, inftead of waiting to be robbed of it in this way, he refolved to fell his genuine copy-right. Therefore it is, as we may fairly conclude, that while the firft part only appears in a very incomplete fhape, the fecond part has descended to us pretty much as it came from the pen of the author.

Who was the bookfeller (asked the Duke) who fraudulently poffeffed himfelf of the firft part, and printed it?

The fame man (faid I) who obtained and printed the complete fecond part, Nathaniel Butter,—a very unfcrupulous gentleman in the trade. But at about this period feveral other publifhers were in the habit of doing the fame thing; and more than one theatre did not fcruple to reprefent any play, derived furreptitioufly and imperfectly from another theatre, which had a fuccefsful run at the rival houfe. The Mafter of the Revels was then the only authority the injured party could appeal to, and he feldom interfered, becaufe his power was doubtful and difregarded.

But is it not fingular (the Duke continued) that the fame bookfeller who had fraudulently obtained the firft part was chofen to be the publifher of the complete fecond part?

Such certainly was not ufually the case (I returned); but as Butter had put forth the firft part, however he obtained it, it would be the better worth his while to print the fecond part; and, as Heywood was always a needy man, perhaps he could procure from Butter more for the copyright than from any other publifher. This, however, is mere conjecture. The fale of the authorifed fecond part would affift the fale of the imperfect firft part, and this might be another motive with Butter, who perhaps had not found the patched-up firft part fo generally acceptable as he wifhed.

D. How utterly lawlefs are both plays as regards the unities, but efpecially the fecond part, where the fcene is made to fkip about from England to France, and from

France to England, juft as fuited the purpofe of the old
dramatift. The unity of time, too, is as much difregarded
as the unity of place, for the piece begins very early in the
reign of Queen Elizabeth, and it ends (like Sheridan's
"Critic") with a blow up on the defeat of the Spanish
Armada in 1588. However, I know from my own reading
that this lawleffnefs was at that period no peculiarity; and if
it had been otherwife, we fhould have been deprived of almoft
every one of the great hiftorical plays of Shakefpeare.

C. True : it is as great a bleffing that he knew nothing
of the unities, as it is that he knew fo little of the claffic
drama, or we fhould have loft much of his fpecial originality. Heywood, his contemporary and fellow actor, was
a fcholar of no mean attainments, but even he has left no
play behind him in which the three unities are ftrictly obferved; and, like Shakefpeare, he availed himfelf of the popular literature of the day, whenever it gave him affiftance.
The play under confideration, " The Second Part of Queen
Elizabeth", is a proof of it, for it is mainly founded upon
a fmall jeft-book, of which the earlieft known edition bears
the date of 1607 ; but, as Heywood's fecond part is dated
1606, there muft have been an earlier impreffion of " Hobfon's Jefts." Heywood's play is full of local and temporary
allufions, and whole fcenes are derived from the merry
old jeft-book.

D. I fancied fomething of the fort as I went through the
different fcenes ; and fome of them on this account, if on
no other, are very amufing, as well as curious. Now and then
the extravagance is carried almoft to the length of ab-
furdity, as where old Hobfon travels to France in his drefs-
ing-gown and flippers.

C. That Heywood had from the jeft-book; and as the incident was well known to the frequenters of the theatre in Southwark (very near to the Globe, where Shakefpeare's dramas were reprefented during the fummer), he thought that he fhould do no unpardonable violence to the truth of nature, if he introduced it upon the ftage.

D. If we take the reprefentation of the dramatift, or if we look at my picture of Southwark (from which, on the title-pages of your three volumes, the wood-cuts are copied), we fhall fee various trees in the immediate neighbourhood of the theatres, and, from what Heywood tells us in his fecond part, they formed quite a wood before a perfon on foot—as Hobfon is reprefented to have been—arrived at Newington Butts. In this wood, and fo on to Deptford, Hobfon loses himself, and applies to another of the characters to put him in the right road :

> " If thou be'st acquainted in these woods,
>   Conduct me to some town, or direct road
>   That leads to London."

C. Newington Butts was then quite a rural village, whither the Londoners ufed to repair for a country walk ; and at the end of it they found, in the fummer, not only tea-gardens and other places of refrefhment, but a theatre for their amufement, where actors not otherwife engaged in London went for employment. This theatre is often men-tioned by Henflowe, the old manager of it, in his MS. diary preferved at Dulwich College.

D. I do not remember that I was ever in that part of the world in my life, and, under your guidance, I fhould like to vifit it. You could point out to me the fites of fome of the old theatres, where moft of the plays in this room

were originally reprefented. It happens that I have no engagement this afternoon, and if you were at leifure we
might fo apply our fpare time.

C. Most willingly ; but you muft not expeƈt to fee any
veftige of fuch buildings. In Southwark there is nothing
left ftanding that exifted in the time of Shakefpeare but a
fragment of Winchefter Houfe. Barclay's brewery covers
nearly all the ground once occupied by three or four play-
houfes ; and the oldeft building in Newington Butts is
perhaps a public-house, called the Elephant and Caftle.

D. Well, never mind ; thither let us go. The whole will
be new to me ; and I ought not, as the owner of fuch a collection of old plays, to be ignorant of the very ground on
which the theatres ftood where they were daily reprefented.

We went accordingly as foon as the horfes could be put
to ; but even the coachman hardly knew the way, and
when in Southwark the Duke was obliged to alight from
the carriage, in order to obtain a notion of the neighbourhood. Afterwards we drove to Newington Butts, where
we faw the Fifhmongers' Alms-houfes and the old Elephant and Caftle, and then along the Kent Road towards
Deptford. All was about as new to the Duke as if he
had been in South America, and he feemed well pleafed.
We did not get back until quite late ; and when I defcribed
our adventures to my wife, with the Duke's foot-pilgrim-
age to St. Saviour's, and through the dirty Borough Market,
fhe laughed heartily.

Aug. 9.—Bartley (the actor, who married Mifs Smith),
from whom I heard the ftory regarding Captain Morris,
and his fong as fung by Sir John Doyle, and the anecdote

of the Captain's difappointment on the death of the late Duke of Norfolk, gave me the following to-day : he fays he had it from Morris himfelf, who was very bitter when he found that the old Duke had left him nothing—not even the houfe he had lived in many years rent-free at Dorking :

EPITAPH UPON JOCKEY, THE LATE DUKE OF NORFOLK.

Of highest *rank* in filth and birth,
A human hog lies here in earth :
His story's told in this short placard ;
He liv'd a beast, and died a blackguard."

I rely upon what Bartley fays, because he knew Morris well, and, when single, had often flept in his houfe at Dorking. Latterly the Captain was peevish and repentant, and hardly ever got out of his chair. The Bible was read to him every morning and evening by an old woman ; and when afked if a young one would not do *better*, his anfwer was that, in that cafe they might do *worfe*. Still, at times he was very good company, and one day repeated to Bartley a joke he had verfified fome years before. I afked Bartley whether the Captain was not, like his old friend Jockey, really a Roman Catholic ; but he replied that he (Bartley) had never inquired enough about his religion to know. He believed that Morris was inclined to the old faith ; but what follows proves that he did not object to laugh at its profeffors :

THE PRIEST AND THE WILL.

A rich old man was dying fast,
All senses well-nigh spent,
While a fat priest drew up in haste
His will and testament,

Leaving his poor relations all
  Entirely in the lurch,
By giving goods and lands, not small,
  To the holy Roman Church.

The dying man could only say
  " Aye, aye", to every question
The wily priest propos'd that day,
  Following his own suggestion

By sticking in new clauses sly,
  All for the Church's good ;
To which the sick man answer'd " Aye",
  But no word understood.

His eldest son was standing near,
  And that son's younger brother,
And griev'd these pious gifts to hear,
  First one farm, then another.

They could not make him understand ;
  " Aye" came at every close,
So that the priest wrote out of hand
  Exactly what he chose ;

Giving the dying man his word,
  That if he gave the whole,
It would in heaven be registered
  And save his sinful soul.

At length the eldest son bespake,
  Close to the old man's ears,
" This wily priest may we not take,
  And fling him down the stairs ?"

" Aye", said the sick man, void of sense ;
  So both the sons at once
Seiz'd his unwieldy reverence,
  And downstairs crack'd his sconce.

Bartley told me now, what he had not told me formerly, that when Morris corrected Sir John Doyle's mode of finging Morris's song, the Duke of York, the Duke of Gordon, Sheridan, Colman, and feveral others were present.

Aug. 12.—Dubois, Judge of the Sheriff's Court, called upon me, and I was very glad to fee his droll, grave face. He is one of the greateft humourifts of our day ; but although fo clever, he has done himfelf injury in his profeffion by ridiculing fome great and powerful people. My knowledge of him began as early as 1808, when he wrote a profe fatire on Sir John Carr and his publifhed travels in Ireland, under the title of "My Pocket-Book", a trial which (in the King's Bench, before Lord Ellenborough) eftablifhed the principle, that any man has a right to criticife a book in any way it deferves, if without malice or perfonality. This was termed the *damnum absque injuriâ* decifion. Dubois was long the real editor of the *Monthly Mirror*, though Thomas Hill obtained the credit for it: it was publifhed by the fame bookfeller as " My Pocket-Book," which had feveral coloured engravings to illuftrate the feverely humorous text. Dubois never obtained higher preferment than as fubftitute for Serjeant Heath in the Court of the Sheriff of Middlefex. In private, and when at his eafe, he was the beft company ; but I have never been very intimate with him : he was capital at a dinner-table, and, not being very rich, he dined out nearly as often as anybody afked him.

Aug. 15.—One of the kindeft and most ferviceable of my friends is Thomas Amyot, with whom my father and mother were made acquainted by H. C. Robinſon, who with him was clerk to an attorney in one of the towns on the borders of Eſſex and Suffolk. They had another fellow-clerk in William Pattiſon, who ſettled at Witham, had conſiderable property left him ; and the two ſons of whom, William and Jacob, were painted by Sir Thomas Lawrence, the picture (boys with a donkey) having been engraved. One of theſe boys—I think, Jacob—married, and went to ſpend his honey-moon among the Pyrenees ; but, embarking on a lake there, the boat was upſet by a treacherous guſt of wind from the mountains, and both he and his young wife were drowned. Old Pattiſon never held up his head after this diſaſter ; and on his death all his property devolved upon his ſon William, whom I remember at the Chancery bar.

Amyot was thus fellow-clerk with Robinſon and Pattiſon. His father was a French refugee on the repeal of the Ediĉt of Nantes, and being a ſkilful mechaniſt, he ſet up in buſineſs at Norwich as a watchmaker. He claimed to be deſcended from the Biſhop Amyot, who tranſlated Plutarch, and from whoſe French verſion our earlieſt Engliſh verſion was made by Sir Thomas North in 1579. The watchmaker obtained great ſucceſs in his trade, became a man of influence in Norwich, and when Windham put up as M.P. for that city, old Amyot ſtrongly promoted his return, and his ſon Thomas was alſo actively and ſucceſsfully employed. After Windham was elected, he engaged young Amyot as his private ſecretary ; and when Windham was appointed Home Secretary in the Whig Government of 1806-7, he made Thomas Amyot his official ſecretary ; and, before the formation of the next adminiſtration, fecured for him a good poft in the Foreign Office. Amyot afterwards got further advancement, and, taking a houfe in Weftminfter, ufed to give rather fmart parties. I remember being at one of them when I was merely a lad, and it was the more remarkable as Windham himself was there ; and not only he but Queen Caroline (who was tried and expired in 1819), fhe being then in difgrace at the court of George IV. Nobody but Amyot's family and Windham knew that fhe was to honour the houfe with her company ; and, as fhe was fond of theatrical difplay, I well recollect that, to introduce her with effect, a dark curtain was drawn acrofs the end of the room, and when it was at a fignal drawn up, fhe was difcovered on a pedeftal, as the ftatue of the injured Hermione in " The Winter's Tale": the underftood inference was, that Queen Caroline's fitua-tion was fimilar to that of the innocent queen of Leontes.

The whole was very well managed, and the effect of the lights behind the curtain on the female ftatue was ex-tremely good. This was the only time I ever faw Queen Caroline in private, and moft people on the Whig fide of the queftion then thought her innocent. I do not think they continued of that mind ; but, whether innocent or guilty, they were afterwards decidedly of opinion that the King was entitled to no redrefs. Such, in fact, was the refult in the Houfe of Lords.

Befides Windham, there were feveral other Whig leaders at Amyot's party, and I call to mind the names of Sheri-dan and Tierney. Tierney was a friend of my father, who had much affifted, at one or more elections, in bringing him into the Houfe of Commons for Southwark. I wanted to fee Whitbread, but he was not there.

E

Amyot continued in his lucrative poſt long after the Tories had returned to power ; but in 1814 he collected and publiſhed his patron Windham's ſpeeches, three vols. 8vo : they did not include his admirable addreſs on the failure of the Walcheren Expedition, in which he introduced, amid ſhouts of admiration from all parts of the Houſe, the ſimile in which he likened the propoſed *coup-de-main* in the Scheldt to a *coup-de-main* in the Court of Chancery, then in inextricable confuſion owing to the doubts and delays of Lord Eldon. I was a delighted liſtener to it in the gallery of the Houſe of Commons. This ſpeech was never reported ; for when it was delivered, the reporters for the newspapers had combined to ſuppreſs it, on account of ſome offence given to them by Windham. The proprietors of newſpapers were then very much in the hands of their reporters, and not long afterwards they put an extinguiſher upon Mr. Spring Rice for a ſimilar reaſon ; and there it was effectual, although the ſnuff of the ruſh-light continued for a while to ſmother and ſtink.

The kind favours done to me by Amyot were innumerable, and one of the moſt ſerviceable was an introduction to Lord G. Leviſon Gower, his old plays and MSS.

Aug. 17.—I entirely forget from whence I derived the main point of the enſuing trifle : perhaps from one of Thomas Deloney's old merry tracts—I rather think ſo— but I have loſt the preciſe reference, and it is not of much conſequence.

SHOEMAKERS AND TAILORS.

Said Jove to Mercury the other day,
" Let's have a walk together in the country :
We'll take our own proviſions for the way,

And thus avoid an innkeeper's effrontery."
  Said Mercury, " I'm your man ; but let me say,
  I'll take no victuals with me, though you may :
I'll bear no wallet ; but I'll lay a wager,
Though you are certainly an older stager,
   I'll fare as well as those with pots and kittles :
   I have my wits, and they shall get me *wittles*."

" Then mind (said Jove) if you run ever short,
  I'll give you nothing from my well-fill'd wallet :
I'll bear no bag for you of any sort ;
  None of my provender shall reach your gullet."—
" Agreed ! (cried Mercury) I don't mean to borrow.
But when shall we depart ? I vote to-morrow :
   The weather is extremely fine just now,
   And birds are singing blithe on every bough,
Mavis for joy, and nightingale for sorrow."

Next morning they both started for their trip :
  Hermes took nought, and trusted all to chance ;
But Jove provided a well-furnish'd scrip :
  And I should say, ere farther I advance,
That both put off their godships for the journey ;
Jove seem'd a bagman, Mercury an attorney.

They travell'd on, perhaps some twenty mile,
  When Jove began to find that he was hungry,
And sat him down upon a country stile
To rest himself, and feed a little while ;
But Mercury did not stop : as he was younger, he
  Said he would step on to the nearest village ;
  Intent, in fact, on roguery and pillage.

When he arriv'd upon the village-green,
  He look'd into a busy tailor's shop,
Where nine men (that's one man, in fact) were seen,
  All eating greedily, withouten stop,

A dish of well-boil'd peas : he gave a hop,
   And laugh'd to see them all, not with a ladle
   Or spoon to eat the peas, but with a needle
Picking them up ; and only one by one
   Into their mouths the single peasen pop,
As if their dinner never would be done.
   Mercury was so hungry, even these
   He envied, picking up their separate peas.

Seeing him look, they ask'd him join the party,
Which he soon did, with appetite most hearty ;
But they would only let him have a needle
To do as they did, picking up each seed ill.
   This little suited Mercury's appetite :
Therefore he drove his needle in the mess
Up to the eye ; and took, indeed, no less
   Than eight or ten at once, much at his ease.
   This sort of dealing did not seem to please
The tailors, who all swore it was not right ;
   And, as he would not fare the same as they did,
   They drove him from the shop he had invaded.

As we have seen a dog turn'd out of door,
   His tail between his legs, so Mercury fled
From the nine tailors.—'Twas not long before
   He saw some jolly shoemakers ; who fed
With spoons and ladles from large bowls of soup,
   Taking at every dip great lumps of meat,
   Such as rejoic'd a hungry man to eat.
The savoury smell made Mercury's hunger more,
And much he long'd to have with them a scoop
   At the rich mess.   They saw him at the door,
And as he wore a cheerful merry grin,
The jolly shoemakers all ask'd him in,
   To do as they did, and to take his ration,
Giving him, too, a ladle to begin.
   Right willingly he took the invitation.

When he had ate his fill they ask'd no payment,
   He was quite welcome ; and so Mercury thought
How much more they deserv'd his warmest thanks
   Than the nine needy stitchers of old raiment
He had at first encounter'd with their peas,
Their bare arms, and cross-legg'd ungarter'd shanks.—
   How to reward the shoemakers he sought,
For their most liberal treatment without fees.

He hasten'd back to Jove in high good humour,
   Whom he soon found, still sitting at his ease
Upon the stile, of his own scrip consumer,
   And finishing his meal with bread and cheese.
"A boon ! a boon ! great Jove," cried Mercury :
"I have a boon to crave," again said he :
   "A boon ! a boon ! compeller of the thunder !"—
"Why, what's up now (said Jove) I really wonder ?
I grant your boon : I think there is no danger,
   You look so cheerfully and well contented,
Though to your roguery I am no stranger ;
   But since I said the word, and have consented,
   Take you your boon."—Then Mercury repeated
How well by shoemakers he had been treated,
   And how he wish'd to make them a return
   By doubling all the profits they could earn.
His boon, he said, was this : that "*ere they spent
A groat, they should earn twopence.*"—"I'm content,
   And swear by Styx (said Jove) ; but how will that
   Make them all thrive, and keep shoemakers fat ?
Nor you, nor they will have much cause to laugh
If they spend groats before they've earned the half.
They'll spend twice what they earn ; and nothing's surer,
The more they spend, they'll always be the poorer."—

"Stop ! stop !" cried Mercury ; "your sentence vary ;
   I blunder'd, and I mean the clean contrary.
Recall your oath : I meant *that they should gain*

> *A groat, ere they spent twopence ; that is plain."
> " It may be so (said Jove) ; my oath is past :
> I swore by Styx : to hope for change is vain,
>   For what is sworn by Styx, you know, must last.
> Shoemakers ne'er will be good fellows thought,
> Spending but twopence while they earn a groat."—

> " I'm sorry for 't (cried Mercury), but I'll teach 'em
>   A trick or two shall make the balance even ;
> A pea-pick tailor never shall o'er-reach 'em :
>   Tailors shall have their hell—shoemakers heaven."

[It may be well to remark that tailors ftill call the recept-
acle under the fhop-board, where they ftow away all the odds
and ends of cloth they can " cabbage", their *hell ;* while the
heaven of fhoemakers is the fhelf above their heads, where
they depofit their waxed thread, bonny-clabber, and fome
of their fmaller tools.]

Aug. 28.—The following dialogue took place this
morning at Devonfhire Houfe.

D. In our various converfations about Old Plays and
Players, you have never faid anything regarding the
dramas imputed, whether rightly or wrongly, to Shakefpeare. I want to know what you think of them, and how
far we are juftified in affigning them, or any of them, to
his genius.

C. It is rather a wide fubjeɛt, confidering how many
plays have been given at different periods to Shakefpeare.

D. I felt myfelf fadly at a lofs only yefterday, where I
dined, and where I fell into converfation with feveral, and
fome of them literary men : knowing that I had the plays
in my colleɛtion, and knowing too that I was often in communication with you, they put the queftion to me, whether

I thought any of the doubtful plays were really Shakefpeare's property?

C. Did they know how many there were that had been,
on various grounds, affigned to him?

D. Certainly not; and you would be furprifed if you
heard how very few people in general fociety could tell you
how many plays by Shakefpeare were contained in the
moft ordinary editions of his works. I remember your telling me that, on one occafion, you dined in a company confifting of modern dramatifts, critics, and actors, and that
the wife of the treafurer of Drury Lane furprifed the party
by afking if "Venice Preferved" were not by Shakefpeare?
Really, people in general, that I meet out in company, are little better informed: I have tried the experiment, and have fometimes put the queftion, how many
plays our great dramatift had produced, and never yet was
correctly and fatisfactorily anfwered.

C. How would you anfwer it? How could I, or any one,
anfwer it pofitively? Among the thirty-feven plays ordinarily printed as by Shakefpeare, there are at leaft two or
three that many have confidered doubtful.

D. Which are they? I fuppofe "Pericles" is one?

C. And "Titus Andronicus" another; but "Titus Andronicus" was included by the Player-editors, Heming and
Condell, in the folio of 1623, and fo far there is diftinct
evidence in its favour; but "Pericles" was abfolutely excluded by them, although it was three times printed (in
1609, 1611, and 1619) in quarto, with Shakefpeare's name
at full length on the title-pages, and all anterior to the appearance of the folio of 1623.

D. Why, then, was it excluded? and was not its exclufion, by the very men who may have acted in it, fufficient to fhow that it ought to be rejected by fubfequent editors ?

C. One would fay fo ; but ftill what can be advanced againft the internal evidence, which I put firft, and againft the fecondary fact that, three years before Shakefpeare quitted the ftage, " Pericles" had come out in 4to, with his name in unufually large capitals on the title-page ? Again, two years afterwards, and one year before Shakefpeare returned to Stratford, it was reprinted under precifely the fame circumftances ; yet it did not obtain a place in the folio of 1623. The popularity of the play was fo remarkable, that Shakefpeare, if he had fhewn the leaft care about his reputation as a dramatift, might have been glad to own it.

D. I fee that, in the edition of Malone's Shakefpeare of 1821, the two plays "Titus Andronicus" and " Pericles" are placed together in a fort of fupplementary volume ; but the circumftances of each were very different : " Titus Andronicus" was never printed with Shakefpeare's name, until it was included in the folio of 1623 ; while "Pericles" was never included in that volume at all, but, as you fay, was printed, with the name of Shakespeare at full length on the title-page, three times,—twice before the date when Shakefpeare returned to his native town, which, as far as we know, he never left till his death.

C. There is reafon alfo to fuppofe that one play, included in the folio without fcruple, was not by Shakefpeare, and that the two player-editors inferted it in order, perhaps, to complete the feries of Englifh Hiftorical Dramas. I mean the "Firft Part of Henry VI", which fome believe was really a production by Robert Greene, a famous and popular author, who died in 1593, not very long after

Shakefpeare had commenced his career. Other plays (not to mention the ftrange jumble called "Mufidorus", performed before James I in 1609, and often reprinted) have at various times and in various ways been attributed to him, befides the feven included in what is ufually known as "Malone's Supplement"—fuch, for inftance, as "Edward the Third", reprinted by Capell, and "Arden of Faverfham", the imputation of which laft to Shakefpeare was, no doubt, fuggefted by the family name of Arden. Tieck, the German critic, very properly thought the laft worthy of tranflation; and he publifhed it in 1823, together with R. Greene's 'Friar Bacon" and T. Heywood's "Lancafhire Witches"— a volume of great merit, if only as tranflations.

D. I have never feen thofe tranflations; and I only know Greene's "Friar Bacon" as it is printed in the edition of Dodfley, which went through your hands.

C. I am glad to hear you ufe the words "which went through your hands"; becaufe, whatever the title-page may fay, it only "went through my hands", excepting as regards the additional plays by R. Greene, T. Nafh, T. Lodge, and G. Peele : thofe, and thofe only, I could be faid to have edited ; but there is not a reprint in the whole twelve volumes that I would not have collated and re-edited, if the publifher could have afforded to pay me. As to the other plays, beyond the four authors I have named, the impreffion of 1825 is an untruftworthy collection, but ftill valuable to all ftudents.

D. What do you fay to the feven plays included in "Malone's Supplement" of 1780 ? Are any of them by Shakefpeare ?

C. Of "Pericles", which comes firft, we have already

F

fpoken. " Locrine", the fecond in the volume, we have good reafon to fuppofe was by the brother of the then Master of the Revels. " Sir John Oldcaftle", in 1600 was printed with the name of Shakefpeare on the title-page, but in the fame year it was cancelled and re-appeared without a name : there is not the flighteft internal evidence for fuppofing that our great dramatift had any hand in it. Malone violently abufes " The Lord Cromwell", but it does not deferve the amount of cenfure he beftows, and my notion is that no lefs a poet than Drayton was importantly concerned in its authorfhip : it is certain, how-ever, that it has come down to us in a very imperfeft ftate. I think " The London Prodigal" was—at leaft in part—by Thomas Heywood, and written after James I came to the throne. " The Puritan" was not in exiftence (I mean printed existence) until 1607, and nearly all the main incidents (as I fhowed for the firft time many years ago) are derived from " George Peele's Jefts", of which there had been a new edition in the fame year : he had died about 1596 ; and the fole ground for imputing the comedy to Shakefpeare has been the initials W. S. fraudu-lently placed upon the title-page, though they may poffibly have been intended for a dramatift of the day with the fame initials, Wentworth Smith.

D. But what do you fay of " The Yorkfhire Tragedy", which comes laft in the " Supplement"? I read it the other day, after you had bought me and brought me a copy of it dated 1608, and with the words " Written by W. Shake-fpeare" at full length upon the title-page. Kemble could obtain no edition of it earlier than 1619 ; but the copy of 1608, which you purchafed for me, proves that it was in

exiftence fome years before Shakefpeare relinquifhed his
connection with the ftage : befides, we are informed on the
title-page that it was "acted by his Majefty's Players at
the Globe", where Shakefpeare muft have feen it performed :
that was his theatre, as it were.

C. My conviction—I do not fay belief—but my conviction is, that Shakefpeare was concerned in the compofition
of the whole piece.

D. I rejoice to hear you fay fo ; for when I read it,
fome of the fcenes produced a wonderfully ftrong impres-
fion on my mind.   What a powerful fpeech is that of the
hero, beginning

> " Why sit my hairs upon my cursed head,"

and containing the frightful couplet,

> " Divines and dying men may talk of hell,
> But in my heart her several torments dwell."

C. True, it is a frightful couplet; and if it had ftood
alone, and the dreadful event to which the play relates, and
on which the whole is founded, had not occurred, and a
tract and broadfide been printed upon it, in 1604, we might
have faid that the drama was written by Thomas Nafh.

D. How fo ?   Do you mean the fame Nafh who in 1592
printed " The Supplication of Pierce Pennylefs"?

C. The fame man, and becaufe the couplet you have
quoted is contained in the very tract you have mentioned :
this fingular fact has never been noticed : Nafh, in an agony
of difappointment and defpair, utters the lines.   But he
died before 1600, fo that he could have no concern in a
drama which arofe out of events in 1604, and which was
printed in 1608.   The fact feems to be that it was got up

in extreme hafte, in order to take advantage of a terrible incident, then making a fudden and deep impreffion on the public mind. "The Yorkfhire Tragedy" was one out of four fhort pieces prefented at the Globe on the fame night, and it was wanted as foon as poffible after the melancholy event in the Calverley family became known.

D. It feems to me that the tenth fcene of the drama is full of fuch writing as might have proceeded from Shakefpeare's ready mind and rapid pen : he was the very man wanted on fuch a fudden occafion ; for, as I have heard you fay, nothing but the utmoft velocity, both of intellect and pen, could have got through the mafs of work which Shakefpeare executed in the twenty years during which he was connected with the ftage in London—nearly forty entire plays (not to fpeak here of their merits), befides others he is known to have affifted in.

C. My opinion is, as regards "The Yorkfhire Tragedy", that every fyllable of it was contributed by him—not merely the ferious portions, but the introductory dialogue of the fervants. There is not a line or a letter, from beginning to end, that does not (if 1 may ufe an expreffion belonging to the cant of criticifm) *bear the ftamp*, the indelible ftamp, of his genius : that is my conviction. Shakefpeare's mind was electrical, and the fparks and flafhes flew from it with a fpeed and brilliancy beyond calculation.

The Duke here pulled out his watch, exclaiming, " Why, we have been talking nearly two hours, and time feems to have flown with fomething like the rapidity you attribute to Shakefpeare's genius. For this day I have troubled you enough, and I thank you heartily." "The labour that delights us phyfics pain" was my anfwer, and fo we parted for the day. Without delay, and without quitting the table, I wrote down notes of what had paſſed.

Electricity ſeems to be the principle of life in man, and according to the quantity of that element he is either clever or dull in mind, and rapid or ſlow in motion.

Sept. 3.—At the Garrick, where Douglas Jerrold told the following anecdote of that impetuous, impulſive, and impatient Iriſhman, Sheridan Knowles. He was jumping out of a cab in great haſte, near one of the theatres, and, toſſing a ſhilling to the driver, was running away at full ſpeed, when the cabman called out to him, "Sir! you have left your papers behind you."—"So I have, my boy," ſaid Knowles. "I thank you;" and he opened the door and took out ſome looſe ſheets of paper, two or three of which were on the ſeat, and two or three others on the floor of the cab. "Faith and troth, it is my new play! Thank you, my boy; thank you. Have you got a pen and ink, or a pencil?"—"No, I have not," said the cabman.—"Never mind;" rejoined Knowles, "what is your name, my boy?"— "John Jenkins, ſir."—"That will do. Wait a moment," added Knowles; "you are an honeſt fellow, and I will give you ſomething." So ſaying Knowles dived into a neighbouring ſhop, and in half a minute reappeared, in a flurry, ſhaking a ſlip of paper in his hand: "There, my boy, take that; it is an order for two to the boxes. Come with Mrs. Jenkins, and ſee me act to-morrow night. You are a good fellow; but I shall be too late for the rehearſal. Mind you come." Allowing a little for Jerrold's dramatic exaggeration, the ſtory was quite true.

Sept. 7.—Talking over the preſent ſtate of affairs in Spain, with H. C. Robinſon and Captain Charles Pycroft, my wife's brother, they reminded me that they had both been at the battle of Corunna, in 1809, having gone together to Gallicia, in order to forward intelligence to the *Times*. They were very nearly caught and made priſoners by the French in the purſuit of Sir John Moore, and only ſaved themſelves by ſcrambling on board a ſmall barque they purchaſed as a re-fuge. H. C. Robinſon and I had previouſly attended the Court of Inquiry into the Convention of Cintra; Wordſworth was there alſo, and wrote a proſe tract on the ſubject. I had ſeen Sir John Moore in 1807, ſitting as junior officer on the court-martial upon General Whitelock for miſconduct at Buenos Ayres, I never shall forget the beautiful harmony of the features of Sir John Moore; but he was very ſilent during the inquiry, and the Court generally left all queſtioning of the witneſſes to Manners Sutton, then Judge-Advocate. To return to Robinſon and Pycroft. After the battle of Corunna, they did not ſave anything but the clothes they wore; but Mr. Walter, proprietor of the *Times*, in whoſe employment they in fact were, took good care that they ſhould be no loſers. He was always on the liberal ſide in money, as well as in politics.

Sept. 13.—A friend has ſent me from Leghorn a copy of a drama by P. Byſſhe Shelley, called " The Cenci," printed in Italy while the author was reſiding there, and intended (they ſay) to have been produced on our London ſtage. This may be ſo, but I am ſure that it was not likely to meet ſucceſs either from the nature of the ſtory or the conduct of the plot. It has been ſpoken, or rather written, of to me as a work of very original genius, but I cannot

agree with the gentleman who forwarded it ; and, whatever
elfe it may do, I do not think it calculated to raife the author's character as a poet. Not a few paffages are almoft
verbally borrowed from Shakefpeare : thus Shelley, in
Act iii, fc. 2, makes one of his characters fpeak of

> " The taunts
> Which from the prosperous weak misfortune takes."

What is this but

> " The spurns
> That patient merit from the unworthy takes,"

of " Hamlet," Act iii, fc. 1 ? Again, in another place, we
are more than reminded of " Othello," Act v, fc. 2, under
fimilar circumftances ; for in " The Cenci", a man intending
to commit murder, exclaims,

> " And yet, once quench'd, I cannot thus relume
> My father's life."

Shakefpeare's words are nearly identical :

> " If I quench thee, etc., that can thy light relume."

In " Richard III," Act ii, fc. 4, we read,

> " I see, as in a map, the end of all,"

and in Shelley's " Cenci," Act ii, fc. 2, -

> " I see, as from a tower, the end of all."

I am not at all well read in Shelley, but I do not confider that thefe quotations tend to eftablifh his originality.
I do not mean for a moment to fay that he wifhed to copy
without acknowledgment, but his mind was perhaps imbued with Shakefpeare, and he wrote down almoft mechan-
ically the expreffions that firft prefented themfelves, not

recollecting at the time where he had found them. Such has been the origin in other authors of many imputed plagiarifms, perhaps fome of my own.

Sept. 20.—As I have a leifure time and an open fpace, I may as well put down here a few notes of the great orators I remember in Parliament in the earlier part of my life.

Addington (afterwards Lord Sidmouth) was Speaker of the Houfe of Commons. He was gaunt and tall in figure, and never loft an inch of his height while addreffing the houfe either from the chair or from the benches. He had a good full voice and a fteady, clear delivery, but he feldom faid anything worth hearing, though he was very emphatic, becaufe he put the higheft eftimate upon whatever he faid himfelf. He was a fine fpecimen of the pompous, and, on the whole, made a good and impartial prefident of the Houfe of Commons.

Pitt I heard once or twice, but not on any very important occafion. He was the model whom Addington imitated : he, too, was tall and fpare, with a very diftinct and not unmufical voice. He ufed little action, but was very impreffive, and was liftened to moft attentively. He was at that time out of office, and fpoke from a bench beyond what was then called the gangway. He came into office again into 1804, but I do not bear in mind any occafion on which I again heard him before his death in 1806.

The firft, and indeed the only, great fpeech I heard Fox deliver was on the affairs of Pruffia, not very long before he died. It did not by any means come up to my expectations. It was well arranged as to matter, but the manner was not good and the delivery in many places catchy and hefitating : he often paufed for a word, and made a fhort cough, as if to conceal the defeft. Neither was Fox's voice good : it was far from fteady and flowing, and was pitched in too high a key, so as fometimes to amount almoft to a fcream. I never heard him fpeak in reply, which I underftood was his *forte :* he feemed too fat in the throat for fmooth delivery.

Though I did not hear Fox, who introduced the Catholic claims in 1805, I liftened to Grattan's maiden fpeech in feconding the motion. His manner was very peculiar, and efpecially antithetical ; but he fometimes dropped his voice in the fwing of his delivery, and one limb of his antithefis was thereby loft. He flourifhed his arms about, moft of all his right, but he never (and I afterwards heard him frequently) carried me away in the tide of his eloquence. He had a ftrong brogue, and made no effort to conceal it.

I was prefent, in May 1805, when Lord Henry Petty (who came forward with greater expeftations than have been realifed) introduced the budget of the Whig miniftry, in which Lord Grenville was Firft Lord of the Treafury, and Fox Foreign Secretary. As Lord Lansdowne, Petty has been always refpeftable ; but his friends did him great harm, in the outfet of his career, by trumpeting him up as having all the requifites of a great orator.

Lord Grenville was a weighty man and a weighty fpeaker : he was diftinft, audible, and confecutive, never indulging in needlefs flourifhes, but always carrying his hearers along with him. During the exiftence of the miniftry of which he was the head, he delivered a great fpeech, the burden of which, at the clofe of nearly every period, was "the balance of power in Europe". I have

G

good reaſon to remember it ; for in the *Morning Chronicle*
of the next day this burden was printed in capitals where-
ever it occurred.   This mode of making it unuſually prominent was much approved by the party and by Perry,
who next day gave me £10 for my extraordinary pains.
This was the origin of my conneÆtion with his newſpaper,
and on a ſubſequent day he introduced me to Whitbread,
Ponſonby, and other Whig leaders.

Whitbread ſpoke coarſely and hoarſely : he was clevereſt
in reply, and not very ſcrupulous : his appearance reſembled
his oratory—forcible, but rather rough, eaſily disconcerted,
and not ready when interrupted : he was like his beer,
heady and strong, and he always looked to me the im-
perſonation of porter.

Perceval, who was taken from the Chancery Bar in 1807
to be at the head of the Exchequer, was always more than
a match for Whitbread, or, indeed, for any other antagoniſt
but Tierney. He was extremely quick, and ſeemed to take
delight in controverſy.   He was irritable, yet never put out
of temper in debate, and in this reſpeÆt he had the advantage of much more powerful ſpeakers. It was an unamiable
pleaſure to liſten to his ſharp voice, when he was making his
adverſaries ſmart by ſaying things as ſharp as his enunciation.   As a man he was inſignificant.

Tierney was the acuteſt ſpeaker of my day—poſſibly of
any day : he played with an adverſary as an angler plays
with a fiſh, which at length he lands.   He often encountered
Perceval, and was put up by his friends for the purpoſe of
anſwering him.   I can recolleÆt Tierney as far back as the
year 1797, when he induced my father to vote for his re- .
turn to Parliament, though he had not any high opinion of

Tierney's political honefty. Tierney's manner was pointed and brief: he never dealt in long fentences, and the dexterous way in which he often tripped up a rival's heels was very amufing: he was never violent, and, though voluble, he never threw away a word.

Of Sir James Mackintofh I muft fay a fentence or two, if only becaufe he was extremely kind to me when I wanted kindnefs. He was a moft painstaking fpeaker, with a moft unfortunate voice—harfh, grating, and diffonant; but, in general, the hearer was fo well fatisfied with what he delivered, that he almoft became reconciled to the mode of delivery. He came out in defence of Peltier, then went to India, returned almoft as poor as he went, but obtained a penfion and a feat in Parliament, where he was trufted by the whole of the Whig party, who paid his debts. In fome refpects he was over-rated; and it was the fafhion of his friends to praife the breadth and originality of his views. He was much liked as a diner-out.

Canning was Foreign Secretary under Perceval, but he did not come out in full bloom, as it were, till after the affaffination of Perceval in 1812: he feemed to keep himfelf in the background, if he were not kept there, and indeed he was not then much wanted. He was the moft elegant and finifhed orator I remember; but in retort and readinefs he was never a match for Tierney, who was quieted, however, by being made Mafter of the Mint. Canning's power of fpeech was not fo vigorous as perfuafive, and his choice of language was not to be furpaffed.

Yet, much as I admired the graceful flow of his ftudied harangues, he never roufed me by the energy and force of his delivery, like Brougham. I liftened to Brougham for

feven hours, without wearinefs, during his fpeech on the
Orders in Council : it had no weak parts, and fome of his
ftrongeft points were worked up to a pitch of enthufiafm,
even upon a queftion fo purely commercial.　He was very
happy at ridicule, and the feverity of his fatire made ad-
verfaries wince.　When he got into the House of Lords
(with the great exception of the Queen's Trial) he loft himfelf : a fhallow fandy foil impoverifhed his roots and ftunted
his branches.

Earl Grey, on the other hand, was heard even to more
advantage there, than when he was Mr. Grey in the
Houfe of Commons.　He was a proud man, efpecially to
inferiors, and always, phyfically as well as metaphorically,
carried his head very high.　His triumph was the paffing
of the Reform Bill.　He was clear, and often forcible ; but
it was very evident, while he fpoke, that he was confidering the dignity of what he called " his order", and even the
pofture that he affumed : he was more ftudied than any
other Parliamentary fpeaker of my time.

I could in this way go through a long catalogue, but I
will only add a few words regarding Sir Robert Peel.　I
watched him from the moment he fet foot in the House of
Commons, and can fay that there never exifted an orator
who took more pains to be both argumentative and impres-
five : he laboured every fentence, and never in his life, as it
were, let go, and trufted to the infpiration of the moment.
He was calm, cold, and calculating : he was encrufted like
an almond, and what was within the fhell was dry, but not
flavourlefs : it required fome maftication.

Sept. 24.—On what authority does Sir W. Scott, in his
" Life of Napoleon", ch. xvi, alter " top" to *type*, in quoting
act iv, fc. 1, of " Macbeth"?

> " And wears upon *its* baby brow the round
> And *type* of sovereignty."

All editions, ancient and modern, read " top" and not *type :* yet " top" and *type* would be expreffed by the fame letters in fhort-hand, if that had been ufed in taking down the dialogue on the ftage. Scott alfo changes " his" to *its.*

Where, let me alfo afk, does Scott obtain the word "aftucious", for aftute, in ch. xvii, etc., of his " History of Bonaparte"? " The aftucious tyrant [Robefpierre] endeavoured to acquire allies among the remains of the Girondifts". There are many fuch Walter-Scotticifms.

Sept. 30.—I have made the Society of Antiquaries a prefent, really of the utmoft intereft and fingularity in its way, although they may not duly eftimate it ; viz., a copy of the very earlieft broadfide in our language, printed, as I am told by very good judges (and as I think myfelf on comparifon), by Lettou and Machlinia, our very ancient printers. It was iffued on a great event, the marriage of Henry VII with the Princefs Elizabeth of York. By itfelf, and in my hands, it feemed worth little ; but, as the Society of Antiquaries poffeffes the fineft and moft complete fet of Englifh proclamations exifting, it is a moft valuable addition, efpecially as they had previoufly none older than the reign of Henry VIII. Still, they feem hardly fenfible of its hiftorical value, and hold in much higher eftimation a fragment of old bronze, or a piece of flint, which they fancy is in fhape fomething like the head of a hammer : they fee comparatively little merit in any literary difcoveries. I found the broadfide as the lining of the cover of a later work.

Nobody ought to purchafe an old book without carefully

examining the fly-leaves: a proof of it occurred to me only
the day before yefterday. I bought a Chaucer, "printed at
London by Thomas Godfray, in the yere of our lorde
M.D.XXXII." The laft leaf of the folio is blank, and upon
it is written, in a handwriting of the time of Henry VIII
(who is defcribed as "by the grace of God King of England and of France, Lord of Ireland and prince of Wales,
and defenfor of the faith, and fupreme head of this Church
of England next under God"), a charter giving to Robert
Syngleton, archpreeft of Dover, "for the behoof of the in-
habitants, the church of the parish of faint Markus, called
the New Work, with the cemetery, there to celebrate and exe-
cute all and divers offices and fervices, fully and perfectly in
all degrees, freely with as much liberty as of good memory
or knowledge, as is perceived to have appertained to the
church of Saint Markus, within the town of Dover, called
the Old Work", etc. This is followed by a fpecial refervation
to the King of the other churches in Dover; viz.,
thofe of Our Lady, of St. Peter, and of St. Markus, "the
Old Work."

The precife date has been worn away at the bottom of
the page; but I only refer to the document (nowhere elfe
mentioned that I can difcover) to illuftrate the importance
of always carefully examining old fly-leaves.

Oct. 2.—The Rev. S. R. Maitland, librarian to the
Archbifhop of Canterbury, is one of the moft acute and
learned men I know: he is nearly related (I think
great-nephew) to John Maitland, long M.P. for Chippen-
ham, and formerly my father's partner in the Spanifh wool
trade: my notion is that S. R. M. was not quite orthodox
in his bringing up, but that he has fince conformed: be

that as it may, I feel fure that he is honeft in his convic-
tions, very clever, very well educated, and very good company, barring a little turn for fatire and ridicule, which
makes his converfation fpicy, but not always pleafant:
people rather fmart under it, and he fpares neither friend
nor foe. In 1828 he wrote, and printed with his own hand,
a pleafant trifle, juft like himfelf, racy, thoughtful, and
cheerful, under the title of " The Owl and the Sun", and
he yefterday gave me a copy of it : it confifts of only
about a thousand lines in couplets ; and, as the little 12mo is
an abfolute rarity, I fhall here make a quotation or two from
it : the author calls it " a didactic poem", and it is in the
form of a Dialogue between the Sun and an Owl, which
the writer fuppofes to be lodged in fome northern nook of
the Tower of London : it begins thus as a converfation between the Sun and the Tower :

> " Quoth the Sun to the Tower of London one day,
> Good friend, I respect, I can honestly say,
> Your comparative age and your pretty square form,
> Which I've gilded and dried after many a storm.
>   The Tower, amaz'd at this sudden address,
> His feelings attempted in vain to express.
> With sunshine and gratitude jointly he burned,
> But to bow was a lesson he never had learned ;
> And his organs of utterance (one cannot say speech)
> Were fit only to make, or to widen, a breach."

This laft line illuftrates the author's faulty verfification,
and there are other inftances of the fame kind : it has a
redundant fyllable, unlefs we pronounce " Were fit" in the
time of only one fyllable. This, however, is a nicety not
abfolutely neceffary in a lively production of this kind,
where the meafure muft be made to run, as it were, trip-

pingly. The Sun proceeds to blame the Tower for being
fo ftationary, in all fenfes of the word, in thefe times of
movement and improvement, and the Tower anfwers that
his interior has undergone many changes for the better,
which, of courfe, the Sun could not fee. At this moment
an old Owl, lodged in a dark recefs of the building, inter-
pofes, and the Sun afks :

> " Who are you ?   But you must be that villanous bird,
> Of whom—though I never yet saw one—I've heard.
> You must be an Owl : and I've heard the moon talk
> Of the wonderful fine ones she sees about York."

Here, again, Maitland fhows fome want of acquaintance
with our beft verfification, or he would not, even in a humorous production, compel "talk" to rhyme with "York";
and juft before he has given us a fpecimen of what we may
call real cockney pronunciation, where he makes "idea" to
found like "fear".

> " All the brickwork look'd brown with amazement and fear ;
> The White Tower was pale at the very idea," etc.

As the Tower was notórioufly a mere Londoner, having
never ftirred from a fpot where he could hear Bow bell quite
diftinctly, this defect might be in him allowed for ; but the
author is here fpeaking in his own perfon, and as it is the only
inftance of the kind it may well be paffed over. I need not
purfue the dialogue between the Sun and the Owl, which
is very characteriftic and lively ; but I will make a quotation from one of the fpeeches of the Owl in anfwer to the
Sun, who had charged him with contracted views and want
of extenfive knowledge.

> " May be so (quoth the Owl) ; I dare say it's all true,
> And that nobody sees half so much as you do ;

Yet, pure creature of light, still a creature thou art,
And though almost all-seeing, thou seest but in part.
When you look on the world all is brilliant and light,
E'en the ditch and the dunghill are sunny and bright :
With a surface of flame the dark muddy stream flows,
And the rock of the wilderness sparkles and glows.
This I know, and am grateful : believe when I say
That I know how to value thy life-giving ray ;
Though unable to bear the full splendour of noon,
And contented to buy second-hand of the moon ;
Yet dark as I am in my turret or tree,
The beauty and value of sunshine I see ;
The bright smile of nature reflecting thy ray,
As it basks and expands in the fulness of day.
Above all I acknowledge your light and your heat."

And fo they proceed, while the Sun, acknowledging the compliments of the Owl, "begins to fufpeᴄt the old bird is no fool"; and they conclude the dialogue very good friends, each admitting the value of the other as works of God. The Tower takes no farther part in the converfation, and he was merely the work of man.

Oᴄt. 5.—The following fingular and interefting advertifement, relating to the greateft poet of the time of Charles II, has never been republifhed in any Life of Dryden to which I have accefs : it is the more important, becaufe it eftablifhes that the date affigned to the beating Dryden received at the hands of the ruffians hired by Lord Rochefter, has hitherto been miftakenly fixed on the 16th, inftead of the 18th December, 1679 : I quote the *London Gazette* from the 24th to the 29th December.

" Whereas, John Dreyden, Esq., was, on Thursday, the 18th inst., at night, barbarously assaulted and wounded in Rose Street in Covent

Garden, by divers men unknown : if any persons shall make discovery of the said offenders to the said Mr. Dreyden or to any justice of the peace, he shall not only receive £50, which is deposited in the hands of Mr. Blanchard, goldsmith, next door to Temple Bar, for the said purpose, but, if he be a principal or accessory in the said fact himself, his Majesty is graciously pleased to promise him his pardon for the same."

It is worth a note to mention that the "Effay on Satire" by Lord Mulgrave and Dryden, which excited the wrath of Rochefter, was fo long popular, that it was printed and publifhed at the price of a penny twenty years after it firft appeared : I have a copy of it in this cheap form in very legible type.

I have alfo a copy of Dryden's pamphlet againft Elkanah Settle, which Dr. Johnfon fo well characterifes ; and, as Settle's autographs are very rare, I may add that I have a remarkable one by him, entirely in his own handwriting : it occupies three folio pages of verfe, and is thus headed: "To the moft renown'd the Prefident and the reft of the *Knights of the moft noble Order of the Toaft*", which was a felf-conftituted body, formed, as it feems, for the laudation of the ladies, and the difcuffion and decifion of matters of tafte, efpecially in relation to the drama : it opens thus :

> " When to the great the suppliant Muses press
> (By a poetic license) for access,
> Like a Court-page they are more bold than rude :
> Custom gives them the privilege t' intrude ;
> But my pen, drawn in your lov'd stage defence,
> For my presumption is a just pretence.
> By you are the dramatic Muses fed,
> Born for your pleasures, in your service bred."

And in the fame ftrain he proceeds, as it were, to blaspheme and blunder, making Mark Antony drink down the draught of·pearl while Cleopatra ftood quietly by, and elevating the "Knights of the Toaft", as they called themfelves, both in dignity and antiquity, above the "Knights of the Garter": it ends in thefe lines, where Settle cenfures Collier by name for his attack on plays and theatres, but only refers to Henningham by initials : he did not fear the pen of the firft, but dreaded the cudgel of the laft.

> "A late traducer's sacrilegious hand
> Has with unhallow'd rhymes your rites profan'd.
> The dove-like Satyrist with his harmless gall,
> Before your own high bar of justice call :
> Do yourselves right and with one sentence damn
> At once our Collier and your H————m.
> The same just doom let them both undergo ;
> Disrobe the Pulpiteer, and strip the Beau."

The following is the precife form in which the Bard of Bartholomew Fair appended his name to his verfes:

> "Here, asking your Honours Pardon for this (I hope) inoffensive Address, I beg your acceptance of this poor Present, which till finisht I durst not presume to lay at your feet.
> "Being in all humility,
>   "Your Honours most devoted servant,
>   "E. SETTLE."

Yet this was the man whom Dryden thought worthy of an anfwer : the "prefent", whatever it were, could hardly have been the tract to which Dryden replied.

Oct. 8.—On the 29th ultimo, I bought a highly curious book : I gave two fhillings for it at a ftall near Clare

Market; and, fhowing it to Rodd, he at once offered me
five guineas for it, which I declined, and keep my treafure:
I really cannot pretend to eftimate the worth of it, either
in a book-felling or book-loving point of view: it contains
feveral very early German plays and poems, dated refpectively in the order in which they occur in the volume, 1538,
1546, 1540, and one with no date: the firft contains on the
title-page and at the end a wood-cut portrait of John Hufs,
and I quote the title-page exactly:

"Tragedia Johannis Huss, welche auff dem Unchristlichen Con-
cilio zu Costnitz gehalten, allen Christen näglich und trostlich zu
lesen. Wittemberg, M.D.xxxviij."

This drama occupies fmall 12mo widely-printed pages as
far as fign. F viij, the repetition of the head of Hufs being
on fign. F vij, and F viij being blank. It is entirely in
verfe, excepting a preface, and a fermon preached by a
bifhop at the commencement of *Actus quintus.*

The tragedy is followed by *Trias Romana, Quaternio
Mundana, Der Welt Gattung,* with frefh fignatures and in
larger type, on two fheets 12mo, mainly confifting of a dialogue between the Father and the World.

Next comes a play with this title:

"Hoffteuffel. Das sechste Capitel Danielis, den Gottfürchtigen zu
trost, den Gottlosen zur warnung, Spielweis gestellet, und in Rheim
verfasset, Durch Johan Chryseum.—Gedruckt zu Wittemberg, Bey
Veit Creutzer. Anno &c. 1546."

It has an Introduction in profe, fubfcribed Johannes
Chryfeus, followed by *Vorrede und inhalt difes Spiels,* to
which fuccecd *Die Perfonen,* etc., confifting, among others,
of Darius, Jofaphat, Narr, Daniel, Sibilla Daniels Weib,
Salomon, Jofeph and Ben Jamin, Daniel's fons, a character

called Hoffteuffel, Cambifes, Michael ein Engel, etc. The
body of the drama confifts of five acts, divided into fcenes,
and terminated by a *Befchlus*, with *Ende diefes Spiels*. The
whole occupies fheets as far as H vj.

The fourth production in the volume has this imprint at
the bottom of the title-page, *Getruckt zum Bern by Mathia
Apiario. Im* 1540 *jar.* The pagination throughout is in
Roman capitals, and it ends on p. LXXXIX with what is
called " Regifter": the whole is entitled

" Ein fast Kurtz wylig Fassnachtspil, so zum Bern uff der Herin-
fassnacht in dem M.D.XXII jar von burgerssonen offentlich gemacht
ist," etc.

The fifth production in the volume has a clever and neat
wood-cut upon the title-page, reprefenting three men, two
women, and a child, the laft bearing an incenfe-burner,
while one of the women dreffes its hair : above the cut are
thefe words :

" Das Barbeli. Ein gespräch von einer muter mit ir tochter, sye in
ein Kloster ze bringen," etc.

It has no printer's nor publifher's names, nor is any place
mentioned, but the whole is in a dramatic form, though
without acts or fcenes, and at the clofe·we read, " *End difs
ffyls. I. F. S.*"

I fpent fome days in making fearches and inquiries
regarding the book, but I could learn nothing fatisfactory,
excepting that it muft be a great rarity in connection with
early German literature and the Reformation. I afked H. C.
Robinfon, and other men more learned on the fubject, without fuccefs, but I muft purfue my inveftigations. One foreign
bookfeller affected to fpeak lightly of it, but, like Rodd,
offered me five guineas for it before I left the fhop.

Oct. 14.—Drayton, in his "Battle of Agincourt", 1627, did not scruple to follow Shakespeare in his "Henry the Fifth", act iv, sc. iii :

> " God's will ! I pray thee wish not one man more", etc.

Drayton has this fine stanza : he seems to have envied Shakespeare, but after his death copied him :

> " When hearing one wish all the valiant men
>   At home in England with them present were,
> The King makes answer instantly again,
>   I would not have one man more than is here :
> If we subdue, less should our praise be then ;
>   If overcome, less loss shall England bear,
> And to our numbers we should give that deed
>   Which must from God's own powerful hand proceed."

" David Gam, Esquire", cuts a considerable figure in Drayton's poem, though he does not save the King's life. In his poem to Henry Reynolds, Drayton hints that his rival Daniel, in his "Civil Wars", was more of a historian than a poet, and says :

> "Amongst these Samuel Daniel ; whom if I
> May speak of, but to censure do deny,
> Only have heard some wise men him rehearse
> To be too much historian in verse."

There is little doubt that Drayton was not free from jealousy of his contemporaries, and in the same poem, only a few lines earlier, he thus grudgingly describes the character and merits of Shakespeare, whom, as we see above, he, in fact, closely imitated :

> "Shakespeare, thou had'st as smooth a comic vein,
> *Fitting the sock*, and in thy natural brain
> As strong conception, and as clear a rage,
> As any one that traffick'd with the stage."

Surely Shakefpeare was as great with the bufkin as with "the fock", but Drayton contrived to forget his contemporary's wonderful performances in tragedy : it was, in part, from envy of Shakefpeare, that Drayton, in the fame poem and almoft immediately afterwards, extravagantly eulogifed Ben Jonfon, by fome called Shakefpeare's rival.

> " Next these learn'd Jonson in this list I bring,
> Who had drunk deep of the Pierian spring ;
> Whose knowledge did him worthily prefer,
> And long was lov'd here of the theatre."

And fo he proceeds to liken him to Seneca and Plautus, and to affert that he was equally eminent for the fock and for the bufkin. No acknowledged drama by Drayton, whether tragedy or comedy, has furvived, but he is well known to have written both.

Oct. 15.—Not long after Charles Dickens had been enrolled in the regular corps of reporters for the *Morning Chronicle*, he was fent in that capacity to give an account of fome public dinner, at which many perfons of diftinction were prefent, and among them Lord Lincoln, then, I think, in difgrace with his father, the Duke of Newcaftle, for votes he had given in the Houfe of Commons. His health having been propofed, it was neceffary for the Earl of Lincoln to return thanks, which he proceeded to do with much hefitation, and at laft refumed his feat without finifhing his fpeech. All that Dickens faid of him in his report was in the feverely quaint words, " Lord Lincoln broke down, and fat down". I remember it well; becaufe there was a good deal of inquiry at the Clubs, and at the Athenæum in particular, who had ventured to write fuch a droll laconic account of Lord Lincoln's failure? I had not heard of it, till I went to the Garrick next morning; and, as people there were aware of my connection with newspapers, inquiry was made of me. I did not at that moment know; but if I had known, I fhould not have divulged what was in fome fort an official fecret: nobody in the *Morning Chronicle* office ufually avowed their acquaintance with fuch matters.

Oct. 20.—Some little time ago, Coleridge wrote a fmall felf-vindicatory poem, which he called "A Trifle", in which he fpoke of himfelf under the rather humiliating figure of a Tomtit—a fmall bird of no fong, and of little apparent ufe. It is not in print, but Martin Burney fhowed me a copy of it, which he had from Lamb. Some people thought it happy, and fo it is in parts; but on the whole a failure. Coleridge has neither kept up the allegory of the bird, nor maintained the character of the man. The following are the opening lines of about a hundred fuch:

> "A bird, who for his early sins
> Had liv'd among the Jacobins,
> Though like a kitten among rats,
> Or callow Tit in nest of bats,
> He much abhorr'd the democrats,
> Yet nathless stood in bad report
> Of ill to Church, as well as Court:" etc.

What had a Tomtit to do with democrats, Church, or Court? Coleridge proceeds to inform us that this fong-lefs bird had neverthelefs learned to pipe "God fave the King": afterwards he abufes the bats, and figures under thefe "blood-fuckers, vampires, and harpies" his own enemies, and thofe of the State, contending

> " That he had never left in lurch
>   His king, his country, or his church,"

when the fact was, that he had found it both right and
expedient, like Southey and others, to come back to
Church and State, after the overthrow of the French Revolution as the hoped-for means of restoring liberty to
mankind. He afterwards tranflates his own initials into
Greek, Εστησε, as if to fhow that *he had ftood*, while others
had fallen, and thus pathetically concludes his apology, for
it does not amount to a vindication :

> " Ah, silly bird ! and unregarded,
>   His lamp but glimmer'd in the socket :
> He liv'd unhonour'd and discarded,
>   Without a penny in his pocket ;
> Nay, though he hid it from the many,
>   With scarce a pocket for his penny."

To keep up the allegory, the " filly bird" ought not to have
had a lamp, a penny, or a pocket. One almoft pities the
great poet while thus condefcending, inftead of fpeaking
out boldly in his own perfon, and fairly confeffing that he
and his Briftol friends had been utterly difappointed by
the refult of the French Revolution. Thoufands of other
fanguine men (my own father among them) had been difappointed alfo. As a counterpoife to this poor ftuff, let anybody read Coleridge's " Garden of Boccacio", or fome noble
paffages in his " Zapolya".

Oct. 21.—I went to breakfaft with Dyce to meet Arifto-
phanes Mitchell, Leigh Hunt, Sandby, and Harnefs.
The eggs, though Dyce faid that he had given three-
pence a-piece for them, were not firft-rate ; and to

I

confole the company, I made them laugh by telling
them what had happened to me, as regards eggs, in 1815,
at the houfe of the lady to whofe daughter I was engaged
to be married.   She lived at Putney, in a good houfe, with
large garden, ftabling, etc., and they kept a confiderable
ftock of cocks and hens: being then devoted to the water,
I ufed to go down in my boat, and fometimes arrived at
Putney after the family, confifting of feveral fingle ladies
(befides my intended, who was the youngeft daughter) had
dined: in that cafe I was provided with a fupplemental
meal, often including eggs boiled in the fhell.   One evening in 1815 I came too late for the family dinner, and
willingly agreed to satisfy my hunger on eggs, the eldeft
daughter, an old maid, affuring me that they happened then
to have a fuperabundance: they were to be brought up for
me one at a time, that they might be hot.   When I broke
the fhell of the firft out rufhed a dreadful hogo of bad air.
The family were aftonifhed: fuch a thing had never happened before, and they could not account for it, becaufe
they always numbered the eggs from day to day, in order
to make fure they fhould be frefh: the ladies were very
forry, and ordered another egg to be brought up.   I broke
the fhell of it, and again came the horrible puff of putrid
air in my face, to the difmay of all, and the fad difcomfort
of my intended: however, they were all fure it could not
happen again, if I would but try a third egg.   I confented,
and that was bad too: a fourth was brought up, and even
a fifth, for being on my Ps and Qs, I did not like to refufe.
"Well", at laft faid the eldeft fifter, who managed the
houfe, "this is wonderful"; and my mother-in-law, that was
to be, afked her to go to the cook and make inquiries; for the

numbers on the eggs regularly followed each other, teftify-
ing the very days when they had been laid. Even the cook
could not account for it; when all of a fudden a light
feemed to break upon the fifter who had the peculiar
charge of the poultry. She exclaimed that fhe could now
explain the myftery : fhe remembered that one of the hens
had laid away in the coach-houfe—that a whole neft of
eggs had been found there, and that fhe had incautioufly
numbered them, not on the days they were laid, but on the
day they were difcovered, and fo on in fucceffion : all, in
fact, were rotten, and five of them had unluckily fallen
to my fhare. This had happened nearly twenty years
before the date when I told the ftory at Dyce's breakfaft-
table, but I could not forget it.

Oct. 24.—Laft night, after my family had gone to bed,
I put into Englifh a fonnet by the old Italian poet, Guit-
tone di Arezzo, with which I had been much pleafed when
in the course of the day it was read to me by a mafter of
the language, to whom I not unfrequently refort when I
meet with any ferious difficulty. I flatter myfelf that I have
not fucceeded amifs, and that I have transfufed into Englifh
fome portion of the grace, eafe, and fimplicity of the original: I therefore fubjoin it here : due allowance muft, of
courfe, be made for the comparative untractablenefs of
our language.

SONNET.

By how much I am troubled by the thought,
   That cruelty has fill'd the world with sighs,
By so much am I in my grief distraught,
   And hope the more as hope rejected flies.
I tell myfelf, what ne'er my heart denies,

That I to earth by weight of woe am brought,
Yet strong desire compels that that be sought
By gaining which the very gainer dies.
Perchance when some few years are gone and past,
When she shall read my loving sighs in rhyme,
Ev'n she will mourn for my untimely lot.
Who knows but she, who deems my love a crime,
Marking the fate which she had caus'd, at last
May shed one tear for me—not quite forgot.

A hint is given in the Giunti *Scelta*, where the above is found, that the sonnet has also been assigned to Triffino, but I feel assured that it is older than his time. Triffino died about the year 1550.

Oct. 27.—I have already mentioned John Hamilton Reynolds, about whom I have taken an interest ever since he published a laudable poem called "The Mermaid", about the year 1820; the writing of it was graceful, and the fancy pretty and novel. It was published by Taylor and Heffey, but it did not fell, and the young man was for some time disheartened. He was, I understand, a son of Frederick Reynolds, the successful but, to my mind, not very meritorious dramatist, who began writing for the stage in 1786, and did not leave off until 1810, having then produced nearly thirty dramas. He was bred to the law, and so was his son, John Hamilton Reynolds, who followed in his father's wake as regards the stage, and was the author of Miss Kelly's Monopolylogue. She was very clever, but not quite strong enough to sustain the weight of a whole piece on her own shoulders. So I may say of the author of the piece: he showed himself very clever, but hardly clever enough to give sufficient variety of gaiety and serious business; and,

on the whole, the reprefentation was not fatisfactory,
nor, I believe, profitable. Still, it was highly meritorious,
and Mifs Kelly gained credit both with her private friends
(among whom C. Lamb and his fifter, and my father
and mother, may be enumerated) and with the public. I
was prefent, but I forget the precife date : it was at a time
when Mifs Kelly had no engagement.

In 1825, J. H. Reynolds and Tom Hood joined in the
production of a little volume which attracted no notice,
and which I had forgotten, until a copy of it was given me
yefterday at the Garrick by Reynolds. It is entitled,
"Odes and Addreffes to Great People", the epithet
"great" being to be underftood ironically : the perfons
celebrated are Richard Martin, Dymoke, the champion,
Grimaldi, Elliston, Dr. Kitchener, &c. There are fifteen
of thefe "Odes and Addreffes", and J. H. R. went over
them with me, while I marked which of the pieces were by
him, and which by Hood. Reynolds appears to have contributed ten, and Hood only five pieces ; and I muft own
that the five are confiderably better than the ten : J. H. R.
is too long and too wordy. There is a great deal of pleafant point in them, but the joke is carried on too long ; till,
in fact, it ceafes to be a joke. Hood's pieces are fhorter and
more pointed ; and as they have not made their appearance
elfewhere, I will here enumerate them. Hood wrote the
Ode to Richard Martin on Cruelty to Animals, the Ode to
Grimaldi (perhaps the beft in the book), the Addrefs to
Sylvanus Urban (alfo good), the Ode to Capt. Parry (only
middling), and the Addrefs to the Dean and Chapter of
Weftminfter (on extorting a fee of 2s. from every vifitor),
which is bitterly humorous.

J. Hamilton Reynolds has loſt his poſition and his money very much by ſitting up late at night. He is very cheerful company, but ſomewhat prone to ſatire, and he cannot reſiſt ſaying an ill-natured thing, if it be but ſmart, and makes others ſmart. On the temporary quarrel between Poole and Liſton, ſomebody remarked that the former was as ſore as if he had no ſkin : "Aye," ſaid Reynolds, "and as if he always wore a coat of pepper and ſalt over his raw hide." Poole never forgave this rub upon his rawneſs.

J. H. R. wrote my name on the title-page of the "Odes and Addreſſes" as a gift "from one of the authors". He is too much in the habit of thinking that converſation is only good as a vehicle for ridicule ; conſequently he makes no friends, though few want them more.

Nov. 7.—It is often very difficult for people of rank and riches to find agreeable employment, and it ſeems that the Duke is about to try the experiment of authorſhip. He has not told me the preciſe nature of the work he projects, but I gueſs that it is ſomething in relation to his own poſ-ſeſſions, in the way of art and virtu. It is only at moſt in embryo yet ; but ſomething that he ſaid to me about private printing leads me to ſuppoſe that he has reſolved to oc-cupy part of his leiſure in this way. He does not intend to include any of his book-rarities, leaving them per-haps for a ſeparate experiment. He is rather myſte-rious with me upon the ſubject, as if he ſuſpected that, if he were quite open with me, I ſhould ſmile at his project—if not openly, at all events in my ſleeve.

By the way, this proverbial expreſſion has puzzled ſome people, but it is derived from the time when hanging-fleeves were in fashion, and when people, difposed to laugh but anxious to conceal it, turned their faces on one fide over their fhoulders, and hid their rifibility, as it were, in their long but otherwife ufelefs fleeves.

A week ago the Duke faid to me, "If you have juft now nothing better to do, I wifh you to accompany me to Derbyfhire, where I have a little bufinefs in which you may aid me." I gueffed the bufinefs; but it fo happened that for the next two days I had a rather important affair of my own to attend to, and when I mentioned it to the Duke, he at once moft kindly gave way, and faid that he would go down to Chatfworth by himfelf, and expect me there in a day or two.

I accordingly joined the Duke there; but we did little more than breakfaft and dine together, for he was very bufily engaged in making notes upon his pictures, ftatues, &c., while I employed myfelf very fatisfactorily in the library. He now and then condefcended to afk my opinion on fuch matters as engaged his attention, and one of them, I remember particularly, was regarding a rofary in fandal wood, moft beautifully carved, as was faid, by no lefs a hand than that of Holbein, and which the Duke had recently bought from Rundell and Bridge, at the coft of two hundred guineas. I had a good deal of time to myfelf, and I efpecially employed it in looking up, and looking over, all the moft famous editions of Ariofto, noticing any variations of text, and tranflating particular portions that took my fancy. I told the Duke how I employed myfelf when not engaged by him, and at his inftance I read to him (for he can always hear me well) the following fpecimen of my labours. Though long, perhaps too long, I copy the whole of it here, as the Duke was pleaſed by it, and as I think it worth the pains of tranſcribing from my own rough ſlips. It is the well-known ſtory of the magic-cup, which ſpilt its contents upon the boſom of any man whoſe wife had been unfaithful. It is from Canto xliii of the *Orlando Furioſo:*

THE CUP OF JEALOUSY.

Fair Mantua is a city, whose high wall
    The limpid waters of a lake surround,
Whose waves expand till in the Po they fall,
    And at Benaco is their well-spring found :
'Twas built when in decay the structure tall,
    Built by Agenor's dragon, fell to ground.
There was I born, though poor, of gentle line ;
A humble roof was all I boasted mine.

If 'twere by fortune at my birth denied
    That I vast hoards of riches should possess,
This one defect by Nature was supplied,
    Who dress'd my person in her loveliness.
Fair dames and damsels for my favour sigh'd,
    E'en in my days of boyish bashfulness :
My manners corresponded with my features,
Although self-praise sound ill from noblest creatures.

In this our city dwelt a man so wise,
    His skill in arts beyond belief was great ;
And when to Phœbus' light he closed his eyes
    He number'd years one hundred twenty-eight.
Till late in life, when love made him his prize,
    He liv'd in free and solitary state :
He then obtain'd a wife ; his riches bought her ;
And in due time she bore to him a daughter.

And to provide that this, his age's child,
    Should not pursue her mother's course, who sold

Her chastity (in marriage undefil'd,
  And of more worth than all his hoarded gold),
Far from the world, upon a dismal wild,
  A lonely spot, barren and bleak and cold,
He by enchantment built a noble palace,
Compelling to the work hell's power and malice.

Chaste, venerable dames alone attended
  On the fair maid, who daily grew in beauty ;
To keep her far from men on them depended,
  Lest youth and flattery draw her from her duty :
Examples of bright virgins who defended
  Their honour, else the lawless spoiler's booty,
And for their virtues justly had been sainted,
Around the walls were sculptur'd and depainted.

Thus did the ancient sire perform his will,
  Until the virgin fruit was ripe to fall,
When 'twas my chance, or call it good or ill,
  To be selected worthiest of all
For such a wife : and many a plain and hill
  For twenty miles around fair Mantua's wall,
Cattle and fisheries, lands all rich and flowery,
He gave me with his daughter for a dowry.

So fair, so courteous, was she, that my heart
  Could never have conceiv'd a better choice :
Her skill so great in every female art, ·
  That Pallas in her might with pride rejoice.
She walk'd as earth had in her frame no part,
  And it was heaven to listen to her voice.
All liberal arts she gain'd, and in the sequel
Her father's learning she could almost equal.

But to her knowledge, wit, and lovely hue,
  Which might to passion almost move a stone,
She join'd the tenderest affection too,
  Whose mere remembrance makes my sad heart groan.

K

She took no joy, no pastime would pursue,
 But in my company, and mine alone ;
And every day we found some new delight :
Fool that I was, such happiness to blight !

For five years only liv'd the wise old man,
 Her father, after our glad wedding morn ;
And then the first of all those woes began
 Which I still feel, and left me thus forlorn.
While 'neath the sunshine my life's current ran,
 So lov'd by her whose love I chang'd to scorn,
A noble dame residing near beheld me,
And to her lawless flame at length compell'd me.

In magic and enchantments such her skill,
 That few or none have ever gone beyond her :
She shook the earth, or made the sun stand still,
 Chang'd day to darkest night, rais'd storms and thunder :
Yet could she not control my constant will,
 Nor my affections from their object sunder.
I could not soothe her passion fierce and strong,
Unless I did my wife a grievous wrong.

Her form, indeed, was fair, her look was pleasant,
 And that she lov'd me passing well I saw ;
But richest promises, and many a present,
 Great as they were, could not my love withdraw.
Her efforts 'gainst my plighted faith incessant
 Gain'd not a look—I weigh'd them not a straw :
I still was faithful to my marriage vow,
Nor other claim would on my heart allow.

The hope, the confidence, the certainty,
 I felt in my wife's chastity and truth,
Would give me power the beauty to defy
 Of one with Leda's countenance, in sooth :
Were all the treasures plac'd before mine eye
 That tempted once the Trojan shepherd youth,

I had rejected favour, fortune, beauty,
And scorn'd their strength to draw me from my duty.

One day when I was near Melissa's palace,
    (Such was her name) she made a new endeavour,
While I was roaming through the flowering valleys,
    To shake my confidence and peace for ever.
By jealousy she strove, with treacherous malice,
    To change my faith, and our true hearts to sever ;
And she began by giving faith applause
Kept to a wife who ne'er broke marriage laws.

" But who (she ask'd) can faith and truth believe
    Who has not seen them prov'd before his view ?
If then you find a wife does not deceive,
    You may, indeed, esteem her chaste and true.
But if alone your lady you ne'er leave,
    And if she see no other man but you,
'Tis but blind confidence ; and breath you waste,
To say you know your untried wife is chaste.

" Let her be prov'd.   Quitting your home awhile,
    Let it be thought some other soil you tread,
While she remains behind, to frown or smile
    On suitors with their messages unread :
If neither prayers nor presents can beguile
    Your wife with guilt to outrage your chaste bed,
When means and secrecy are both allow'd,
Then of her truth you may be justly proud."

These words and others like them she employ'd,
    And in the end so much upon me wrought,
That I agreed my dwelling to avoid,
    That to the test my wife's faith might be brought.
" Suppose (I said) my bliss should be destroy'd
    (Of which I will not entertain a thought),
Or be preserv'd, how shall I know the time
To recompense her love, or blaze her crime ?"

" I will a drinking-cup for thee provide
    (Th' enchantress said) of virtue great and strange :
Morgana made it, when her brother tried
    Whether Genevra's faith had known a change.—
The man whose wife is true may from its side
    Drink without fear ; but if her passion range,
The wine, although he think himself most blest,
Runs o'er the brim, and flows upon his breast.

" To try it if you wish before you go,
    Your dress will be unstain'd, as you expected ;
For yet your wife, no doubt, is pure as snow,
    But wait what in your absence is effected :
When you return try what the cup will show ;
    And if the liquor's course be still directed
Between your lips, nor o'er your bosom run,
On happier man than you ne'er shone the sun."

I freely took the cup, she freely gave it—
    I made the proof, and to my wish succeeded :
My wife was chaste and pure (so Heav'n would have it)
    As chaste and pure as fondest husband needed.—
" Now quit your dwelling ; if there's danger brave it,
    (Melissa said) and leave your wife unheeded
But for a month or two ; and then forget not
To try the cup—but mind your breast you wet not."

To me the parting seem'd the most severe :
    Not that I felt the slightest cause to doubt her,
But that of absence I could hardly hear,
    Though for a day, an hour to be without her.—
Melissa said : " The truth shall still appear,
    And you remain conceal'd, unknown, about her ;
For you shall change your features, dress, and speech,
If you pursue the course that I shall teach."

Not far from hence a town the Po defends,
    Spreading its branching horns on either side :

The jurisdiction of it far extends,
    Ev'n to the borders of the ocean-tide.
It is not very ancient, but contends
    With its near neighbours both for wealth and pride :
'Twas founded by an exil'd Trojan crew,
When from the scourge of Atilla they flew.

A youthful knight, rich, gallant, debonair,
    Rules o'er the land of which I now am telling ;
And, following once his falcon flying there,
    He found a ready entrance to my dwelling.
He saw my wife : charm'd by her beauty rare,
    His heart th' impression kept, and love impelling,
He us'd all arts, far more than I can mention,
To bow her virtue down to his intention.

So often she repuls'd him, that at last
    No further efforts he resolv'd to make :
Yet though the fury of his love were past,
    Her image would not his sad heart forsake.
Such magic spells Melissa round me cast,
    She soon enabled me his form to take :
How she transform'd me can I not devise,
Nor how she chang'd my speech, face, hair, and eyes.

Having already to my wife pretended
    A tedious journey on affairs of weight,
As her young suitor (when the change was ended
    In mien, dress, face, the knight to imitate),
And by Melissa, as my page, attended,
    I reach'd one afternoon my castle gate.
The richest gems, and numberless, we bore,
That ever burn'd upon the Indian shore.

I who, of course, knew every avenue
    Enter'd unseen, Melissa still behind,
And with occasion to my purpose true
    My lovely wife I unattended find :

My suit I proffer'd ; and then forth I drew
  The incentive to all vice with human kind :
Diamonds and rubies, emeralds, I showed,
For which the coldest bosoms oft have glowed.

Yet spoke I of all these as trifles merely,
  Compar'd with what hereafter she might have ;
Then dwelt on the occasion blest, which clearly
  The long-wish'd absence of her husband gave.
I next reminded her how long, how dearly
  I had ador'd her as a humble slave ;
And vow'd my love, so constant and intense,
Deserv'd from her some answering recompense.

At first she felt resentment, and her cheek
  Grew red with anger : she refus'd to hear me :
But then the gems most eloquently speak,
  And melt her heart, as she beheld them near me :
Her speech became more kind, her heart more weak.
  At last, in words that were design'd to cheer me,
But which I shall remember till I die,
She promis'd me in secret to comply.

Her words shot through me like a poison'd dart
  That in my inmost soul had found its rest :
Like ice it froze my blood and beating heart,
  And chok'd my palsied voice within my breast.
Melissa at that instant drew apart
  Enchantment's veil, and there I stood confess'd !
How, think you, look'd my wife, who ne'er expected,
And least of all by me, to be detected ?

We both became as pale as ashy death,
  To think that with such ease my gifts had won her :
And scarce could I recover speech and breath,
  While bending my accusing eyes upon her,
To utter, " Could'st thou thus betray my faith,
  And sell at such a price thy husband's honour ?"

She could not answer, scarcely seem'd to hear,
But bath'd her breast with many a bitter tear.

Much shame she felt indeed, but more despite
    For the most cruel artifice I tried :
It still increas'd, and grew to such a height
    That in the end her hate all bounds defied.
She soon resolv'd from me to take her flight,
    And when the sun repos'd on western tide,
She plac'd herself on board a rapid bark,
And still urg'd on impetuous through the dark.

And in the morning she herself presented
    Before the knight who long had vainly mov'd her,
And in whose shape I basely had consented
    To tempt her love, and to my grief had prov'd her.
I need not say that he was well contented,
    For still with the most ardent flame he lov'd her.
From thence she sent me word I might despair
Ever again her once-priz'd love to share.

Alas, alas ! from that sad day to this
    She lives with him, and both make me their scorn,
While I, the murderer of my perfect bliss,
    Survive to curse the day that I was born.
All thoughts of future peace I now dismiss,
    Still dying by degrees, unlov'd, forlorn.
I think the first year I had surely died,
But to my grief one comfort was supplied.

That one sole comfort is, that all of those
    Who for the last ten years have been my guests,
And who to drink from out the cup propose,
    Have ever spilt the wine upon their breasts.
Full many partners in my lot, Heaven knows,
    I found to ease the woe that still molests ;
It is my joy to hand the cup and fill it,
And still more joy to see them always spill it.

Nov. 16.—A curious literary incident happened to me to-day. I was praifing to Lord Morpeth Wordfworth's notion as to Dryden's mode of tranflating, viz., that he firft thoroughly imbued his mind with a paffage in the original, taking in its full meaning, and then, throwing the book afide, confidered how it could beft be expreffed in Englifh. Lord Morpeth thought the fuggeftion happy, and added that only a day or two ago, reading Sir Walter Scott's "Life of Napoleon", he had met with what he confidered a good illuftration of it. Opening the book (which by accident lay upon the table), Lord M. turned to a note in chapter IV, where Scott quoted three lines from Virgil, and followed them by fix lines of tranflation. "At any rate," I obferved, "that is an expanfion," and Lord M. admitted it, adding that it was alfo an improvement, and fhowed the way in which Dryden, writing in his own language, and carrying out the ideas of the original, increafed the beauty of that original. His lordfhip then rather pompoufly, and like a fchool-boy, as I thought, read the following paffage from Book III of the Æneid :

> "———— procul obscuros colles humilemque videmus
> Italiam : Italiam ! primus conclamat Achates :
> Italiam ! læto socii clamore salutant."

"Now, this," added he, " is Dryden's *original tranflation* if I may fo call it, for it does not read like a mere rendering of the Latin into Englifh : it is given at the bottom of Scott's page, and is followed by the name of Dryden in capitals :

> " Now every star before Aurora flies,
> Whose glowing blushes streak the purple skies,

When the dim hills of Italy we view'd,
That peep'd by turns, and div'd beneath the flood.
Lo! Italy appears, Achates cries,
And Italy, with shouts, the crowd replies."—DRYDEN.

" I admit," said I, "that what you have read are good lines, but, in the firſt place, we have not the *primus* before Achates, and next there is nothing in the original about the hills peeping and diving."

" Which laſt," ſaid his Lordſhip, " I conſider one of Dryden's poetically-deſcriptive touches, and an illuſtration of what you ſtated as the opinion of Wordſworth."

" Let me ſee," added I, " how the lines are introduced by Dryden ;" and I took down his tranſlation of Virgil, and opened Book III, where we could not find the paſſage quoted by Scott as from *Dryden's tranſlation ;* but at the place referred to, I read preciſely as follows :

" And now the rising morn with rosy light
Adorns the skies and puts the stars to ſlight ;
When we from far, like bluish mists, descry
The hills, and then the plains of Italy.
Achates first pronounced the joyful sound,
Then Italy ! the cheerful crew rebound."

" This is ſtrange," obſerved Lord Morpeth : " I wonder whether what I read juſt now is a tranſlation by. Scott him-ſelf : I should not be ſurpriſed."

" I do not think that likely," ſaid I, " becauſe Scott, who clearly wrote his hiſtory at speed, in order to ſatisfy the public and the publiſhers, would hardly pauſe for the pur-poſe of giving a new rendering : it ſeems to me more likely that he took the quotation from ſome other author, who gueſſed it was by Dryden. Let us look at the only other

L

modern tranflation I know of Virgil in Englifh : the lines
may poffibly be by Chriftopher Pitt."

It was fome time before we could find a copy of Pitt's
Virgil, but when we did the matter was cleared up at once,
for there we faw the very lines quoted by Scott as from
Dryden.

" Here," said Lord Morpeth, "is one proof of what Johnfon
faid, viz., that ' Dryden's tranflation would be read, and
Pitt's quoted.' Scott quoted Pitt, and did not know that
he was not quoting the much more popular Dryden. He
muft, as you fay, have taken the lines in a hurry from fome
other author, who had miftaken Pitt for Dryden."

" At all events," added I, " Wordfworth's criticifm does
not apply in this inftance." Walter Scott's next quotation
from Virgil, in chapter viii, we found was not in the fame
predicament : there the tranflation was, as he ftated, from
Dryden's, and not from Pitt's tranflation.

Nov. 19.—Madame de Stael came once to my father's :
it was when H. C. Robinfon was ftaying with us, and her
vifit was, in fact, to him, as fhe knew nothing of our family.
I cannot at all fix the precife date ; but it was fomewhere
about 1810. I remember that it was long before my marriage, and my intended wife was in the houfe, and fhe
did not like the politico-literary lady. I confidered her
efpecially ugly, and very unfeminine. She clearly gave
herfelf fuperior airs, or airs of fuperiority, which did not
fuit my father, who efpecially difliked in a woman anything
that was mafculine. She fpoke loud, and that he did not
at all approve ; fhe talked faft, and that he did not think
becoming. I cannot call to mind anything fhe faid,

but fhe feemed anxious to produce a notion that fhe had been very intimate with Buonaparte, and indeed with moft of the crowned heads of Europe. On the whole, the impreffion fhe made upon me was unfavourable. There was a degree of falfe energy when fhe fpoke, and to my ears her voice was not mufical : befides, fhe rather bounced about the room while talking.

She was at this date banifhed from Paris with Madame Recamier ; but they were only alike as fellow-fufferers, for Madame Recamier was all beauty and delicacy, while Madame de Stael was all coarfenefs and confidence : ftill, there was fomething likeable about her, and if fhe talked loud, fhe talked well. At this date a ftory was current that, fhortly before fhe was fent away from Paris, fhe had told Buonaparte "to confide in her advice, for that fhe and he were born to act in concert; and, if they did fo, they could rule the deftinies of Europe." She did not remain long in our houfe, and fhe quitted England within a week afterwards : fhe had come to London from St. Petersburgh.

Nov. 23.—I do not know what the original paffage in Cervantes may be, as I have no Spanifh Don Quixote ; but it feems to me that when Shelton tranflated it firft into Englifh, in 1612, he had in his memory that fine direction of Hamlet to the players, where he tells them that the purpofe and end of playing, "both at the firft and now, was, and is, to hold, as 'twere, the mirror up to nature", &c. Shelton puts the following words into the mouth of the hero: ' I would have thee, Sancho, to efteem of them, and confequently the actors too, and the authors, becaufe they are the inftruments of much good to a Commonwealth, being, *like looking-glaffes, where the actions of human life are lively reprefented;* and there is no comparifon that doth more truly prefent to us what we are, or what we fhould be, than the comedy and the comedians". (Shelton's " Don Quixote," Part I, p. 69, ed. 1612.)

It may be only an undefigned coincidence, and the thought might naturally occur both to Shakefpeare and Cervantes ; but I muft look at the original. " Hamlet" was firft printed in 1603, and "Don Quixote", Part I, in 1605, I believe. Biographers tell us a ftill ftranger coincidence, namely, that Shakefpeare and Cervantes died on the fame day, 23rd April, 1816. Has not this fact been difputed ?

I have very recently bought a book, publifhed at the very time when " Hamlet" was in its firft run, that may be faid to fupply another note to the fame tragedy : it is Florio's tranflation of Montaigne's Effays, folio 1603 (my copy be- belonged to James I, as attefted by his fignature). Shake- fpeare makes his hero (act iii, fc. 2) fpeak of a player who " tore a paffion to tatters, to very rags"; and Florio, in his addrefs " to the reader", mentions a *" tear-a-rag* player" who acted " the princely Telephus with a voice as ragged as his clothes". Florio was brother-in-law to Samuel Daniell, the poet, and was one of the tutors to Prince Henry.

Nov. 27.—Cino da Piftoia is fo old an Italian poet as to have obtained the praifes of two fuch mafters of his art as Dante and Petrarch : he is fuppofed to have died before 1340, and was one of the men who, though ftudying and practifing the law, alfo cultivated poetry. He never en- tirely abandoned either for the other, but left few produc- tions in verfe behind him. He is fometimes obfcure ; but for his age his lines are harmonious, and even elegant. The following is one of his beft fonnets ; and, in putting it into our language, I have endeavoured to give some notion of its fubtlety and refinement. I copy it here as a trifle of mine of many years' ftanding, and perhaps I could not do fo well now. I take it from Mathias' *Componimcnti Lirici*, I, 116:

If he who breathes for thee his heavy sighs,
　And whose sad soul dwells in a sorrowing heart,
　Cannot e'en die, he must endure the smart,
While thou inflict'st on him new agonies.
Yet in his grief all others sympathise,
　Who mark his state beyond the power of art,
　And think they see Death with his mortal dart
Within the hollow circuit of his eyes.
But thou wilt neither health to him restore,
　Nor kill him quite ; but keep him lingering still,
Like some strong man in death's last agony.
　Thine eyes possess a power, unknown before,
　And draw from pleasure's self the cruel skill,
Still to revive the heart that else would die.

Dcc. 1.—A friend—indeed, a relation—of mine this morning fent me the third edition of "Punch and Judy," with illuftrations defigned and engraved by George Cruikfhank, bearing the date of 1832. I knew that the book had come to a fecond impreffion only a week or two after the firft had been brought out in 1828 ; but I had not heard of a *third*. I am glad it has fucceeded fo well.

It was, if I may fo call it, "a ferious *jcu d'esprit*" of mine, to which I had, however, no inclination to put my name, and it originated thus. The brother of Septimus Prowett, the publifher of the new edition of "Dodfley's Old Plays," came to me one morning and afked me to do him a favour.

Edward Prowett was a young man whom I wifhed to oblige,
and I afked what he wanted. He anfwered that George
Cruikfhank, the admirable comic illuftrator, had made fome
etchings of fcenes and incidents in the *immortal tragedy*
(for fuch it unqueftionably is) of "Punch and Judy." He
had heard, as the fact was, that when quite a boy I had written down the dialogue, fongs, and defcriptions of fcenes belonging to the performance, and he (Prowett) wanted them
for Cruikfhank's ufe. I replied that they were in a moft
rough and unfinifhed ftate, and that, even if put into fhape,
they would not anfwer the purpofe without fome fort of "introduction". He caught at the word, and added that that
was juft what he required. He then offered me £50, if I
would let him have the dialogue and fongs of the drama,
preceded by a few pages on the hiftory of Punch and Judy,
particularly in this country. I told him that I had no objection, provided I was not required to put my name to the
fmall volume, becaufe my materials were few and disjointed;
and although I might be able to put together what would
anfwer his purpofe, I doubted if it would anfwer mine.
Befides, he wanted the MS. immediately, or as foon as pos-
fible, and what I fhould have to do would afk time and induftry. He faid that he could allow me no more than
three weeks, and that moft of Cruikfhank's etchings were
quite ready, having been made from the original puppets
belonging to an Italian of the name of Picini, who was in
the habit of exhibiting both in London and the country.

The conclufion was that I agreed to do the work for him;
and as foon as he went away I set about it, rummaging out
all my materials, and among others the words and rhymes of
the "Punch and Judy" I had put down in writing when I

was certainly not more than fourteen or fifteen years old.
It had been done at Brighton, when I was ftaying there
with my uncle, and when I frequently faw the piece reprefented, following the fhowman from ftreet to ftreet for the
purpofe. The drama, as publifhed by Prowett, was made
up from thefe reprefentations, corrected by those of Picini,
to whofe place of refidence (somewhere near Field Lane
and Saffron Hill) I went with Cruikfhank. This interview was a very droll one; and there we had an opportunity of being introduced to Mr. Punch, Mrs. Judy,
pretty Polly, Toby, and the reft of the *dramatis perfonæ*,
off their ftage. Cruikfhank made his fketches from the
very dreffes of the characters, and to their ridiculoufly life-
like refemblance I can bear witnefs. I never had a more
amufing morning, for Picini himfelf was a ftrange character:
the dirt, darknefs, and uncouthnefs of his abode, together
with the forbiddingnefs of the appearance of Mrs. P., I
fhall never forget. She was an Irifhwoman, and he an
Italian, and the jumble of languages in their difcourfe was
in itfelf highly entertaining.

I found my undertaking as to the "Introduction" in fome
refpects more difficult than I imagined; for the materials
were not only fcanty but fcattered, more efpecially in foreign
authorities: however, I finifhed my part of the bufinefs
within the time ftipulated, and Cruikfhank's cuts were, like
nearly all his productions, inimitable: the beft thing in the
letter-prefs of the book is, I humbly think, the mock-ballad
headed "Punch's Pranks", going through the chief events
of his life, and ending with his triumph over the devil.
Befides the twenty-three etchings, the artift furnifhed two
wood-cuts even better than the etchings, particularly the
one upon the title-page, fo full of truth and life.

After the work was publifhed, Cruikfhank made me a prefent of a fet of the plates coloured by his own hand, and with original fketches on the margins, one of them a likenefs of his own really handfome features. Many, indeed moft, of his works muft be immortal.

Dec. 5.—I have juft returned from Cambridge, whither I went to fee a Shakefpearian book of the higheft value and importance, only found there, in the library bequeathed to Trinity College by Edmund Capell. It is called, in the original title-page, "The Hiftorie of Hamblet", and this copy was printed in 1608: it muft have been originally publifhed before 1587, becaufe at that date there was acted a tragedy founded upon the ftory, and the copy of 1608 is only a reprint, after the tract had been at leaft twenty years in circulation. I apprehend that Shakefpeare conftructed his tragedy with the aid, not merely of this old profe narrative, but of the ancient drama which had been founded upon it previous to 1587, and to which reference was made in many contemporaneous tracts, efpecially in thofe by the famous Thomas Nafh. How far that ancient but loft drama was an improvement upon the old ftory cannot be known, fo that we cannot judge what degree of affiftance Shakefpeare derived from it. The mere profe ftory, as it appeared in 1608, is fo bad that, without important changes, a drama, conftructed merely upon it, could hardly have been palateable even to the audiences of 1587.

In the fame collection I alfo faw the unique editions of "The Paffionate Pilgrim" in 1599 and 1612. I am quite fatisfied that there muft have been intermediate impreffions, but not one is extant. It is this tract which contains two poems which Richard Barnfield printed as his in 1598, but withdrew them in 1605, when he republifhed his " Lady Pecunia." The keepers of the Library of Trinity College are very obliging, but on the day I was there the light was not good, and it feemed out of the queftion to be permitted to remove the book even to a larger window.

Suppofing Shakefpeare had had only the " Hiftorie of Hamblet," on which to build his " Hamlet," nothing could more aftonifhingly fhow the wonderful variety and amount of his own refources : Ophelia in the novel is a mere proftitute, and fo fhe is reprefented by Belleforeft, whofe bald narrative the profe verfion pretty exactly follows. I have compared the two.

Dec. 7.—As I am now in middle age (*nel mezzo del cammin di noftra vita*), I may be allowed to fay, whatever be the fate of my later productions, that I hope thofe of my extreme youth may never rife up in judgment againft me. I wrote many things in my boyhood, of which I can now never think without fhame—utterly difgraceful to any period of life, and I ftate it with unfeigned humility. I began authorfhip before I was fixteen; but when about two years older, I looked back with fcorn at the unredeemable rubbifh I had put upon paper. I adopted Walter Scott as my firft model, and compofed a poem, in four or five cantos, upon a ftory in fome refpects refembling the " Alonzo and Imogine" of Monk Lewis. Still earlier I had written fome ballads ; and even now I remember one or two fragments in that form. In one of them, of a myftical character, I defcribed my hero as arriving, by moon-lit midnight, at a large and fmooth piece of water, and being furprifed at the

M

fights and founds that met his eyes and ears from the furface of it: four brief defcriptive ftanzas remain in my memory, and I venture to quote them here:

" Low strains from out the waves ascend,
  Like steam at summer noon ;
And thousand varying colours blend
  Beneath the silent moon.

" Yet could I not one tuneful song
  Distinguish as I stood,
Nor see one form or figure long
  Upon the tranquil flood.

" Colours and sounds in union meet,
  And mingle in delight,
While sight and sound, combin'd and sweet,
  Show'd lovely to the night.

" Now fancied forms in vision fair
  In streaked robes went past ;
Now all was gone, and some new air
  Began, but did not last."

I can remember no more, nor do I know in what way thefe ftanzas contributed to the fubject of the forgotten ftory. There was no end to my literary ambition ; and firft I wrote a comedy, in which, I recollect, an Irifhman played a prominent part. A tragedy on a merely-invented fable followed ; and, not to leave any department untried, I put together the words of an opera, in which my principal finger was imprifoned, and (of courfe) freed by his miftrefs. I am fure there were not fewer than twenty fongs, and pieces of concerted mufic in it, but no trace of one of them remains in my memory—nor, I fincerely hope, anywhere elfe.

Dec. 8.—I mentioned to the Duke, a day or two ago, that Charles Lamb had brought me as a prefent a copy of his "Adventures of Ulyffes." He afked me to lend him the book, as he did not think he had it. He returned it to me this morning, obferving, as was very true, that it was written with even forced fimplicity, and that it read, in fome fort, in the ftyle of the Bible, fo much fo that feveral paffages were abfolutely imitated : the very conclufion was an adaptation of the words of Scripture—"for he that had been fo long abfent was returned to wreak the evil upon the heads of the doers ; in the place where they had done the evil, there wreaked he his vengeance upon them."

I admitted that this remark was juft, and added that Lamb had, in fact, written the fmall volume for the ufe of young people, who had learned almoft only to read out of the Bible ; the imitation had been intentional, and even proper, as I thought.

"I am furprifed," continued the Duke, "that Lamb left out, near the clofe, the very interefting and characteriftic incident of the recognition of Ulyffes by his faithful old dying dog, Argus, thus verfified by Pope :

> " ' The dog whom fate had granted to behold
> His lord, when twenty tedious years had roll'd,
> Takes a last look, and having seen him dies :
> So clos'd for ever faithful Argus' eyes.' "

"Give me leave," I interpofed, "to fhow you with what forcible fimplicity old Chapman rendered the paffage not far from 300 years ago :

> " ' But by the dog no sooner seen but known
> Was wise Ulyffes, who now enter'd there :

> Up went the dog's laid ears, and coming near,
> Up he himself rose, fawn'd and wagg'd his stern,
> Couch'd close his ears and lay so ; nor discern
> Could evermore his dear-lov'd lord again.' "

"Pope," remarked the Duke, "is briefer, quite as intelligible, and, to my ear, much more harmonious."

"True," faid I ; "but not fo minute or picturefque."

"Be it fo," added the Duke ; "but you know that, like you, I am a lover of dogs, and Lamb does not do them juftice when he makes fuch an omiffion as to their faculties and fidelity. Otherwife, I think that he has well condenfed the twenty-four books of the Odyffey. In Homer the conclufion has always feemed too much drawn out ; but, of courfe, I fpeak very diffidently on fuch a point : the reader has, I think, arrived at the conclufion long before the poet. I fhould like to fee more of Lamb's writings ; but, I affure you, among my acquaintances he is comparatively little known. Have you other books by him ?"

I anfwered that I had nearly all he had printed, including efpecially his "Elia," confifting of very pleafant original effays, of which he had infcribed a copy to me, in return for one of my *Poet's Pilgrimage*. I have alfo his "Tales from Shakefpeare," fome of the beft of which were written by his fifter.

In the end I promifed to fend the "Elia" to the Duke ; but he did not appear to care much for the "Tales from Shakefpeare," perhaps, becaufe the plots of the different plays were fo well known to him.

Dec. 9.—I have had the following letter by me for above a dozen years ; and, as in 1821 I kept no diary, it has obtained no place. It is from a dear kind old friend, and, relating to my firft publifhed work, I copy it:

" May 16, 1821.

" DEAR J. P. C.,—Many thanks for the 'Decameron': I have not such a gentleman's book in my collection : it was a great treat to me, and I got it just as I was wanting something of the sort. I take less pleasure in books than heretofore, but I like books about books. In the second volume in particular are treasures—your discoveries about 'Twelfth Night', etc. What a Shakespearian essence that speech of Osrades for food ! Shakespeare is coarse to it, beginning 'Forbear and eat no more'. Osrades warms up to that, but does not set out ruffian-swaggerer. The character of the Ass with those three lines, worthy to be set in gilt vellum, and worn in frontlets by the noble beasts for ever—

" 'Thou would, perhaps, he should become thy foe,
        And to that end dost·beat him many times :
        He cares not for himself, much less thy blow.'

Cervantes, Sterne, and Coleridge, have said positively nothing for asses compared with this.

" I write in haste ; but p. 24, vol. i, the line you cannot appropriate is Gray's sonnet, specimenifyed by Wordsworth, in first preface to L. B., as mixed of bad and good style : p. 143, 2nd vol., you will find, last poem but one of the collection on Sidney's death, in Spenser, the line,

" 'Scipio, Cæsar, Petrarch of our time':

This fixes it to be Raleigh's : I had guess'd it Daniel's. The last after it, 'Silence augmenteth rage', I will be crucified if it be not Lord Brooke's. Hang you, and all meddling researchers hereafter, that by raking into learned dust may find me out wrong in my conjecture !

" Dear J. P. C., I shall take the first opportunity of personally thanking you for my entertainment. We are at Dalston for the most part, but I fully hope for an evening soon with you in Russell or Bouverie Street, to talk over old times and books. Remember *us* kindly to Mrs. J. P. C.

" Yours very kindly,

" CHARLES LAMB.

" I write in misery.

" N.B.—The best pen I could borrow at our butcher's : the ink, I verily believe, came out of the kennel."

At this date Lamb and his fifter in the winter refided over a large fhop at the corner of Ruffell Street, Covent Garden, but in the fpring they rufticated at Dalfton. With the above I find, folded up in it, a note to my father from C. Lamb, and, as it intimately relates to William Hazlitt, it is worth tranfcribing here : my mother has indorfed the date upon it, " 1812 or 1813":

" DEAR SIR,—Mrs. Collier has been kind enough to say that you would endeavour to procure a reporter's situation for W. Hazlitt. I went to consult him upon it last night, and he acceded very eagerly to the proposal, and requests me to say how very much obliged he feels to your kindness, and how glad he should be for its success. He is, indeed, at his wits' end for a livelihood; and, I should think, especially qualified for such an employment, from his singular facility in retaining all conversations at which he has been ever present. I think you may recommend him with confidence : I am sure I shall *myself* be obliged to you for your exertions, having a great regard for him. " Yours truly,

" Sunday morning." " C. LAMB."

The refult was that my father procured for Hazlitt the fituation of a parliamentary reporter on the *M. C.;* but he did not retain it long, and as his talents were undoubted, Mr. Perry transferred to him the office of theatrical critic, a pofition which was fubfequently held for feveral years by a perfon of much inferior talents.

Dec. 10.—I received a very kind, complimentary note from the proprietor of the *Times*. I well remember my father's firſt interview with Mr. John Walter (*junior* he then was called). His father had for ſome years eſtabliſhed and conducted the newſpaper, having commenced printing it with logographic types, repreſenting words, not letters. I have alfo a ſmall book, entitled "Letters between an Illuſtrious Perſonage and a Lady of Honour" (Mrs. Fitzherbert), which was iſſued from "the Logographic Prefs, and fold by J. Walter, Printing Houſe Square, Blackfriars," but without date. Prior to the iſſue of it, Mr. Walter, fen., had kept a firſt-hand and fecond-hand bookfeller's ſhop at the corner of a court in Fleet Street, leading down to Whitefriars, the fame, I was told, which, many years afterwards, was kept by William Hone (the parodiſt), and there I bought a copy of "Howell's Letters," ſtill in my poſſeſſion.

From the office of the *Times*, in 1804, came Mr. John Walter, junior, to call upon my father, then living cloſe to Weſtminſter School, and having previouſly written fome approved articles for a newſpaper called the *Oracle*, proprietor'd (if I may uſe the American word) and edited by Peter Stuart, the brother of the Stuart who afterwards owned the *Courier*, for which, while ·I was ſtill a boy, Coleridge had been engaged to write. William Combe (the author of "Dr. Syntax") at about that date furniſhed the *Times* with political articles, and my father's aid was not wanted in that department. Mr. Walter wiſhed to engage him as law reporter; and he was well qualified, becauſe, when our family was reſiding for two years at Thames Ditton, my father was ſtudying for the bar. He had no regular engagement with Peter Stuart, and Mr. Walter offered my father fomething over £200 a year, if he would furnifh an account of the proceedings in the Court of King's Bench, then prefided over by Lord Ellenborough, whom my father had known in Yorkfhire, and who had married a lady from a family with which my mother was acquainted.

At that date £200 a year was a moft important addition to our family income ; and my father continued in this employment for fome time, until indeed Mr. Walter wifhed for his aid elfewhere on the newfpaper. I was then under twenty ; but Mr. Walter put me in my father's place, continuing for fome time the fame falary, but foon afterwards, and not at all at my inftance, Mr. Walter raifed it to £250 a year, and fubfequently to fix guineas a week.

I continued thus employed when I married in 1816, and fubfequently involved the *Times* in a fcrape, from which I extricated it so well that Mr. Walter prefented me with £100, as I have elfewhere related. Such was the origin of my connection with newfpapers. My father had fubfequently a difference with Mr. Walter (though they always remained private friends) : he went to the *Morning Chronicle*, under Perry, and I foon followed him there, with no increafe of falary, but a change to lefs arduous duties. While under Perry my father's income was raifed to £1000, or £1500 a year, not merely for work done for the *Morning Chronicle*, but by reafon of a political correfpondence he had eftablifhed with various country newfpapers. To this fort of employment I fucceeded on my father's death, and carried it on so fuccefsfully that (as the two things were not compatible) I long deferred my call to the Bar—too long to give me any chance of fuccefs ; efpecially as I had in the meantime written fome effays upon candidates in the profeffion, who were not very well pleafed with my criticifms. Sir James Scarlett, whom, on the whole, I had praifed, was my chief enemy; and once, when I held a brief as his junior, fo pertinacioufly placed his large figure between me and the Bench, that the judges felt obliged to interpofe, in order to give me a chance of being heard, or even feen. I was, however, heard, and with fuccefs. Having a wife and fix children, I could not afford to relinquifh the income I derived from other fources, and hence my long connection with them. I never engaged but with the *Times* and *Chronicle*, and my work for country newspapers was both political and literary—comments and criticifms.

Thus my pen had pretty conftant employment; but ftill I did not neglect other fubjects, though fometimes, looking back to my career, I cannot but wonder how I found opportunity for doing even what I have accomplifhed in various departments. The fact is that I confidered newspapers tafk-work, and, when that was performed, I went with increafed zeft to other purfuits and employments; hence what little fuccefs I may have experienced. I publifhed my "Poetical Decameron" in 1820: in 1822 I privately printed my "Poet's Pilgrimage"; and in 1831 I put forth my three laborious volumes on the early hiftory of our Stage and Drama.

My education was as complete as my father and tutors could make it, for I never was at fchool or at college: I was a ready, but not a fteady learner; and there were four years of my life, not long after I married, when I read nothing, and did nothing, but amufe myfelf and my children with my boats on the Thames, on the bank of which, near

N

Chifwick, I refided : four happier or idler years I never fpent. Still I read, even on the water, and it was then that I ftudied (as far as I did ftudy it) Italian ; and I got through Boiardo, Ariofto, Pulci, Taffo, and feveral other romancers, together with as many of the novelifts as I could lay my hands upon ; for I had then refolved not to look into any book that was not in the language of the garden of earth and heaven—of flowers and poetry.

Thus I have put down a few particulars of my early and later life ; but I am almoft afraid to look back at what I have written, left I fhould be tempted to tear the leaves out of my Diary. I fhall, however, let it ftand, becaufe I have made many quite as worthlefs entries. What I have faid may be ufeful to ftrugglers hereafter, by fhowing what induftry, painftaking, and love can accomplifh, even under the numerous difadvantages to which I have at times been unavoidably expofed.

Dec. 12.—Ludwig Tieck, the great Anglo-German fcholar, has fent for my guidance and information a lift of Old Englifh Plays (with his opinions upon moft of them), which he thinks ought to be included in my once projected, but now unluckily abandoned, Continuation of Dodfley. The enumeration, and Tieck's judgments upon their merits, are well worth preferving ; and H. C. Robinfon has aided me very kindly in making out his difficult handwriting, and in tranflating his remarks : both run thus, and I put the criticifms in italics.

Look About You. 4to. 1600. *Excellent, full of character and wit.*

Shoemakers' Holiday. 4to. 1637. [1600]. *Very good.*

A Warning for Fair Women. 4to. 1599. *This piece, which, according to some fragments, must be excellent, was not to be found entire in* 1817 [when Tieck was in England].

The Birth of Merlin. 4to. 1662. *Very excellent: it is one of those I caused to be copied. Probably Shakespeare had a hand in it.*

Fair Maid of the Exchange. 4to. 1637. [First printed in 1607.] *By Heywood: very good.*

If You Know not Me You Know Nobody. 4to. 1623. [1605. 1606.] *In two parts, by Heywood.*

The Lancashire Witches. *By Heywood: good.*

If this be not Good, the Devil is in it. 4to. [1612.] *By Deckar.*

Orlando Furioso. [1594.] *By Greene.*

A Maidenhead well Lost. 1634. *By Heywood.*

Two Angry Women of Abingdon. *By Porter.*

The Arraignment of Paris, by Peel. [1584.] *Remarkable by its antiquity.*

The Battle of Alcazar. 1594. *Remarkable for being so much in the style of " Locrine".*

The Fair Maid of Bristow. 1605. *Remarkable for its antiquity.*

The Gentle Craft. *Very good and popular.*

Jack Straw's Life and Death. 1593.

Mucedorus. 1668. *Very remarkable, and leading to interesting reflections.*

Nobody and Somebody. *Excellent, and one I copied.*

Patient Grissell. [1603.] *Probably by Chettle.*

The Travels of Three Brothers. *Very curious, and fit for representation.*

The Life and Death of Capt. Stukely.

Antonio's Revenge, by Marston.

Wisdom of Dr. Dotypol. 4to. 1600. *Not very good.*

Shoemaker a Gentleman. 1638. *I caused it to be copied.*

The whole of the above is authenticated by the signature of the writer in this form, but without date.

Boeckhaus in Leipzig,
LUDW. TIECK.

I may add, that if I had been able to carry out my scheme of a Continuation of Dodsley's Old Plays, I should hardly have omitted a single drama in the above list. Some of them have since been reprinted by Dyce.

Dec. 14.—I think that my version of the following sonnet by Guido Dalle Colonne is worth a place in my Diary, and I give it from the collection by Muratori, 1, 8.

> That pride becomes thee not, I will not say,
>   Though pride and beauty cause me bitter pain ;
> For pride befits fair ladies, that they may
>   Keep beauty's state, and its high worth maintain :
>   But too much haughtiness is beauty's stain,
> And ev'n in thee unseemly its display.
>   Then, lady, thy proud cruelty restrain,
> Or change it into pity ; for delay
> Will quite destroy me, dying day by day.
>   The sun pursues his journey through the sky,
> And throws his beams upon reviving earth,
>   Shedding more light as he ascends more high :
> So let thy lofty beauty's glittering ray
> Shine down on me, and turn my grief to mirth.

Dec. 15.—I had mislaid the following, when I formerly mentioned, that Thackeray had requested me to endeavour to obtain for him some employment in connection with newspapers, as he was then in difficulties, with two daughters, and an invalid wife. He had first called upon me in London, and subsequently from Paris he sent me the following note :

"68, Grande Rue de Chaillot à Paris, April 22.

"MY DEAR SIR,—I have only five minutes, and this dirty scrap of paper, to ask for your aid and assistance in a matter pending between me and the *Morning Chronicle.*

" It appears that the proprietors intend to send a correspondent to Constantinople : I have already applied for the place ; only as I can produce no proofs of my capability in the columns of any newspaper, I am obliged to ask my friends to vouch for the same.

" Do you think that your knowledge of me, and our conversations at the Garrick, will allow you to speak a word or two in my favour, and will excuse the liberty I take in asking for your aid ?

" If so, perhaps you will mention it at head-quarters : a word from you, I am sure, will be all-powerful ; and thus I shall be able to realise a favourite dream of mine, and fill my Sketch-book to my heart's content.

" Pray remember me to all our old Garrick friends : I wish there were any such pleasant place here, or a few such good fellows, to delight me with their social converse.

" Ever, my dear sir, faithfully yours,

" W. M. THACKERAY."

Happily, the proprietors of the *Morning Chronicle* did not accept the propofal to banifh our great novelift, and fagacious obferver and depicter of human nature, to the Bofphorus ; and Thackeray, at his wits'-end for remunerative employment, was compelled to continue that literary career which has given him fuch deferved diftinction, and us and pofterity fuch inftructive amufement. Much genius and learning have, from time to time, been buried, as well as developed, in newfpaper-offices : *haud facilè emergunt* when once an entrance has been effected.

Jerrold's note to me, with the fimilar object of employment on the *Morning Chronicle,* as a Parliamentary reporter, was in thefe terms : here, again, we may rejoice that the writer was driven to other expedients, by which all of us have been made both merrier and wifer.

" Thistle Grove, Little Chelsea [no date].

" MY DEAR SIR,—I am much indebted for your cordial advocacy

of my interests. I could not expect, and indeed ought not to hope, that Mr. Black would accept an untried, and consequently unskilful, person, over a gentleman long practised in his craft. I shall, however, be farther obliged to you for a line to the editor of the *Mirror of Parliament;* for, as he is compelled to enlist new recruits, I may stand a fairer chance among the raw volunteers. I can only wish that I had been as intimate with St. Stephen's gallery, as I have unhappily been with the galleries of Drury Lane and Covent Garden. Thanking you most heartily for your kindness, and with best respects to Mrs. Collier, believe me

" Your truly thankful

" DOUGLAS JERROLD."

Having failed with the *Chronicle*, I gave Jerrold a note to the *Morning Herald*, which was more successful, but the connection did not last long : Jerrold was too truthful and bitter. It was about this date that he expressed his deep regret that he had not continued in the navy : his father had been an actor, but of small repute —never in London, I think.

Dec. 16.—Leigh Hunt called upon me, and gave me some copies of his *Tatler :* he asked me to contribute to it, and I promised that I would. I kept my word, anonymously, for some little time, until his energies began to slacken; which they almost invariably do as soon as any of his literary undertakings promise to be successful : then he grows weary of, and even indifferent to, them. This is the great fault of his character ; and but for his brother John's steady application to business, even the *Examiner* would perhaps not now have been in existence : hence the number of Leigh Hunt's enterprises, and the small profit of many of them.

I have known him, more or less, for the last twenty years, ever since his imprisonment in 1812 for the libel on George

IV," the firft gentleman of Europe", as he was called by his admirers. I ufed to go to Horfemonger-lane Gaol two or three times a month, in company with Thomas Barnes, Mitchell, and fometimes with my father and mother, while L. H. was confined there for a couple of years. There are few men fuperior to L. H. in converfation for an hour or two : his obfervations and criticifms are clever and fprightly, though not very original. His attainments are rather elegant than fubftantial, and his wife is a very flimfy fort of perfonage. In 1818, two years after I married, having had confiderable experience by attending courts of juftice, I had written for the *Examiner*, as already mentioned, fome off-hand papers, called " Criticifms on the Bar": they were liked by moft people, excepting certain members of the profeffion, to which I myfelf was deftined to belong. The collected articles afterwards appeared (always anonymoufly) in a fmall volume, which had a confiderable fale, and upon the title-pages of fome copies of which my name was furreptitioufly inferted. I was wrong in ever confenting to write the effays ; but, although the addition of my name was calculated to do me harm, I never thought it worth while to take any fteps to punifh the offenders, and thereby make the matter more notorious.

Dec. 18.—I yefterday entered the Duke's ftudy (I may call it, where he ufually receives morning vifitors) when fome gentleman, whom I did not know, was juft making his bow on going away.

" That man", obferved the Duke to me, "is as rich as a Jew, has a charming wife and a nice family, and yet I believe him to be one of the worft fatisfied and worft tempered men in the world : he always looks difcontented, and is what he looks. The fact is, that he has nothing to wish for; he wants nothing : Bacon, as you know, for I have heard you quote the paffage, fays that ' men in great place are thrice fervants—of fame, ftate, and bufinefs'; but my friend holds no office, and has more than once refufed public employment : he is clever and well-informed, and all his connections are anxious that he fhould have fomething to do : he will not even manage his own eftates, and yet he is always on bad terms with his agent. I really pity my poor friend. He keeps himfelf, like bad beer, in a ferment, and nobody about him is at cafe."

"The fource of all this", faid I, "is that he has nothing to wifh for. I often wonder whether you yourfelf would not be happier, if you had lefs money and lefs attendance —had a wife and half-a-dozen children, as I have, for whofe wants you might have to provide."

"Ah", continued the Duke, "matrimony is out of the queftion with me. I have been from my birth a predeftinate old bachelor, and as ' Bachelor Bill' you will fee me introduced into ' Paul Clifford'. Did you ever read that book ?"

"One volume of it," I anfwered, " which the author afked me to read, and which I did read ; but I own I could get no farther : it was my fault, not the fault of the book ; but excepting fuch novels as ' Robinfon Crufoe', ' Tom Jones', ' Jofeph Andrews', ' Clariffa Harlowe', ' Roderick Random', and a very few more, they form a clafs of reading for which I have no partiality, and for which I have, I believe, no tafte. I have tried over and over again."

"You lofe, then, a great deal of pleafure," rejoined the Duke ; "though I think I like novels almoft too much."

"If novels", faid I, "give me little pleafure, I, of courfe, loſe the leſs in every reſpect by not reading them ; and let me aſk, in the purſuit of knowledge, what do I loſe by not reading novels ?"

"Knowledge of the world and knowledge of the human heart," anſwered the Duke—"both very important."

"I admit it," I obſerved ; "but can we be ſure that we gain real and valuable knowledge of the one or the other? Are not manners often groſſly miſrepreſented, and motives often miſinterpreted ? You may ſay that plays, eſpecially old plays, of which I am ſo fond, are only novels, uſually in verſe, divided into ſcenes, and ſupported by characters : that is true ; but however they may pervert facts, or dis- tort characters for the purpoſe of the ſtage, at all events they often afford us moſt beautiful ſpecimens of poetry. Here is an old drama by Thomas Heywood, who was a playwright and actor nearly all the time Shakeſpeare was connected with theatres. I will venture to open it at random, and I am ſure we ſhall find ſomething worth reading and remembering : the play is 'The Fair Maid of the Weſt'; and the heroine is declaring to one of the characters the ſincerity of her attachment to the hero of the ſtory : only note how prettily, and how naturally, ſhe illuſtrates the truth and purity of her affection.

> ' Thou resemblest *him*
> For whose sweet safety I was every morning
> Down on my knees, and with the lark's sweet tunes
> I did begin my prayers ; and when sad sleep
> Had charm'd all eyes, when none but the bright stars
> Were up and waking, I remember'd *thee.*'

Juſt obſerve how naturally, though addreſſing a third per- ſon in the outſet, when ſhe comes to the cloſe, ſhe cannot avoid apoſtrophiſing the object of her devoted affection. It is a charming touch of nature."

" And how ſweet the verſe," interpoſed the Duke, "as if the writer's mind were ſo overflowing with poetry that he could not avoid alluſions to the ſong of the lark at day-break, and to the ſparkling ſtars at night time."

" Even taken ſeparately, and as a merely accidental ex-tract," I added, "it claims our warmeſt admiration ; but, read with the context, in every ſyllable of this dialogue the great poet breaks forth and ſhines : in theſe ſix lines we have the very muſic and the brilliancy he introduces almoſt throughout. Coming back to the point from whence we ſtarted, let me aſk (in comparative ignorance, I own) where in any modern novel will you find ſo much that is admir-able in ſo ſmall a compaſs ?"

" That queſtion is not eaſily anſwered," the Duke re-joined, " if we take into account only the multiplicity of volumes ; but I maintain that in modern novels there is an aſtoniſhing quantity of good writing, and good think-ing too. The characters are often drawn with truth, de-licacy, and diſtinctneſs."

" There muſt alſo," I remarked, " be great intereſt in the ſtories, or they would not be ſo generally read as they are the quantity of invention in this reſpect ſeems wonderful."

Here the Duke was called away, and our converſation ended for the day.

Dec. 19.—Having ſent to Sir Walter Scott (on a kind hint given me by Mr. Hallam that he would like to have it) a copy of my " Hiſtory of Old Engliſh Dramatic Poetry and the Stage", I received from him ſome time afterwards the following letter, written at the commencement of that illnefs which in a few months proved fatal : it is of great intereſt as, I believe, Scott's lateſt letter of the kind. I had been introduced to him by Campbell a year or two before.

"Abbotsford, August 27, 1831.

"DEAR SIR,—I safely received, some weeks since, your very interesting volumes upon dramatic antiquities, and have to thank you very much for the curious information I derived from them. I should long since have assured you of this, but my medical friends, till of late, have restricted me chiefly to vegetables and water in point of diet, and in my studies are not desirous I should go beyond 'Cinderella, or the Little Glass Slipper'. I am, however, much better, and emancipating myself gradually from my restrictions.

" I have some thought of going in the winter to Italy, to try what a warmer climate will do for me. In that case I will be anxious to trace the origin and progress of the Comedy of Character, where the use of a dramatic poet was in a great measure dispensed with, or at least only required in condensing the intricacies of a prepared plot, which the actors filled up according to their various characters previously fixed and settled.

" I am sure that when I am able to read your valuable dissertations with the attention they deserve, I shall find something throwing light on this curious subject, which would go far to decide the question whether mummery and masquery did not precede the proper drama in the infancy of that interesting art. I am scarce sufficiently strong to enter upon the particulars at present. I would willingly hear that you were not only encouraged to republish the " Annals of the Stage", but to meditate a complete history of Dramatic Art, as it took its rise in England. As you yourself well observe, while we justly rely much on our English Dramatic Poetry, we should at the same time not suffer its history to rest upon the snatches of intelligence which have been gleaned together for the illustration of Shakespeare—an object, to be sure, most worthy in itself. But, I apprehend, it will not require less than the exclusive knowledge which you have displayed on the subject to draw a general history out of the Annals which you have collected with such uncommon diligence; and your accurate acquaintance with the Museum and the Duke of Devonshire's Collection has paved the way so far as to render the labour of doing so, however great to another, a mere trifle to you, as the erecting of a building is but a trifling labour when the collection of the materials has once simplified it.

"Pray, dear sir, be so good as to accept a hurried and confused letter, as intended to convey the best thanks and assurances of interest in your labours from

"Your most obliged humble servant,

"WALTER SCOTT."

Dec. 22.—I have already, I think, said something of the ridiculous quarrel between Poole and Lifton, who, I hear, came to blows after a good deal of abuse. Several satirical *skits* were circulated on the subject, the point of which mainly depended upon the names of the belligerents—therefore not very good, nor worth copying here: the rhymes were inevitable, and one of them, tolerated with respect to Whifton in the time of Swift, could not be used now. Poole's "Paul Pry" is an excellent comedy, though bordering upon farce; and if he wrote anything before that excepting his "Hamlet Travefty", I never heard of it: his "Paul Pry" was acted at the Haymarket more than forty times in succeffion in 1825, and again at Drury Lane four years ago. Mrs. Waylett, a pretty little woman, tried her hand at the male part of the young sailor in it, and I have fince seen her as the waiting-maid, originally reprefented by Madame Veftris, and then by Mrs. Humby, regarding whom Charles Lamb's unrepeatable joke became current.

Poole began life as clerk to a ftockbroker, and he was ftill no higher when he publifhed, in 1811, his "Travefty", which many have, and the author wifhed to be, forgotten.

It was good in its way, but it was a bad way : fome of the fongs, as parodies, were excellent. Kenney was clerk to a banker when Poole was clerk to a ftockbroker, and thus they became acquainted. Kenney told me that he advifed Poole againft printing his burlefque upon " Hamlet", but Poole perfevered, and did the fame for " Romeo and Juliet"; but the laft met with no fuccefs, while the firft, being the earlieft of its kind, came to a fourth edition before the end of 1812 : the public thought one dofe quite enough. Kenney urged Poole to try his hand for the ftage, and the refult was " Paul Pry", which, Poole admitted to me, Kenney read before it was acted, and fuggefted various improvements, one being the fong of " Cherry ripe", which Madame Veftris was often called upon to repeat three times : originally her part was without it, but it was wanted by the finger and by the fcene.

I never could meet with the firft edition of " Hamlet Travefty": it was in 8vo, while the three fubfequent impreffions were in 12mo. Poole gave me my copy of it.

I have ftated elfewhere that I never faw any rhymes by Dyce excepting in one of the " annuals", I entirely forget which ; but I fince find that I am miftaken, and that three comic octave ftanzas, which he addreffed to me, are in exiftence among my unforted papers. At Chriftmas 1831, I invited him to meet a family party on a Sunday at my houfe in Hunter Street. He made no fcruple as to the day ; but as he had recently, and I may fay fulkily, regaled himfelf on a turkey and game fent to him by his friend Sandby, without inviting anybody to partake of them, he was afraid that he fhould not be able to do juftice to our comparatively poor fare, and therefore fent me the fol-

lowing preliminary poem, to account, as I ſuppoſe, for any
apparent abſtemiouſneſs when he came.   The ſtanzas run
as if he were not unaccuſtomed to that ſpecies of verſification, but I never heard of any others.

"TO J. PAYNE COLLIER.

" I really feel that I should be unable,
    Unless I make confession of my sin,
To show my visage at your Sunday table ;
    And though I'm most reluctant to begin,
Know that (upon my conscience I don't fable)
    Three weeks ago came safely to Gray's Inn
The bountiful old Sandby's Christmas present,
A turkey—yea, besides, a hare and pheasant.

" But I had promis'd Mrs. Childe that I
    Would have no parties (swearing it by Avern),
And my new system of economy
    Forbade my giving ' blow-ups' at a tavern ;
So I determin'd I would gradually
    Devour them, like a boa in his cavern :
I ate the birds first, with much self-applause,
And with a little pepper and bread-sauce.

" As to the hare, it was a different matter,
    For Mrs. Childe quite spoil'd it in the cooking :
She tried to make it into soup, and (rat her !)
    The sight of it had well-nigh set me puking—
A long lank body swimming in brown batter !
    You never saw a thing more horrid-looking :
And so that day I was oblig'd to mess on
Beef from a cook-shop.   This is my confession.

"ALEXANDER DYCE."

It ſhould be noted that Mrs. Childe, here mentioned, is a
fat good-tempered woman (nearly all fat women are good-

tempered) and Dyce's laundrefs; and fhe takes care of him and of his chambers, four ftories high in Gray's Inn. Alexander Dyce is fix feet five inches tall, and when I fometimes jeer him about his verfes, his anfwer generally is that he writes nothing but *Alexandrines.*

Dec. 26.—Till yefterday, when I read the following in Drayton's "Moone-calf" (firft publifhed, as far as I can trace, early in the reign of James I), I was not aware that the ufe of white hair-powder by ladies was fo old in England : the poet is fpeaking of an extravagant full-dreffed beauty.

> " Ere she be drest, she seemeth aged growne,
> And to have nothing on her of her owne :
> Her black, browne, aburne, or her yellow hayre,
> Naturally lovely, she doth scorne to weare :
> It must be white to make it fresh to show,
> And with compounded meale she makes it so ;
> With fumes and powdrings raising such a smoke
> That a whole region able were to choke,
> Whose stench might fright a dragon from his den :
> The sunne yet nere exhal'd from any fen,
> Such pestilencious vapours as arise
> From their French powdrings, and their mercuries."

My ignorant notion was that hair-powder did not come into ufe in France till the reign of Louis XIV, and that we had it afterwards from thence. The whole poem of the " Moon-calf" is a fevere fatire (though not fo called) upon the people and manners of England.

The Rev. Mr. Barham, knowing how deeply I am interefted by anything connefted with the name of Shakefpeare, has forwarded the following to me : I cannot find that the Shakefpeares here fpoken of were in any way related to the great dramatift—moft likely not ; but the name is enough to excite curiofity.

"MY DEAR SIR,—In looking over the Registers belonging to my old living, St. Gregory by St. Paul's, London, I find two entries of baptisms, which I inclose.

"'*John, sonne of Thomas Shakespeare, Gentleman :* 18 *July,* 1619.'

"'*Thomas, sonne of Thomas Shakespeare :* 6 *Oct.,* 1620.'

"I do not know whether these good folks have any connection with the 'Swan of Avon' or no : you probably will.

"There is also a marriage of a Mr. John Shakespeare, of Portsea, with Mary Higginson, of St. James's, Westminster, widow, 25 April, 1747 ; but it is impossible that any descendant of the bard could have allied himself to so unpoetical a name.

"*Valeant quantum valent.*

"Yours ever,   "R. H. BARHAM.

"Amen Corner, St. Paul's, Nov. 7, 1833."

Sheridan Knowles, who is always beginning, has commenced a new drama : he called upon me, and read part of it.   The ftory relates to the conteft between the Chriftians and Turks, in the middle of the fifteenth century, and there is to be a good deal of bloodfhed and love in it : the name of the Turkifh hero is Amurath, and of the Chriftian Tancred, as in Taffo.   He left one act with me for re-perufal ; and I copy from it the following fpeech, in which Othman, an old foldier, endeavours to wean Amurath, his Sultan, from the pleafures of the harem to the raptures of the victorious battle-field.   Knowles may never finifh the play, and I do not altogether like the fpecimen.

"OTHMAN. Courage, my prince, and be your former self ;
Bold as the lion of your native forests,
And fierce and subtle as the tiger there.

Remember whence you sprang : let Amurath,
Your royal father, be your great example,
And make the Christians tremble, as he wont,
Shaking and falling like the timorous leaves,
When the dread lion in his anger roars.
   "AMURATH. Say on, say on; but ware his indrawn fangs.
   "OTHMAN. Where now the mighty deeds, the foughten fields,
Made Amurath the terror of the west,
And emperor of all the subject east,
When Stamboul fell, and all her chivalry
Ow'd even life to his forbearing sword.
Rouse thee, my liege ! strike terror to thy foes,
And arm thy friends with thy enduring courage.
Leave, for a while at least, effeminate
And idle toys of love and lethargy :
Then, having first subdued thyself, lead on
And conquer all our crescent's enemies.
   "AMURATH. Speak on, speak on. (*Aside.*) Ah, how his
         ardour stirs me !
   "OTHMAN. Methinks I see thee in thine armour bright,
And plumage waving o'er thy turban'd head,
Return to her you love with victory,
And doubly dear for all thy triumphs won.
She will receive thee then with open arms,
Who now laments thy feeble, womanish,
And wanton ways, degenerate from thy stock.
Forgive, great sir, thine ancient soldier's words,
Or strike me down : my spirit still shall soar,
And o'er thy standard watch its victories.
   "AMURATH. No more, no more.—My falchion and my
         steed !"   [*Calling to Attendants.*]

This is fpirited and dramatic—perhaps melodramatic—
but ftill fpirited, and like Knowles. He told me fomething
of the plot, but not connectedly, and I doubt how far he
has yet fettled it. He writes by fits and ftarts, and fome-

times paufes, even in the ftreets (I have feen it), to put down fome lines, or a fudden thought.

Dec. 29.—The Duke and I had a good deal of converfation to-day on the comparative merit of four different ages of our poetry : we divided the periods thus—1, *Ancient*, from the time of Chaucer to that of Henry VIII ; 2, *Old*, from the time of Elizabeth to that of Charles II; 3, *Middle-aged* (not mediæval), from the time of Anne to that of George III ; and 4, *Modern*, from the time of George III to the time of Victoria.

I have not an opportunity juft now of giving any details, but I was particularly ftruck by a remark the Duke made anent Goldfmith's " Traveller": he liked it better than the " Deferted Village"; and his obfervation related to a ftrange difference of manners, as illuftrated in the very commencement. Goldfmith dedicated it to the brother, whom he moft affectionately addreffed in the firft ten lines, ending with the well-known quatrain,

> " Where'er I roam, whatever realms I see,
> My heart untravell'd fondly turns to thee ;
> Still to my brother turns with ceaseless pain,
> And drags at each remove a lengthening chain."

" How ftrange it is," obferved the Duke, " that in fpite of the ftrong affection betokened by thefe couplets, Goldfmith dedicated the whole poem to that brother, addreffing him in profe merely as ' *dear fir!*' Which is the truth, the warmth of the poetry, or the coldnefs of the profe ?" I could not give any anfwer fatisfactory to the Duke or to myfelf, merely faying that the hyperboles in the beginnings of modern epiftles were then unknown. Certainly there was an apparent contradiction ; and it feemed very probable that had Goldfmith been addreffing his brother, in an abfolutely private letter, he would have called him "dear Henry" or "dear brother".—"Why (inquired the Duke) fhould he have been apparently afhamed of the public exhibition of fraternal affection ?"

Goldfmith, of courfe, belonged to the fourth period of our poetical divifions. Our talk lafted for nearly a couple of hours, and I was fomewhat furprifed to find how wellread the Duke was in the writers of verfes anterior even to the reign of Elizabeth : he was acquainted with the collections of Cooper, Headley, Ellis, Campbell, etc., and in fome confiderable degree with the books to which they had reforted for their fpecimens. All I can here fay is, that we traced our Englifh poetry in a continuous ftream from the fountain-head (as far as it was difcovered) down to our own day, noting its turnings and windings, its fwellings and its fhrinkings, its broad expanfes and its narrow ftraits, always connected and continuous, and never abfolutely dry, though fometimes choked by extraneous and offenfive matter caft into the clear current. I could eafily fill a dozen pages with what paffed between us on this delightful fubject. The Duke again preffed me to accept another hundred a year from him, but I refolutely, refpectfully, and fuccefsfully refifted.

Dec. 31.—As I muft now, in confequence of other and imperative engagements, difcontinue my Diary, at leaft in its prefent detailed form, I wifh to conclude it with fomething, not indeed my own, but as much my own as love and admiration can make it : it is the tranflation of a moft charming fonnet by Dante, and the words of the original may be feen in the *Scelta di Sonetti* of 1709, p. 12. If I did not think my verfion rather happy, I would not infert it here, as my lateſt performance of the kind. Nothing can exceed the ſimple and tender feeling of the Italian.

SONNET TO HIS LADY.

My gentle lady wears so pure a grace,
    While she salutes with modest courtesy,
    That every tongue is silenced tremblingly,
Nor eye presumes to look upon her face.
To shun our praises she forsakes the place,
    All clad benignly in humility,
    And seems as she had only left the sky
To show a miracle to mortal race.
    In hearts of those who dare to lift the eye
Her beauty pours a flood of sweet delight,
    Which some, who prove not, cannot understand.
    Between her lips a spirit mild and bland,
And full of love, appears to take its flight,
    And whispers to the soul enraptur'd, " Sigh!"

The heart abfolutely expands (at leaſt mine did) when one reads the exquiſite original.

J. P. C.

————————

———— *nec turpem feneɛtam
Degere, nec cithara carentem.*

FINIS.

www.ingramcontent.com/pod-product-compliance
Lightning Source LLC
Chambersburg PA
CBHW032009110726
47901CB00004B/1023